TITANICUS

Discover the war machines of the Imperium in

• IMPERIAL KNIGHTS •
By Andy Clark

BOOK 1: KINGSBLADE
BOOK 2: KNIGHTSBLADE

WARLORD: FURY OF THE GOD-MACHINE
A novel by David Annandale

IMPERATOR: WRATH OF THE OMNISSIAH
A novel by Gav Thorpe

SERVANTS OF THE MACHINE-GOD
An anthology by various authors

TITAN
A graphic novel by Dan Abnett and Anthony Williams

Tales of the Adeptus Mechanicus

• THE FORGES OF MARS TRILOGY •
By Graham McNeill

BOOK 1: PRIESTS OF MARS
BOOK 2: LORDS OF MARS
BOOK 3: GODS OF MARS

• ADEPTUS MECHANICUS •
By Rob Sanders

BOOK 1: SKITARIUS
BOOK 2: TECH-PRIEST

TITANICUS

DAN ABNETT

BLACK LIBRARY

The author would like to thank Big Steve for his loan of the ancient archives, and Richard Dugher for his engine-painting labours.

For Dju and Sylvia.

A BLACK LIBRARY PUBLICATION

First published in 2008.
This edition published in Great Britain in 2018 by
Black Library,
Games Workshop Ltd.,
Willow Road,
Nottingham, NG7 2WS, UK.

10 9 8 7 6 5 4 3 2 1

Produced by Games Workshop in Nottingham.
Cover illustration by Fred Rambaud.
Map by Adrian Wood.

A CIP record for this book is available from the British Library.

ISBN 13: 978 1 78496 816 8

Printed and bound by CPI Group (UK) Ltd, Croydon, CR0 4YY

It is the 41st millennium. For more than a hundred centuries the Emperor has sat immobile on the Golden Throne of Earth. He is the Master of Mankind by the will of the gods, and master of a million worlds by the might of His inexhaustible armies. He is a rotting carcass writhing invisibly with power from the Dark Age of Technology. He is the Carrion Lord of the Imperium for whom a thousand souls are sacrificed every day, so that He may never truly die.

Yet even in His deathless state, the Emperor continues His eternal vigilance. Mighty battlefleets cross the daemon-infested miasma of the warp, the only route between distant stars, their way lit by the Astronomican, the psychic manifestation of the Emperor's will. Vast armies give battle in His name on uncounted worlds. Greatest amongst His soldiers are the Adeptus Astartes, the Space Marines, bioengineered super-warriors. Their comrades in arms are legion: the Astra Militarum and countless planetary defence forces, the ever-vigilant Inquisition and the tech-priests of the Adeptus Mechanicus to name only a few. But for all their multitudes, they are barely enough to hold off the ever-present threat from aliens, heretics, mutants – and worse.

To be a man in such times is to be one amongst untold billions. It is to live in the cruellest and most bloody regime imaginable. These are the tales of those times. Forget the power of technology and science, for so much has been forgotten, never to be re-learned. Forget the promise of progress and understanding, for in the grim dark future there is only war. There is no peace amongst the stars, only an eternity of carnage and slaughter, and the laughter of thirsting gods.

Western Prospection
(the deadlands)
Old Semik Wharfs
Jeromihah Subsids
Prospect Highway
Argentum Hive
Gox Subsids
Undergox Edge
Shaltar Refineries
Lexal Refineries
Fidelis Highway
Vassal Townships
The Astrobleme

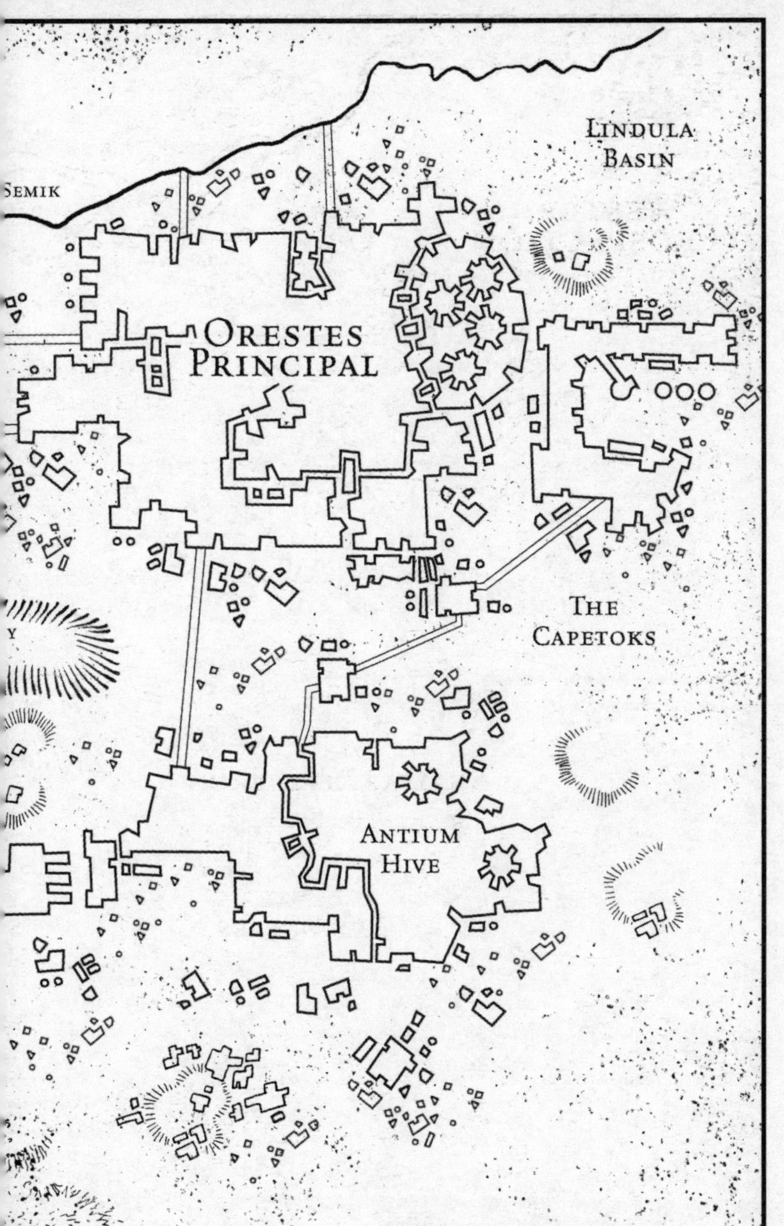

SEMIK
LINDULA BASIN
ORESTES PRINCIPAL
THE CAPETOKS
ANTIUM HIVE
ORESTES
CIRCA M.41.779

<[exloaded from] Crusius, magos executor fetial, Legio Invicta (110011001101, code compression zy) [supplementary data modules appended, stream 2] [begins]

Pursuant to proposal of execution K494103, I have opened negotiative discourse with the Orestean magi. Access supplementary module 1100, and you will inload a detailed fact audit of the situation on Orestes. This assessment has been verified by our executer remotes. The Orestean magi have made an accurate representation concerning the crisis. Aggressive hostiles, including one hundred and seventy-four [one seven four] identified gross war engines of the Primordial Annihilator, have begun prosecution of Orestes Principal and adjacent subhives, Argentum Hive, the assembly yards at Mount Sigilite, the finishing silos at Gynex Subhive and Antium Hive, the Western Prospection and various vassal communities in the Astrobleme. In consideration of execution K494103, the Orestean magi propose to extend full refit and overhaul processes to Legio Invicta, without delay, tariff or reimbursement, in return for prophylactic action. My recommendation, pending your authority, is that we execute. Notwithstanding the offer of refit, I believe that we are duty-bound to make this execution, and we would be derelict to ignore the plight of this sacred forge world. I trust the magi probandi will verify the legality of this, but I believe that this execution supersedes Imperial Order 475:3Ae472 [Macaroth]. I submit this recommendation, in the name of the Omnissiah, to the wisdom of my trusted seniors, this day of the Imperium, 223.779.>

<[exloaded from] Kovenicus, magos navis, Legio Invicta (0011101010011101, code compression twa) [supplementary data modules collated, stream 2] [begins]

I have inloaded your statements, Crusius, and I concur. I have ordered the fleet to stand by, and am ready to divert and make shift to Orestes if Gearhart assents. I await confirmation of orders.>

<[exloaded from] Bohrman, first princeps, Legio Invicta (1110101101101111, code compression cfn) [supplementary data modules collated, stream 2] [begins]

Documentation re: execution K494103 inloaded and reviewed. I do not believe we have a choice, legality or no legality. No matter what the Imperial Warmaster demands, we cannot bypass and ignore a Martian dependency in extremis. We should walk. Why is Gearhart taking so long to consider this?>

* * *

<[exloaded from] Lau, commander skitarii, Legio Invicta (44 decimal 8, code compression exk) [supplementary data modules collated, stream 2] [begins]

Bohrman is correct. Orders be damned! The skitarii stand ready. Execution must begin and Orestes rescued. I implore my Lord Gearhart to make his decision quickly.>

<[exloaded from] Gearhart, princeps maximus, adept seniorus, bearer of the Seventh Seal of Mars, first commtator, master of the Manifold, called the Red Fury, blessed of the Deus, Legio Invicta (11101101101111100, code compression kln) [supplementary data modules collated, stream 2] [begins]

So impatient, you young devils. Steel abides longer than flesh. I have inloaded and finished my review. Kovenicus, make shift. Bohrman, wake your MIUs. Lau, data-load your forces.

We will walk upon Orestes.>

TITANICUS

I

Gristle-faced and lipless, the regiments of the dead howl out their awful calumny as your footfall passes. Dun smoke fills the massive cavity of space. Oh machine! Oh divine engine! Furnace hot the welter of your combustion, buckling the rancid air of heaven's arch and fusing the mould of the ground to glass. The princeps in his amniosis, drinking liquid data, broken by the beautiful agony of being so mighty, feels the burden of your great walk as surely as if he had carved the mausoleum plaques of your every last victim alone, by hand, until finger bones peep through eroded flesh. Oh metal god! The union is fierce, like a maelstrom in black water, like a seething cauldron on a fire in which you boil and cook together, no start of one, no end of another, but both admixed, like an alloy. To be clutched by god! To feel the incendiary hunger ring in your marrow! Oh lucky man!

Do you ever really sleep? In the long between-times, in the silences wasted in oily holds and scaffold frames, do you sleep then? When the enginseers reduce you to dormancy, is that sleep for you? Do you dream then, great engine?

What do you dream about?

1

The auspex returns seemed to suggest that the engine had retreated behind the burning shell of the tannery and moved away, but the auspex had been dropped several times and had taken at least one las deflection that had crazed its screen. Its main display kept milking out, and Goland trusted it about as far as he could sling it.

Goland had a nasty feeling he *would* end up slinging it. When the moment came, he and his men would have to throw everything they had at the enemy, literally everything.

It was the middle of the day, but it felt like the middle of the night. The sky was low and filthy black, and the only illumination came from the burning ruins around them. Acid rain sheeted down, transmuting the thick brick dust underfoot into a squelchy paste. Though torrential, the rain was failing to quench the firestorms. There was a constant, pressurised sizzle as water met fire, and veils of steam, rolling like fog, further occluded their visibility.

This was what hell looked like, Goland decided. He corrected himself. This *was* hell.

Daric Goland knelt down in the mire and fumbled with the auspex set. His wet fingers kept slipping on the handheld's fascia. Somewhere behind him, a man was shrieking long, awful screams into the rain. There was no pain relief left, no ampoules of morphine, no medics, no hope.

The auspex started to give Goland a partial bounce, a freak return. He cursed quietly. What did that mean? Was there something lurking behind the tannery or not? He shook the device, and slapped it against his thigh, hoping the bounce was just an imaging artefact conjured by the cracked display.

Some heavy structure, possibly an arch or a retaining wall, suddenly fell in a few hundred metres to his left. It made a noise like an avalanche as it toppled into the inferno that had brought it down. Sparks burst up like a swarm of fireflies, and the rain consumed them. The shivering crash set his men off.

'Settle. Settle!' Goland yelled. 'It's just fire-damage! Hold your places!'

Their nerves were shredded. It was a wonder most of them hadn't run already. They had been mobilised against an enemy that outclassed them in every detail and dimension. This was no infantry war. This hadn't *ever* been an infantry war.

To them, and to Goland, the collapsing structure had sounded like the doom-step of an engine. In these tight, high-walled manufactory streets, as they had learned to their cost, a collapsing wall was often the only warning they got of an engine steering in to attack.

A noxious odour began to drift down the narrow sub-street. Goland gagged slightly. The fire in the tannery had reached the hide stores, and the air started to reek of burning flesh and melting fat.

Goland rechecked the auspex. The bounce had vanished. The damaged screen was now only showing topographic solids and the energy wash of the fires. Was that the truth, or just another display error?

'So, do we move, leader?' Trooper Kiner asked. Goland looked over at him. Kiner was huddled in a broken doorway, corrosive rain streaming off his helmet, his slicker and his weapon. Six days earlier, in the friendly warmth of PDF company barracks, they had celebrated Maki Kiner's twentieth birthday. To Goland, Kiner's pinched, white face looked no more than twelve years old.

'I want to be sure that bastard monster has gone before we advance,' Goland told him. 'Hold tight, all right?'

Kiner nodded.

Somewhere to their left, a kilometre away, an engine cannon licked off. Despite the distance, it shook the ground with its thunder. Goland and Kiner flinched.

'Shitting hell!' Kiner yelped.

'Hold tight,' Goland said. 'Trust me, Maki, just hold tight and I'll get you out of this.'

'Vox. Vox!' a lost voice called out behind him.

'I'm over here!' Goland yelled, rising to his feet and waving through the rain. Tertun, the squad's caster man, ran up, and dropped to the ground beside Goland.

'Signal from Principal!' Tertun spluttered, wiping the rain off his face as he proffered the speaker horn of his set to Goland.

Goland took it and crouched down beside his caster man. 'Xeres Five PDF, come back.'

'Xeres Five PDF, this is Principal. Report your position.'

'South of Gynex Subhive, Principal. I daren't send you the precise co-ordinates because they're listening.'

'Query, Xeres Five PDF?'

'The enemy. They've synched into all our comms and systems. They're listening to us!'

'We are advised. Is this Major Kairns?'

'Kairns got killed about an hour ago. This is Sergeant Goland, acting. We've got three, possibly four, engines busting up through the agro-burbs. Serious collateral damage. Nothing's slowing them.'

'What is your strength, sergeant?'

'Stand by, Principal.' Goland looked up, blinking the scalding rain off his eyelashes. 'Sound off!' he called into the downpour. Eighteen voices answered him, some distant and muffled, just eighteen. That morning, walking behind Kairns, Goland had marched out with seventy-five PDF troopers.

'One eight, eighteen,' Goland rasped into the vox. 'We're getting hammered down here. Please advise, Principal, where is Legio Tempestus? We were told to expect Tempestus.'

There was a long pause. 'Tempestus is unavailable at this time. We are routing six Vultures to your position.'

'Vultures?' exclaimed Goland. 'Vultures aren't worth a damn! We've got engines here! Three Reavers, maybe four Reavers, and a Warlord too! I'm not joking, Principal, we're getting steamed and we need engine support!'

'Stand by, Xeres Five PDF,' the vox chattered.

It went to dead air.

They tell me to stand by, Goland thought, and I tell the boys to hold tight. We're all caught in a holding pattern, waiting for hell to claim us and suck us down.

'Frigging idiots,' Goland told his caster man, tossing the horn back to him. 'They haven't got a clue.'

He got up, and looked back down the demolished street. The surviving members of his unit were cowering in rat-holes and craters behind him, clagged with mud and pissing themselves with fear.

'Xeres Five, listen up.' Goland called out. 'Cannon? Any cannon left? No? Any demolition? Any plasma?'

No one answered.

'A flamer, at least? Anyone?' Goland asked desperately.

He waited in vain for a reply, but instead of an answer, he heard the terrible, drawn-out thunder of collapsing stone.

'Oh shit!' Tertun squealed.

Goland turned.

The burning tannery's high walls and chimneys were falling down. They were falling down because they were being knocked down.

It hadn't gone. The auspex had lied.

Brickwork, stone blocks and reinforcing girders spewed down into the street like a rockslide, bouncing and tumbling, swirling with flames. Mud and sparks sprayed into the air, and the pelting rain turned the up-churned dust into falling beads of liquid tar.

As the walls came down, the searing fires inside the tannery sucked in oxygen and gleefully gusted up, yellow and white, sixty metres and more into the black air. Something loomed in the sheeting flame. It had the rough shape of a man, a man magnified until it was over thirty metres tall.

The engine stood behind the curtain of fire like a silhouetted god and stared out at them.

'Run! For frig's sake, run!' Goland cried.

The men of Xeres Five PDF were already running.

Giant hydraulics hissed, vast gears engaged, massive metal joints groaned and clanked. The engine took a step, and the ground quivered. Masonry debris scattered like shingle off a shin with an eight-metre girth.

'Move! Find cover!' Goland yelled as he ran. He glanced back.

Emerging from the fire, the great engine remained a silhouette. It was caked black with carbonisation, the patina of its hull thick with surface soot. Residual combustion crackled and fluttered in the cavities and joints of its structure. It took two more reverberative steps, and then seemed to stoop slightly, as if noticing the tiny, fleeing men for the first time. It paused. It swung down its smouldering right limb, locked it out, and opened fire.

A turbo-laser on auto sounded like the death scream of a sun. The hailing, incandescent blast pattern overtook Xeres Five PDF like a surge tide as they ran for their lives down the back street. Caught in the rolling blitz, fleeing troopers ignited and evaporated almost instantly. The onslaught levelled the entire length of the thoroughfare and ripped the ground down to fused bedrock.

Maki Kiner disintegrated mid-stride in a puff of ash flakes that billowed like confetti. The last thing Goland saw of Tertun was a cooked spine, skull and single shoulder blade, tumbling out of the chasing fire-wash like part of a puppet, still articulated, thrown on by the roasting fury of the attack.

Goland turned, screaming, and hurled the treacherous auspex like a discus at the great engine treading down the street behind him.

He didn't live long enough to see if it had struck its mark. Mass laser discharge vaporised the flesh off his bones, and then, a millisecond later, over-pressure scattered his skeleton like twigs into the rain.

* * *

>

They had become so habituated to the state of war that when it finally stole in upon them personally, it seemed to take them by surprise.

The folk of Orestes, Imperial and Mechanicus alike, had long believed themselves to be far from the hot lines of the contested front. The crusade raging through the Sabbat Worlds was months away to spinward. The folk of Orestes thought they were safe.

Lights seen at night in the desert extremes of the Astrobleme signalled the start of the unthinkable. Vassal communities dwelt in that punishing hinterland, the scarred entry wound of a prehistoric meteor, and it was these, the tribal moots, the mobile prospector colonies, who first saw lights in the sky over the emptiest quarters of the wracked lands, and wondered at them. Messages and signals swirled, like gossip and rumour, through the vassal communities, through the subhive marketplaces, and north to the Hive Principal. By the time they were taken seriously, it was far too late. Bulk landers had set down, secretly, in the planet's most dead areas, and unberthed engines of war. The dark mechanics of the Archenemy had blinded and tricked the vigilant sensors and watch satellites of the Orestean PDF, and the legions of Urlock Gaur had been unleashed to neuter that vital source of materiel supply, Orestes Forge.

One morning, the third day of Makefuel, the seventh month of the Orestean calendar, twenty-nine days before Daric Goland's fused bones were scattered into the rain, slow bells began to peal across Orestes Principal. It was barely dawn. The bells woke Captain Erik Varco, in his dormitory bed, and he roused, understanding without the need for words that his life was about to change entirely. They disturbed Cally Samstag, waiting listlessly in her cramped sink hab for her husband to come in from his late shift at the docks.

They rang along empty walks and under copper arches. Their dull tolling echoed through low sinks and high avenues. In his bed, Lord Governor Poul Elic Aleuton stirred as an aide tapped persistently on his chamber door. In his garrison cot, Daric Goland woke with a heavy head and a sour taste in his mouth, and hated the day for all that it brought. In her manse on Southern Cliff, Etta Severin paused over the trade report she'd been up all night working on, and listened to the chimes, frowning. Dozing in his amniotic sleeve, Solomahn Imanual, the Adept Seniorus of the forge, felt a surge of data and realised that bells had been ringing in his binary dreams.

The chimes echoed through the dark heart of the forge, along causeways and radiating tunnels, under the heavy loops of fat fibre-trunking that clung to the ceilings and walls like succulent vines, through assembly vaults where manufacture never ceased, through the climate-controlled crypts of the vast cogitators. Magi gathered in the workshops and monitor points, puzzlement bristling across their epidermal haptics, questions pulsing in their floodstreams. They watched with mounting disbelief the telemetry flow casting live from the southern hives: the rolling, scrolling, mocking data that filled the lead-glass screens and declared invasion as a fact, daring them to believe otherwise.

'Is this an exercise? A simulation?' asked Adept Feist, trying to process the full measure of what he was reading.

'This is no simulation,' replied a nearby magos logis.

* * *

The bells continued to ring. A cold, pre-dawn light scoured the sky. The Worthies Garden, a walled, tree-lined lawn beneath the eastern elevation of the Chancery, was empty at that time of day. Unable to sleep and summoned by the bells, Moderati Zink came out of his hut and regarded the day. Despite his age and infirmity, Zink still walked with the stiff-legged gait of a man who had been mind-bonded to a great engine.

A flock of tiny, twittering zephyrids was preening on the southern part of the lawn, keeping to the only part of the grass that the newborn sun was touching. They milled and scudded like dry leaves caught in an autumnal gust. Zink buttoned his coat, fetched his withy broom from the hut, and began to sweep the paths.

Bells that didn't sound the hour. That was a novelty. Zink wondered what their ringing meant, but came to no conclusion. He wasn't sure of much on any given day, so he got on with his meticulous sweeping. He was a shell of a man. Pain, delivered by a gargant's fury, had fried his Manifold receptors and his haptics during an engine war eighty years earlier. The shock had burned out all of his acceptors and rendered him machine-dumb. The Mechanicus had provided him with a service pension, and Zink's princeps had secured him the job, as caretaker of the garden. Zink swept the paths, tidied and trimmed the lawns, and cleaned the busts of the worthies.

Zink had observed a curious process. Every year or two, servitors came into the Worthies Garden and removed some of the busts, usually the oldest and the most bearded with moss and lichen. Zink wasn't sure where the servitors took them. Fresh, new busts were then planted on the vacated pedestals. New heroes to replace the old.

As he swept and raked the lawns, hearing the bells striking out of hours, Zink gradually appreciated something.

A great many worthies were about to be martyred, and a lot of pedestals were going to be needed.

>

Riik! Riik! Riik!

Slowly, ponderously, the Titan advanced upon its enemies, one step, then another, *thunk, thunk, thunk*. Then it halted, whirring. Its weapon limbs swung up and down, and sparked with light, destroying all before it.

'Monstrous! Monstrous!' Zember cackled, clapping his arthritic hands together.

The pale dolls looked back at him, blank-eyed and unimpressed. The candle perched inside the hemisphere of a dirty, cracked glow-globe, guttered. Zember's cackle turned into a cough.

He took hold of the Titan to stop it trudging off the edge of the workbench. It was the height of a man's forearm, and reassuringly heavy. Iron cogs weighted the clockwork heart cased inside the tin armour. He had painted the tinplate himself: cobalt blue, the colour of Tempestus. As he lifted it, its legs thrashed helplessly back and forth.

Manfred Zember was the third-generation proprietor of the little emporium, *Anatometa,* in the level eighty-eight commercia of Orestes Principal, Ironwright Row, tucked between the poultry market, with its metallic stink of blood and corn, and the studio of a society miniaturist. Across the narrow thoroughfare, a chandler's, a dye-maker's, a wool-carder's and a hosier's clung together, shabby, their slumping premises embracing like a group of friendly drunkards. Zember's grandsire had limned the shop sign by hand – A N A T O M E T A – in gold and red. Back in the day, it had been a thriving proposition, selling mannequins and automata to the wealthy and the privileged from Summittown and Southern Cliff. A cherished family story told of the day the Lord Governor himself had come to buy a mechanical simian for his youngest daughter. The simian had worn a jester's mop and clashed brass cymbals together when it was wound up and set to run. 'Very marvellous,' the Lord Governor had declared. That had been sixty years ago. Time had passed, tastes had changed, and the sign had faded.

Zember considered that his main profession was now as a kind of physick to invalid toys. There was little money in it. Customers came by infrequently, clutching bald dolls, dislocated dolls, mechanicals that refused to walk or dance or twirl. He took his coin from such repairs. Zember could restring a doll in five minutes, paste back together a broken ceramic or papier maché face as brilliantly as any cosmetic medicae, replace a faulty spring or a toothless cog, make the damaged and the broken walk and whirr and spark and delight like new.

But he could not, as simply, restore his own fortunes.

The hour-less chiming of the bells made him rejoice. Waking, as per his habit, at four, he had shuffled down to the busy dining-hall on Congress for a mug of caffeine and a crust of yesterday's bread. The late and early shifts had been overlapping, purchasing breakfast or supper. When the bells began to peal, the manager of the hall had turned on the public vox, and the steamy hall had gone quiet as the patrons listened to the broadcast.

War had come to Orestes. The southern hives were reporting early assaults. The Lord Governor had requested calm, and the forge had declared that Tempestus would walk.

There had been consternation. Zember had ignored it, and trudged back to his premises, clutching the hot tin cup of caffeine to his pigeon chest.

The Titan had taken him three weeks to build, and it had stood on a shelf at the back of the store for nine years. Zember had taken it down, dusted it carefully, and wound it up. Dolls, tired and broken, awaited his ministrations in the hospital his store had become. He regarded them wearily: a doll for restringing, a clown with a broken eggshell head, a tired princess anxious to have her faded beauty repainted, a soldier automaton that had been lamed on some carpet battlefield.

Let them wait.

Its motor winding down, the Titan marched ever more slowly. Zember set it on the bench. It made a final, fitful sputter with its guns.

This would be his remaking: an engine war. He would build the toys and they would sell, as souvenirs, as trophies, as keepsakes, as lucky charms: little clockwork Titans.

Riik! Riik! Riik!

He wound the toy up again and let it go across the bench. It seemed to pace in time with the bells. The dolls watched, silent and wide-eyed.

The Titan toy would save his business. After all, weren't the Titans supposed to save them all?

10

'Will they walk?' asked the Adept Seniorus. He framed the question in binaric cant, and issued it as a data-blurt of rapid pulses through augmitters built, like gills, under the corners of his jaw. The speed and pitch of the blurt conveyed the nuance of his impatience and concern.

The executor fetial was named Djared Crusius. He bowed respectfully before the august assembly. He stood alone on the wide marble dais, the focus of their attention. More than five thousand notables had gathered that afternoon to hear his answer. Numinous silhouettes, they filled the rings of seats below the dais, bathed in a haze of late summer sunlight that flooded the vast auditorium through the panes of the domed roof. Crusius kept his eyes, dutifully, on the Adept Seniorus.

'Honoured lords,' he replied in clear, precise Low Gothic. 'Etiquette obliges me to conduct this conference verbally. Not every person present is binaric-fluent.'

The Imperial high officers and grandees in the chamber clapped in approval. They were outnumbered almost three to one by the magi of the Orestean Mechanicus.

'Thank you for the courtesy, executor,' said the Imperial Governor, rising from his seat. 'Given the import of this session, I would prefer not to listen to baffling machine sounds for the duration. With respect to my honoured friend the Adept Seniorus, of course.'

Governor Poul Elic Aleuton was a dignified, charismatic man juvenated to look sixty, a quarter of his meat-age. He wore the heavy white plate of the Orestean Pride Guard comfortably, thanks more to a lifetime of formal duties and state parades than actual military service. In him, the power of the Golden Throne was invested. He was the voice of Terra on Orestes, the proxy of the Council, and his voice commanded all of Orestes and its system holdings. Still, he looked deferentially across the sunlit auditorium at the Adept Seniorus. Solomahn Imanual, red-robed, ancient, and ninety-one per cent artificial, was the master of the Orestean Forge. Imanual nodded back graciously.

'My apologies, Lord Governor,' Adept Seniorus Imanual replied, also rising to his feet, 'my frustration got the better of me.' His fleshvoice came out clumsy and nasal, like the speech of a man profoundly deaf. The Adept Seniorus was unaccustomed to verbal exchanges.

'I may not know cant, but I can guess the adept's question,' Aleuton continued, looking up at the executor. 'Will they walk?'

Djared Crusius, like most executors fetial, had chosen to receive only subtle or encysted augmetic work. He presented as a tall, handsome male, with regal cheekbones and cropped silver hair, his height emphasised by the crisp drop of his simple black robe. He was an ambassador, a go-between, an arranger, and his appearance was skilfully designed to be reassuring and comfortable to non-Mechanicus parties. Most of the legio's negotiations, down the years, had been conducted with Imperial agencies. Only his uniform robe, and a slight, electric green cast that filled his eyes when the light caught him at certain angles, betrayed his fealty to Mars.

Crusius was also a master of the dramatic pause.

'They will walk,' he said, nodding.

The magi seated in the marble circles below him exhaled a general wheeze of relief, even though most of them no longer needed to breathe for any practical purposes. There was a flutter of applause and a few triumphant cries from the Imperial contingent.

Crusius raised an elegantly gloved hand. 'Understand, please,' he said, as the applause died away, 'my legio requests supportive statements from all of you. We are breaking with our orders to come to your aid, and those orders were issued by the Warmaster himself. He is expecting us to join him at the Sabbat front in sixteen weeks.'

'He will be disappointed,' said a magos called Egan. Crusius knew all their names. His adapted eyes saw what the Imperials present could not: the limnal skein of the noosphere, a green aura that read data transfers as zips of light, and appended to each and every magos present an overlay spec declaring their name, biography, specialisation and vital record. To Crusius, to all of the Mechanicus personnel gathered in the massive auditorium that afternoon, the air shimmered with columns of visible data and the synaptic fizzles of information exchanges.

'He will,' Crusius agreed, 'but explanatory statements from the elders of Orestes should ameliorate that disappointment.

It is important that Warmaster Macaroth understands why we have diverted. Bad feeling between the Mechanicus and the Warmaster must be avoided.'

'I will transmit an explicatory apology to him before nightfall,' said Governor Aleuton.

'Thank you, sir,' said Crusius.

'I will do likewise,' said the Adept Seniorus, gnawing the words out with his clumsy tongue.

'Again, my thanks,' said Crusius.

'What is your current strength, executor?' asked a red-robed magos, rising to speak from the row behind the Adept Seniorus. The noosphere told Crusius that the magos's name was Keito.

Despite his earlier remark, Crusius half-opened his lips and replied with a ten-second data-blurt of soft, rapid squeaks that issued from the augmitter in the roof of his mouth.

'Forty-eight engines,' said Keito, his eyes mirroring slightly as he reviewed the data suddenly scrolling across his retinas.

'Forty-nine, Brother Keito,' replied Crusius, 'if the Warlord *Dominatus Victrix* can be made battle-ready. It is eager to walk too.'

'The plants at Antium are ready to receive it,' another magos responded. 'The fabricators have been roused and fully stimulated. Given your summary of the damage to *Dominatus Victrix*, the fabricators estimate eight days.'

'Ryza would do it in six, Brother Tolemy,' Crusius said, smiling.

The Adept Seniorus gestured dismissively with one of his tailored steel manipulators. 'Ryza is Ryza. They do everything the day before they were asked. This forge's resources are more limited. Eight days.'

'Eight days is perfectly reasonable,' Crusius replied.

'Invicta has been fighting the eldar?' asked Egan. 'I see this from the inload. Eight years in the Beltran Cluster?'

'Seven years of actual combat, brother,' Crusius corrected, 'the last year has been spent in transit. The Beltran Campaign was a demanding walk. The eldar produce subtle, swift engines. We lost eight units.'

'I would be most gratified to inload your data experiences of that war,' said another magos called Talin. 'Any supplementary throughdata would be welcomed.'

'It's yours,' Crusius replied. 'I will exload what I have via your grafts. When the legion deploys, I will instruct the princeps to transfer all gunbox data to your archive deposit.'

'I am gratified,' said Talin.

'I believe our business is concluded,' said Crusius. 'I thank you for your patience, lords.' He made another bow. 'The Legio Invicta is at Orestes's command.'

>

'But we're breaking orders,' Famulous Sonne complained as he scurried along behind Crusius.

They were out in the open sunlight, walking the long processional that linked the auditorium to the set-down annex. Lines of intricate topiary half-shaded the processional path. Below them, the magnificent sprawl of Orestes Principal fell away.

'Your point?'

'Macaroth will be pissed off with us, won't he?'

Crusius halted and looked down at his famulous. 'Of course he will. Additional: where did you learn a phrase like that?'

Sonne shrugged. 'I... I don't know.'

'*Pissed off*. That's very earthy. Very Imperial. What's the rule?'

Sonne sighed. 'We of the Mechanicus prefer cant and system code imagery to biological ones.'

'So?'

'Macaroth will be very error shunt abort with us.'

'Better.'

Sonne snorted. 'I thought executor training meant we had to embrace and acknowledge unmodified bio-traits, so as to better understand the Imperials we have to do business with?'

'It does,' said Crusius. He frowned. 'That sounds like part of a lecture.'

'One of yours, six months ago. I 'chived notes.'

'Well done.'

They started walking again. 'Besides,' said Sonne, '*pissed off* has a certain phlegmatic power.'

'You're not wrong,' Crusius admitted. He looked down at his apprentice. Sonne was sixteen, and virtually unplugged. 'It must be so hard for you,' said Crusius, 'opting out of the standard upgrades.'

'I want to be an executor fetial,' Sonne replied. 'I understand the demands. Next year, I'm assigned to receive my amniotics, my subtle haptics, and my noospheric receptors.'

Crusius smiled. 'Already? Rudimenting: it seems like only yesterday you were an unmodified boy sent to me for specialisation.'

'Have I disappointed you, sir?' Sonne asked.

'Glory, no,' Crusius replied. 'You keep on this way, another sixty or seventy years, and I'll recommend your full biosheafing for executor status.'

Sonne's eyes were wide. 'Sixty or seventy...?' he began.

'What?' Crusius winked. 'Can't I make a joke? Binaric humour bores me so.'

Sonne laughed.

'So, to review, yes, Warmaster Macaroth will be pissed off with us. There's nothing we can do about it.'

'Because Orestes is a Mechanicus colony?'

'Because Orestes is a Mechanicus colony, and it is under attack, and the Warmaster can just learn to live with it.'

'In six thousand years,' said Sonne, 'the legio has seldom disobeyed an edict from the Imperium.'

'Recite, date and circumstance.'

'Decanting: the War of Lochrisus, 412.M35. Warmaster Gallivant ordered the Legio Invicta to Shackropal, to stem a swarming by the lethids. Gearhart refused, claiming it would be a waste of engines. The Shakropal sun ignited the next year, and the lethids were immolated without need of execution. That was the last time.'

Sonne looked pleased with himself.

'Good,' said Crusius, 'but actually, thirty-eight years ago, Gearhart countermanded the orders of Warmaster Hengis on Talphus VII.'

'Really? *Really*?'

'Hengis was clinically insane. We were forced, eventually, to annihilate him.'

'I never knew that,' said Sonne.

'We keep it quiet. It's sequestered in the archives. What are you doing, Sonne?'

'I'm incanting the data to my memory buffer.'

'Well, don't. Objection tone: it's sequestered. Didn't I just tell you it was sequestered? Wipe your buffer this instant and decant me a wipe-memory record.'

'Sorry.'

Crusius blinked as the record arrived in his noospace.

'That's better. By the way, when you refer to him you might at least call him *Lord* Gearhart.'

'Sorry,' Sonne repeated.

'It's all right. Sonne, our legio has functioned for almost twelve thousand years. Once in a while, we are faced with a task that leaves us with no choice.'

'Like pissing off Warmaster Macaroth?' asked Sonne.

'Exactly like pissing off Warmaster Macaroth,' Crusius agreed.

>

Adept Feist took a sip of nutrient fluid from the straw-sac attached to his left wrist, sighed, and returned to his work. His fingers played in the warm air in front of him; the subtle haptics laced through his epidermis actuated and sorted the data drifting in the noospheric realm in front of his eyes. He closed images, opened others, scanned and stacked, enlarged, tightened, enhanced. It was slow work. The data source was crude, to say the least.

<Pan two eighty,> he whispered to the noosphere. <Hold. Rotate. Hold. Magnify four hundred. Hold. Embellish. More. Stop. Enhance box eighteen. Impose character recognition. Request match.>

No match occurs in the Orestes archive, the noosphere told him in soft green binaric script.

Feist sighed again. He rocked back in his seat and rubbed his eyes. The Analyticae was working to capacity again, nine hundred adepts and logis, toiling at their cogitators like communal insects. Day and night, for over a month, since the war began, shift teams had been reviewing any and all data received from the fighting zones, no matter what the quality, and processing it, hunting for any clue, any tactical advantage. The air smelled of clammy metal, heated coils, and sweat: human sweat and the odd secretions of those adepts modified for floodstreams.

Magos Egan was running their section that evening, wandering between the busy adepts, examining any finds or curiosities. Egan had set them, twenty of them, to the job of close scanning all extant pict capture of the Archenemy engines, most of it gun camera footage or auspex targeter feed. It was poor quality stuff, most of it risibly fuzzy, and it frequently cut short in disturbing ways.

These are things people have seen in the seconds before they die, Feist thought. What a terrible thing to die with this as your last sight.

For an hour, he had been trying to discern surface detail from a pict feed showing the head of an enemy engine as it approached through drifting smoke.

He wasn't getting anything.

<Crusius, the executor fetial of Invicta, has personally charged us with this task,> Egan had told them all at the pre-shift briefing. Red-robed, his mechadendrites flexing anxiously, he had looked each one of them in the face. They had all been selected for their keen processing skills. <We're looking for weaknesses, my brothers and sisters, anything that might aid Invicta as it makes this execution on our behalf.>

<What exactly do we look for, magos?> a junior adept next to Feist had asked.

<Identifying marks. Insignia, especially defaced or excised markings,> Egan had canted. <Remember, these vile engines were once ours. They were lost to us, but we made them, may the Omnissiah forgive us. Yes, they are changed and corrupted, manifestly so, but if we can, by any means, identify or isolate their original model, origin, pattern or derivation,

we might be able to pull up early specs held on archive and pinpoint characteristics or weaknesses.>

<Query: do we hold specs that old, magos?> Feist had asked, raising his hand.

<If we don't, we can request them from Mars, adept. The Mechanicus never deletes anything.>

They laughed. It wouldn't have sounded funny in human words, but in binaric cant the phrase was a neat numeric pun that lifted their spirits. Egan was trying to keep them lively, focused.

<You're tired, adept,> Egan canted.

Feist looked up and found the magos standing at his shoulder.

<I'm fine, magos,> he replied. < It's just that I've been studying this image for over an hour…>

Egan smiled at him. <Advisory: don't break yourself. You're no good to me burned out, Feist. I see from your skein you've been inloading at a high flow-rate. Your cortex will suffer. Take a few minutes' rest.>

<I'm really all right,> Feist replied. <Thank you for your concern. I want to do this, for the forge, for all of us. This pict just won't give up its secrets.>

Egan bent down and looked over Feist's shoulder so he could accept the noosphere as Feist saw it. <Inloading. You've enhanced?>

<Yes, magos. I've washed it through all the advanced modifiers. It's a Reaver.>

<It most certainly is. When was this caught?>

<Four days ago at Gynex, the gun-box feed of a Vulture. You see the head here? Near the neck joint? Some marking has definitely been excised.>

<Yes, you're right. Nothing from the archives?>

<No match at all.>

Egan straightened up. He patted Feist gently on the shoulder with the manip of his lower left mechadendrite.

<All right, Feist, nothing more you can do. Move to the next one. In fact, go for a walk and cool your head. Then move to the next one.>

Feist nodded. <I wish the data we were getting was cleaner, magos.>

<So do I,> Egan agreed.

Feist pointed to the frozen image. <Two seconds more, and this one cuts off in noise. You can hear a man screaming like–>

<Take a walk. Then move to the next,> Egan advised.

Feist sat in his seat and stared at the image a while longer. Why was there no match in the archive?

The Mechanicus never deletes anything.

Pithy, clever. True.

Except…

Feist stood up. 'Magos?' he called.

Egan, busy with another adept, turned and walked back to him. 'Feist? What is it?'

'We never delete anything,' Feist said.

'No, we don't.'

'So how much do we sequester?' Feist asked.

11

When he came in from his long shift, he found her in the bedroom of their little hab, packing a few belongings into a bag. For a few seconds, he couldn't think of a single reason why she might be doing that. Then he saw the look in his young wife's eyes.

'No,' he whispered.

'It was always a possibility.'

'I can't believe it.'

'It was always a possibility, Stef,' she repeated.

'When?' he asked.

'Tonight. Midnight. The slip's on the table,' she replied, continuing to pack the bag with such serious intent it seemed that packing was an end in itself.

'I can't believe it,' said Stefan Samstag. The slip, a message wafer in a foil tear-bag, lay on the little plastek table in the living space, beside a stack of unwashed beakers and a half-eaten loaf of spelt bread in a wax wrapper that they'd been saving for supper.

Stefan picked up the slip and read it.

'Oh, Throne,' he sighed. He was bone-tired from his double shift at the docks, and all the way home his dearest wish had been that the hab would have enough juice to heat some water to wash in, when all the time he should have been wishing this away.

He looked up, and his eyes found the little votive aquila hanging in the hab's domestic shrine. The posy of flowers in the little offering bottle was fresh. Despite everything on her mind, Cally had remembered to change them. That was duty. Stefan felt monstrously let down by the powers represented by the little brass icon.

The Samstags had been on Orestes for eighteen months. They'd grown up in the sinks of a subhive on Castria, five months' shift away. The Sabbat Crusade, a campaign that seemed set to last forever, had been sucking resources out of Castria at an infernal rate. The planet had become an impoverished pit of systemic crime, corruption and bleak futures. Stefan Samstag's most likely career paths had been either mindless sweat-work in the Castrian arsenals, milling shells for the war effort, or the Guard. Since the Sabbat Wars had begun, twenty-four years earlier, nine and a half million young men and women of Castria had shipped out to the front in Guard foundings.

Stefan had toiled hard instead to earn his wharfinger certificates, slaving unpaid hours in the Castrian docks to get his supervisor's papers. As soon as he had qualified to grade six, he had applied for emigration passes. Orestes, a thriving forge world closer to the Sabbat systems, had publicly advertised its need for certificated cargo handlers to help deal with its munitions output. For those with the proper accreditation, Orestes was willing to pay set-up and relocation expenses.

Orestes had promised a new life, away from Castria's slum sinks. With his papers and work record, Stefan had been accepted automatically. He'd had to apply for a permit to bring his new wife along with him. Cally, a junior data-loom clerk, was not qualified in a reserved occupation, and thus various conditions had been made.

There was only one that counted. Cally Samstag would be obliged to serve, four weeks a year, in the tertiary reserve of the Orestean Planetary Defence Force.

Cally was small and athletic, and she'd been a volunteer in the Castrian scholam cadet force, so it hadn't seemed like a terribly big deal. She quite enjoyed the camaraderie and teamwork of a week with the reserve PDF, running exercises, survival hiking in the Astrobleme, drill training.

'You realise I could get called up, don't you?' she'd once said to him.

He'd shrugged. 'Of course, but since when did things get so bad the tertiary reserve got activated? Honestly?'

Stefan tossed the wafer back onto the table. It missed, and fell onto the floor. He made no effort to pick it up. He felt like he'd somehow, elaborately, manoeuvred his wife into harm's way.

'I'll go in,' he said.

'What?' she asked from the bedroom.

'I'll go in. Have a quiet word with Reinhart. Maybe he can do something.'

'He won't be able to do anything.'

'He's a port supervisor.'

She stuck her head around the door. 'Stef, your overseer won't have any sway in this. Don't ask him, please. I signed the papers. This was a condition, and I agreed to it. Now shut up and put a brave face on.'

He shook his head again. 'You're tertiary reserve, Cally, tertiary reserve. Since when did tertiary reserve get a call-up?'

'It must be really bad,' she replied from the bedroom.

He sat down on the worn couch beside the table. 'I just can't believe it,' he muttered.

In the tiny bedroom, Cally Samstag stopped packing her bag for a second. Her hands were shaking. She closed her eyes and clenched her teeth. She'd known Stefan would take it this way. She loved him, but sometimes he could be such a child. He wasn't the one being called to war. He wasn't the one being sent off into who knew what. Why weren't his arms around her? Where were his reassuring whispers that everything would be all right? Stefan was a strong man, physically. She'd seen him heft cargo crates as if they were empty, but she was the strong one when it came to holding them together.

She had less than an hour before she was due at the muster. She knew she'd be spending most of that time keeping him contained.

'Stef? It will be all right, Stef,' she called out. Her hands wouldn't stop shaking.

Cally took the maglev cross-hive to Perpendicular and Congress, and then changed to a south-bound mag that crept along the low, dark tunnels under Southern Principal as if it was a worm, eating its way through the soil.

Saying goodbye had been hard. Stef had tried not to cry, and hadn't been very good at it. It was painfully hard to make your farewells when you didn't know when you'd be coming back.

Their little hab in Makepole sink hadn't honestly been much better than the dwellings they'd shared on Castria, but it had been a start, and at least there'd been the prospect of a future. Stef's superior, Reinhart, had promised Stef a promotion, which would have come with a better place in the Loric Projects, possibly a quad-room hab with sanction for children.

Cally would have liked that. Perhaps it would still happen. The future had suddenly become cloudy and unreadable.

She got off the mag at Counter Point, and walked up the long marble steps to the windy surface streets. She'd never told Stefan, but she didn't much like Orestes. It didn't feel like a proper Imperial world. The Mechanicus was everywhere, and they were strange folk. It wasn't so much the augmetics or the gross implants, that was all superficial. It was the attitude. They were a race apart. It was like two races living under one roof, co-existing but separate.

Approaching the place of muster, she spotted Golla Uldana, trudging along, a bag on her shoulder.

'Golla!' Cally called, running to join her.

'Cally-girl! How frigged up is this?' Golla asked. Golla was a hefty forty-five-year-old woman who worked as a midwife in the inner habs of Principal. 'I joined tertiary for fun, and to meet a nice man, not this,' she complained.

'A nice man?' Cally asked.

Golla shrugged. 'How much more wrong could I have been?'

They chuckled.

'How's that nice man of yours?' Golla asked.

'Pissed off that this is happening.'

'Men, kind and thoughtful.'

'Stef's not that bad,' Cally said.

'Whatever you need to tell yourself, little sister,' said Golla.

They walked together for a while in silence.

'This must be really bad, mustn't it?' said Cally.

'Why do you say that?'

'A call-up for the tertiary reserve?'

Golla nodded. 'It must be a frigging nightmare. It's strategic, isn't it?'

'Is it?'

Golla rolled her eyes. 'You're so naive, Cally. This shit-storm was just waiting to happen. Orestes Forge is one of the main supply worlds of the whole frigging crusade! Yes, we're a target! I just thought, you know, that the Warmaster, in his infinite wisdom, might have had us covered.'

'I've heard its engines,' said Cally.

'And the rest,' said Golla. 'War engines, the whole thing, but there's good news.'

'There is?'

Golla nodded again. 'I have a friend who has a friend who knows a fellow in Protocol, and the word is that the Lord Governor was taking meetings this afternoon with an executor from another legio.'

'Really?'

'Invicta, he said. A whole Titan legion coming to save our lardy arses, how fine would that be?'

'Very fine.'

Golla smiled. ''Sides, I have a special itch for one of them handsome moderati types.'

'You're a terrible person,' Cally told her.

'Catch,' said the officer. He threw the MK2-sk lasrifle at Cally Samstag and she caught it.

'Learn it, use it,' the officer said.

It was as blunt as that.

Four hundred tertiaries had gathered in the dingy municipal hall requisitioned for the muster. A PDF quartermaster was issuing kit and ammo. Numb, bemused men and women were wandering around with arms full of equipment.

'Excuse me,' asked Golla Uldana. 'How long do you think we'll be out for? I left a stew on a low boil.'

'Until this ends,' said the officer. 'They're all over us. The southern hives are burning. We lost eight thousand PDF in two days. That put a smile on your face?'

'Not at all,' replied Golla Uldana.

'Oh, Throne,' whispered Cally Samstag.

>

The Lord Governor's residence was situated at the very summit of Orestes Principal, and sunset always came a little later up there. As the vast hive below sank through dusk into night, sunlight still lingered on the summit tower.

Waiting in an anteroom for her appointment, Etta Severin watched the postponed sunset through tinted ports that ran from floor to ceiling. Everything was washed in a pale, tobacco haze. It was as if the sun respected the authority of the Lord Governor, and kept its light on him for as long as possible.

She walked right up to the window ports, and pressed her forehead against the glass, so she could peer down. Below, in the pooling darkness of a night that had not yet reached her, the colossal hive was invisible apart from a trillion pinpricks of light, scattered like stars.

Etta Severin, twenty years a consular officer attached to the Munitorum's Trade Service, was not easily impressed, but the view was undoubtedly impressive. She reminded herself that she spent too much of her life poring over paperwork and data-slates, making small talk with shipmasters and merchant envoys, and negotiating tariffs and residuals in windowless rooms, and not enough time opening her eyes and observing the world.

She sighed. It wasn't working. Her forced admiration of the view, her deliberate thoughts that life quality might be improved if only she took the time to step back, these were just exercises, brain-game techniques designed to use immediate surroundings to negate stress. The view was magnificent, but she was still tense.

The Lord Governor had summoned her. She awaited his pleasure.

'Mamzel?'

Severin hadn't heard the servitor enter the anteroom. She jumped back from the window, feeling foolish to have been caught with her head pressed to the glass like a child.

'Yes?'

'The Lord Governor is ready for you,' said the servitor, in a voice as soft as the whisper of burning paper. It was an artful thing, its cowling worked in gold to resemble the empty face of an angel. 'The Lord Governor apologises for making you wait.'

She nodded graciously. She had a horrible feeling that pressing against the glass might have left a red mark on her forehead.

'This way,' said the servitor.

It led her out of the anteroom, down a carpeted corridor past huddles of gubernatorial lifeguards in full body-armour, and through two huge, noisy chambers where aides and adepts milled about in urgent activity. Business had not closed for the day. In times of war, the Lord Governor's offices bustled on past nightfall, however delayed that might be. Severin saw several high rank officers of the PDF, and at least three generals of the Imperial Guard, all representing Orestean units, mixing with Munitorum staffers, senior members of the Ecclesiarchy and the Telepathicus, and provincial nobility. They muddled around, reviewing data, sharing wisdoms, calling out for confirmations and updates. Aides and servitors hurried to and fro, bearing communiqués, freshly loaded slates, rolled charts, and trays of caffeine. There was an air of duty, of urgency, of solemn attention. Ignored by the throng, the beautiful antique busts and priceless paintings adorning the grand staterooms seemed to gaze down with mute amusement.

Following the servitor, Severin arrived at a pair of dark nalwood doors, twice as tall as necessary. Two lifeguards stood on watch. She recognised them both: Major Gotch and Major Tashik, junior only to Senior Frenz, master of the gubernatorial lifeguard. She'd encountered them both at various formal functions, escorting the Lord Governor. Their robust physicality alarmed her. They were big men, ex-Guard storm troopers, distinguished in their crimson coats, black drill breeches and silver cuirasses. They wore glinting beak helmets with huge crinières of white feathers. Gotch had a spectacular horseshoe scar that hooked around his right cheek and split down through his lips. Chromed hellguns hung over their shoulders. It was quite telling that the Lord Governor had posted two of his very best men to watch his door.

'She is expected,' the servitor told the lifeguards.

Gotch stepped forwards. 'I know she is. Good evening, Mamzel Severin.'

'Good evening, major. I trust you are well?'

'Fit to bust. I'm sorry about this, mamzel. It's just protocol.'

Severin nodded. She held out her biometric and let his sensor wand sniff it.

'Perhaps a twirl?' he suggested.

She smiled back, and rotated slowly, self-consciously, on the spot as he ran the wand up and down her figure. There were deep mirrors set into the wall on either side of the heavy doors, and as she turned, she caught her reflection. No red mark on her brow, thank the Throne. She saw a handsome woman of forty-eight, dressed in a sober gown and mantle of grey wool, turning sheepishly as an ogre with a white cockade played a sensor over her body. Her red hair, cut short and businesslike, looked good in the mirror, and the money she'd spent on that last juvenat process had been worth it. Not a blemish, not a sag, full lips, artfully plucked eyebrows, eyes that a man might die for.

Not that any ever had.

'You're clean,' said Major Gotch, switching off his wand and returning it to its holster.

'You expected me not to be?' she asked, with a brave laugh.

Gotch smiled back at her. The smile did something disconcerting as it met the scar. 'Just protocol, mamzel,' he said. 'We can't be too careful. Anyone can steal a face these days.'

'So I hear,' she replied.

'They'd have to pay a lot for yours,' he added.

She baulked and blushed. Had he just flirted with her, or was that some kind of rebuke, a reference to her expensive juvenat work?

She groped for a reply. Before one could form, Major Tashik had pushed a coded stud on the wall and the heavy doors had opened on electric hinges.

The bisected smile still on his face, Gotch bowed and gestured for her to go in.

'Thank you, major,' she said.

The inner office was a huge, circular chamber with skylights that allowed the dying light to seep in like honey. To one side, a high-backed leather throne stood behind a gigantic ormolu desk, backed by a state portrait of Franz Homulk, the first governor of Orestes. Glow-globes floated around the rim of the ceiling. Hololithic wallplates silently scrolled data feeds and news squirts from the territories.

Aleuton was not at his desk. He was sitting in a nest of leather sofas off to her left, talking quietly with an ancient, palsied man in snow-white robes. Severin knew the old man by sight. He was Gaspar Luciul, the Prelate Ecumenic of the Ministoria Orestae. Gowned Ecclesiarchy aides stood attentively behind the sofas, and seraphic ward-drones floated above them. Nearby, a magnificent mahogany walking carriage awaited, like a confessional box on spider legs.

'Mamzel Severin,' the servitor announced. The drones whipped around at the sound of its voice, and armed their thermobaric weapons. Several of them puffed out their cherubic cheeks and hissed.

'Disarm,' said the prelate with a gentle wave of his purple glove. The seraphs floated back to standby. Severin thought that the old man's hand had far too many rings on it.

'Etta, so good of you to come,' said Governor Aleuton, rising from his seat.

As if I had any choice at all, she thought.

'I won't keep you any longer, my honoured lord,' Aleuton said to the Lord Ecumenic. 'I thank you for your time and consideration.'

Luciul rose to his feet, a movement that was accompanied by a whirr of hidden augmetics. 'Always a pleasure to converse frankly, Poul, even in times like this. The Ecclesiarchy stands four-square behind you. I know, in my heart, that you will see Orestes through this difficult period.' He held out his hand. The Lord Governor leaned down and kissed the Warpmaker's golden ring.

'The Emperor protects,' said the Lord Ecumenic.

'My trust is, as always, in the Throne of Terra,' Aleuton replied.

Assisted by his aides, Luciul clambered arthritically into his walking carriage. The seraphs buzzed overhead. An aide closed the carriage door, and the machine started forward, clicking across the tiles of the stateroom. The aides fell in step around it, one swinging a censer. With the drones trailing behind the carriage in a rising line, like notes on a stave, Luciul slowly made his exit from the chamber. He halted the carriage to regard Severin as he passed her.

'Mamzel,' he said, looking down at her through the knotwork screen. His face was as lined and creased as a walnut. She could smell the sweet odour of his anointing oils.

'Holy lord,' she replied, bowing.

'Be well, my child. I believe the Lord Governor has work for you. Serve him as you would your own father.'

'I will do my duty, holy lord,' she replied. Her father, an intersystem trader and fleetmaster, had been a gladstone addict and fond of his fists. Severin intended to serve the Lord Governor a great deal better than she'd ever have served the old man.

The nalwood doors closed behind the Prelate Ecumenic and his retinue.

'Etta,' said the Lord Governor.

'My lord.'

'Come, sit.'

The Lord Governor was wearing the heavy, white plate

armour of the Orestean Pride Guard. As he took his seat, he seemed uncomfortable.

'It's been a long day,' he admitted. 'I usually only get dressed up like this for state occasions.'

'You look very handsome, sir,' Severin said as she sat down on the sofa opposite.

'Thank you. Do I?'

'Yes,' she said. 'Dignified and regal.'

'Well, thank the Throne for that. If Orestes burns, at least I can die looking dignified and regal.'

Aleuton stared at the tiled floor for a few seconds and then looked up at her. 'My apologies, Etta. It's been a long day. As you may know, we're in it up to our necks.'

'I am privy to certain data, sir,' she replied. 'I understand that the situation in the southern hives is reaching critical.'

'They're overwhelming us, Etta,' he sighed. 'War has come upon us, and we are found wanting. Three hours ago I authorised the call-up of the tertiary reserves of the PDF.'

'The tertiary? Goodness!'

Aleuton nodded. 'It's come to that. Oh, those poor souls. Not a proper warrior amongst them, but I have to be seen to be doing my duty.'

'I understood that Legio Tempestus had engaged with the enemy, sir.'

Aleuton sat back and sighed. 'Eight days ago. They're getting hammered. Twenty-two engines, that's all Macaroth allowed us to keep here as a standing defence. The enemy has at least seven times that power.' He reached over and picked up a sheaf of black-edged papers. 'You see these? Death notices. Eight of them. Eight engines dead. What does that tell you?'

'That the Orestean Mechanicus must be in mourning,' she

replied. 'That we have suffered humiliating losses, and that Warmaster Macaroth has left us woefully undefended in his race for glory.'

Aleuton shrugged. 'Are you sure you're not a military advisor, Etta? Because that's exactly what my aides keep telling me. Twenty-two engines. That's nothing like enough to guard a forge world. Macaroth has drained us empty, and left us exposed to the wolves.'

She smiled. 'Why am I here, sir?' she asked.

Aleuton tossed the black-edged documents to the far end of his sofa. 'Today, thank the Throne, we have secured military assistance from another legio. Invicta. It was in transit, heading for the Sabbat front. They have forty-eight engines. They have agreed to divert, to bolster our efforts.'

'Thank the Throne,' she said.

'It may turn this war around,' said Aleuton. 'Let's hope it does. Invicta makes planetfall in two days, translation permitting.'

'The question remains, sir,' she said. 'Why am I here?'

'Am I the most important man on Orestes, Etta?' he asked.

'Of course. You are the Lord Governor. You rule this system and its subsidiary holdings.'

Aleuton smiled. 'I wish that were true. Orestes is a forge, Etta. The Mechanicus rules. My authority, the Imperial presence itself, is accepted under sufferance.'

'The Mechanicus serves the Throne of Terra,' Severin said bluntly.

'The Mechanicus is a race apart,' said Aleuton. 'They work to their own agendas, and the Imperium is grateful whenever those agendas match our own. Since the dawn of this age, we have been two species of humans, working towards a common goal.'

Severin exhaled slowly. 'I know we have our differences. Throne knows, I've spent enough hours trying to negotiate treaties with the magi. They are very closed. But really, sir, they're as true to the Emperor as we are, aren't they?'

Aleuton gestured to the waiting servitor. 'Amasec, one measure,' he said. 'Etta?'

'I'm fine, sir.'

The servitor strutted off to obey the command.

Aleuton leaned forwards. 'Mars is an entirely separate enterprise from the Imperium. We work in concert, and we depend upon them for tech, but they are not Imperial. If push should come to shove–' He broke off.

'What, sir?' she asked.

The servitor brought the Lord Governor's drink over on a golden salver. Aleuton took it and sipped.

'I have no doubt, Etta, that the Mechanicus would cut us off, ditch us, the moment they sensed that Imperial ideals were contradicting the Martian ethos.'

She sat back. The servitor hovered behind the sofas. 'Maybe a small fortified wine?' she said. 'Or sacra, if you have it?'

'We have a stock of Tanith sacra, mamzel,' said the servitor. 'Ten or twelve years?'

'Twelve, please,' said Severin. She looked at Aleuton as the servitor moved away. 'Is it really that tight?'

Aleuton nodded. 'This is rapidly turning into a Mechanicus war. Engines against engines. Though our world, and our lives, are at stake, we are trusting the magi to deliver us. I feel helpless. I need to know what's going on. I want you to be my eyes and ears.'

'How?' she asked.

'Invicta sent us an envoy, an executor fetial. His details are combed in this.' Aleuton tossed a data-stick to Severin.

'Crusius. He seems a decent fellow. I want you to join his staff, as my designated observer. I've made arrangements.'

Her eyes widened. 'Sir, surely a military expert would be better suited. A Guard–'

He shook his head. 'I've already considered that. General Paske was willing, but a military observer would be sidelined and shut out. You're Munitorum, a trade representative. They will let you in. You will accompany the executor into the field and report back to me, directly. The Imperial holdings of Orestes need to know what's going on.'

The servitor had returned with her drink. Severin knocked it back in a single gulp.

'I'll do my best,' she said.

'I thought you would. I'm sorry to ask this of you.'

'I'll do my best,' she repeated, rising to her feet.

Aleuton stood up. 'Thank you, Etta.'

'The Emperor protects,' she said.

'Of course, but I've assigned you body protection anyway. Major Gotch will accompany you.'

'Gotch?' she said, smiling. 'Fantastic.'

>

Dawn was still an hour or two away, and Erik Varco doubted it would bring any good news. His tanks galloped west up Prospect Highway at a hard lick, fuming rain-spray out behind them. They were running, lights out, auspex only. Stretches of the vast arterial, the principal link between Argentum Hive and the Western Prospection, had been chewed up so savagely by shelling that the squadron had to pull off sometimes and run parallel to the road along embankments and brackish watercourses so as not to lose momentum.

Jolting in his seat in the turret cage, Varco kept one eye on the threat detector and the other on the soft green cursor that was blinking in the middle of the terrain reader's fuzzy screen. A locator fix. Nine days of fighting had taught the men of Orestean Pride Armour Six not to trust vox or squirt signal. The enemy was listening.

It was stinking hot in the Vanquisher's dark cabin. Varco could smell his own rank body through the oil fumes and grease. He hadn't washed in a week, and he was still wearing the kit he'd set out in eleven days earlier.

'Coming up on it now, chief,' his driver called from the pit below.

'I see it,' Varco replied. 'Signal the train, lamps only. Then pull us over. Keep her running.'

'I was hoping to shut the plant down to work on that busted seal,' said Koder, the crew's enginseer.

'Negative,' Varco replied. 'It'll have to wait. Remember what I was saying about pants-down situations?'

'I do, captain,' said Koder dubiously.

'Well, good,' Varco said. If they shut off the Vanquisher's plant, a restart might take a full minute or more, not counting the wait time needed to rebuild the electronic mapping and propitiate the machine spirits, and if shit pounced, that was time they couldn't spare. Koder knew that. Frigging Adeptus, it was all about the cogs to them.

'Additional: I am concerned about fuel tolerances,' Koder said.

'I know, I know,' Varco snapped.

'If we sit running, we are burning fuel,' said the enginseer.

'Do me a favour,' Varco suggested. 'Don't talk to me for a while.'

The signal flashed back along the train of vehicles, top

lamp to top lamp, and the convoy began to slow, tracks churning through the pools formed in the pitted road surface.

Varco's Vanquisher, nicknamed *Queen Bitch*, rumbled to a standstill on the highway's rockcrete shoulder. Varco popped the top hatch and hauled himself out into a night that felt like it was sweating rain.

He took a quick look back down the line as the armour pieces he commanded drew up behind him. The wet air clung to the petrochemical stink of their exhausts. The low sky was a deep, hot brown, and amber vapour draped across the broken landscape. Somewhere back there, twenty kilometres away, Argentum Hive lurked, invisible. Argentum Hive. *Soak Town*. Someone had coined that a few days before, and now they were all using it. Soak Town, because it was soaking up the punishment that would otherwise have come straight at Orestes Principal. With the southern hives and sub-habs in tatters, Argentum was the only thing standing between the enemy and the heart of Orestes.

Varco slithered off the turret's wet metal onto the sponson and jumped down into gritty puddles. He was unsteady on his feet. Been sitting in that rig chair too long, Varco thought. How many hours, how many days, since I last walked?

He stretched out his legs to fight off cramps, made a respectful aquila to the tank to thank the machine spirits for their diligent protection, and touched the little medallion of the Omnissiah fixed to the skirt armour for good fortune. Then he jogged across the drenched rockcrete towards a knot of habitents pitched at the roadside. There were vehicles parked nearby, light transports, a Chimera, and a pair of red Mechanicus rollers, high-sided track units with thick armour.

He glanced at the open highway. It was wide and empty, scarred with craters and blast holes. He'd often patrolled its length, in better days. He was used to seeing it in daylight, choked with heavy cargo trucks rolling in from the Prospection with loads of mineral ore. Now it looked heartbreakingly forlorn.

Varco ran towards the tents. The rain was warm on his shoulders. He realised he was still stripped down to his vest, his tags dancing around his throat, his lower half heavy in padded breeches, high-laced boots and a weighty equipment belt. There was no time to go back for his jacket and cap.

Sentries in the white plate of the Pride came towards him, bayonets rising.

'Varco, commanding the OPA Six out of Argentum,' he said.

'Let's see your biometrics,' said one of the sentries.

Varco jerked a thumb at the growling, revving tank behind him. 'I believe that proves I'm who I say I am,' he said.

'Yes, sir,' the sentry replied. The men stood aside.

Varco entered the habitent.

'Captain Varco,' he announced.

'Colonel Habers,' replied a stout man in white field dress, coming towards him at once. They gave one another the aquila and shook hands.

'Tough run?' asked Habers.

'Tough is only ever what you let it become, sir,' Varco replied.

Habers led him towards a portable chart table that had been set up in the centre of the habitent. A chem lamp hung from a hook overhead, illuminating three figures poring over the charts.

'You could use a shave, soldier,' Habers said amiably to Varco.

Varco rubbed his bristly chin.

'I could, sir,' he replied, 'along with a shower, a square

meal, twelve hours' sleep, a large amasec, and a bout of restorative, uninhibited congress with an athletic girl. I'm guessing you're not going to be able to help me with any of the above.'

Habers snorted. 'Sorry, captain,' he said. He held out his hand to introduce the others. 'Jael Hastrik, from Tacticae.'

'Hello, Erik. How're you holding up?'

'Not so bad, Jael,' Varco said, smiling and shaking the tactician's hand.

'Von Maes, my adjutant,' said Habers.

'Captain Varco, a pleasure,' the young adjutant said, saluting.

'And Magos Logis Stravin, from Legio Tempestus.'

Stravin was a tall, stern female in a red gown. The left side of her face was a mask of engraved black bionics. She bowed her head to Varco, and knotted her knuckles together to make the meshed cog sign of the Cult Omnissiah.

'Captain.'

'Magos. May I say what a fine job your legio is doing in this dark hour,' said Varco.

Stravin hesitated. 'We are beleaguered, captain, and our engines have suffered terribly. I–'

Habers coughed uncomfortably. His adjutant and Hastrik shuffled awkwardly.

'I'm sorry,' said Varco. 'I was being sarcastic. I thought you realised.'

'Oh,' said Stravin. 'Processing. I see. Sarcasm is an unmodified behavioural pattern that we of the Mechanicus find hard to distinguish.'

Varco shrugged. 'You should get out more.'

'Out?' replied the magos.

'He's doing it again,' said Habers. 'Can we just get on?'

'No,' said Stravin. 'I wish to pursue this. Captain, I identify hostility from you. A criticism of the Forge Mechanicus.'

'There you go,' said Varco. 'That wasn't so hard, was it?'

'Captain Varco,' Habers snapped, 'while I'm happy to make allowances for the pressure you've been under, this isn't the time or the place to–'

'I believe it is, colonel,' Stravin interrupted. 'If not now, when? Captain?'

She looked at Varco. Her artificial eye glowed in its knurled socket. Her real eye simply did not blink. 'Say your piece, openly.'

Varco stared back at her. 'I've lost fifteen crews. We're running blind, jumping at every auspex shadow. Their engines are all over us. Tanks against engines? No contest. Isn't that why we trust in the forge? To protect us?'

'Of course,' said Stravin.

'So where's Legio Tempestus? Famous, lauded Legio Tempestus? Where are the frigging Titans? It feels like we're fighting this war on our own.'

'Now I understand,' said Stravin. 'You feel as though the Mechanicus has let you down?'

'That's putting it mildly,' replied Varco.

Stravin nodded. 'Then I share your anger. The Mechanicus *has* let you down. It has let Orestes forge world down. We have been woefully under-provided. Legio Tempestus is not a full-strength force. It is token. It is barely able to match the enemy forces unleashed against us. The Warmaster's constant demands have drained us of resources and forces. Orestes Forge has been left weak in the face of attack.'

Varco blinked. He had never thought to hear a member of the closed and guarded Mechanicus speak so frankly.

'Who's to blame, then?' he asked. 'Macaroth?'

'One might blame the Warmaster for his demands,' Stravin replied. 'One might blame the Adept Seniorus for acceding to those demands. One might also blame the Magi Council for ratifying the Adept Seniorus's decision to send so much of this forge's strength off-world. But blame is an unmodified quality, a luxury. Dwelling upon it wastes time. We are at war. We should focus on the now.'

'Well said!' said Habers enthusiastically.

'Your criticism is not misplaced, captain,' Stravin said to Varco. 'As for your sarcasm, I cannot tell. It is alien to me. You should know that Legio Tempestus, under-strength though it is, has been fighting at the front since day one. Tempestus has suffered fifty-three per cent casualties.'

Varco sighed. He felt as if the whole weight of *Queen Bitch* had been slowly lowered onto his shoulders. 'I apologise, magos,' he said. 'I spoke out of turn and my sarcasm was unforgivable.'

'A man who speaks the truth should not feel the need to apologise,' Stravin replied. The flesh part of her face seemed to smile kindly, but it was impossible to tell if the smile was genuine. The engraved half of her face could not match it.

'I am not at liberty to discuss details,' said Stravin, 'and I trust you will all keep this close. But I want you to know that there is another legio coming, a war-ready legio.'

Varco nodded. 'Thank the Throne for that,' he said.

'The Throne has nothing to do with it,' replied Stravin.

'Shall we, uh, turn to the chart?' asked Habers hopefully.

'That would be prudent,' said Stravin.

They closed around the underlit table. The magos reached out with her hand to indicate various details. Varco cringed inwardly to see that two of her fingers had been replaced with snaking silver mechadendrites. 'Data informs us that an engine is moving up through the ruins of the Shaltar Refineries here. It has already wasted the ore silos and the worker habs at Jeromihah. A Warlord of Legio Tempestus, *Annihilus Ventor*, is pursuing it along this vector, hoping to surprise it here and make a clean engine kill.'

'Where do we come in?' asked Varco.

'The enemy engine is moving with speed,' replied Stravin. 'There seems to be a real danger that it will outrun the *Annihilus Ventor*. Pride Armour Six is tasked to swing in here, across the river, and lay down pattern fire to drive it back. When the engine turns, it will meet our Warlord head on.'

'You think we can do it?' asked Varco.

'I know you can,' replied Stravin. 'Additional: the Mechanicus would appreciate any pict-feed data you might collect.'

'Why?'

'These engines were ours, once. Before the Fall, they belonged to us. Pict-feed data might help us identify them and identify any weaknesses.'

Varco nodded. 'Done, lady.'

'Thank you, captain,' she responded.

Varco produced a slate from his belt pouches and quickly scanned in the table's data.

'The Emperor protects,' said Stravin.

'You have my promise,' Varco said. He saluted Habers, and shook hands again with Hastrik and the adjutant. He turned to Stravin and clumsily made the meshed cog sign with his fingers.

'Right over left,' she advised.

'Sorry,' he said, correcting his knuckles.

She made the sign back to him with practiced ease.

'Remain vital, captain,' she said.

'I'll do my best, magos,' Varco replied.

* * *

Varco ran back out into the rain and scaled the side plates of *Queen Bitch*. 'Rev her up!' he yelled.

He dropped down into his rig seat and slammed the hatch, buckling up. 'Let's go. Signal the train, running order, follow me.'

'Yes sir!'

The Vanquisher's engines roared and blue smoke spurted from its exhausts.

Varco plugged his slate into the side of the auspex and inloaded the data.

'I have a target vector,' he said, pulling on his headset. 'Load HE shells, track loose, and wait for my command.'

'Aye!' the gunner and loader sang out together.

'Roll!' Varco commanded.

The Vanquisher lurched forwards, turning hard right. The convoy woke up and sped after her. Varco used the top lamp to flash a quick instructional brief to the train. He watched for the acknowledgement signals.

'You seem... cheerful,' Koder remarked.

'I just found out we're going to win this,' said Varco.

'We are?' asked Koder.

'Just you wait and see,' said Varco.

>

The tanks crossed the river at a ford offered by the spans of a collapsed rockcrete bridge, and squirmed up the mud banks on the far side. It was time to risk the vox and make sure his pack was tight and together.

'Varco to elements,' Varco said into his vox horn. 'I trust HE is loaded. We're the beaters, all right? All we have to do is scare the prey up and push it back. No heroes. I repeat, no heroes. Pattern fire only.'

They voxed affirmative replies back, one by one.

The Vanquishers toiled up the slope and crested the ridge.

On the far side, the world was ablaze. A hundred ignited promethium wells, surrounded by lakes of burning fuel, filled the plain ahead. The air, bright with flames and heavy with smoke particulates, became solid and yellow. The skeletons of ruined derricks rose out of rippling fire. The night sky, filled with rising sparks, had turned the colour of old straw.

'Steady as we go,' said Varco.

'Pict feed on,' said Koder. 'Gun cameras active.'

'Where are you, you bastard?' Varco whispered as he watched the threat display. The heat-read of the fires around them was confusing the motion sensors. 'Pride Armour Six, fan out.'

The tanks pulled out around *Queen Bitch*, muzzles raised, targeters hunting. The machines clunked and rumbled down the slope through the next wash of blazing fuel. The flames parted before them like a theatre curtain.

'Throne of Terra!' Varco exclaimed in dismay.

A Titan lay on its back right in front of them. Tumbled, crumpled, its gigantic structure burning, it lay like a cadaver on a funeral pyre. Volcanic fire sheeted out of its inner cavities. It was vast. It felt as if they were advancing towards the corpse of a fallen god. Varco heard a cracking sound, and realised that *Queen Bitch's* treads were rolling over shards of plate shrapnel spalled off the monster's hull.

'It's dead,' voxed one of the tankers.

'Someone got here first,' crackled another signal.

'No, no,' Varco murmured, 'that's ours. That's one of ours!' On the display in front of him, pattern recognition systems had identified the wreck as *Annihilus Ventor*.

'But, sir–' one of his tank chiefs began to say over the link.

'Alarm! Alarm!' Varco yelled. 'Watch the scopes for Throne's sake!'

He felt acid in his belly. His optimism gushed away. Magos Stravin's intelligence had been seriously flawed and Pride Armour Six had just rolled into a very bad place.

The threat detector began to chime.

'Contact!' Koder announced. 'We have just been spectrum-painted by an aiming beam!'

'Where?' Varco demanded. He twisted around in his seat, checking the physical scopes.

'The auspex refuses to fix,' said Koder. 'Too much background heat.'

'Fine! Where is it?' Varco insisted.

The tank beside them, *Victoria*, commanded by Gem Larok, one of Varco's oldest friends, abruptly disintegrated. Varco flinched away from the scope, temporarily blinded by the flash. *Queen Bitch* shook on her axles, and metal fragments rained off the hull like hailstones.

'Turn! Turn!' Varco ordered. Another Vanquisher, *Havoc*, was torn in two as a rip of turbo laser fire cut across it. Its rear portion rocked up into the air in a vomit of shrapnel and engine debris.

Varco suddenly heard the hollow bang of tank weapons firing. Three vehicles to his left were pumping off rounds into the night, their barrels elevated.

'Traverse! Traverse!' Varco's gunner shouted. 'I think I see it!'

'How can we not see something so frigging big?' the loader moaned.

'Grid 81!' the gunner replied. 'It's right there!'

Varco looked at the auspex. It was finally fixing. The enemy engine was coming for them through the firestorm, cloaked by the heat wash of the burning wells. It came gunning, limb and carapace weapon mounts sizzling with sensor noise.

It was behind them.

Varco traversed *Queen Bitch's* turret cage hard, making the collar motors squeal, until they were aiming backwards.

'Fire!'

The main gun exhaled deafeningly.

'Again!'

His gun crew struggled to reload. They got off a second shot.

Nothing. The giant engine strode on, closing ground. Its vast left heel mashed a Vanquisher underfoot and kicked the mangled wreck aside.

'Full ahead!' Varco yelled. *Queen Bitch* hurtled forwards, and the gun team got off a third shot. Varco saw the shell burst like a firework against the tarnished chest plate of the advancing monster. The turbo laser fired again, a blizzard of light.

The Vanquisher *Heat of Battle* went up, its magazine lighting off as the chewing trace of turbo fire stitched through its hull. *Heat of Battle's* entire turret blew off as the tank's chassis exploded and came spinning through the night like a discarded frying pan. It crashed into *Queen Bitch's* flank with bruising force. Varco was thrown sideways in his seat. Damage alarms began to sing.

'Hit it again!' he ordered.

His gunner thumbed the fire switch and a round boomed out of *Queen Bitch's* raised muzzle. It struck the advancing engine in the throat, and made it rock back a step.

'Again!' Varco bellowed.

The *Victory March* went up. Metal fragments whizzed in all directions. Two of them struck *Queen Bitch's* turret sensors and knocked out the auspex. A third, white-hot, punched through the mantle armour, severed a sheaf of cables and eviscerated the loader. He fell down into the gunwell, screaming, clutching at his exploded torso. Varco blinked away blood. Blood had hosed the entire turret interior and coated every surface.

He unbuckled his restraints and jumped down into the well. 'Koder! Help him! I'll load!'

He knew it was pointless. The loader, writhing and shrieking in pain, was past saving. His intestines were strewn across the tank floor, and his smashed ribcage was sticking out through his torn tunic.

How are you even alive, Varco wondered? He grabbed a fresh shell from the sleeve, and rammed it into the breech.

'Aim!' he told the gunner. Pasted and dripping with his loader's gore, the gunner hesitated.

'Aim it!' Varco screamed.

It was too late. The engine had reached them.

100

When the time came to wake him, he was already dead.

'How is that possible?' Moderati Tarses had asked.

Tarses had spent his life surrounded by the impossible. The engines, the war they unleashed, the arks that carried them, the manner of their delivery, the song of the Manifold, these were all things of a magnitude beyond comfortable human comprehension. Tarses dealt with such things matter of factly. But the death, the death seemed an impossible thing.

They had come to wake him, to break the anointed seals of the hiberberth, and gently coax his vital systems out of suspension, and they had discovered him to be dead.

'How is that possible?' Tarses had asked. He had a cold, clear memory of asking the question, asking it as calmly as a moderati would call for a routine sweep.

'It would seem that, despite our best efforts, he perished from his injuries,' the magos organos had replied. 'Statement: we mourn the loss. Legio Invicta will mourn the loss.'

'I don't understand,' Tarses had said. 'How is this possible? It cannot be possible. You had him suspended on full-spectrum restoration, monitored and supplemented.'

'The very best care, with constant monitoring on a cellular level,' the magos organos had replied. 'Unfortunately, as happens sometimes in cases of severe trauma, we–'

'Let me see him,' Tarses had interrupted.

Tarses looked down. Uplift winds shivered the train of his robes. Lights fizzled and blinked in the black chasm below. Some of them were guide lights, winking in strings, others were the running lights of small pilot craft, chasing down ahead of the gently descending lander. Two thousand metres below him, the roof hatches of the silo were slowly opening like giant petals, exhaling golden light. It was like peering down the throat of a slowly waking volcano.

Tarses searched for a name. Antium, that was it. This place was called Antium, a bulk fabrication plant. It was night down below, and the massive plant, as big as a modest city, was locked in darkness, but it was a false night, a shadow cast by the sheer size of the settling lander as it shut out the Orestean sun.

There would be storms later on. A vessel as large as the lander did not penetrate a world's atmosphere without consequences, no matter how slow and delicate its descent. Standing on the open-mesh gantry fixed to the underbelly of the leviathan, Tarses could smell ozone and hear the pop and squeal of ruptured atmospherics.

Sirens sounded from far below. The crane ships were deploying to begin delivery.

The sirens sounded thin and sad, like a mourning wail.

They had come to wake him, and he was dead.

'How is that possible?' Tarses had asked.

The hiberberth was open, and there was a sweet odour of corruption. Servitors had been scooping out the suspension jelly, but the magos organos ordered them to halt so Tarses could come forwards and look in.

Tarses remembered seeing teeth bared in a frozen rictus, and eyes screwed shut and plugged with jelly residue.

'Begin emergency resuscitation,' he had ordered, turning away.

'It's too late, moderati,' the magos organos had said. The magos organos's name had been Kercher.

'Begin–'

'It's too late,' the magos organos had insisted. 'We have run emergency resus eight times, and additionally boosted vitals with a simulated MIU shunt. There is nothing more we can do.'

Kercher. The magos organos's name had been Kercher. Tarses had not gleaned the data from the noosphere because no moderati were modified for noospheric interface. It conflicted with their direct-plug connection to the Manifold. They were crew, and all crew were direct-plugged.

The magos organos had identified himself by name when he had come to find Tarses. Kercher. 'My name is Kercher, moderati,' he had said, 'from hibernautics. I need to speak to you. I have some terrible news to exload.'

Delivery began. The crane ships moved in like floating islands, skeleton frames of girder-work around huge, whining lifter plants. The uplift wash picked up, until Tarses's robes began to flutter, and he braced one hand on the gantry rail.

Kercher. The magos organos's name had been Kercher. Kercher had come to wake him, and found him to be dead.

'How is that possible?' Moderati Tarses had asked.

'Was it a sudden deterioration?' he had pressed, aware that his voice was changing in pitch. 'Organ failure? Surely organs can be re-grafted? I don't understand what you're telling me. The Mechanicus can defy mortality! How can he just be dead?'

'He's dead,' the magos organos, Kercher, had insisted.

'But–'

'It was no one thing. It was systemic. The wounds he received on Tara were critical. He–'

I was there, you wretched man, in the thick of it. I was beside him when he took those wounds, yelling orders, watching the autoloader count, keeping my eye on the auspex, snarling at my steersman to come around. Thick jungle, the enemy engine darting away like a white ghost through mist and uprooted trees. So fast, those eldar engines, so fleet and light, mocking Victrix, *mocking her stubborn advance. We soaked it up, our void shields absorbing everything our dancing enemy spat at us. They were fast, but they were frail, and one clean shot from the destructor, one clean shot was all we needed. Dogged* Victrix, *slow and heavy, but a brute killer compared with the eldar machine. One shot. One clean shot.*

We were a pico-second away from target solution when the shield popped. Narler yelled out from his sensori station: 'Shield gone, shield gone!'

I remember him shouting that.

The eldar beam trepanned Victrix. *It cut through the outer casing, the intermediate, the internal subcutaneous, spalling white hot shards in all directions and spurting out fat globs of superheated, liquid metal. The upper arrays went, the forward scopes, exploding in sheeting sparks. Narler lost his left arm at the elbow. Gylok, the famulous, was cut in two at the waist. The rear cabin bulkheads blew out as the beam passed through them and murdered tech-priest Solium in his aft compartment. Then the rear cranial generators blew.*

The beam missed him, but the blast effects caught him. Shrapnel and metal chips from the rear cranials blew out like a razor storm, shattering the back of his casket, shredding the principal plug sheafs, the central MIU trunking, and bursting his amniotics.

Pain shot through the MIU link. It was so fierce, I had to unplug before it killed me.

I shouted, 'Princeps! My princeps!'

'I was there,' Tarses had said to the magos organos. 'I was there, on Tara. I know what wounds he took.'

'Then you'll understand, moderati,' Kercher had said.

Kercher.

'I don't understand,' Tarses had said. 'He should be alive. You had him suspended on full-spectrum restoration, monitored and supplemented. The long sleep from Beltran, that should have been enough.'

'We believed so, but we were wrong,' the magos organos had said. 'It is as though, in stasis, he lost the will to live. That he faded away, unwilling to visit the pain of flesh-life again.'

The magos organos's name had been Kercher.

The crane ships delivered *Dominatus Victrix* to the fabrication silo. A scaffold cage awaited to hold and restrain its titanic form. As it settled in, the pneumatic buffers gasped, and servitors swarmed across its hull to detach the delivery lines.

Tarses fell from the lander in a shuttle, alone. The shuttle picked up a blinking pilot boat and followed its signals down the black gulf, along the guide light pathways, into the bowels of Antium.

No one spoke to him. Orestean magi, ferrying tools from carts and calling up noospheric specs to begin repairs, saw the look on Tarses's face. He climbed the steps, moving up the scaffold cage, hearing the pop and hiss of machine tools at work, seeing the flare and ghost light of welding work already underway.

At the scaffold summit, he walked across the extended link bridge to the rear cranial hatch.

The bridge space was unimaginably cold. *Victrix* had ridden in a void vault during transit. There was thawing frost on all the surfaces. Tarses stepped inside.

This was his entire place in the universe, his chosen and appointed place: split level, circular, the command seats – moderati, steersman, sensori – set in the chin, the princeps's amniotic socket raised behind them. Loose cables, severed cables, draped the floor. The hard surfaces had spots of dried blood on them. The bridge space was open to the false night sky. Tarses looked up. Buckled, torn metal, cut through to the inner skin, curled away. There were puncture wounds everywhere, in the old, rich, red leather upholstery of the command chairs, in the deck, in the roof, in the stations. Several screens were cracked or smashed.

He rested his left hand on the back of a leather seat. It was cold to the touch. His right hand reached around to his back. Still sore. The blast had caught them all. Tarses hadn't even realised he'd been slit by a shrapnel splinter until much later.

'Moderati, you're bleeding,' Sensori Narler had said, which had been funny as Narler had been bleeding chronically at the time, clutching his severed arm to his chest like a surprise gift.

'Oh,' Moderati Tarses had said.

Like yesterday.

Cold. Cold metal and cold leather. Cold glass fragments crunching underfoot. Dead cold. Awake, *Victrix* had been so alive. The metal itself had been alive: a living thing, an engine, a Titan.

The MIU had been closed down into dormancy before they'd made shift. It could and would be revived, but the pain would linger.

There was a dark stain on the deck plates that marked where Gylok, the famulous, had died so terribly and so suddenly. Tarses peered at it. The mark looked like rust.

Both of them.

Tarses sat down in his seat, feeling tiny lumps of armourglass crunch under him.

Kercher. The magos organos's name had been Kercher. They had come to wake him, and he was already dead.

'Zane?' Lau called out. 'Are you in here?'

The Master of the Legio Invicta Skitarii clambered into *Victrix's* bridge through the rear hatch, his hefty boots grinding fragmented glass underfoot.

'I'm here,' Tarses replied, rising slowly from his seat. He looked across the bridge space at Lau. 'It's you then, is it? Not Bohrman?'

Lau nodded. He was a massive, armoured creature, clad in the hawked colours of the foot warriors, designed to threaten, designed to terrify. His gun arm rested limply at his side.

'Zane, I'm so sorry,' Lau said. His voice thundered up out of his augmitters like a freight train on an incline.

Tarses sighed and walked up the bridge steps to face him.

'So am I. I regret my actions, of course. I understand the consequences.'

Tarses knelt in front of Lau, his head back. Glass crackled under his knees. 'Make it quick, Lau, that's all I ask.'

'Get up,' said Lau.

'What?'

'Get up, Zane.'

Tarses rose to his feet and looked up at the skitarii monster. 'The standard punishment is death, Lau. I understand that. I embrace it. I had hoped that Bohrman might have had the decency to finish me, but I appreciate he doesn't want to get his hands dirty. Just get it over with, quickly. Arm that limb of yours and fire.'

'Zane, Zane,' Lau said, shaking his head. He reached out his left hand, the one that wasn't fused into a weapon, and set it on Tarses's shoulder. 'You've really messed up this time.'

'I know I have.'

'But we need you. *Victrix* must walk again.'

Tarses snorted. 'Without a princeps or a famulous to be anointed in his place?'

'*Victrix* must walk again.'

Tarses shook his head. 'Skaugen's dead, Throne help me, and his apprentice was slain. Solium too. There's no–'

'The forge of Orestes has promised to provide a candidate. We will make do.'

'So… *Victrix* will walk under another master. Good. I'm gratified. She will walk without me.'

'Gearhart has ordered the crime to be overlooked,' said Lau.

'What?' asked Tarses.

Lau looked down at him. 'Overlooked. *Victrix* needs her moderati. It was unfortunate. Charges have been suspended.'

'I killed him,' Tarses said.

'In extremis,' Lau nodded. 'The magos organos–'

'Kercher,' said Tarses.

'What?'

'The magos organos's name was Kercher.'

'I didn't know that,' said Lau.

'Unwilling?' Tarses had said. 'Are you suggesting that Princeps Skaugen, my princeps, would shrink from life like a coward?'

'That's not what I'm saying, moderati,' Kercher had replied.

'You said that, in stasis, he lost the will to live, that he faded away, unwilling to visit the pain of flesh-life again. My master Skaugen was no coward! He would not have given up like that!'

'Moderati! I–' The magos organos – Kercher, *Kercher* – had choked as Tarses clamped his fist around his wind pipe.

'You insult his name, you despicable bastard!' Tarses had growled, tightening his grip.

'It was murder, a capital crime,' Lau said. 'The circumstances allow some leeway, but not much. That's why I'm here and not Bohrman. The legio understands you were out of your head with grief. This mitigates.'

'I killed him.'

'You did, Zane.'

'So, just execute me. A magos, I butchered a magos.'

'You did.'

'His name was Kercher.'

Lau sighed. '*Victrix* is to be repaired. It will be given a new princeps and a new tech-priest. You have to stay plugged to this crew. You're the moderati. We can't afford to lose you too. You know the engine, it knows you. You have to ease the new princeps into meshing. No one else can do it.'

'But I killed a man.'

Lau shrugged. 'After this war is done, we will make amends. Punishment may be due. Bohrman told me that the Order Execute will be at the discretion of your new princeps.'

'I'm tired,' said Tarses.

'Of course you are' replied Lau. 'No one suffers the loss of a princeps easily. He should not have died in his sleep.'

'He should not have died at all,' replied Tarses.

But he had.

They had come to wake him, and they had found him dead.

>

'If I might be permitted to say, mamzel–'

'What?' Severin replied, cupping a hand to her ear. The great ceremonial horns on the summit of the hive and the main forge ziggurat had just blared again, an ear-splitting noise that rolled out across the hive and eclipsed Major Gotch's words as comprehensively as the bulk lander overhead was eclipsing the daylight.

'If I might be permitted to say, mamzel, it is quite a spectacle,' Gotch repeated.

'It is, major,' she agreed.

From the parapet of the Covenant Gardens, beside the Munitorial Halls, they could see across inner terraces of the mid-hive, across streets and sinks, belltowers and pylons, stacks and spires, all the way to Kiodrus Square and the Field of Mars, behind which the bastion of the High

Forge rose like a sooty cliff, its detail hazed by the distance and the coldly eclipsed light. West of them rose the summit of Orestes Principal, a mountain of lights where, for once, the evening rays had been stolen early.

The bulk lander held its station less than a thousand metres above the highest spires of the hive, scorching credulity with its mass and its defiance of gravity. Its belly-holds were open, pouring out shafts of pale radiance as soft as moonglow, and crane ships as big as entire hive stacks, but diminished by the shape of their parent vessel, were slowly trafficking the air, manoeuvring massive cargoes down onto the Field. They moved ponderously, as if they were sticking to the air like molluscs sticking to glass.

'How does it hang there?' Gotch wondered aloud.

'I presume that was a rhetorical question, major,' she replied.

Gotch nodded.

'Good, because I couldn't begin to tell you.'

Bells were pealing across the hive, from every tower and campanile, but not the ominous tolling that had presaged the war. The ringing was jubilant. Legio Invicta had arrived.

What seemed like the entire population of the great hive had taken to the streets to watch and celebrate the moment. Etta Severin saw them swarming below her, choking the sink avenues, the conduit terraces, every balcony and observation, cheering, waving, and brandishing flags and banners, some handmade for the occasion, others old emblems of Imperial and Orestean significance reverently unfurled.

The multitude was flecked through with red. The servants of the Mechanicus had emerged from their fabricatories in astonishing numbers, to mix with the citizenry and welcome salvation.

'There's another,' remarked Gotch, and pointed to the eastern sky. Out in the smoky blue of the evening sky, beyond the skirts and outreaches of the hive and under the lip of the bulk lander overhead, Severin saw a second superheavy ship, forty kilometres away, a pale ghost like an oblong daytime moon, holding its station and waiting to approach the hive as soon as the first lander cleared away.

The horns sounded again, spurring another roar from the watching crowds that ran, doppler shift, from street to street across the hive. Trooper transports, tiny compared to the toiling crane ships and their bulky cargoes, were beginning to fly down from the bulk lander's holds towards the Field of Mars.

'The foot troops,' Gotch said.

'Skitarii,' said Severin.

'They're the ones,' Gotch nodded. 'Not like the Guard, I hear. Not regular. All plugged up and bionic.'

'You've never seen them?' asked Severin.

Gotch shrugged. 'Of course, time to time. Living here, you can't but help it. State dos, ceremonials, that sort of thing. But I've never served with them, never fought with them.'

'That would be the true measure of them, would it, major?' she asked.

He sniffed. 'That would be the true measure of anyone, mamzel.'

She checked her chronometer. He was late, but she was hardly about to complain. They'd arranged to meet via courier messages, and he had seemed to agree without any qualms, which she'd taken as a good sign. He'd chosen the place, the Covenant Gardens. She had a good idea why, and it wasn't the view. The executor fetial was playing games right from the start. She silently cursed the mortal soul of Governor Aleuton for dropping this onerous duty in her lap.

She took a breath, and tried another of her brain-game techniques to calm her mood, with no success. She felt unprepared. She'd spent the past two days studying protocols, archives and summary accounts, trying to supplement what she already knew about the Mechanicus and its customs. The process had simply served to emphasise how little she knew, how little the Imperium knew, to be frank. *The Mechanicus is a race apart,* Aleuton had said.

'You're not joking,' she whispered.

'Mamzel?' asked Gotch.

'Nothing. No matter. I was just talking to myself.' All the files, all the data, proof that not only were there things about the Mechanicus she didn't know, there were things she didn't know she didn't know.

'No, mamzel,' Gotch nudged, 'I meant... he's here.'

Gulping in surprise, a gulp that turned into an awkward cough that she fought to contain, she turned.

The executor fetial was advancing towards them across the twilit lawns of the Covenant Gardens. He was strikingly tall, and cruelly handsome, with sculpted cheekbones and cropped silver hair. His robes were soft black, and he strode with the long, elegant steps of a dancer, not like a member of the Mechanicus at all, not at all. Only that emerald flash in his eyes gave it away.

He was escorted by a slender, shaven-headed youth with ferociously intelligent blue eyes. The youth, significantly shorter than the executor, was also dressed in black. His famulous. That will be his famulous, Severin thought. Sonne. A famulous is an apprentice or adept trainee.

The executor smiled as he saw her. It was a warm and human smile, and this surprised Severin more than anything.

'How do I look?' she whispered sidelong to Gotch, smoothing the sides of her simple grey gown.

'How do *I* look, mamzel?' he countered.

Surprised, she looked at him. Gotch had opted for battle-dress, not the ritual armour he'd greeted her in two nights before. His heavy frame was cased in a matt-brown body glove, covered with khaki webbing, and his boots and gloves were thick-laced leather. He wore a Cadian-style moulded helmet, buckled under his chin, and the hellgun in his paws was matt black.

'You look... impressive,' she replied.

'Good. You look a lot more impressive than I do.'

Severin blinked. 'Thank you.'

Gotch nodded and smiled at her. The horseshoe scar made his lips curl the wrong way. 'Then we're set, aren't we?' he mumbled.

Severin, flushed with a refreshed confidence, turned back to face the approaching executor. She speed reviewed all she had gleaned about him.

Djared Crusius. Executor fetial of the Legio Invicta. En route to the Sabbat front from the Beltran Campaign. Forty-nine war engines, plus a skitarii force. Skitarii, not skatirii. Remember the pronunciation, for Throne's sake. His famulous is called Sonne. Invicta is an ancient legio, much honoured. Crusius's job is to smooth the way. He is an ambassador, a facilitator. He was purposely designed to interface with Imperials. Legio Invicta's princeps maximus is named Gearhart. Forty-nine engines. They derive from Proximus forge world, close to the Imperial heartworlds. Invicta is an ancient legio, much honoured. Forty-nine engines. His name is Djared Crusius–

'Mamzel, my name is Djared Crusius. I apologise for my tardiness.' His voice was so much softer than she'd imagined.

Fleshvoice. They call it a fleshvoice.

'Executor,' Severin replied, bowing her head and expertly making the cog sign with her hands, only to find that the executor had made the sign of the aquila to her.

Crusius's smile broadened. 'It's like a game. Stone, paper, blade.'

Blushing, Severin parted her hands.

'I meant no disrespect,' Crusius said. 'In my experience, few Imperial souls can make the Icon Mechanicus without laboured unfamiliarity. You must have practised.'

'I did,' she nodded.

'Thank you for that. I genuinely appreciate the effort. Few bother.'

'You do not need to apologise for your timekeeping, executor. I was admiring the view.'

Crusius looked up at the bulk lander filling the heavens, and his eyes tracked the slow descent of the latest crane ship. They flashed green for a second.

'I can appreciate why. In fact that's the reason I chose the Covenant Gardens as our meeting place.'

She nodded. *As if.*

She began. 'I am Henrietta Severin, consular officer first class, attached to the Munitorum Orestes Trade Service. This is my bodyman, Major–'

'Zamual Gotch, Orestean Pride, now of the gubernatorial lifeguard,' Crusius took up smoothly, giving his hand to the soldier. Gotch took it and shook it warily, as if he were being offered something unusual to hold.

'Eight decorations for valour, including the Emperor's medal,' said Crusius. 'I must hear that story sometime, major, if you'd be inclined.'

'Yes sir, anytime,' said Gotch, taken aback.

'This is–' Crusius began, turning to his companion.

'Your famulous, Sonne,' said Severin quickly. She nodded to the boy, who bowed to her in a dignified manner.

'Well,' chuckled Crusius, 'shall we get past this game of who owns the most data? Because, I assure you, mamzel, I will win it.'

'Really?' asked Severin with a fake smile.

'Really,' Crusius nodded. 'I should address you as Consular Severin, but informally, if such time should come, I should call you Etta, as this is the diminutive you prefer. You were born in Antium Subhive forty-eight years ago, but you don't, I may say, look anything beyond twenty-five. Your father was a fleetmaster with an inner spinward charter. He was domestically violent. He died eight years ago, of an addiction-related illness. Your mother resides in Antium still. Chloris Rhoweena Severin. How's her hip? It was playing her up, rheumatic. An augmetic would repair her.'

'My mother is... well,' said Severin, tight-lipped.

'Good. Do we have an understanding?'

Severin nodded. 'I don't much like your manner, sir,' she said.

Crusius frowned. 'I apologise. That was not my intention. I simply wished to establish the breadth of my data resources.'

'You've surpassed yourself,' muttered Gotch.

'Behave!' Severin hissed.

'My master is sometimes forward, lady,' Sonne said. 'No offence is intended. We of the Mechanicus are used to immediate inloads of personal data. No... uhm... what is the word, executor?'

'Small talk,' said Crusius.

'Ah, yes. I will incant the term to my vocabulary index. We are not used to small talk, lady. Are you noospheric, at all?'

'No,' replied Severin.

'Data-inload formatted in any way?'

'No,' replied Severin, more firmly.

Sonne looked up at his master. 'Remedial: I fear we are getting off to a bad start.'

Crusius nodded. He looked down at Severin. 'Etta… may I call you Etta?'

'No you frigging mayn't,' growled Gotch.

Crusius ignored him. 'I understand what this is about. The Lord Governor feels uneasy. A Mechanicus war, driven by the Mechanicus, on a world that should be his. That's why he's sent you to me, to observe, on his behalf. A clever choice: female, non-military.'

'Seems you have the measure of us, sir,' Severin replied.

'I welcome your involvement,' Crusius said, turning to look at the crane ships crawling through the air.

'You do?'

'We stand together in this venture, Etta: Imperium and Mechanicus. We were born together, and we rose together, and the Imperium is as nothing if we don't stand together now. Legio Invicta is not offended by the Lord Governor's desire to spy upon us. Behold! Watch us work. Send me more Etta Severins, in fact. You will come with me and I will show you everything, Etta, everything. Are you ready for that?'

She nodded. 'I find your attitude surprising, Djared. May I call you Djared?' she added snidely.

'Of course.'

She bowed her head slightly. 'I know why you wanted to meet me here,' she said.

'Do you? Why?'

'The Covenant Gardens. Established in the second century Orestean to commemorate the tacit union of forge and Imperium. You were making a point.'

'Was I?' asked Crusius. 'What might that have been?'

'You were reminding me how Imperial and Mechanicus interests always mesh, especially at times of war.'

Crusius smiled and shook his head. 'I was simply offering you a grandstand view of the proceedings. There was no significance in this choice of venue apart from the view it claimed across the hive. Engines are so massive when you see them close up. I wanted you to observe them from a proper distance.'

'You did?'

'I most certainly did. See.'

Severin turned. Far away, across the hive, the Titans were assembling in a row on the Field of Mars, where the crane ships had deposited them. Eight of them. They looked like a small honour guard standing to attention, like soldiers dressing ranks, except the scale was off.

They weren't men. They were giant constructs in the rough shape of men.

'Invicta alights,' said Crusius. 'Would you like to see them close up, Etta?'

'I would,' she replied.

'I didn't know your name was Zamual,' she whispered to Gotch as they followed Crusius to the steps.

'You never asked,' he returned.

>

There was something going on. The bells were ringing again. In the Worthies Garden beneath the Chancery, Moderati Zink sat back on his heels and stopped tending. A small basket sat beside him, full of weeds uprooted from the flowerbeds.

Twilight had come early, and the bells were ringing. In the

streets beyond the garden's walls, Zink could hear a swarming multitude, cheering, chattering, singing. The hive horns boomed. Zink saw banners fluttering past behind the top of the walls.

Was it a feast day? Candlemas already? Zink wasn't sure and couldn't remember. Perhaps someone would come and tell him. They often did that when he became befuddled.

He got up, stiff and unsteady, and carried the basket of weeds over to the incinerator behind his hut. He plodded, shoulders slowly swinging, like a war engine steadily walking towards its prey. The twilight had turned the garden into a cold, grey space. Where had the sun gone?

He looked up to find it. Something was filling the sky, a vast shadow with square holes in it, out of which beams of heavenly light were falling.

The hive horns boomed again.

Zink couldn't find a name for the thing filling the sky, but he knew he'd seen one before. It made him shudder, not the awesome sight of it, but the partial memory it conjured in his broken head.

Tears sprang up in his sunken eyes, inexplicably. His gnarled hands, unconsciously remembering an old habit, made the sign of the cog.

Crowds mobbed Perpendicular and the public squares under Congress. They formed a jubilant avenue, millions strong, through the Bulwarks and down onto Kiodrus Square, cheering the procession of the Prelate Ecumenic of the Ministoria Orestae as he made stately progress from the Basilica down to the Field of Mars to greet and bless the arriving princeps of Legio Invicta. The prelate, Gaspar Luciul, waved at the multitude from his walking carriage. He advanced with an entourage of a thousand priests and two thousand Ecclesiarchy aides, a river of golden gowns, scarlet velvet, fur trims and silver staffs flanked by the glittering white lines of Ministoria pikemen and halberdiers. A constellation of seraphic wards skimmed over the cavalcade, supporting the long, flowing banners of the Ecclesiarchy in tribute.

Banners and flags were everywhere, brandished, waving, draped from hab balconies, or lowered down the front elevations of state buildings: aquilas, cogs, the emblems of the Guard and the Fleet, the austere insignias of the Munitorum, the gaudy banneroles of merchant houses, public placards proudly denoting particular hive quarters and trades, the crests of nobility, the quirky motifs of artisan guilds and trade associations, the solemn brands of colleges and academic brotherhoods, even the dark, dismaying standards of the Orestean ordos.

In the level eighty-eight commercia, as in every other mercantile node of the hive, premises had stayed open into the evening, past the usual end of business. The concourses and alleys, lit by naphtha flares, were thick with pedestrians, some intoxicated, some eager for intoxication, flooding to the taverns and dining halls, buying souvenirs and trinkets and lucky charms, badges with religious mottos, pendants with the markings of the Orestean World Crest, little tin aquilas, pins of the Orestean regiments, wardsafes, mementos, touchstones, hopefasts. In *Anatometa*, Manfred Zember almost cackled aloud as he sold his twenty-ninth Titan doll of the day. He had employed a small machinist in the west end of the commercia to mass produce them to his design, a hundred units, a daring investment. If the dolls hadn't sold, he would have never been able to pay the machinist off, and the city bailiffs would have taken *Anatometa* away from him, and marched him off to debtor's gaol.

He would have to order more. Twenty-nine dolls had earned

him, in less than five hours, more than he'd usually make in a quarter. He could already pay the machinist off, place a down payment on fifty more, and still have coin in his coffer.

'These are very marvellous,' the next customer announced, just like the Lord Governor had remarked to Zember's grandsire, sixty years earlier. How times had changed.

'May I see it walk?' the customer inquired.

'Of course you may, sir,' Zember replied, taking up a clockwork Warlord and winding the key in its back.

Riik! Riik! Riik!

He set it walking across the show bench.

The customer clapped his hands. 'I will take two!' he decided. 'They are quite the most ingenious things! Are you of the forge, perhaps, sir?'

Zember bowed. 'I am but a modest doll-maker, sir,' he replied, 'and you are very gracious in your compliment.'

'Two then, one for each of my sons. Another couple of years, and they will be old enough to enlist in tertiary.'

'You must be very proud of them, sir,' said Zember.

'I am. Two, then. Two, I declare. The blue Reaver there, and that crimson Warlord walking before us.'

'Shall I wrap them, sir?' Manfred Zember asked.

Stefan Samstag closed the door of his little hab and locked it. He couldn't bear the noise. The whole of Makepole sink was shaking with footsteps and voices. The hive had gone mad, and he knew the uproar would continue long into the night.

He had worked a shift and a half. His supervisor had ordered the port's cargo decks to be cleared out to make space for the materiel coming in with the new legio. Brute work, no time for chat, no time for rest, working the wharf end to end, hauling the wheezing hydraulics of the pack-loader back and forth to pick and move the crates. Loading space would be at a premium.

Most of his workmates had quit the shift and headed off to join the celebrations in the bars and taverns along Garnet and Homulk. Reinhart had given each of them a silver florin and a smile. 'Good work! Have a drink to victory on me, boys,' he'd said.

'Have you heard anything?' he'd asked Stefan.

'Not a thing,' Stefan had replied.

Not a thing.

The little hab was cold, but Stefan felt no inclination to fire up the heater. The place was so small, but it felt enormous without her in it. The slip, the message wafer in its foil tear-bag, still lay on the little plastek table in the living space, beside the unwashed stack of beakers and the half-eaten loaf of bread gone blue with mould.

Nothing. She'd been gone these few days, and not even a word to say where she was or when he might see her again, or if she was even alive. He thought of her: her smile, the sound of her voice, the movement of her short blonde hair, the scent of her body, the taste of her mouth, the reassurance of her fingertips, the little golden wheel.

Weary, shaking, he knelt down in front of the hab's domestic shrine, made the sign of the double eagle, and looked up at the flimsy brass icon. The posy of flowers in the little offering bottle had withered.

Stefan began to pray to the God-Emperor, for deliverance, for strength, for Cally, wherever she was.

In the hall outside, revellers began to shout and sing, banging on doors, and breaking the intensity of his prayer.

He leapt up, furious, and hammered his fists on the inside of the locked door.

'Shut up! Shut up, you bastards! Leave me alone!'

No one heard him. They were making too much noise.

The Analyticae was almost silent, just the buzz and hum of working systems and processing cogitators. Despite the prospect of the spectacle outside, and in spite of the permission of the magos, most of the nine hundred adepts and logis had voluntarily remained at work.

Adept Feist marked the latest block of pict-feed sampled to him *'undecipherable'*, and discarded it. His head was throbbing, and filled with images he would have given several high-end modifications to forget.

A manip gently tapped his sleeve. Feist looked up.

'Magos?'

Egan smiled down at him. 'Reviewing: what have I told you, adept?' he asked, kindly.

'Take a break once in a while, magos?'

Egan nodded. 'Agreement. Your skein is inloaded to bursting point. I fear for your cortex, Feist. Take a walk, for my sake if not yours. Suggestion: why don't you stand down and let another take your station? Go out and enjoy the ceremony. Or at least watch it here.'

Feist nodded.

'Good,' said Egan. He turned to move on.

'Magos?' Feist called out.

'Yes, Feist?'

'My suggestion, magos? Has it been actioned?'

'It's pending, Feist. I exloaded the query directly to the Adept Seniorus and the executor fetial, requesting their comments. I have received nothing back so far. It's possible they're busy.'

Feist grinned. 'That's a reasonable supposition, magos,' he said.

'Even if they agree, adept, the process may take time. Permissions and code authorities will have to be obtained. Sequestered material is inaccessible for a reason.'

'Of course.'

Egan nodded, his mechadendrites writhing like a mantle of snakes. 'If they grant permission, Feist, I'll put you on it. Team leader. An advancement for you, I think.'

'I'm gratified, magos.'

'You deserve it. A step on the way to magos modification. Your hard work and insight should be rewarded. Now relax, please, for a moment at least.'

Feist turned back to his hololith. His fingers played, haptically cancelling out his work dossiers and moving them to a side field. He accessed the direct feed from the state pict-flow. An image, three-dimensional, blossomed across his noosphere: the Field of Mars, live feed, ebullient millions, singing and cheering. Switch view: the banners flapping above the ranked figures of the Imperial Guardsmen. Switch view: the dark line of Titans, Legio Invicta Titans, drawn up like an armoured wall, too large to be appreciated by the pict's limited field of vision, just legs like gigantic tree trunks, martial banners draping into view from gun-limbs out of shot: class symbols, victory banners, kill pennants. Switch view: the Prelate Ecumenic, in his mechanically elevated pulpit, arms outstretched, singing the psalm of invocation, a thousand-strong choir of clerics behind him. Switch view: there, the Lord Governor, Aleuton, flanked by crested lifeguards, side by side with the Adept Seniorus, waiting to greet the arrival.

'Audio,' said Feist.

The sound swam up. Hectic crowd noise, overwhelming: the boom of the forge horns; bells, chiming fit to crack; voices, mass voices, massive, swelling voices.

'Dim sound,' said Feist. He wiggled a finger. Switch view: an angle aimed up at the vast lander eclipsing the field. A drop-ship, thorny and armoured, ramping down into focus on blazing spurts of retrograde thrust.

'Show,' Feist instructed.

The drop-ship set down in the open heart of the field, rocking on hydraulic limbs. The ceremonial carpet was buffeted by the underwash, and Guardsmen hurried forwards, heads down, to set it flat again. On the side wall of the hulking drop, the emblem of the Legio Invicta. The waiting multitude went wild with cheering and yelling.

The side hatch of the drop-ship clunked open. Petals and confetti filled the air like a snowstorm or bad pict feed disruption.

Emerging, slowly, majestically, Lord Gearhart of the Legio Invicta and First Princeps Bohrman, side by side, conducted in their amniotic caskets by dozens of adepts and skitarii. The Legio Invicta adepts wore damask robes, and spurred the upright caskets along with their mechadendrites and manipulator poles. The Invicta skitarii, a throwback to more savage times, were fearsome beasts, striped and extravagantly marked, their armour built for threat, their genes selected for bulk. Muscular arms gleamed in the odd light. Heavy boots thumped in marching unison. Weapon limbs snapped up to salute as one. Feather plumes, ivory ornaments, leopardskin capes, modified fangs. The skitarii roared at the sky like predators, as fearsome and bestial as Space Wolves.

Feist shuddered. The skitarii thumped their fists against their breastplates and howled again. Barbarians, Feist thought, so unlike our own. How can we be bred of the same stuff? They are like another race.

Another howl, so loud, the audio dampers on Feist's feed cut in automatically and muted the noise.

Feist switched view back to Gearhart and Bohrman. Their amniotic caskets slid forwards on suspensor bearings, spurred and directed by the flocking adepts. Both men were naked, beautiful flesh and bionics intermixed, riding nobly inside their data-liquid worlds like gods, their forearms, hands, shins and feet enveloped by the dense bundles of plug sheathing that connected them to the inner surfaces of the caskets. The amniotic fluids were soft pink with blood. Trunking cables and implants snaked out of both men's eyes and scalps, writhing and wobbling in the viscous fluid. Gearhart's body was sixty-eight per cent bionic; Bohrman's was forty-two. Feist marvelled at the intricate work that had fashioned them into monsters.

For monsters they most surely were.

Both armourglass caskets were studded with amniotic plugs, ready for connection. Sockets in the heads of the mighty engines waited, breathlessly, achingly, to receive their fit.

Gearhart opened his mouth.

'Audio up,' Feist instructed.

'Lord Governor Imperialis Poul Elic Aleuton, Adept Seniorus Mechanici Solomahn Imanual,' Gearhart said, his augmitted voice deep, like the plutonic grumble of a dying sun, 'the Legio Invicta greets you both.'

Aleuton bowed and made the sign of the Icon Mechanicus. Imanual bowed and made the sign of the aquila.

Gearhart grunted his approval. 'Know then,' he growled, 'that Legio Invicta is here. Know then that the Legio Invicta will walk upon Orestes.'

* * *

>

Fidelis Highway, running south-west out of Gynex Subhive, rain coming down out of the russet night like spittle. The subhive behind them, a grease-black skeleton of girders and derricks, spires and stacks. They were still passing through the hinterland of processors and sub-silos that skirted Gynex, dingy outlying suburbs and satellite plants; left of the highway, industrial refineries on fire, stuffing the air with a hot, petrochemical stink that made their eyes sore and their throats tight; right, bulk smelteries and ore works like giant iron buckets. The flames of the refineries reflected in the rainwater caught inside the shell craters pocking the road surface. Wind levees had come down somewhere south of them, and sand had blown in from the Astrobleme, dusting the road and drifting in the gulleys like stained snow.

Cally Samstag recognised the sand, the peachy pink of it. She'd enjoyed tertiary PDF's exercises out in the Astrobleme. It had all been hiking, map work, range firing, hunt and hold games. They'd been adventures to her, out in the hollow wilds of the ragged planet, setting up habitents under the huge bowl of the night sky, learning to navigate by unfamiliar stars, sniping sand-rabbits for food, listening to the ordinary stories of ordinary hive folk just like her. Once, last trip out, her platoon had encountered a vassal tribe on the move, out past the first line of impact cliffs: mobile prospectors, riding crawlers and dune tractors, pulling their habs behind them on heavily treaded trailers, mangy livestock following along in long, tethered teams. Handmade banners, bleached by sun and dust, faded robes, battered rebreathers turned into heathen fright masks. Savage people. To Cally, they'd seemed like the most alien things she'd ever met, out there in the peachy pink wastes under the startlingly blue sky, a landscape she didn't belong to.

The platoon had been wary. Mister Sarosh, their veteran sergeant, had explained to them that it was an excellent opportunity to practise stop and search protocols. They'd advanced and hailed the slow convoy. Men had shouted back guttural cries and jumped down from the halting procession, waving las-locks and staves. Mister Sarosh had spoken with their leaders. A tense moment waiting, then a broad welcome. There had been the ritual exchange of water and alcohol, toasts and handshaking, the etiquette of the deep desert. Everyone had been obliged to drink a sip of the tribe's caustic homebrew, and surrender a sip of their amasec rations. Then began the bartering, the trading: Imperial coins for anthracite beads and polished seashell fossils, a uniform-issue sand scarf for a belt of worked leather, water purification tablets for uncut gems and rough stones, a habitent pack for a beautiful prayer kite.

They had searched the wagons, compartment by compartment, trying to be polite and uninvasive. Each compartment had been dark, sun-blinds drawn, dust-drapes down. The wagons had smelled of spices and heat, and warm dusty bodies, but not, as Cally had been afraid, of filth or disease. The hab interiors, lit by hanging brass prom-lamps, had been wonderfully decorated in brass, rich fabrics and astonishing carved wood. Inlays and veneers had shone through ancient lacquer. Silver kettles with long swan-neck spouts had simmered on coal stoves, issuing the sweetest, thickest aromas. Women, so gowned and veiled you could only see their eyes, clutched infants to their breasts and watched warily as the clean, drab troops of PDF tertiary moved through the wagons. Children, wild-eyed and wondering, had peered out at them from overhead bunks or underfloor stow-spaces. *We are the aliens,* Cally had realised.

A woman, dark brown eyes showing through the slit in her purple silk robe, had approached her, speaking to her in a low but insistent way. The woman had pointed to the silver aquila Cally was wearing around her neck. Stef had bought it for her, as a good luck charm, the night before they'd left Castria for Orestes.

The woman had shown Cally a golden medal, a little, intricate wheel of dark gold on a golden chain. It was the most beautiful thing Cally had ever seen.

'She wants to trade, Samstag,' Mister Sarosh had told her. 'Always trade. Keep them sweet.'

Cally had hesitated. Stef had given her the aquila, as a good luck charm. She was sure he'd understand, but–

'What's the hold-up, Samstag?' Mister Sarosh had asked.

Cally had explained her reluctance.

Mister Sarosh had looked at the golden medal the woman was proffering. 'That's just good luck in another language,' he had told her.

Cally had carefully taken the silver aquila from around her neck, and made the exchange. The woman had hugged her quickly, gratefully, and then vanished forever into the shadows of the compartment.

Cally had worn the little golden wheel around her neck ever since.

When she'd come home, back to the little hab in Makepole sink, Stef hadn't minded. 'Heavy gold. Worth a bit more than the double eagle I gave you,' he'd admired.

Her pack, her bedroll and her boots had been full of peachy, pink sand and its pungent, graphite smell, residue of the Astrobleme, a reminder of her adventures.

Coming up the wounded Fidelis Highway, Cally saw the sand again, blowing in mournfully from the outer dark. She smelled the same pungent, graphite smell on the wet air, and felt happy memories thudding back into her as painfully as lasrounds. All those adventures, those innocent adventures, back when being part of tertiary PDF meant fun and exercise and comradeship, and coming home each time, after a week away, to Stef and the little hab in Makepole sink. He'd be cooking dinner, slow and tired from his last shift. He'd take her into his big arms with a mouth kiss and a husky 'Welcome back'.

'What's that smell?' he'd ask.

'Just the dust. The dust in my clothes. Gets everywhere.'

'Smells good. Smells real.'

Adventures. A laughable notion now. This was a real adventure, the rest had all been rehearsals. She'd said so to Golla Uldana. Golla had laughed.

'Cally-girl, they weren't adventures. Tertiary out in the 'bleme was just exercises.'

'But–'

'Listen to Golla, little sister. Adventures, *real* adventures, are never fun while they're happening.'

They were Activated Twenty-Six, shipped to Gynex from Principal, four platoons under a master sergeant called Chine, who Cally hadn't met before. Mister Sarosh had been reduced to a platoon leader. Light infantry, no heavy support or ordnance except a single autocannon lugged along by a team in third platoon. Cally only knew some of the faces. Golla, of course; Binderman, a bird-like scholam tutor who'd been with them the day they'd met the tribe; a hard woman from Lazarus sink called Reiss; Johan Farick; Franz-Alfred Koch with his wall-eyes and his continued insistence on the use of his full, ridiculous name; Bohn Iconis; Gerhart Peltze; the posh girl from Summittown whose name Cally could never remember – Janny, Janey, was it?; Kyril Antic, who liked to play the joker; Lars Vulk, the big nung from the Bulwarks who tried to persuade everyone he was a moody hammer when in fact he was a junior at a Bulwark bakery; Cefn Shardin, a seamster; Osric Muldin, the idiot from Congress who'd so dismally failed to erect his habitent on the first Astrobleme exercise and had become a standing joke; and a few others.

The rest were unknowns, and all of them were in this with her.

'Break over!' Master Sergeant Chine yelled out. 'Come on, come on! Let's be having you!'

Cally had slipped away into a storm gulley to take a pee. She heard the master sergeant's shout, and struggled to empty her bladder, squatting in the basin of the gulley, her PDF breeches pulled down around her bare knees.

'Come on! Come on!'

'What are you doing down there?' Golla called. 'Cally-girl?'

'Taking a wiz!' Cally yelled back. 'Cover for me!'

'Taking a wiz,' she heard Kyril Antic laugh, as if it was a brilliantly crafted joke.

'Front and centre, Activated Twenty-Six!' she heard Master Sergeant Chine yell.

Done, *done*. Cally hauled up her breeches and buckled her belt. She began to clamber up the gulley side, her fingers pulling uselessly at the pink sand. Sliding down into the gulley had been easy. Cally hadn't realised how hard it would be to get out again. She began to panic, trowelling at the sand flows with her hands. She smelled the pungent, graphite smell and felt the sand underneath her fingernails.

Shit. Oh shit.

A metre up the bank, then rolling back. A metre up again, down she went.

Oh *shit*.

'Sound off, Activated!' Chine bellowed.

They began to sound off, trooper by trooper.

I'm stuck! I'm stuck down here! Help me, I'm stuck in the storm gulley, Cally wanted to shout out. How would that look? How would that end? PDF officers had commissarial powers. Chine was a miserable piece of work. He'd shoot her in the head.

'Where's Samstag?' Chine shouted. 'Where is she?'

Silence. Cally tried to ascend again, but slithered back to where she'd started.

'Sir, Trooper Samstag is taking a relief break, sir,' she heard Golla call out.

'A what?' she heard Master Sergeant Chine reply.

'Sir, a relief break, sir.'

'A piss?'

'Yes, sir.'

Cally heard Kyril Antic sniggering.

'Shut your laughter, funny man!' Cally heard Master Sergeant Chine shout at Kyril Antic.

'Sir, sorry, master sergeant, sir.'

A pause.

'Activated Twenty-Six, you are such a bunch of idiots,' Master Sergeant Chine complained. 'You don't even know the protocol, let alone the rules.'

Thirty-nine voices said, 'Sorry, master sergeant.'

'Find Trooper Samstag and bring her to me,' Chine yelled. 'I don't even care if she's finished pissing. Bring her to me now! I'll frigging show you what discipline means!'

'Master sergeant, please,' a voice said. Sarosh. It was Mister Sarosh.

'What, Sarosh?'

'These are not experienced troopers, master sergeant. They are tertiary PDF. They are attempting their best. You must give them some room to learn. If a young woman like Cally Samstag needs to relieve herself, we should let her, not discipline her. These men and women have offered their lives to defend the hive, but they are not Guard like you. You must allow them some space to learn.'

There was a long silence, broken only by the noise of the wind and the boom of the distant Gynex horns.

'Have you finished, Sarosh?' Cally heard Chine ask.

'Yes, master sergeant.'

There was the sound of a slap, a callused hand whipping across a cheek.

'Frig you, Sarosh, telling me how to run this outfit.'

'Yes, master sergeant.'

Cally tried to squirm up the gulley again, sure she could get there, failing to do so.

'I'll tell you nungs what I'm going to do,' Chine began. 'I'm going to–'

There was the sound of a slap, like a callused hand whipping across a cheek, but not stopping this time. A slap that went through flesh, fat, bone, through teeth. Someone screamed.

The highway air was suddenly squealing with lasrounds. Cally dropped back into the gulley and instinctively pulled herself into a ball.

She heard puncture shot after puncture shot, and flinched and moaned at every one. Lasbolts into flesh made freakishly different sounds to lasbolts hitting asphalt or rockcrete. They made wet sounds, splattering sounds, frying meat sounds. Activated Twenty-Six was screaming. Some of the screams were panic. Most of the screams were pain: pain, or death noise.

Cowering in the bed of the gulley, her arms around her head, Cally heard other noises: the pneumatic clatter of armoured limbs, the manic chatter of binaric code spooling out of machine mouths, frantic, rapid, like cackling laughter.

The sky above the gulley lit up with fierce lasfire. Sand and spray and pellets of mud rained down on her. Bodies came tumbling and scrabbling down into the gulley beside her. Some of them landed on her. Cally saw Golla Uldana, Binderman, thin limbs milling, the hard woman from Lazarus sink called Reiss.

There was no order, just a blur of thrashing limbs and wailing voices. People were falling over, crashing into each other as they tried to run in opposite directions. Binderman was barely back on his feet when Lars Vulk came tumbling down the slope and knocked him over again.

'That way. Get up. That way!' Cally heard Sarosh shouting. She saw him sliding down the gulley bank towards them, his face and the front of his jacket soaked in blood. He was pointing along the gulley.

'That way! Get up and run for your lives!'

They started to crawl, scramble, run, heads down, along the gulley in the direction Mister Sarosh had indicated, to wherever the gulley led to, as long as it was away.

Cally Samstag ran. She ran, to her shame, like a terrified child. There was pink sand in her eyes, in her mouth, the pungent taste in her mouth.

There were some troopers ahead of her, some behind, all

running, no formation, no discipline, just frantic flight. She'd lost sight of Golla. Behind them, weapons continued to discharge, rapid bursts from the enemy pod-lasers, each shot like the snap of a lash, and the occasional crackle of returning PDF small arms.

The gulley petered out after half a kilometre, and they ran, piecemeal, across bleak waste ground, tufted with lynchweed and strawgrass, away from the highway, towards the blown-out ruins of a refinery complex. There were bits of metal debris scattered across the waste ground, and several people fell, tripping on lengths of broken pipe or plating buried in the strawgrass.

Cally reached the outer structure of the refinery, a forest of twisted pipework and charred structure frames, industrial skeletons that showed where outbuildings and substations had stood: ghost buildings, zombie structures. Chemical fires had turned all the metal shapes still standing white, their surfaces flaking like scurf. A weird, dry smell lingered in the air, like cooked bleach.

She saw a large chunk of heavy iron ducting ahead of her, rising from underground pipe systems like a pollarded tree, ran behind it and crouched down. Her legs were shaking, and she was on the verge of hyperventilating. She could hear a drum, and realised it was her own heart.

It had gone very quiet. Occasionally, the stillness was broken by someone running past, off into the depths of the refinery ruin. Cally raised her head and opened her eyes.

She was still holding her weapon, a MK2-sk lasrifle, short form, bullpup pattern, type 3 cell rear of the firing grip, integral scope, lugs for optional bayonet and grenade launcher fitments. *That's it, that's right, focus on something you know.* Very slowly, her hand quivering violently, she reached behind the grip and switched the weapon to armed. A little green tell-tale lit up on the side plate.

Then, and only then, did she look back.

From her cover, she could see back across the waste ground to the road. Fidelis Highway stretched away north-east, broad and pitted and empty. The sky looked like embers. Gynex Subhive loomed through the haze and the intermittent rain.

About half a kilometre back down the road, where Activated Twenty-Six had rested, where she'd slipped off the highway into the gulley for a relief break, things were burning: small bonfires, scattered across the road surface, bright flames and billowing black smoke. She raised her weapon and trained it so that she could look through the integral scope. Her hands were still shaking badly. It took a moment to focus.

Image swim, fuzzy, then sharp. Crackling flames. Cally nudged the magnification. Image swim, then sharp. The bonfires were bodies, immolating. Blackened, wretchedly twisted, horribly reduced, dozens of human corpses littered the roadway and burned. Cally stifled a sob. There was no way of recognising any of them. Pieces of PDF kit, helmets, fallen weapons, parts of a webbing set, were scattered pathetically across the punctured rockcrete.

There was no sign of whatever had slaughtered them, no sign at all of what had made her run in childish terror.

She was lowering the scope when she glimpsed movement, and snapped the weapon up again. Image swim. What had she just seen? Something had moved, something had–

The killers appeared. They had been cloaked by the foul smoke of the incinerating corpses. The killers were moving again, coming towards her position. Was that just coincidence, or had their sensors picked up the fleeing scraps of Activated Twenty-Six?

There were six of them. Cally had to fight to keep them in focus, and fight just as hard to bite down her panic. They were, she was sure, what the PDF briefing officer back at the place of muster had called *weaponised servitors*. 'They look like heavily armed bugs,' Golla Uldana had said out loud, without meaning to. 'Shockroaches!' Kyril Antic had joked, hopefully, working the crowd, trying to establish his role as platoon jester. No one had laughed.

The things Cally's scope held in focus didn't look much like the hololith examples the briefing officer had showed them. His picts had been Tacticae impressions and work-ups of walk-frame platforms surmounted by weapon systems, ridiculously top-heavy and an easy target for Antic's vapid wit.

These things were bad dreams. They were heavy, sleek, each one striding along on a set of four insectile limbs. The metal limbs supported heavy, burnished abdomens, plated in loricated armour. The torsos were raised vertically, supporting twinned pairs of heavy gun-pods in place of arms: a vile, ischiopagal body geometry. They had faces, heads with faces, raised high and proud and eager. The faces were leering masks, gold and silver, their frozen smiles so disturbing, they made Cally Samstag shudder. Pieces of broken chain and razorwire decorated their crimson-painted farings like victory wreathes. Necklaces made of white and beige beads dangled from their chassis. Cally magged her focus and sucked in her breath. The beads were human skulls and pieces of bone. As the weaponised servitors – *shockroaches*! – came forwards, the grisly pendants swung. Their strutting insectile hooves advanced oblivious of the burning corpses on the roadway. They trod on some and kicked others over, making them roll and blow out puffs of sparks.

There were some markings, insignia, on the hulls of the advancing shockroaches. Cally trained her scope on one of them and–

She projectile vomited. The choking spasms and throes kept coming, uncontrollably, until she was down on her hands and knees, gagging, her stomach empty, her throat sore, her lips drooling.

Cally Samstag groaned. She spat, wiped her mouth, spat again, and got up. Her hands were shaking. She almost dropped her weapon.

'Golla?' she called out, cautiously. 'Golla?'

She found Golla Uldana nearby, through the forest of scurfing pipework. Golla was with Bohn Iconis, Kyril Antic, Lars Vulk, the big nung from the Bulwarks, and a few others, all of them hunched over in exhausted shock.

'They're dead. They're all dead!' Antic was wailing. Golla looked at Antic disdainfully.

'Shut up, you little frig,' Golla told him.

She turned to look at Cally as she walked through the zombie structures of the refinery to join the little group of cowering survivors.

'Cally-girl? You all right?'

Cally nodded, knowing that she had vomit speckling the front of her tunic, and stomach acid on her breath.

'We have to move,' she told Golla.

'But they're all dead!' Antic gabbled. 'The master sergeant! Farick! Frigging wall-eyed Koch! Peltzer! Shardin! I saw him go down! His head just popped, Throne save us! It just popped! Idiot Muldin, him too! Boom! Like that! Boom!'

'Antic, please shut up,' said Cally.

Half-lost in the wind, the horns of Gynex Subhive boomed

out behind her. 'We really do have to move,' Cally said. 'The weap– the *shockroaches* are coming for us.'

Antic sniggered despite himself.

'I'm with her,' said the hard woman from Lazarus sink called Reiss, getting up.

'Samstag knows what she's doing,' said Binderman, rising to his feet.

'I really don't,' Cally replied, 'I just know we should move. Please, get up, move off.'

'Who put you in charge?' the posh girl from Summittown asked Cally.

'No one,' Cally told her. 'What's your name?'

The posh girl faltered. 'Janny Wirmac.'

'We have to move, Janny,' Cally told her softly. 'We can't stay here. Shockroaches are coming. We've got to find somewhere to hide.'

The survivors rose to their feet and began to follow Cally through the charred ruins of the refinery.

'Anyone seen Mister Sarosh?' Cally called back over her shoulder.

'Yeah. I saw him. I saw him cut in two,' replied Janny Wirmac. 'Can I go home now?'

101

The walk had begun. Execution K494103 was underway. Moderati Tarses observed the news via a data-feed from Orestes Principal. It was the only news any of the feeds were carrying. At noon on the third day following surface delivery, Legio Invicta had formally ignited its drive plants.

Huge, cheering crowds had turned out to watch Gearhart, Bohrman and eight other renowned princeps interface with their engines. The gun-servitors had already been installed and sanctified, one by one, to the cooed wonder of the gathering crowds. At noon, the data-feed carried dizzy footage of the amniotic caskets being lowered into their sockets. Tech-priests ceremonially connected the MIU links while servitors power-tooled the retaining bolts shut, and celebrant choirs sang hymns of investment and benediction.

The crowds had roared at the first grumble of main drive auto-start. Exhaust fumes puffed like noxious, rank breath out of the gas exchangers poking out from under the shoulder blades of the giant engines.

Gearhart, the Red Fury, had always been inclined towards theatricality. Tarses loved him for that. Gearhart's Warlord, *Invictus Antagonistes*, had been the first engine to move. The multitude had roared once again as it took its first step. Gearhart had ordered his steersmen to take *Invictus* forwards five paces, and then had paused to execute a clumsy little bow of the engine's head.

The crowd had screamed in delight.

Bohrman's machine, *Divinitus Monstrum*, had followed *Invictus* forwards. Then the others, one by one, moved out of their echelon to plod across the Field of Mars. Prayers, both vocal and digital, filled the air. Prayer texts scrolled down across the data-feed that Tarses was watching.

Weapon limbs swung up and locked out. Tarses noticed the blink and flash of auspex and targeter beams test-firing from under the engines' heavy brows. The Titans strode towards the hive's Great South Gate in slow formation.

A three kilometre-long convoy of skitarii armour had led the procession – tanks and guntracks and mobile Hydra platforms. Vultures and, higher up, Thunderbolts, had skimmed down the line of the convoy like dense flocks of migrating birds.

Outside the Great South Gate, the crowds still thronging on either side of the highway, the skitarii forces had parted to create an avenue through their ranks. The Warhounds, *Lupus Lux* and *Morbius Sire*, had begun to lope forwards, ahead of the big, pacing Warlords.

Tarses watched this part of the data-feed several times, looping it back and cueing it again on his picter. At the start of his career, before his promotion to moderati, he'd been a steersman on a Warhound, and he still missed the aggressive speed and fleetness of foot achieved by the small scout engines. With their hunched posture and reverse-jointed legs, the Warhounds ran like saurian raptors, like flightless birds, sniffing the ground for blood-scent, and moving far faster than any machines that big had any business doing.

The princeps commanding the two Warhounds were close friends of his: Leyden Krugmal, presiding over *Lupus Lux*, and Max Orfuls, princepting *Morbius Sire*. They were free-plugged in their seats; only the legio's Warlords required full amniotic interface, a legacy to darker times. Tarses envied them: to be walking already, to be moving clear of the pack into the hunting zone, to be graced with such speed. Tarses remembered what it felt like to be in a Warhound cockpit, embracing the Manifold, while the war engine moved at flank pace. His body keenly remembered the sensations: the rapid, shuddering *thump* of every footstep, the repetitive clunking *hiss* of the massive hydraulics, the rapid play of the auspex sweep, sliding across all senses in a blur: fast, agile, muscular.

At Tarses's last periodic review, Bohrman had hinted that Tarses was set for a Warhound princepture the next time a vacancy came up.

'Thank you, sir,' Tarses had replied. 'I would relish it.'

Little hope of that now. Not now, after Kercher. There would never be a *Princeps Tarses*.

Red-robed and introspective, Tarses submitted himself for routine biological inspection at Antium's medical facility. As he underwent tests, stripped naked, he continued to half-watch the feed on his picter.

'Something interesting, moderati?' one of the magi organos asked as he did the bloodwork.

'Invicta is walking,' Tarses replied.

'Praise be the Omnissiah,' the magos said.

The organos staff were treating him warily. Tarses had almost forgotten why.

They know what I did, he reminded himself. They know I choked a magos organos to death in my rage. They're all afraid I might snap and do it again.

'I won't hurt you,' he said. Out loud, it sounded like a stupid thing to say.

'Of course you won't, moderati,' the magos replied.

Tarses looked up from his picter and realised how many extra skitarii had been posted around the lab. They were all watching him, weapons slung but ready.

'Really, I won't,' he insisted, laughing awkwardly.

'I know you won't,' the magos replied. He swabbed the cannula valves in Tarses's inner elbow and spritzed counterseptic.

'I'm not a killer,' Tarses said.

The magos shrugged, sorting the bloodwork vials ready for the centrifuge. 'You're Zane Tarses, aren't you?'

'Yes.'

'Then you are a killer, sir.'

Tarses blinked. 'No, you–'

The magos stared back at him coldly. 'Do you plug into that Warlord? Do you fight? Yes? It's in you, then. The instinct, the lust. Omnissiah help us all that we must make men like you.'

'The galaxy makes it so,' Tarses replied.

'Pity us all that this is the galaxy we are made to live in, then,' the magos said, turning away. Such was the gulf between the active hard-plugged and the smoothly interfaced noospheric.

The machines purred.

'What's this?' Tarses asked, as an injector lowered towards him.

'A glycoprotein booster,' said one of the magi, 'admixed with a shot of synthetic hormones. Your D-cell count is low.'

The needles of the injector slid into his primary venus catheter and the solution shunted.

'You will have met Prinzhorn, of course,' a magos remarked.

'No.'

The magos offered his hand to help Tarses up. The moderati rose from the couch, his head swimming from the solutions mingling in his bloodstream.

'This way,' the magos said, leading him.

Naked, Tarses was presented to the man who would be his new princeps.

Guido Prinzhorn floated in his amniotic casket as if asleep. All Proximus-pattern Battle Titans required amniotic connection. He seemed young, far younger than Tarses, a boy. The electoo of Legio Tempestus Orestae stood out, on his pallid left forearm, bold and hard.

Prinzhorn's eyes flicked open.

'You're Tarses?' Prinzhorn asked in binaric cant, his signal issuing from the augmitters in the base of his casket.

'I am, princeps.'

'Tarses the murderer?'

'I–' Tarses began and then shut up. He bent his head. 'There was an incident.'

'You murdered a magos organos,' Prinzhorn said, his data-burst clipped and elegant.

Tarses nodded. 'I did. The heat of the moment. My princeps was recorded dead. I lost control.'

In his vat of thick, gluey fluid, Prinzhorn nodded. 'I have, after consideration, decided that I will serve with you. I will measure you as we go along. I understand from the back-logged data that you are competent.'

'I try my best, sir.'

'I prefer binaric, Tarses.'

<Apologies,> Tarses replied, switching from vocal to binary cant. The response flickered out of his augmitters in quick pulses. Skaugen had always preferred voice.

<I am not Skaugen,> Prinzhorn said. <I taste your sympatico with the deceased in the back of your head. I am not Skaugen. I hope we can overcome this. *Dominatus Victrix* must walk again.>

<She must,> Tarses agreed with a binary spurt.

<Query, moderati: how is she?> Prinzhorn asked, bubbles boiling up through his amniotics.

<Sir?> Tarses asked.

<*Dominatus Victrix*, how is she? What are her qualities as a war engine?>

<Surely you've incanted the MIU logs, sir?>

<I'll try not to be offended by that question, Tarses. The logs are committed to my engram buffers in full. I was asking you for a personal appraisal.>

Tarses felt suitably chided. He waited while two magi stepped in and attached metalloproteinase receptors and oncostatin flush pipes to valves in the side of Prinzhorn's casket. As they moved away again, consulting diagnostic data-slates, he framed an answer.

<*Victrix* is a fine engine. Her systems are responsive, and she develops power well on the lower ratios, faster and more rapidly than many Warlords her age or spec. Her gyros are especially stable for a platform her size.>

<You've made comparisons?>

<I've decanted MIU logs from other Warlords, for training purposes. Some Warlords, in my experience, have a tendency to shake or fluctuate when firing carapace weapons at more

than fifteen degrees waist traverse. *Victrix* stays true at up to thirty degrees.>

<Noted.>

<Her auspex has a propensity to ghost when running hot.>

<Ghost?>

Tarses coughed. His throat was not used to sustained canting. <I mean to say, it sometimes clouds, or resolves false imaging artefacts. Only briefly, but–>

<This must be repaired,> said Prinzhorn.

<It has been. The auspex has been overhauled and refitted several times. The aberration persists. I believe it is part of her spirit's character.>

Prinzhorn did not reply. Tarses felt a need to qualify his comment.

<I'm sorry, sir. It's my belief that every engine has a unique character, complete with its own foibles and quirks. No two are alike, even if they are of the same pattern. They are, by the grace of the Omnissiah, living things, after all.>

<Noted,> replied Prinzhorn. <*Victrix* is a Proximus-pattern Warlord, is she not?>

Tarses nodded. <Legio Invicta is a Proximus legion, sir. All our engines are Proximus-pattern. Proximus is our homeworld, our forge.>

<A venerated world, moderati,> Prinzhorn replied, <an old and noble forge. The honour of taking a princepture with your legio does not escape me, nor does the burden of adapting our amniotics to match your pattern. Orestes is a younger world, a younger forge. We acknowledge the legacy of your ancient tradition, although, I hope, the perfection of our manufacture will one day be equal or even superior. I am an Orestes man, Tarses. Does it shock you, a warrior who has walked on many worlds, to know that I have never left my home soil?>

<I have complete faith in your abilities, sir. You would not have been recommended if you were lacking in skill. May I ask, how many actions have you seen?>

<Two hundred and thirty-five,> Prinzhorn blurted. <Some as steersman, some as moderati, the last ten as princeps.>

<Then I am content.>

Prinzhorn stared at him through the fluid and the armour-glass. <Your level of contentment matters little to me, moderati. Like me, you serve the Omnissiah. That is all that matters.>

Prinzhorn closed his eyes. Tarses understood that he was dismissed.

>

Tarses submitted to further tests: bone density, lung capacity, hand/eye examinations, beta phase interleukin and plasminogen typing, Kohl-Borgeat redundancy sampling, dopamine receptor assay. His blood was taken out, washed, and put back, his plugs were cleansed and scoured, and his peripherals were wiped and rewritten. He was told to report back the following day to have three of the graft plugs in the top of his spine replaced.

'They're worn and loose,' a magos told him, 'and the tissue around them is necrotised. We'll regraft them tomorrow. It should only take eight or nine hours. Once that's done, we'll certify you as field ready.'

Tarses left the medical facility and walked back to his quarters through Antium's echoing corridors. The only signs of life he saw were scurrying sub-servitors. He felt numb, and slightly disorientated, the usual consequences of having his peripherals rewritten. Tarses understood the importance of washing old, clotted data out of his subcutaneous circuits. A bridge officer had to be clear-headed and clear-sighted, but a peripheral rewrite always left him heartsick and uncomfortable, his fingers and toes tingling with pins and needles. He would suffer the usual migraine before the night was done.

Prinzhorn. Quite a man. Tarses had an ugly suspicion that their relationship would not be a comfortable one. That fact alone boded ill for the *Victrix*. The union of princeps and moderati was a singular thing, the most important detail to get right if an engine was going to function at its full potential.

He thought, for a moment, about Skaugen, and salt water briefly welled from the aluminium rinse ducts embedded under his eyes.

They had issued him with quarters under west-lock eight, two rooms, once the home of a Tempestus moderati. The place had been stripped bare of all personal effects, and Tarses had no clue as to the identity of the previous incumbent. He wondered what the man's name was, and what engine he served with. He wondered if the man was still alive out there, fighting the Archenemy in one of the few Legio Tempestus engines still walking. Or was he already dead, and never coming back to reclaim his rooms?

There was a bunk, a chair and a small desk, and a washroom behind the sleeping chamber. There were also wall-sockets for direct plugging into the finishing plant's data feeds and the noosphere.

Tarses showered for a long time, reaching up to feel at the sore plugs in his neck. Of *course* they were worn and loose.

Shrapnel and metal chips from the rear cranials blew out like a razor storm, shattering the back of his casket, shredding the principal plug sheafs, the central MIU trunking, and bursting his amniotics.

Pain shot through the MIU link. It was so fierce, I had to unplug before it killed me.

I shouted, 'Princeps! My princeps!'

When Skaugen died, Tarses had been forced to wrench out his plugs to save his own life. Pain had been screaming into him. He'd grabbed the knot of thick cable and jerked them out. His mind had gone blank for a moment, severed from the glorious dream of the Manifold. He'd fallen to the deck, retching.

It was little wonder he'd damaged the sockets.

Skaugen, my princeps…

He let the washroom's air-jets blow him dry, and then lay on the bunk for a while, staring into space.

He thought about Magos Organos Kercher, and despised himself.

His Icon Mechanicus hung on a wall stud above the bunk. It was the only gesture he'd made to personalise the room. *Omnissiah, God-Emperor made steel, watch over me now…*

Tarses sat up, and reached under the bunk for his kit bag. He pulled out a sheaf of direct-plug couplings, and connected himself to the room's wall-sockets. He used the secondary plug points built into the wrist of his left arm. His top-spine plugs were too painful.

Tarses linked, and inloaded a status on *Dominatus Victrix*. Four days into a projected eight-day refit, and the Orestean forge was anticipating no more than two days to finish. Omnissiah bless them! *Victrix* would walk again, two days sooner than the estimate.

'Prinzhorn,' Tarses canted.

Data buzzed up across his eyes. What did he want? *Biographical? Medical overview? Background and training? Certification?*

'Edit. Bio, basics,' Tarses instructed.

The feed began to exload, sliding data windows up, one over another.

Guido Pernall Jaxiul Prinzhorn, born 322.760.M41.

'He's nineteen?' Tarses barked.

Query: do you wish to continue?

'Proceed. Still already, *nineteen*?'

Two hundred and thirty-five actions.

'All successful?'

All successful.

'Impressive.'

All simulated.

'Simulated?'

Princeps Prinzhorn has not experienced actual combat. His exemplary record is based upon his high scores in test simulations.

'He's never been in live combat?'

No, Moderati Tarses.

'What the hell does Legio Tempestus think its doing?'

Enter: query/unknown.

'Rephrase. What does... Never mind. Cancel.'

Tarses slumped back on his cot and unplugged.

'So you're checking out your new princeps's bio, are you?' asked a voice from the doorway.

Tarses sat up.

A girl stood there, smiling at him. She was tall and slender, with cropped brown hair and a handsome nose at odds with her thin features. She wore a short red robe over a brown bodyglove, and Tarses could see that she was hard-plugged in a rudimentary fashion.

'You are?' asked Tarses.

'Apologies, moderati. I am Fairika, Princeps Prinzhorn's famulous. Is this a good time?'

'I am unclothed,' Tarses replied, reaching for his robe. 'How did you get in? The door was closed.'

Fairika wiggled the cog-form pass-pendant that hung around her neck. 'All doors in Antium open for me, sir.'

'Lucky you,' Tarses replied, buttoning his robe. He stared at her.

'Come in,' he said.

'Thank you, moderati,' she replied, and stepped over the threshold.

'So, you're checking out your new princeps?' she asked, mildly.

'I like to know what I'm up against,' Tarses replied.

'Interesting. Rumination: you perceive Prinzhorn in an adversarial way?'

'I didn't say that. Prinzhorn will be my princeps. That's all I need to know.'

'But you resent him?'

'What is this? An ordo search? I consider him as I consider him.'

Fairika shrugged. 'Fair enough. He has no time for you either.'

'Really?'

'Neither do I.'

'Is that so?'

'You are weak, Tarses. You killed a magos. No self-control. That is weakness.'

'Is that what you think, famulous?' Tarses asked.

She shook her head. 'That's what I know.'

Tarses sat back on his cot. 'You don't seem especially inclined to get on my good side, famulous,' he said.

Fairika beamed at him. 'I don't care,' she replied. She looked up at the Icon Mechanicus hooked to the cell's wall, and bowed.

'The Emperor protects,' he muttered.

'The Emperor?' she asked, sharply.

'Of course.'

'You surely mean the Omnissiah, moderati?'

'I mean what I say. They are the same, are they not?'

'No,' she replied. She stared at Tarses. The playful smile had left her face. 'I am disappointed to discover that you are of the *new way*.'

'The what?'

'The *new way*. Is this view a personal one, or do all the servants of Legio Invicta believe that the Omnissiah and the God-Emperor are one and the same?'

'Of course we do,' he replied.

'Ah,' she said.

'You don't?' Tarses asked. He was tired, and he didn't feel like engaging some insolent, cocksure famulous in a semantic debate. The ideological split was ages old, and lurked beneath the surface of all Cult Mechanicus beliefs. The matter was sometimes referred to as *the Schism* by those adepts especially exercised by its implications. In the inner circles of some primary forges, the issue was argued and explored by councils of magi, but in ordinary, everyday life, it was largely ignored, and held as a matter of personal conviction. It was generally decided that the Deus Mechanicus, the Machine-God, and the God-Emperor of Mankind were both aspects of the same divinity, from which all machine spirits originated.

'I don't,' replied Fairika, as if enjoying his annoyance. 'The magi of the Orestean forge are taught to regard them as separate entities.'

Tarses shrugged. 'I had heard that some of the younger forges favoured that philosophy, but the union of Mechanicus and Imperium depends upon an implicit faith in the God-Emperor.'

'Perhaps,' she said, 'but he's not my god.'

There was a long pause. 'Well, thank you for sharing your opinions with me, famulous,' Tarses said. 'Query: was there anything else?'

She nodded. 'One last piece of business. I need your authority on this.'

She unhooked a data-slate from her belt and handed it to Tarses.

'What is it?'

'A refit order for *Victrix*, in addition to the work already being carried out. As moderati, you need to notarise it.'

Tarses studied the slate. 'This is ordering the installation of a new auspex system.'

'It is.'

'It's not necessary. I explained this to Prinzhorn.'

'The princeps feels it is necessary, and has insisted upon it.'

'Damn it, this will add to the refit timetable.'

'Just two days,' she replied.

'We don't have two days,' said Tarses. 'This order is a waste of time.'

'Are you going to tell the princeps that?' she asked. 'I assure you that the only time-wasting will be due to you delaying your authority.'

Tarses scowled. He slid out the stylus, and countersigned the slate.

>

Outside Soak Town, outside old Argentum Hive in the smoke-clogged grasslands of the refinery belt, they nursed their wounds and tried to keep moving. Smoke haze from the burning wells draped like lank fog in the sickly yellow light, or billowed poisonously whenever the rain and wind picked up. They clung to the verges of Prospect Highway, looking for signs of life.

Signs of death echoed through the filthy air: the *boom* and *crump* of heavy weapons, the chattering squeal of engine mounts, a flash in the oily fog, now and then. They had no vox, nor would they have used one even if they had managed to recover a set from the burning wreck of *Queen Bitch*. The airwaves were crackling with the enemy's ominous scrapcode.

There were eight of them: Varco, his enginseer, and his driver, Sagen, the only ones who'd managed to pull clear of *Queen Bitch's* death fires; Gram Hekton of the *Merciless* and one of his gunners; the driver and one of the loaders from *Treadfire*; and a second enginseer, whose mind was too deeply traumatised and his clothing too badly burned for them to identify which crew he had belonged to. Hekton thought it might have been the *Havoc*, but there was no real way to be sure. The enginseer, his skin variously blackened and raw, his eyes empty, refused to respond to any questions, and Koder was unwilling to attempt a direct interface.

'His mind is gone, captain,' Koder said. 'Look at him. If I plug into that, I'll lose my wits.'

'You don't know him?' asked Varco.

Koder had shaken his head.

The ruined enginseer followed their small party like a stray dog.

Varco didn't know if anyone else from Pride Armour Six had made it out alive. There was a possibility that other crews had ejected or fled during the fight, but it had been four days, and there had been no sign of anyone. The engine had systematically murdered Varco's formation, and then vanished away into the smoke banks, as if disappointed that its gleeful sport was over.

They'd spent the first night huddled in a culvert, and had then begun to pick their way east. Varco and Hekton had agreed that they should attempt to make their way back to the hive. They had little in the way of supplies: four water bottles, one medical kit, no food. Varco and Hekton had their sidearms, and *Treadfire's* loader, Kazan, had a lascarbine he'd pulled from a rack during his rapid exit from the tank's gun-cage.

They made good progress for the first day, taking cover whenever the menacing sounds of battle rolled too close. On the second day, they watched Imperial air cover pounding a sector to the north-east of them for over an hour. On the third day, after two hours of good progress just after dawn, the route east became impassable. An artillery barrage opened up, annihilating the zones ahead. Due to the bad atmospherics, it was impossible to tell the range or direction of the shelling, or even which side of the conflict was laying it down. They waited, heads low, pummelled by the detonations. Sagen had to pull the mute enginseer down into cover.

The shelling began to creep.

'We can't stay here,' said Varco.

They doubled back, moving south and west through the ruins of smelteries and bulk fabrication plants, the bombardment thundering on behind them. Their bellies were growling, and the last drops of the water sloshed just as emptily in the bottles. They stopped for the night in the shell of a manufactory, where half-charred canvas sheeting hung from the roof spars and swayed like tattered sails. Outside, light blistered the darkness as the bombardment rolled on.

Varco woke in the dead hours to silence. The shelling had

ceased and an awful emptiness had filled the night. Cold and numb, he left the others sleeping in the dust and began to explore the manufactory. He found a standpipe, but the tap grated open, dry, and he cut the heel of his palm on the rusty metal. With a sigh, he pulled a grubby kerchief out of his hip pocket to wipe the cut, and something came out of the pocket with it. It fell on the ground with a small clink.

Varco bent down to find out what it was. In the dusty gloom, he saw the little medallion of the Omnissiah that had been fixed to *Queen Bitch's* skirt armour. There was no mistaking it. Varco had no idea how it had come to be in his pocket. He crouched in the darkness, staring at it in wonder.

Someone walked past him, just metres away on the other side of a broken pipework hub. Varco leaned back into full cover and watched. The figure moved clear of the hub, and advanced across an open stretch of hardpan.

It was a skitarii trooper of the Dark Mechanicus, tall framed but hunched, its weapon limb toothed with jagged blades. It ambled forwards, swinging its head left and right as it prowled. It was hunting. Varco glimpsed the luminous blue of its visor slits. Uneven spikes protruded from the hump of its carapace like thorns. He could smell its blood and its plastics, the stink of dirty flesh and discharged waste. He could hear the scrapcode gurgling in its augmitters. He marvelled that it could not detect his heat or scent, and prayed for that miracle to continue.

It reached the far edge of the hardpan, half-hidden from his view by overhanging ducts. It stopped, scanned around once more, and issued a quick scrapcode blurt that was answered by another unit close by. Then it moved off into the manufactory away from him.

Varco waited for a moment, the pulse in his neck pattering

as fast as a boxer going at a speed bag, and rose to his feet. He realised that if he'd been upright when the skitarii first appeared, the creature would have seen him instantly.

But he hadn't been upright. He'd been crouching down, retrieving something that shouldn't have been in his pocket to begin with.

Varco slipped back through the ruin to the part of the manufactory where the others were sleeping.

'Get up, no noise,' he whispered to each one in turn as he shook them. 'No noise, your life depends on it.'

They left the ruin, and fled west into the hazy night, crossing over a storm drain and under an elevated pipeline. The route brought them to a cratered service road, and then down a weed-strewn embankment and across the gleaming litter of an ore bed. Even the mute enginseer seemed to appreciate the urgency and the need for quiet.

They found a block of bombed-out worker habs on the far side of the ore bed, and took shelter there. From the window holes, they looked back on the ruins they had abandoned. Lights were playing inside, stab-lights and torch beams. They could hear the rattle and chatter of badly maintained power plants, light armour and transports toiling up into the ruins. Behind the manufactory ruins, the eastern sky was lit by vast fires on the horizon. Three tall figures stalked in silhouette against the flames: war engines, Reavers by the shape of them, advancing several kilometres away.

'We got out of there just in time,' Hekton said.

'We should go south, then,' said Sagen, 'try and work our way around them.'

'I think that would be suicide,' replied Varco.

The others began to discuss their options, all agreeing that it wouldn't be long before the skitarii started to search the habs too. Varco tried to recall which pocket he'd put the medallion in. He slid his hands into his hip pockets, and found it in the left one.

'West,' he said. It had saved them once, and he trusted it. The machine spirits were looking out for them.

'West?' asked Koder.

'We go west,' said Varco.

They went west, through the fourth day's dust, through the twisted remains of the industrial suburb, listening for traces of movement behind them. Once, just before noon, they heard a vast detonation to the north-west that sounded like a full magazine torching off. A fat plume of black smoke climbed above the horizon like an exclamation mark.

The streets had become low-order hab blocks, rows of modular accommodation, rusted and flaking. Some had burned out, others shelled flat, and others were curiously intact and deserted, as if the war had skipped over them. Doors and window shutters swung loose in the breeze and personal possessions – clothes, bedding, housewares – lay discarded in the dust. There was no power, and the water mains were dead, but in one vacated hab they found a basin that had been left full of water, and they were able to refill three of the flasks. In another, Leopald, Hekton's gunner, discovered three cans of Munitorum-issue pressed meat. Varco found him trying to open one with a chisel.

'Not here,' he said. 'Bring them.'

'I'm so hungry, sir,' Leopald replied.

'I know, but it's not safe here. We have to keep moving. Bring them.'

* * *

Not long after that, as the afternoon began to slope towards evening and the daylight began to discolour, the war caught up with them again.

It came suddenly, as if it had been lying in wait. They were crossing a street, a low paved walk between a hab sink and a public hall, when holes began to speckle across the rockcrete wall of the hab, big holes, punching through the material as if it was soggy pulp-board. Varco heard the cycling whine of heavy drum cannons.

They started to run, Varco dragging the mute enginseer by the hand. What had started as a lazy hail of cannon-fire became a thoroughly murderous blizzard. Walls simply disintegrated in showers of rockcrete chipping and whizzing slivers of rebar. Bolt rounds chewed up the roadway and tossed fractured paving slabs into the air like loose sheets of paper in a high wind. The noise was immense and continuous: furious, blitzing detonations, the spatter of atomising rockcrete, the grinding shriek of high-fire-rate cannons. Dust fumed and billowed.

Two tanks came through the smoking shell of the hab stack, ploughing down what remained of the shot-riddled walls. Their heavy tracks made a loud, shrill clatter. A third tank followed them, its hull rising snout-up as it negotiated a massive stone lintel. The lintel suddenly perished under its weight in a cloud of pulverised stone-smoke, dropping the vehicle back level sharply.

The survivors of Pride Armour Six had reached the partial cover of an underwalk beside the public hall, and fled along it as bolter rounds scorched over their heads. Varco looked back. For a second, his spirits lifted.

The tanks were Imperial.

They were Vulcan-variant Macharius heavies, wearing the

silver and green of the Third Argentum Mobile. Instead of long main weapons, their rear-set turrets mounted thick, blunt Vulcan mega-bolters, lending them a stunted, truncated look, like attack dogs that had been de-fanged back to the gums.

If they'd only stop shooting, Varco thought, I could signal them and–

But they weren't going to stop shooting. The massive main weapons lit up with blooms of burning gas, and screamed as they spun and pumped out torrents of bulk-calibre rounds. They seemed intent on levelling the entire district. It was likely they had no clue they were chasing friendly personnel with their monstrous fire patterns.

Varco and the others ran, throwing themselves flat every time the salvoes dipped too close overhead. The top of the underwalk wall got chewed away in a flurry of brick waste, and then part of the public hall's north wall simply folded over and came slithering down like a landslide. Trask, the *Treadfire's* driver, was almost buried by the avalanche, and Varco and Hekton nearly died when they scrambled back to help him and the hall's unstable roof section fell in.

Coughing, half-blind with dust, they reached the end of the underwalk, where the others grabbed them and bundled them over a sump wall into a drainage ditch. They cowered in the ooze, feeling the ground shake and the world come to pieces above their heads, until Varco realised that they had to risk moving again.

He had begun to hear the enemy. Skitarii and weaponised servitors of the Dark Mechanicus invaders were pouring in through the suburb from the north to meet the Macharius heavies. The glowering daylight began to strobe with lasfire.

The eight of them were stuck in a ditch directly between the contesting forces.

Despite the protection offered by the ditch walls, Varco knew that they would be better off getting out of it. If anyone, the skitarii especially, got a line of sight on them from, say, the ditch bank, that would be it. They had no cover.

Varco led the others south along the ditch, hunting for a likely looking place to clamber out and hide. A series of brutal, deep explosions went off behind them, showering them with grit and metal fragments, and cudgelling them with over-pressure. They kept going. The screaming Vulcan fire from the tanks seemed to increase in pitch. Sound was rebounding in all directions. It was impossible to tell where anything was any more.

Several footbridges crossed the ditch. Varco wondered if one of them might offer a good hiding place. He heard Hekton curse.

Three skitarii brutes had suddenly appeared on the bridge ahead, just thirty metres away. They were ghastly hybrids, cyber-organic by-blows covered in scare-patterns and thorny armour, intently crossing the bridge to engage the tanks. One of them, the largest, had some kind of plasma beamer, an anti-armour weapon, built into its hulking carapace. Varco froze. If any of them glance over the rail, if any of them turn, or sense anything–

One turned, and saw the pale, helpless men trapped in the ditch. Without hesitation, it rocked around and aimed its weapon-limb. Totally exposed, Varco and his men dived into the mud, or pressed their bodies into the ditch sides as if they hoped the walls would swallow them up.

Except Kazan.

Treadfire's loader, wide-eyed and frantic, raised the carbine he carried, and opened fire. His wild shots slapped and gouged off the iron rail and struts of the footbridge, and grazed across the back plates of the largest skitarii.

A nanosecond after Kazan started shooting, the skitarii that had spotted them fired back. Its weapon-limb spat out a stream of overpowered lasfire. Several shots struck the wet ooze in the bed of the ditch and made ferocious, quenching geysers of vapourised mud. Two passed clean through Kazan. The skitarii weapon was a form of hellgun, designed to cut armour. Kazan didn't lurch or fly backwards off his feet. The superheated shots imparted no recoil. They simply made huge, cauterised holes in him, one through his chest, the other through his head. Kazan rocked and fell flat on his face. There was an unholy stench of cooked bone and burned blood.

Varco stared up at the skitarii on the bridge. All three had turned towards them. Time turned to sludge. He felt his last heartbeat thud in his chest. He saw nothing except the blue-slit visors of the invaders, magnified by his terror, as they made micro-second target adjustments that seemed to last forever.

Then they were gone. They shredded into metal fibres, into flesh sprays, into violent bursts of pink mist. The footbridge went with them. The metal handrails stripped back, curling and thrashing like whipped ropes, and the bridge decking and sub-frame deformed and unravelled from the right-hand side to the left, reduced in the blink of an eye to astonishing metal confetti.

A Macharius heavy, somewhere off to Varco's right, out of sight behind the buildings, had read the superheated signature of the hellgun and made its kill.

Varco tried to find his voice.

'Run,' he urged, hoarse with shock. The others started to

run, stumbling in the mire. Varco began to follow them. He paused, and went back to pluck the carbine from Kazan's dead hands.

Then he ran too.

The street battle raged through the suburb behind them well into the night. Weapons fire, both heavy and light, rattled through the dark streets, punctuated by the occasional scream of a Vulcan cannon, the crash of a falling wall or the rush of a fireball heaving sparks up into the sky.

They found their way up out of the ditch through a grating at its north end, ran across a dark concourse, and clambered through the torn hem of a chain-link fence. Broken country lay before them, ragged levels of wetland and scrub stretching away into the night.

They did not stop running.

Just before midnight, their flight reduced to little more than a weary trudge, they found the roundhouse.

It was a squat, drum-shaped post made of processed rockcrete, with an adjoining annexe.

'PDF station,' said Hekton.

Varco nodded. The hinterlands around the hives were studded with listening stations and strongpoints, most of them left locked and unmanned unless the defence force mobilised.

Varco gave the carbine to Leopald, and they approached the place on foot, Hekton and Varco leading the way with their pistols drawn.

There was no sign of life, but there was no apparent sign of damage either. They moved closer. In the dark, their initial impressions had been wrong. Something had happened here. The main hatch was open.

'Stay here,' said Varco.

'Erik...' Hekton warned.

'Do as I say.'

Varco approached the main hatch. There was no light from inside and no sound, but no smell of death, either.

He edged inside. It was cold and pitch-black. His eyes, adjusted to the amber gloom of the night outside, strained to see. He found a light switch just inside the thick inner jamb of the reinforced hatch, and threw it. Nothing happened.

Varco stumbled forwards, still blind, and knocked into something. He felt it. A chair, a metal chair. He moved around it and encountered another.

Something spluttered behind him and made him jump in his skin. He wheeled around, aiming the pistol into the dark.

'Who's there? I'm armed!'

Another splutter, a gurgle, and lights came on. Varco blinked. They were low-level, emergency lights, dull green. The spluttering was coming from a small portable generator in the corner. He'd woken it by throwing the switch, but it had taken its time to come up to power.

He lowered his pistol. He was standing in a block room, spare and crude, with hooded weapon ports in the curved outer walls. Along an inner wall, two hatches led into other chambers, and there was a row of steel-frame desks bolted to the rockcrete. The desk supported three pieces of modular equipment: voxcaster, tactical plotter and auspex. All three appeared to have been disabled by blows from an axe or entrenching tool.

Hekton and Koder entered the block room.

'Power, huh?' said Hekton.

'Not much,' replied Varco. He nodded to the enginseer,

inviting him to look over the station's electricals. He investigated the adjoining chambers with Hekton. They found a wardroom with six bunks, a half-filled water-reclaim drum and a stove, a chemical toilet, three dedicated gunport silos without weapons, and a locked hatch that evidently gave access to a store or magazine.

'It's digitally coded,' said Hekton.

'Know the number?'

'Not off the top of my head,' Hekton replied. 'You realise this station's entire stocks of food, pharmaceuticals, weapons and munitions could be in there?'

Varco made a face and nodded. They walked back into the block room, where Koder was fiddling with the generator in the green half-light.

'What's your thinking?' asked Hekton.

Varco shrugged. 'It's a minor watch facility, probably staffed by secondary or even tertiary PDF. When this shit started, they abandoned it, either because they were ordered to, or because they panicked.'

Hekton nodded. 'Place certainly wasn't overrun. Why do you reckon secondary or tertiary?'

'Look around,' Varco replied. 'Front-line troops would have crippled this place so it couldn't be used by the enemy. They'd have burned out the wardroom, mined the magazine, and either smashed or removed the equipment modules.'

'Someone took an axe to them,' Koder said.

'Yeah, but half-heartedly,' said Varco, 'as if they were a little freaked out they might get blamed for damaging Munitorum property. That to me says low-grade hab-worker on temp duties, drilled and obedient, but reluctant to do the job properly for fear of charges. Besides, when do frontliners make their beds before leaving?'

Hekton grinned. The bunks in the wardroom had been neatly turned out, as if by the hands of youngsters still scared of a drill instructor's wrath. 'You're right. The stove was clean too.'

'Captain?' said Sagen, entering the block room. 'My apologies,' he added, nodding to Hekton, 'captains?'

'What's up?' asked Varco.

'Come look at this.'

They walked out into the pitchy night and followed Sagen around the skirt of the blockhouse to the annexe. Leopald and Trask were waiting for them. The annexe was essentially an armoured garage, and a large generator unit sat in one corner.

'Someone's disabled the generator,' said Leopald.

Varco wasn't looking at the generator. Half of the garage space was empty. The other half was filled with a PDF Centaur towing a field piece, a heavy quad launcher on an iron-wheeled cart.

'Fuel?' Varco asked.

Trask shook his head. 'Tanks have been drained.'

'Loads for the quad?'

'Nothing in the limber or the ride itself,' replied Leopald.

'Any sign of the pintle weapon?' asked Hekton.

The Centaur's turret mount was vacant.

'No, sir,' said Trask.

'So we've got everything and nothing,' said Varco.

They assembled in the block room. 'I'll tell you what we have, then,' said Varco. 'We've got a roof over our heads and somewhere to sleep for the night. We've got water, we've got three cans of pressed meat and we've got a stove to keep us warm. That'll do for now. Tomorrow we decide what happens next.'

They all nodded. They were dead on their feet, but the prospect of a little food and water was keeping them awake.

'Someone stands guard through the night. We'll take it in turns. I'll take the first watch. Six sleeping and one awake. That'll solve arguments over the bunks, at least.'

'There are only six of us, captain,' said Sagen.

'What?'

'My fellow enginseer,' Koder said. 'Somewhere in the panic, we lost him.'

Varco cursed. The poor bastard, whatever his name was, hadn't deserved to get left behind. They'd all been so scared, though, coming out of that suburb, so desperate and petrified.

Still, it wasn't good enough. Yet another regret for Varco to file away. Somehow, he felt the loss of the poor bastard enginseer more keenly then he'd felt the loss of the formation.

They got the stove going with pieces of flake wood gathered from the surrounding scrub. It burned dirty, stinking the place with a sappy smoke, but the warmth was welcome. Leopald portioned out two of the cans, and they ate mechanically recovered meat by-product, the best meal they'd ever tasted, and drank metallic water from the reclaim tank, sweeter than any wine. Then Sagen, Trask, Leopald and Hekton slept, instantly and deeply.

Varco stayed up, prowling the premises with the carbine in his hands. Koder insisted on working on the broken equipment for a while. The enginseer never seemed to need much sleep. Varco watched as Koder extruded mechadendrites from his bulked forearms, and probed the innards of the vox and auspex.

'Anything?' Varco asked.

'The damage is superficial, captain,' Koder replied. 'I believe

I can repair the vox and the tactical plotter. The auspex, though, I'm not so sure about.'

'Well, that's a start.'

'The problem is, we don't have enough power to run any of them,' Koder added. 'The portable generator is barely keeping the emergency lights on.'

'You'll think of something,' Varco said.

Koder raised his eyebrows. 'Your faith in me is misplaced, captain.'

'My faith is in the Emperor, the Omnissiah and the spirits of the machine,' replied Varco. 'They've kept us alive this long.'

'Some of us,' said Koder, 'a few of us. On balance, I hardly feel they deserve congratulations.'

'We'll thank them for whatever we get.'

'Yes, captain.'

Varco paused. 'Koder?'

'Yes, captain?'

'Did you, by any chance, place anything in my pocket?'

'No, captain. When, captain?'

'I'm not sure,' said Varco. 'That night. It was you that pulled me out of *Queen Bitch*, wasn't it?'

'Sagen and I, together. Everyone else was gone, and you were unconscious. It seemed churlish to leave you there.'

Varco laughed. '*Churlish*, now?'

Koder shrugged. 'If we'd left you there, captain, you'd have missed all this fun.'

Varco snorted. Magi seldom made jokes that Imperials could appreciate, but when they did, they were often mordant and ironic. 'So you didn't?'

'Place anything in your pocket? No, captain. What sort of anything, may I ask?'

Varco took the medallion out of his pocket and held it up so that Koder could see it.

Koder blinked. His nictitating secondary eyelid slid down in surprise as he scanned and enlarged the item.

'That was in your pocket, captain?'

'I found it there. How odd is that?'

Koder meshed his hands into the Icon Mechanicus and whispered a binaric prayer.

'Yeah, that's what I thought,' said Varco.

He went outside. Heavy guns and field weapons were drumming in the distant east, lighting up the muggy sky with dull flashes and airbursts. Varco knew it would be no more than a day before skitarii hunt packs came their way. They would have to be gone by then, but gone to where? He and his pitiful survivors had been given a reprieve, but it wouldn't last.

Every time he closed his eyes, he saw the engine, the flames, the brave vanquishers of Pride Armour Six blowing out in withering hails of debris.

They ought to be dead already.

In all practical terms, they were.

>

Adept Feist woke to the urgent pulse of his biometrics. It was dark in his cell, and he canted lights. They came on softly.

It was early, too early. His bio-status monitor flashed a display up in front of his eyes, rebuking him for curtailing his rest period, and displaying the consequent health and nourishment deficits. He closed the display with a blink.

This wasn't his regular wake-alarm. It was something else.

Feist made a gesture, and his haptics conjured a fresh noospheric display: a message link.

<*[exloaded from] Egan, magos analyticae, Forge Orestes (110011001101, code compression tze) [begins]*

Feist. Please attend me at the High Forge as quickly as you can. My apologies for rousing you. As quickly as you can, adept.>

Feist had been sleeping in his bodyglove, too tired to peel it off after a long shift in the Analyticae. He washed his face and hands in the cell's water sink, and pulled on his dark red robes.

The tails of it flying behind him, he ran down the corridor outside his cell, leaping over the early shift servitors scrubbing the deck.

He took a rocking, empty transit up through Perpendicular to Seneschal and then rode the maglev all the way in to First Forge Transit. The booming flares flowering from the apex of the mighty ziggurat shook the early sky. Magi milled around on the marble concourse, and he pushed through them in his haste.

'Watch where you're going, youth!' an angry skitarii from Tempestus yelled.

<Apologies,> Feist canted back to him.

He entered the core, and chose a riser chamber.

State business and request deck, the noosphere inquired of him.

Magos Egan. I am anticipated, he canted back, flashing his biometric.

Request ratified. Magos Egan's bio-template located. Selecting deck, adept.

The riser chamber shot up like a bullet, with Feist inertially damped inside.

Deck seventeen hundred, the Audience.

The chamber hatch opened. A quartet of thuggish skitarii glared at him as he came out of the riser.

'Biometric!' one demanded.

He had it noospheric and ready.

'Pass,' the monster augmitted.

He entered another open concourse in the upper tiers of the vast pyramid. Angled panels of glow-light filled the air with a daylight radiance. The dark marble pavers were edged with gold. Hololithic threads of data-light rose from deck projectors like incense smoke. Small knots of people, dwarfed by an immense space as lofty as any templum, stood waiting in conversation.

<Feist!> A sharp data-cant.

'Magos?'

Magos Egan approached him, smiling, but looking tense. 'You came. Good boy, good boy. You came.'

'Of course I came, magos. You summoned me. Is this about–'

'Yes, Feist. Brace yourself. The Adept Seniorus has sent for us.'

'Omnissiah! I'm not ready for this.'

'Of course you are, Feist, of course you are.'

'But, sir–'

'You've been my brightest and best, Feist, and this is all down to you. Don't let me down. Don't let Analyticae down.'

The Analyticae was Magos Egan's department and, though Egan was a senior magi, it was often overlooked. Feist realised the significance of the moment, and what was depending on him.

<Who are the others, magos?> he canted quietly.

<Read them for yourself, adept,> Egan canted back with a jittery display that betrayed his nerves.

<Please, sir, I don't want them to know I'm searching them noospherically.>

<Very well, Feist. That's the executor fetial of Invicta, Crusius, with his famulous. Over there, that beast is Lau, Master of the Invicta Skitarii. Conversing with him is Enhort, executor fetial of our own Tempestus. Beyond them, the congregated magi of the archives, led by Magos Tolemy, and the magi of fabrication, led by Magos Keito.>

<Who's that female with Crusius? And the Imperial warrior beside her?>

<Oh, some lackey of Aleuton's, and her bodyman.>

<And the princepture casket?>

<That's Prinzhorn, the boy-princeps we're giving to Invicta to get their last engine operational. Hush now, Imanual approaches.>

Feist had never been in the Audience before. He took a sharp breath as the massive Icon Mechanicus bas-relief on the rear wall turned with the sound of grating stone, and the wall opened like a sliding cliff. Gilded choir platforms extended through the opening and unfurled, like the spreading wings of a giant metal bird. The choristers were singing complex mathematical melodics in thirteen part binaric cant, and as the sounds left their augmitters, they turned into hololithic data-streams that wound away into the air like scrolling banners.

The Adept Seniorus's throne descended between the wings of the choir platforms onto the floor of the Audience in a column of golden light.

Solomahn Imanual was old and almost entirely bionic. He sat back in his throne like a feudal king, plugged into its matrix through wrist, heart, spine and armpit. He grew out of the seat like a carving.

The throne made a soft thump as it met the platform. Imanual raised a hand and noospherically bade the choir to cease.

<Thank you for attending me so early,> he canted.

<Honoured lord,> Crusius canted in reply. <I request we use vocals for the benefit of my guest.>

The noosphere suddenly went dark. Imanual inclined his head and looked down at Etta Severin.

'Lady,' he said, slurring, 'you are the Lord Governor's elected witness?'

'I am, sir,' she replied.

Feist felt for her, to be surrounded by so many modified humans.

'Welcome, lady. The forge welcomes you. Where is Adept Feist?'

Feist suddenly felt terror in his guts, and no longer sympathised with the Imperial female.

Egan nudged him. Feist moved forwards.

'I am Feist, lord.'

'Let me look at you. Hnh. Well-enough constructed, I suppose. You have disconcerted many with your suggestion, adept.'

'I apologise, my lord.'

'I don't think he has any reason to apologise, Adept Seniorus,' said Crusius.

'Clarification: the adept's suggestion essentially implies that there is a flaw in our archiving process,' said Magos Tolemy.

'Not a flaw so much as a loophole, Tolemy,' Crusius replied.

'Are you suggesting,' asked Enhort carefully, 'that Orestes Forge is ill-prepared for this war?' As an executor fetial like Crusius, Enhort was reserved and polite, but there was an offended tone in his voice.

Crusius shook his head. 'If Orestes Forge is ill-prepared, the blame does not rest on this planet. I'm sure we all agree with whom the fault lies. That issue is not for debate here. Orestes is at war, and we must make the best use of all available resources if we are going to win.'

'No argument, executor,' said Tolemy, 'and as such a resource, the archives are supplying all the data they can.'

'Up to certain permission tolerances,' Crusius replied. 'Magos Egan and his Analyticae have been processing tactical data from the warfront since the conflict started. At my suggestion, they began identity analysis on the enemy engines. All Titans were ours once, even these abominations. I believe that we can learn a great deal of strategic value if we identify these machines and examine their histories and technical specifications. Which brings us to the loophole. Adept Feist?'

Crusius glanced at Feist and nodded supportively.

Feist cleared his throat. 'My experience has been that, while many identifying marks or inscriptions can be detected in the tactical footage, none of it compares to anything we hold on record. Requests for comparative schematics are repeatedly returned to us as data/not found.'

'But you believe we have the data?' asked the Adept Seniorus.

'I am sure of it,' said Feist, 'but it is simply not kept available in the open record. We have the data, but we can't get at it. The engines we are attempting to analyse may date back to the Horusian strata of the archive, and all such material is sequestered.'

'For many good reasons,' replied the Adept Seniorus. 'Much of it is dangerous and imprecise. Most of it is touched by the Heresy. However, Feist, I have carefully reviewed your petition, and I believe that the Analyticae should be granted access extraordinary to the sequestered material.'

'Those are forbidden coils, Adept Seniorus,' Magos Tolemy reminded the master of the forge. 'Access privilege must be obtained from Mars.'

'I will request it personally,' replied Solomahn Imanual. 'Work must advance without delay. I commend Magos Egan and Adept Feist for bringing this issue to our attention.'

'You look bemused, mamzel,' Crusius said to Etta Severin as they left the Audience.

'Slightly,' she replied. 'Am I to understand that the forge possesses a significant databank, sections of which may be vital to this fight, and is only using a part of it?'

'In a manner of speaking,' Crusius replied. 'May I ask, mamzel, have you ever had a memory so unpleasant that you wished you could *un*-remember it?'

Severin shrugged. She felt uncomfortable being asked such personal questions with Major Gotch in earshot. 'I suppose I may have, executor,' she said.

'The data we have just obtained permission to open is just such a memory. It relates to early history, to dark times, things we had shut away so we didn't have to contemplate them.'

He paused, and looked back at her. 'The war is opening old wounds, mamzel. It is forcing us to delve into things the Mechanicus would prefer to forget.'

>

She smelled the pungent, graphite smell of the Astrobleme, and wondered how long it would be before the pink sands blew in and covered her corpse.

'You all right, Cally?' asked Binderman, the tall, skinny scholam teacher.

'I'll do. Just thinking.'

'That's something I'm trying not to do,' Binderman admitted.

'What's taking them so frigging long?' complained Kyril Antic.

'Maybe they have a problem?' suggested Lars Vulk. 'You understand what a problem is, don't you, Antic? It's like you not being able to keep that whiny trap of yours shut for even five minutes. Or like us having to live with you.'

'That's enough, Lars,' soothed Binderman. The big nung from the Bulwarks looked at the scholam teacher sourly, but fell silent. Vulk could break Binderman like a stick, but he seemed to respect the teacher's calm manner.

'Someone's coming!' hissed Lasco, a weaver's mate from Gynex. He was crouching nearby in a knot of broken pipework. Quick as a fingersnap, they all raised their carbines and aimed.

Three figures darted towards them through the dry ruins of the refinery.

'Safeties!' Cally hissed. 'It's them.'

Golla Uldana, Bohn Iconis and the hard woman from Lazarus Sink called Reiss covered the last few metres and dropped into cover beside them. They were all breathing hard.

'Well?' snapped Kyril Antic.

Golla shot him a look.

'It's clear for about a kilometre,' she said, panting, 'then there's a road, a spur off the highway, I think.'

'Pretty open there,' said Iconis, 'not much cover at all.' Iconis was a good-looking, dark-haired man with intelligent eyes and an attractive down-turned mouth. As far as Cally could remember, his job in real life was as a hydroponics steward in the farm galleries.

'Bohn's right,' said Golla. 'It's not at all inviting.'

'We shouldn't head that way,' said Reiss. Her voice, with its sink-slang accent, was thin and nasal. 'If anything found us on the spur, we'd be dead.'

'Well, we can't go back!' Antic snorted.

'No, we can't,' Binderman agreed. 'It's times like this, you know... a map.' He made a sad, empty gesture with his hands.

The only charts issued to Activated Twenty-Six had been kept in the possession of Master Sergeant Chine, Sarosh, and the other three platoon leaders, none of whom had escaped Fidelis Highway alive. Tertiary PDF, even activated ones, weren't ever trusted with much in the way of tactical aids, data or autonomy.

'Look, I hate to bring this up,' said Cally, 'but before we worry about which way we're going to go, shouldn't we consider what it is we're trying to do?'

'Stay alive,' said Lars Vulk.

'I hear that,' muttered Antic.

'Of course,' said Cally. 'Survival's our immediate concern, but after that? Do we find a bolt hole, dig in and wait for the war to end? Do we try and make our way back to the hive? Or...'

'*Or*, Cally-girl?' Golla asked.

'I don't know, Golla. Do we try and find a friendly unit and hook up with it? Do we try to... stay operational?'

'You mean keep fighting, Cally?' asked Binderman.

'I wasn't aware we'd started,' said Antic.

'I don't know what we'd do,' said Cally, 'but this zone is hardly short of viable targets. They sent us out here to fight a war. Maybe we should be fighting it.'

'Stuff that,' said Antic. The others were silent.

'I think we should go home,' said Janny Wirmac. 'I–I think... I think we should go home.'

'I'm with her,' said Lasco.

'I think we should find another unit,' said Iconis. 'Someone's got to be close. If we head for the hive that's a long, damn trek.'

'Bohn's talking sense,' said Golla.

'We could elect a leader,' said Reiss. 'They could make the decision for us.'

'Who did you have in mind?' asked Vulk.

Reiss shrugged. 'Golla? Everyone likes her. Binderman? Samstag? They've got their heads screwed on.'

There were several grumbles of disapproval.

'I don't want to lead,' said Binderman. 'Really, I don't.'

'Samstag gets my vote,' said Iconis.

'No one's getting anybody's vote!' Cally said. 'We just stay low, keep together, and find a friendly unit. It's simple.'

They were all looking at her.

'What?' she asked.

'Looks like we didn't need a vote at all, Cally-girl,' grinned Golla.

'Yeah, Samstag,' said Antic, 'what do we do?'

>

Coming into Jeromihah Subsid from the east at full stride, the rain on their skin, watching the haze for spoor, Max Orfuls called out for a dead stop.

'Dead stop, aye,' his moderati, Strakhov, echoed, and the engine slowed to a shuddering halt. Hydraulics hissed under them as the beast settled back on its hips, its body-bulk swaying slightly. The idling power plant grumbled behind them in its steel safe like a fretful ogre. Some portion of the chassis subframe creaked as it took weight. The only other sounds were the thin patter of rain on the armour plate and the cockpit ports, and an occasional ping or chime from the consoles.

Strakhov turned in his chin-seat and looked back at Orfuls in the main chair. 'Anything wrong, princeps?' he asked. It was Strakhov's duty to ask, even though he knew full well that nothing was amiss. This was one of Orfuls's regular combat rituals. Most princeps began their execution logs the moment they plugged in and linked to their MIUs at drive-start. Orfuls preferred to wait until he was about to step into the shooting zone.

'Everything's fine, Strak,' said Orfuls. 'Indulge me a moment, if you will.'

'Aye, sir,' Strakhov replied, and returned to his station. He and Orfuls had served together for a long time, and their relationship was good enough to be classed as a friendship, but once Orfuls was plugged in, Strakhov knew to treat him with cautious respect. Once Orfuls was plugged in, he wasn't quite Orfuls any more.

Max Orfuls looked down at his hands, resting on the arms of the main chair. The leather sleeves of his jacket lay against the cracked leather upholstery. His pale fingers twitched slightly to the beat-pulse of the plant.

He closed his eyes.

His left hand became a Vulcan mega-bolter. His right hand became a plasma blastgun. His sleeves, his leather jacket, became dense ceramite armour, twenty centi-measures thick, the rain tapping off it. His legs became back-hinged limbs with vast, metal toes splayed in the Orestean mire. His heart became a furnace that throbbed unpleasantly like a chained sun. In his mind, another intellect, invasive and alien, bristled and growled like a hunting dog, an angry, barely trained attack dog ready to snap its choke-chain and–

Restraint!

Orfuls opened his eyes. He was back in the small, sloping cockpit, his steersman and moderati waiting for his orders in the chin-seats in front of him. The air smelled of heated plastics, of circulating lubricant and damp sweat, of the unguents and sacred oils that the tech-priests had used to propitiate the machine spirits at drive-start.

The feral thing growled again in the back of his skull, like a predator lying in wait at the darkest part of a lightless cave.

Be calm! Wait a moment longer!

There were no subtle haptic options on a battle engine, no noospheric links. Such nuances perished in the grind of combat, or were too easily compromised. In a battle engine, everything was hard-plugged and hard-switched. Orfuls pulled a brass lever on his left hand arm-console.

<active…>

'Maximillian Filias Orfuls, princeps, Legio Invicta. I am linked to the mind impulse unit of the Warhound *Morbius Sire*. Is my authority recognised?'

<recognised…>

Orfuls manually entered the date, time and location using the punch-keys. 'We are now commencing Execution K494103. Begin log recording.'

<recording…>

Orfuls felt bilious and uncomfortable. He was still getting his engine legs. He'd been away from the plugs and the MIU for too long, and his head ached from the sting of reconnection. The princeps of the mighty Warlords remained in their amniotics at all times, soothed and pampered by permanent remote congress with their MIUs. No such luxury for hard-plugged Warhound commanders. Away from active duties, in transit, it was their lot to have their links disconnected, and they struggled with withdrawal shakes, limb cramps and night terrors, all the while longing for the joy of re-plugging.

It was never a joy when it came. The ancient mind impulse units of the veteran engines were surly and cantankerous, resentful at being woken, forwards in their response to instruction. It always took a while to regain trust and re-establish cooperation. It was like breaking in the same, rebellious steed every time you saddled it, or bringing to heel a ferocious dog.

Morbius Sire was an obdurate creature. Orfuls had guided its MIU through seventeen execution campaigns, during which they had made six hundred and eight confirmed kills on targets classified as *heavy armour (various)* or above. Even so, it still fought him. It still tested him, despite the tally they had chalked up together, tonne for tonne the best kill ratio in Invicta. *Morbius Sire,* like all Warhounds, was a tough princepture. Orfuls reassured himself that this was what made *Morbius Sire* such a murderously effective engine.

He cleared his throat and the power plant automatically revved in response. 'Moderati?'

'Princeps?'

'Do I have the Manifold?'

'The Manifold is yours, princeps,' Strakhov confirmed: another ritual, for the benefit of the recorded log. Orfuls had possessed the Manifold since drive-start on the Field of Mars. This exchange marked his formal acceptance of that fact.

The Manifold was the hard-plug equivalent of the noosphere, an immersive and interactive sensory space through which a princeps comprehended his engine and realised his environment. Orfuls settled back and let the Manifold flood him properly for the first time since plugging, until it felt as though it was seeping in behind his eyes and soaking into his brain. *Morbius Sire's* truculence ebbed away, as if the Warhound knew that the bloody game was on at last.

Orfuls breathed gently. He could see and sense everything to a minute degree of sparkling clarity that had an almost lysergic quality: the loose weight of the munitions in the autoloaders, the *ping* of raindrops on the hull, the pulse rates of his moderati, calm and steady, and his steersman, eager and tense. He could feel the obedient low-brain murmur of the two weapon-servitors wired into his shoulders, and the steady, meditative vigilance of the tech-priest, Magos Zemplim, in the armoured enginseer cabin aft of the cockpit. He could feel the dull throb of the power plant in his belly, the ache from one leg where a piston needed to be re-set, the dirty heat of the plasma weapon's reservoirs.

He could feel the bestial needs of *Morbius Sire*, attack dog, the thick, wet purr of a carnivorous predator.

Enough! Be patient!

'Ahead, walk pace,' Orfuls signalled.

The power plant snorted. Zemplin uttered a benediction to god-in-the-machine. The engine began to walk, its body rocking with each heavy pace.

'Arm primary left,' ordered Orfuls.

'Arming primary left, aye,' Strakhov and the port weapon-servitor responded in unison. The autoloaders rattled, and the mega-bolter cycled out to ready. Orfuls felt the tendons in his left wrist twitch, like a neurotic tic.

'Arm primary right,' he ordered.

'Arming primary right,' Strakhov and the starboard servitor chorused. Exhaust wash vented from a thermal exchanger as plasma levels built. Orfuls felt his right wrist prickle with heat-rash and bead with sweat.

'Low stride advance,' Orfuls ordered.

'Low stride, aye,' replied Strakhov. The Warhound began to pick up speed, the cockpit rocking ever more steadily.

'Light auspex.'

'Auspex alive,' Strakhov answered.

Data plots began to slide and drift across Orfuls's Manifold vision. Data, almost an overload of data, bombarded him visually and acoustically. Using his sub-links, he intuitively blanked off the clutter, and refined the auspex feed down to the four essential combat principals: heat, motion, mass and code activity.

Spoor.

The Manifold field cleaned up rapidly. Data streams eroded and vanished. The core essentials remained fixed and bright in the middle of his field of vision.

'Begin data streaming,' he instructed.

A sub-mechanism chattered, and a coloured pattern started to blink in the lower left-hand periphery of Orfuls's view. *Morbius Sire* had begun transmitting its inload directly back to the rest of the pack, ten kilometres behind them, in a continuous, live feed.

The vox crackled. 'Sire, sire, this is Bohrman. We are receiving your feed signal. Clean transmission. How does it look, eyes on?'

'Pretty murky, sir. Jeromihah Subsidiary is a shambles.'

'That much was a given. Scout the ground.'

'My purpose in life, sir,' Orfuls responded. 'Anything from *Lupus Lux*?'

'Negative at this time, Max. Good hunting.'

'And to you, sir.'

The vox went dark. Orfuls expanded his view to three-sixty, taking in the monolithic bulk of Orestes Principal one-fifty-six point three-five kilometres behind him, the delicate peak of Mount Sigilite one-twenty-six point two-four kilometres to the south, and the heat-bleed of Argentum Hive eighty point two-two kilometres ahead. There was a lot of fire smoke coming from Argentum. The peak of Mount Sigilite was as cold and hard as ice.

Orfuls switched to a tactical appreciation. He'd reviewed tactical data of the surface dozens of times on his way in-planet, immersing himself in the topography, learning it, but he called it up again anyway: suburb plan, block plan, street plan, overlay, pinpoint. Jeromihah Subsid was a vast outer-urban worker sprawl that almost but not quite connected the edge of Argentum Hive to the skirts of Orestes Principal. It was typical of the populous outspread found on many hive worlds, where low-grade worker domiciles erupted like plague pustules or virile weeds around key labour sites. The population of Jeromihah, little more than an authorised shanty town at best, worked the vast refineries at Shalter and Gox. Maglevs had been laid to allow the workforce to commute. Templums had been constructed, scholams, commercias. In ages to come, Jeromihah would become a hive and then it would join Orestes Principal and Argentum Hive together. Then all three would meld into a true super-hive spread.

If they survived this war...

Orfuls was able to determine their precise position. They were moving at low stride along Pax Divisible, a ten-kilometre avenue that ran through the heart of Jeromihah Subsid.

The hab-town was dead. Many of the street rows and sinks had been knocked flat or razed, others were on fire. *Morbius Sire* trod upon spilled rubble as often as it did open rockcrete. Via the Manifold, Orfuls was privy to a Munitorum inload that listed every hab, every registered identity, every family no longer living in the demolished dwellings.

Everywhere he looked, he could read the names of workers, their wives and children, people who would never return, families that hadn't made it out alive, the dead, the missing, the unidentified.

'Cancel population census manifest,' Orfuls instructed.

The tiny, painful script of the overlay vanished.

'Omnissiah grant me a target today,' he muttered.

The thing in his head snarled in sympathetic agreement.

The Warhound ran like a flightless bird.

It was heavy and hunched, snout down, weapon limbs held out at its sides like the stubs of vestigial wings. Its footfalls, like drum beats, shook water up out of shell holes as it passed by. It ran through the ruins of habs, sinks and manufactories, along shattered streets, down road cuttings, under shot-pocked viaducts, pausing to listen, to sniff.

From his chin-seat, Strakhov glanced back at his princeps. Orfuls was alert, focused, engaged. He was hunched over in his seat, unconsciously aping the posture of the Warhound. *Morbius Sire* was inside him, snuffling, growling.

They passed weed-littered empty lots, the roasted shells of once-fine buildings. In the Manifold, Orfuls switched his gaze left and right: a tangle of razor wire, the hull of a burned-out tank, and a row of iron street lamps bent over by the passage of some vast weight, twisted back like trees in a typhoon.

The heavy rain lent the Manifold a quality like smoked glass. Orfuls kept blinking away raindrops that weren't actually beading his eyelashes. He smelled wet rockcrete, leaking promethium and dank brick.

He heard sounds.

Distantly, hauntingly, the wild soar and squeal of sensor patterns and the strange whoops and wails of electromagnetic activity sang out. They came and went, like anguished voices, moaning for a moment, then silent, high-pitched and musical, then low and guttural. Interference, audio artefacts, bits of corrupted data and sensor noise were loose on the wind like lost souls.

Along with little harsh blurts of scrapcode.

'Dead stop.'

'Dead stop, aye,' Strakhov returned. *Morbius Sire* came to a halt inside the cavernous wreck of a municipal templum. 'Orders, sir?'

'Wait,' hissed Orfuls.

Pale, furtive beams of daylight poked in through shell holes high overhead. Echoes surrounded them. The rain dripped from the burst roof. Charred walls, three times the height of the crouching Warhound, loomed above them.

'What are we doing, princeps?' Strakhov asked.

'Listening,' Orfuls replied. 'Hush.'

At the *hush* command, they killed the main drive and systems, almost asphyxiating the power plant. *Morbius Sire* was running at its most basic levels, a simple tick-over, just alive. Anything less, and they'd go dormant and have to restart. Outside, silence and the plip of water.

'I can taste something,' Orfuls muttered.

Ripples pulsed across the sheet pools around the Warhound's feet, as if a wind had picked up and flurried. There was a distant boom and then the *chug* of rapid fire.

'I think we have a contact,' Strakhov agreed.

Orfuls nodded. 'Three and a half kilometres east, heavy weapon discharge.'

He listened, his head craned to the right. Vox transmits and little squirts of scrapcode came and went.

He could indeed taste it: something dark, something made of black metal and rage, something that stank of aggression and filthy oil.

'Orders?'

'Boost the auspex,' said Orfuls.

Hard return. The bastard was big. Three thousand and six hundred metres away to the east, an engine was in motion. It was betrayed by its heat signature, the wash of its weapons and its metallic bulk.

'A Reaver,' said Strakhov, consulting his console. 'A Reaver, at least. Has to be.'

Orfuls nodded.

'It's firing again. Throne, that was a main weapon discharge!'

Orfuls nodded again. 'Walk us on, left, left, to the edge of the structure. I'll task the weapon systems for a firing solution.'

Re-igniting, *Morbius Sire* began to walk, creeping along the length of the bombed-out templum. Rainwater drooled off its heavy carapace.

Orfuls sat back in his chair, trying to clear his head. He had the taste in his mouth, the noxious taste of the foe. All he could see was screaming black metal, steel teeth and flames. The image scorched his mind. Orfuls knew he was gathering the raw ingredients of un-plugged nightmares yet to come.

Vox bursts suddenly lit off, back and forth, bright and urgent across the Manifold. Orfuls was hearing the transmissions of an armoured artillery company, Pride Eighty-Eight: Thunderers, Bombards and Manticores, the crews screaming at each other for a target solution, for instruction, for a way out. Transmissions kept going dark, in gritty blizzards of white noise, as the tanks died, one by one.

Orfuls didn't communicate. There was no point identifying himself and his location, but as each tank shrieked its last, he was able to add relative positions to his target plot.

'They're dying out there, princeps,' Strakhov said.

'I know, Strak, I know,' Orfuls replied, concentrating on his complex vector maths.

'We should move in. Help them,' said the steersman.

Strakhov slapped him hard. 'Keep to your place and shut your mouth!' he hissed.

'Of course, moderati,' the steersman replied.

'The princeps will move us when the time is right.'

'Yes, moderati.'

Move us now, Max, move us now, Strakhov willed. *They're dying, one after another*.

The target pipper suddenly chimed, fixed on the source of heat and light.

'Left, left, forwards,' said Orfuls.

'It hasn't seen us,' said Strakhov.

'It's too busy murdering,' Orfuls replied. 'Come around point two-one.'

The steersman obliged.

'That's it. Just as we are, on the creep, steady, steady.'

Broken brickwork crunched under the Warhound's feet. The east wall of the ruined templum lay directly ahead of them.

'Full stride, now!' Orfuls cried.

'We've got a wall in our face!' Strakhov replied, dismayed.

'Since when did that stop us? Full stride! Full stride!'

The Warhound took off, moving from idle to sprint in less than twenty seconds. Snout down, it crashed through the wall, bursting the bricks asunder like a ram. As it came through, the entire wall collapsed, and brought what was left of the templum's roof down after it.

Morbius Sire was already clear and running, hungry, malicious. Behind it, the fabric of the templum spilled to the ground in an avalanche of bricks and tiles. The plasma blastgun was going to be his best bet. Orfuls channelled the solution to his right hand.

<target now fixed.>

'Thank you,' said Orfuls.

The Warhound stormed forwards, past the burning wrecks of Hellhounds and Basilisks.

The enemy engine, a haggard Reaver, was standing at the junction of Pax Divisible and Compromise, surveying the blazing ruins, sporadically belting out gunfire across the subsid at the retreating components of the armoured artillery company. It was an ugly thing, twisted and deformed, blackened and rusted. Lube oil wept from its joints and it seemed, to Orfuls, to be breathing hard.

Just his imagination.

The Reaver swung its head around as it sensed *Morbius Sire's* rapid intercept.

'Raise shields,' Orfuls ordered.

'Void shields, aye,' replied Strakhov.

Orfuls accessed the pre-set target. Throne, it was a big, ugly beast, twice the height and mass of *Morbius Sire*. The Reaver turned to engage them, its limb weapons stiffening to power.

Orfuls could feel the heat of them as they built.

They crashed heedlessly through several rows of dwellings, splintering walls and shingles around their steel shins.

'Stay on target,' Orfuls cried out. 'Aim primary right!'

'Primary right, aye!' Strakhov yelled back.

Final target overlays swung down across Orfuls's Manifold vision.

The enemy engine fired its turbo. Hard-light bolts lacerated the air, missing *Morbius Sire* by less than five spans. The enemy fired again, locking its auspex down onto the charging Warhound.

'Voids hit!' cried Strakhov. 'Void shields holding!'

<Fire!> Orfuls told *Morbius Sire*.

The blastgun retched. Burst after sizzling burst struck the Archenemy Reaver.

It reeled. It wavered. It rocked back a step or two, rank oil spraying from its loose seams.

'Again!' Orfuls yelled. His voice had become a growl, a carnivore's purr.

The blastgun fired again. They were sixty metres away from the enemy Reaver, and it was swinging up its morning star to greet them, hand-to-hand.

Then it died.

The enemy Reaver suffered catastrophic shield failure. It exploded from the waist up. The light blast overwhelmed the Manifold for a second.

'Full reverse! Pull us back!' Orfuls cried out, momentarily blinded.

'Aye,' replied Strakhov, wincing.

Orfuls felt broken pieces of ceramite casing rattling off his skin. Ablaze, the Reaver toppled over in a welter of flames and sparks. As it went down, a ruined manufactory died along with it, crushed by the falling weight.

Orfuls realised he was growling and mewling. He damped down the feral intellect at the back of his brain. Synthetic hormones were rapidly attempting to negate the massive testosterone levels in his bloodstream.

'Princeps?'

'I'm all right. That was a damn fine kill. Thank you, all crew.'

'Princeps?'

'Signal Bohrman,' Orfuls ordered, shaking his head and trying to collect his thoughts.

'What signal should I send, princeps?' asked Strakhov.

'Signal received from *Morbius Sire*, princeps,' Bohrman's moderati announced.

Bohrman swung around in his amniotics. 'Relay it to me at once.'

'Yes, sir. Signal reads "First blood, Invicta",' the moderati replied.

Bohrman smiled.

110

Etta Severin woke with a start and couldn't remember where she was.

She was lying on a day bed in a small cabin. The recessed orbs were set at half-glow.

'Hello?' she called, befuddled.

Gotch appeared in the cabin doorway immediately, a pistol in his hand.

'What's the matter?'

She sat up and sighed, remembering.

'It's all right,' she said, feeling foolish. 'I couldn't... I was just confused for a moment.'

Gotch holstered his pistol. She noticed that he was refusing to look directly at her. Though fully clothed and in no way indecent, she was still technically a high-born female in bed, and Gotch was averting his gaze. His gallant propriety was somehow charming.

Etta stood up and stretched. 'Where are we?'

'Entering the northern belt of the subsid,' he replied. 'The executor signalled about ten minutes ago that we were approaching the staging point.'

'Why didn't you wake me?'

Gotch shrugged. 'It seemed to me that you needed the rest.'

Etta nodded. 'Thank you, major. We'd better go up.'

The executor fetial's retinue had left the western gates of Orestes Principal before dawn, moving out into the sub-hive levels to form part of the rear column supporting the main advance. Etta had wondered if she'd have to request a formal place in the retinue, but Crusius had taken it for granted that she would accompany them. He seemed to be going out of his way to accommodate her.

Etta had been mulling over her role. Lord Governor Aleuton's brief had been simple, but in hindsight she recognised his disingenuity. Given the orbitals, the PDF arrays and the military data-feeds, the governor's command and control networks would have no trouble maintaining an ongoing assessment of the fighting. She had not been sent to gather tactical information, which was beyond her expertise anyway. Aleuton had despatched her to observe the political and strategic aspects of the execution. This was a role she was more than qualified for, but it seemed distasteful. Aleuton had singularly underestimated Crusius's perceptive skills. The executor fetial fully understood Etta's agenda, and was evidently aware that she knew he understood. His courtesy and openness made her role all the more uncomfortable.

The executor's transport was a giant armoured crawler. Sonne, the famulous, had mentioned the vehicle's pattern name and type at some point, but Etta had forgotten the details. Five decks and an observation bridge rode on three pairs of heavy-gauge treads, protected by a ceramite reinforced hull and void shields. Its progress was slow and smooth, with barely a hint of ride motion.

Gotch waited at a respectful distance while Etta filed and sent her latest report to the Lord Governor's office. Then they walked together along the vehicle's spinal corridor and climbed the through-deck ladder to the bridge.

The observation bridge was principally crewed by servitors, each one bearing the insignia and hallmark of the Legio Invicta. Most were plugged directly into their stations at waist-level. Etta doubted they had legs. She wondered if they detached from their legs in order to plug in. Were the legs stored somewhere while they were on-station? Were they permanently on-station?

Fearsome skitarii warriors, eight of them, stood in alcoves around the bridge area, on watch. The bridge was nominally under the command of a man called Lysenko, who wore the fatigues and jacket of an engine crewman and carried the honorary rank of moderati.

Crusius and Sonne were at the central chart table, skimming through hololithic data. Though he had his back to them, Crusius seemed to be aware of them the moment they emerged on deck.

He turned and smiled. 'Mamzel, are you well rested?'

'I'm fine,' she replied.

'Join us, please.'

With Gotch in tow, she walked over to the chart table. She noticed that Sonne quickly cancelled and stored the data files under review, and replaced them with a terrain montage. Crusius evidently read something in her face.

'My apologies, Etta,' he said. 'We were just reviewing the

first of the data inloaded from the sequestered archives. It is sensitive material, I'm sure you understand.'

'Of course. Anything of use?'

'Nothing so far, mamzel,' said the famulous. 'It is still being run through the Analyticae.'

'We are two minutes from the first staging point,' Crusius said. He indicated the terrain montage. It meant little to Etta: a shifting, constantly updating three-dimensional map of street plans and structure markers. She vaguely recognised the layout of certain blocks.

'Noospherically, that conveys an adequate picture,' said Crusius, 'but it's a poor alternative to eyes-on.' He turned and called to Lysenko. 'Moderati? Lose the shutters, if you please.'

'At once, executor,' Lysenko replied from his station, and gestured a haptic command to the invisible noosphere. External shutters immediately withdrew, like eyelids opening, and the entire observation bridge became a dome of glass. Etta blinked as hard daylight replaced the ambient gloom of the bridge.

The observation bridge was a blister of armoured glass at the prow of the crawler. Ten metres above ground, it afforded a panoramic view of the location. Etta turned slowly, taking it all in.

They were coming down Principal Highway, down the slope of Semple Heights, a steep borough of hab-stacks and domiciles that formed foothills beneath the rising bulk of Principal. The highway, a broad chasm of rockcrete and aluminium palings, dug through the angle of the hillside in a series of deep cuttings. The buildings were piled on top of one another, teetering cliffs of domestic architecture overhanging the deep road cutting and clinging in tiers to the hard incline.

Etta had always loved Semple Heights. In better years, she had often travelled out there on the maglev from Congress, to spend her off-duty afternoons haunting the shabby tract markets and bibelot stalls, the book dealers on Castigate Walk, the cage-bird auctions in the Dwell, walking up and down steep public staircases mysteriously shaded by the mounted buildings, lunching in over-hang cafés where the air was filled with the music of mandolins and klusepipes. It had always been her place of escape, a world outside the oppressive totality of Hive Principal. It had owned a roguish air, a tawdry ebullience, a sense of life. She remembered a caffeine house on Soulpike, serving the best caff she'd ever tasted.

The war had not yet entered Semple Heights, but its high stacks and teetering footwalks were empty. Habs were shuttered and businesses shut up. War might not have arrived, but the odour of it had. Looking out from the crawler's dome, Etta sensed fear and alarm, the tension of the imminent. The population had shut itself away, or fled up-hive into Principal, to share rooms with friends, or bed down on the floors of in-hive relatives.

The morning was bright and innocently cheerful. She could see for tens of kilometres. Eastwards, behind her, above the heaped stacks of Semple, she could see the vast bulk of Orestes Principal, engulfing the sky with its hazy blue mass. Whether she was inside it or outside it, the sheer size of the main hive always stunned her. It filled the horizon, and its bloat dwarfed the sky. Its upper spires, one of which she had been standing in just days before, scraped the top of the world. *Nothing that vast could ever fall, could it? Could it*?

Ahead of her, down in the lowlands, the vast urban spread of the subsid ran all the way down to the distant mountain that was Argentum. According to Gotch, they were calling

Argentum 'Soak Town' now. Gotch hadn't been sure why. The pale sky above the faraway hive was bruised with smoke and soot: the line of war, she realised.

The executor's crawler led a van of fifty similar vehicles, most of them ammunition carriers, some of them troop transports. Light armour and weapon platforms scooted along beside them, and flocks of Vultures and Valkyries droned overhead in close escort. Crusius's transport alone had eight Hydra platforms and six skitarii quick-guns slaved to it, their raised weapons constantly circling and switch-targeting any potential threat. They moved and reacquired like phototropic plants. The retinue convoy was a small army in itself.

Hosts of the skitarii marched with them, rowdy and alarming. To Etta Severin, the skitarii seemed the polar opposite of the Guard or the PDF. They were gaudy, bestial, loud and brutish. They chomped for war, and uttered terrifying group yells of testosterone-fuelled antipathy. They were also non-uniform. She had never seen such a hybrid mix of feathers, furs, inbuilt weapons, claws, augmetics, engineering fangs, plumes, body armour, decorations and jewels.

She knew that Gotch was nonplussed. He simply did not know what to make of the barbarian skitarii. They were not common soldiers, the type he had been trained with.

'If you'll look west, Etta,' Crusius suggested.

She looked to the west. Vast figures stalked the subsid in the strong sunlight between her and the distant hulk of Argentum. She counted fifteen Warlords of Invicta, trudging west towards the line of war. They were immense, towering incongruously above the suburbs.

'So, this is what an engine war looks like, Crusius,' she said.

'Mamzel, not at all,' he answered. 'When they start firing, then you'll see what an engine war looks like.'

'I find that they scare me, executor.'

'That's the point of them, Etta. They are supposed to scare anyone who sees them.'

Her bodyman was staring at the distant engines. 'Old wars,' he murmured, to himself.

'Major Gotch?' Crusius asked.

'Sorry, thinking aloud,' Gotch replied.

'Of what?' asked the executor.

'Of books and slates that I read as a child, of records and tractates I was obliged to study in my years training: the accounts of old wars, the myths of epic campaigns from early eras. I never thought to see such scale unleashed upon Orestes.'

'I have, of course, been required to study such material myself,' said Sonne. 'It is indeed stirring to see the engines walk.'

'I didn't mean it was stirring,' said Gotch, 'though I'll grant you it is. In the old wars, worlds were split apart and turned to cinders. The old wars always cost the most.'

One of the distant, plodding figures, away to the north-west, suddenly lit up, sizzling with light.

'The day's work has begun,' said Crusius.

>

Invicta's first major engagement lit off in the northern hem of the subsid, where the shelving piles of Semple Heights began to level out into the warren of lawless streets and sinks at Old Silo.

Old Silo was one of the hive spread's most miserable black slums, jutting into the oozy inlets of the Semik. The dwellings there were propped on stilts, and the highest tides filled the ditches around Saint Satis Island, and crept in up the lower boundary streets. It was a destitute area, the cesspool home of thieves, debtors, bawds and outcasts where even the Magistratum and the social missionaries of the Ecclesiarchy were unwilling to tread.

Although the main eastward thrust of the Archenemy advance was being met at Argentum and the western limits of Jeromihah, Gearhart's tacticians had predicted that a flanking effort might be attempted along the basin and fens of the Semik. Several engines had been pushed wide to the north with skitarii support to watch for such an approach.

The Warlord *Sicarian Faero*, principted by Vancent Kung, led the way. Clear of the main arterial, roadways large enough to allow for the passage of Titans, engines such as Kung's were forced to cut their own pathways. It had been a long time since *Faero* had walked in a city, and Kung dropped back to low stride. Collateral damage was a given, but he had no wish to brutalise parts of a hive-spread which he was supposed to be protecting, just to get at the enemy.

Even at low stride, *Faero* left a trail of destruction in its wake. Its bulk brushed down walls in narrow streets, or crushed through mouldering hab blocks in the absence of clearance.

In this district, many of the structures were already ramshackle and derelict. Stonework and timbers were blackened with age and pollution. The hulks of four- and five-storey structures stood unroofed, and *Faero* snagged on overhanging eaves and rotten support frames as it crunched forwards, demolishing moribund slum buildings that had stood for six or seven hundred years. It manoeuvred through murky nests of by-courts and back-land alleys with the effect of a mobile earthquake, accompanied by the constant rumble and slither of falling masonry, the smash of glass, the shatter of tiles. Where it passed, harsh daylight, laced with dust, fell into exposed rooms and gutted underwalks that had been dark for generations.

Kung was disheartened by the number of vital traces that his auspex was showing. Although damned and dilapidated, Old Silo was not abandoned. Unlike their wealthier neighbours in Semple Heights and its adjacent boroughs, who had the means and opportunity to evacuate into the main hive, the wretched gutter-poor of Old Silo had remained in their slums. They were cowering out there, in the dank and flooded basements, in undercrofts and noxious cellars, waiting and praying for the war to end so that they could come out and resume their putrid lives.

As *Faero* advanced, Kung watched the auspex. At every step, at every crash of a falling side wall or roof, the clusters of vital traces moved, billowing in front of the engine, and scattering into the surrounding streets. Like vermin driven from their lairs, the residents of Old Silo fled before the engine's catastrophic advance, though they waited until the very last moment, until the doom steps of the approaching Titan could no longer be ignored. Then the resolution to stay put and hide was overwhelmed by mortal fear, and they ran, dragging children and livestock, clutching belongings, into the adjoining alleys and by-courts as their homes and shelters perished.

'This sector should have been cleared,' Kung murmured.

'With respect, I doubt the forge or the governor has any sway over these wretches,' replied his moderati. 'This is a black slum. There is no authority here.'

'So, how am I supposed to like this?' Kung asked. 'Am I to consider myself a force of urban renewal?'

His moderati laughed at the suggestion.

The Titan emerged from a dark sub-street into a court bordering a row of rotting slaughtersheds. Brown tide water had welled up across the ditches, and each giant step sloshed foam and froth across the court so hard that eddies broke like dirty surf against the fronts of the surrounding buildings.

Kung's moderati let out a cry of surprise. Mobs of local residents had gathered at the edges of the court, baying and jeering at the advancing engine. Some appeared in windows, or even on the broken-backed roofs. They began to pelt *Faero* with slabs and rocks. Kung could feel tiny *clicks* and *pings* as tiles and lumps of paver bounced off his skin.

'There's gratitude,' he said.

He sounded *Faero's* great warhorn, and the angry rebuke of the ancient engine made the mobs disperse in fear. Some re-formed behind the Titan, hurling missiles and abuse intended to drive the engine out of their lives.

'Damn it,' said the moderati. 'Don't they understand what we're trying to do for them?'

Kung wasn't listening. Something had just flashed across the Manifold and he triggered a retrocognition pattern to replay and lock it.

'Contact!' he bellowed, adjusting his position in the amniotics and focusing his will. *Faero* abruptly came under simultaneous fire from seven ground positions in the streets ahead. Flak and hard cannon flashed off its armour.

'Voids to full!'

Flights of shrieking rockets spat in over the rooftops and burst in sheets of flame across the shields. Heavy cannon-fire ruptured walls and timber frames in its eagerness to greet them. Several of the densely-packed buildings ahead of them disintegrated as the shuddering barrage robbed them of all integrity.

The onslaught turned the flooded court into a thrashing forest of waterspouts, mud-wash and flying debris. Dozens of civilian protesters were cut down or blown apart. Those with enough wit left to flee ran headlong into the nearest alleys and sub-walks.

They did not escape. The enemy brought up heavier shelling to target *Faero*. Ranged shot, from modified Bombards and Earthshakers, rained down across the court and the slaughtersheds. The Archenemy's aim was not precise. Falling shells detonated in the sub-streets and alleys behind the Titan, gouging out deep craters and exposing foetid cellars. Firewash boiled along narrow thoroughfares and belched through the shells of buildings. The mobs, scattering, burned in the blast-flash or were killed by sheets of scalding floodwater. The steady impact of the shell-fall was so heavy that *Faero* rocked back on its heels slightly.

'Voids holding!' the moderati called out.

Kung responded aggressively, blitzing turbo fire from his left limb. Traversing, he levelled an entire block-row with the turbo, and took out one of the concealed enemy ground positions with it. He was reading scrapcode and motor noise. The ambushers were trying to re-task and readdress their mobile batteries.

Kung sourced the motor noise and let the turbo laser pump again. The fury of its scorching emissions shivered tiles off roof slopes and shattered windows. The auspex showed a heat flash as a guntrak or weapons carriage cooked off. Positive kill.

'Ahead, flank stride!' Kung ordered.

'Flank stride, aye!'

Kung's sensori was calculating target solutions as the source data came in. Any heat spot showing up amongst the cold, dark stone of the immediate vicinity, any blurt of scrap-code snatched from the ether, became viable spoor. Kung felt the veins in his forearm throb as the Vulcans kicked in, switching from one solution to the next as fast as the sensori supplied them.

<Exload situation, *Faero*!> Bohrman was demanding over the Manifold link.

Already doing twenty things at once effortlessly, Kung data-squirted the tactical picture in response. He was aware of the skitarii forces swarming up in his wake in support, and of *Vengesus Gressor* moving in from the south.

He didn't require the assistance of either.

>

Crusius watched the inloading feed intently.

'Kung,' he murmured.

'What?' asked Etta Severin. The hololithic display was moving faster than she could follow, blink-overlaying data too rapidly for an unmodified soul to track.

'Princeps Kung,' said Sonne, 'walking *Sicarian Faero* in the Old Silo area. The princeps has engaged.'

'Successfully?' asked Etta.

'The engagement is ongoing, mamzel,' said Sonne. '*Sicarian Faero* is undamaged at this time, and has made kills on nine ground targets.'

'Ten,' Crusius corrected, without looking at either of them. The crawler's noosphere links were proving to be too flimsy for effective combat observation. Crusius deployed a discreet mechadendrite from a wrist socket under his cuff and plugged into the console directly. Hard-plugged, if only in a limited capacity, Crusius interfaced with the Manifold.

Etta watched him. The executor fetial seemed to be staring into empty space, his brow furrowed. Every now and again, a slight reactive expression creased his lips or forehead.

'It would appear that Lord Gearhart's speculation was correct,' he said. 'The enemy has attempted a flank move along the Semik. Indeed, they have advanced further than expected. *Faero* is encountering ground units, light motorised gun platforms, weaponised gross servitors.'

Etta looked towards the windows. Even from the open vantage of the observation bridge, the battle was too far away for her to make out any detail. Kilometres away to the north, fire patterns were flashing in the sky, and smoke was rising. The engine they had seen light up with gunfire had vanished from view.

'What are enemy numbers like?' Etta asked.

'Princeps Kung is currently tagging forty-eight sources of ordnance or heavy weapons fire.'

'Forty-eight?' asked Etta. 'He's taking fire from forty-eight sources?'

'His shields are holding, mamzel. He is eliminating them at an admirable rate.'

'He is?' she echoed.

'Of course,' said Crusius. 'He is *Sicarian Faero*.'

>

Kung's Warlord burst through the old Almonry at the end of Solehouse Passage, disintegrating in a matter of seconds an Old Silo landmark that had presented its flaking, moss-black features to the Orestean sky for a thousand years. Granite columns, hung with ivy, toppled like trees into the street beyond, and the Almonry's west wall slowly curled over and fell away like a breaking wave. The roar of wholesale destruction was drowned out by the squeal of turbo lasers and the searing spit of plasma mounts.

Scuffing through the rubble, *Faero* came out onto Birdmarket, a broad thoroughfare that ran south towards the commercia at Gox from the old Semik wharfs. About a dozen weaponised servitors, heavy-frame models, were snapping around *Faero's* heels like pit bulls baiting a brute ursid. They darted in, leg mounts scurrying, and pulsed off shots at close range with their engine-killing plasma mounts, before retreating.

Kung was tired of their sport. A dozen brutes like them already lay broken and burning in *Faero's* wake. He lowered the declination of the turbo laser and raked the roadway around the Titan's feet, swivelling the engine at the waist to increase the cone of fire. The harassing servitors suffered for their daring. Two vapourised. Another three took such severe damage that their carriages were flung aside in pieces. Having cleared the Almonry, Kung resumed full stride and crushed another two underfoot. *Faero* trembled as plasma reservoirs combusted. For good measure, Kung turned one powerful stride into a crude kick that caught one of the servitors head-on and sent it crashing and bouncing down the street.

The remainder backed off, firing parting shots with traversed weapons as they scuttled away down the cratered road surface. Further along Birdmarket, the Archenemy tanks and self-propelled guns that had shelled *Faero* at the slaughtersheds grumbled into rapid retreat as the Titan loomed. Kung aimed his quake cannon and his turbo and began to pick them off as he advanced. They had trusted their massed firepower to finish *Faero* before it reached the open roadway. That trust had been rash and foolish.

Tank hulls began to explode. Turrets burst or tore off and went whirling into the air. Magazines detonated with thunderclap violence. Entire gun platforms were blown in half or over onto their sides. Those that were spared by the first salvoes increased their rate of retreat, some of them reversing off the roadways through walls in their effort to escape a direct confrontation.

'Maintain full stride,' Kung ordered.

Even as they withdrew into the slum warrens off the open road, knocking holes through buildings with their fenders, the pieces of enemy armour remained visible to him. Kung's sensori was still patiently tagging every piece of spoor the auspex registered: scrapcode, motor noise, exhaust heat, motion tremor. He was even pinpointing the target vectors indicated by sloughing masonry. Kung's mind, alive with the bestial wrath of the MIU, moved between his suite of weapons, multi-tasking, agile, selecting the type of ordnance suitable for each target, and making the kill. The wounded structures of the subsid were not sparing the enemy units: the stone and rockcrete walls neither hid them from *Faero's* gaze nor protected them from its reach.

The engagement had lasted nine minutes. In that time, *Sicarian Faero* had levelled five blocks of Old Silo and made thirty-four kills. In his amniotic casket, Kung was swept up in war-rapture. His head was locked back, his mouth open in a snarl and his hands locked into claws. He was letting go to *Faero*, allowing the machine spirit to lift his performance to an intuitive, instinctive level.

Daross, his moderati, kept a careful watch on the vital

monitor. At this pitch of battle, it was not unknown for a princeps to stroke out, suffer a grand mal, or snap his sanity completely and become lost in the screaming maelstrom of the MIU. Through the Manifold, through the tingling surge of the hard-plugs, Daross could feel Kung's experience, second-hand but still intense: the overload of sensory images and target mathematics, the limb power, the braying rage of the weapon servitors, the racing reactor, the sizzling shields, the machine code running down his spine like molten lead, the spirit in his heart like steel, the joy–

Weapons lock suddenly sounded. A warning cursor like a blood bruise lit up on the Manifold.

<Engine! Engine!> the sensori canted.

The fight was about to go up a gear.

It ploughed towards them through the dusty granaries beyond Birdmarket, striding hard across the ditches and underwalks that criss-crossed the back-land. It kicked down walls and shouldered aside towers and eaves in its aggressive lust to reach the Imperial Titan. It tore through an overwalk bridge that blocked it at chest level, twisting and snapping the metal frame like a winning sprinter breaking the ribbon. Debris from the bridge sparked and bounced down into the street below.

It was called *Nekromant Invidiosa*. It made no effort to disguise its name, but rather broadcast it aloud as howling scrapcode through its augmitters, screaming it on all frequencies as if the words were some kind of weapon. Its toxic rasping made the Manifold tremble and distort at the edges. Kung growled and dimmed the audio receptors, cutting off a dozen non-essential channels to kill the noise.

The malign scream lingered. The utterance 'Nekromant

Invidiosa' echoed around the Manifold, the MIU, the imagination, as if it had been branded there with a white-hot iron. The name stank. It reeked of death and murder. It tasted of some unholy, lightless place beyond the known stars, and its phonetic structure was composed of abhuman noises.

The enemy engine was spiked and malformed. It was black like burned meat, but there was no way to tell if it had been deliberately painted black or had carbonised as the result of previous actions. Rust ate into its body plates like ulcerated sores. Blood-red light shone out of its cockpit ports. Locked up, it fired first. Some kind of turbo retched a bar of light at *Faero*, a blast so bright that it left a livid after-image scarring the retina.

Kung winced as the shot struck his voids at the abdominal rectus, flaring out a shower of energy dissipation. The voids held, but an angry psychostigmatic welt appeared on the flesh of Kung's washboard stomach. The enemy engine fired a second shot that glanced off the deltoid voiding. Kung heard vicious animal laughter cackling from his enemy's augmitters.

The disfigured enemy Warlord fired again and *Faero* took a second hit to the abdominal rectus. Kung gasped in pain and a shield warning sounded.

'Shield impairment, location 883,' Daross relayed.

Cunning and deliberate, *Nekromant Invidiosa* was purposefully retargeting the wound, trying to pop the shields. It uttered a primeval chortle, a thick autochthonic gurgle that was part gleeful laughter and part corrupted code.

Kung flexed his right shoulder and the starboard carapace mount woke and armed. The mount was a box-form launcher, which *Faero* carried on its broad right shoulder like a hod. It carried a payload of five missiles. The firing baffles and tube lids flipped open.

<Come about, two ten,> Kung canted.

'Two ten, aye,' replied the steersman.

<Target solution.>

'Target solution, aye,' replied the sensori.

<Flank stride.>

'Flank stride, aye,' replied Daross.

Faero moved out of the enemy engine's angle of fire, and turned in to engage. *Nekromant Invidiosa* didn't break stride. The kill banners swinging from its weapon limbs – tatty, blood-stained tallies – billowed in the hot wind as it began to traverse at the waist for another shot. Kung snap-fired the turbo three times, scoring two deflections off the machine's shimmering voids and decapitating the chimney of a manufactory plant one hundred and fifty metres behind it. Stung by the deflections, *Nekromant Invidiosa* took a step back and began to execute a full turn to face its Mechanicus foe.

Kung launched his first missile. It whooped out of the carrier on a cone of burning gas, and struck the enemy engine head-on.

The detonation was considerable. Electromagnetic pulse-shock scrambled the Manifold for a second. As he regained the link, Kung saw that the enemy Warlord had rocked backwards, stumbling. It was still intact, but its frontal voids were writhing and crackling with overload. Traceries of sparks and electrical discharge danced in the air around it.

He hit it again.

He heard scrapcode howling. For a moment, he thought he'd brought it down, but the bestial thing was still on its feet, staggering, lit up with corposant and buckled energy.

It turned and began to stride away.

'It's running,' Daross called in approval.

<We're not going to let it.>

The moderati glanced back at the amniotic casket and grinned. 'Full stride!' he yelled. *Faero* lurched into pursuit.

The enemy engine was topping out at maximum stride, but there was a limp to its gait as if it were hurt. It was retracing its steps, retreating along the gouge of destruction that it had cut through the granaries. *Faero* left Birdmarket and plunged into the thickets of old buildings and decaying hovels, exploding a path of its own through the black slum. Old walls and roofs burst apart before it, entire block rows collapsing like dominoes. Moving on a parallel course, Kung drew everything he could from the reactor, and closed the distance, snatching off shots with the Vulcans and the turbo.

The paths of the two striding engines were slowly converging. *Faero* began to draw level, separated by less than two sink-blocks from the enemy. It was visible from the waist up above the roofline, wading through the slum.

Still striding, *Nekromant Invidiosa* traversed its torso to starboard and began to pump its turbo as it ran. Coming alongside, *Faero* twisted its torso to port and returned fire. Side by side, the two engines kicked and stamped their way through the slum, blasting freely at one another. The wild crossfire lacerated and disintegrated the tops of the buildings between them, spraying tiles, bricks and mortar into the air. Three long trails of smoke and dust climbed into the air behind them, one from the wake of each Titan, and one from the collateral devastation in between.

An old templum, Saint Laera in the North, loomed before them, taller than both. They passed on either side of it. Neither suspended their firing patterns. The templum was raked from end to end as they passed, its whole structure shivering and dismantling like a storm of dead leaves. The ancient spire collapsed down into itself in a bloom of white dust as if the ground were swallowing it.

They came past the temple, still blazing at one another. The wide grey band of the river lay ahead, fringed by knots of post-set dwellings, warehouses, wharf cranes and the dank mollifying beds of the northern reservoirs.

'Its shields are going!' Daross yelled above the savage percussion of the autoloaders. 'I'm registering a thirty-six per cent integrity loss on its starboard voids!'

Kung selected missile lock and launched his third payload element. It struck *Nekromant Invidiosa* just below the starboard carapace mount and the huge fireball that resulted suddenly jerked and frothed, as if caught in a typhoon wind of savage cross-current.

Kung recognised the signs. The enemy engine's shields had blown out, had blown out *hard*, and the pressure flash had distorted the firewash like a backdraft.

The enemy Warlord stumbled, righted itself with a scream of gyro-stabilisers and stumbled again. Its right carapace was fractured, and parts of its plating were dangling on threads of reinforcement wire. Its wretched kill banners were burning. Secondary detonations, small but vital, were firing off down the right-hand side of its hull, showering off hunks of red-hot plating and fragments of subcutaneous armour.

Staggering, its gyros straining beyond tolerance, the enemy Warlord reached a rockcrete platform beside the principal reservoir, knocking down a stork crane and tearing through overhead powerlines that broke and sparked. The jetty platform cracked under its weight.

It turned to face them, its bulk sagging to the right. Smoke was pouring out of its torso and pluming up across its cockpit.

<Dead stop.> Kung ordered.

The two engines faced one another for a moment: *Faero* rigid, robust and locked out, its weapon limbs raised, its back hunched, *Nekromant* slack and swaying like a punch-drunk prizefighter. The dust and smoke of their vast contest blew in around them from the devastated streets.

<*Nekromant Invidiosa*!> the engine howled defiantly through its augmitters.

'You already said that,' replied Kung, and fired his quake cannon: a single shot to the head.

The enemy Warlord's cockpit exploded, the top and rear of its armoured cranium punching back through the overhang of the carapace. Power relays blew out around its shoulders and elbows. It swayed back, and the sway kept going, past the point of return.

Nekromant Invidiosa slowly toppled backwards, ablaze, and fell into the reservoir bed, taking a row of cranes and cargo-lifters with it. The impact crashed foul water high into the air, as if a submarine charge had been detonated, and a flash flood drowned the wharf platform, sucking back as fast as it had come. A vast eagre churned across the reservoir, and violently overwhelmed the weirs and filter barriers at the river end. The engine's subsystems continued to explode as it sank, and bubbling geysers broke the choppy surface, venting steam.

'Weapons to safe mode, recharge and reload,' Kung said. 'Let's find another.'

111

Varco tried to get his bearings. He hadn't gone far from the PDF post, no more than half a kilometre, but the dawn had come up thick with mist, and it was hard to see far in any direction.

The mist wasn't natural. It was a fug of propellant vapour and smoke residue drifting slowly off the main zone, out into the wetlands. It was white, like steam, and turned the air into a soft, pale solid, backlit by the sunlight: a bright, cloudy nothingness, like a child's idea of the afterlife.

Varco and Sagen had gone out early to reconnoitre the area. It was unnervingly quiet, and the mist both muffled and magnified even small noises, like the sound of their breathing, the friction of their garments and the skitter of stones under their boots.

They had found a rockcrete gulley a short distance from the post. They had almost fallen into it, in fact, coming up on it by surprise in the soft mist. It was part of the old wetland drainage system, an ancient network that had fallen into disuse long ago. The rockcrete walls were flaked and stained, and knotty weeds clustered along the sticky, half-dry bed.

'You walk that way for a little bit,' Varco said. 'I'll go this way. Don't leave the edge of the gulley, or you'll get lost. Let's see what we can find. Turn back in five minutes and we'll meet up again here.'

Sagen nodded and slowly faded into the mist.

Varco began to crunch along the ragged lip of the gulley. He passed a group of weed-choked chutes where another branch of the watercourse had once fed into the main gulley from the north-west.

Varco was jumpy. He kept his hand on the grip of his holstered sidearm. The place was so strangely quiet, the light and lack of distance so ethereal, it seemed oppressive. He could feel his heart bumping.

There was a cry. Varco started. Muffled by the bright fog, the cry seemed to have come from all around and nowhere. It sounded like the raw squawk of an estuary seabird.

He drew his pistol and armed it.

The cry came again. This time, his brain deciphered it. It was Sagen, calling his name.

Varco turned and began to hurry back along the rim of the gulley. Pebbles scuffed out under his feet and a few flew down into the gulley, pinging and bouncing off the rockcrete with little cracks like snapping bird bones.

He heard Sagen call again. The cry seemed to come from behind him, but Varco knew that was impossible. He pressed on.

Shapes loomed in the mist. Varco slowed down, and advanced with his weapon raised. A burned-out PDF transport truck lay on the edge of the gulley, listing on fractured axles. It was a blackened wreck. A tarry, spindle-limbed shape sat grimacing behind the glass-less frame of the windscreen, clutching the heat-twisted steering wheel. Other burned remains were fused into the payload area, and littered the ground. Flames had reduced the bodies to sooty bones, clad in only the merest shreds of flesh or clothing. They were withered, scarecrow shapes reduced by the blaze.

'Captain? Captain Varco?'

Varco edged around the dead truck. A PDF Centaur lay nose-down in the gulley, its back-end raised against the side, its nose buried in the bed. Its dozer blade had rammed upwards, like a horribly dislocated jaw. It had clearly driven off the lip and plunged, nose down, into the steep, four-metre ditch.

'Sagen?'

'Sir. Down here!'

Varco looked down into the gulley. Sagen had clambered down somehow and was poking around the wrecked Centaur. The Centaur hadn't burned. The quad launcher it had been towing had been dragged into the ditch behind it, wrenching around as it fell. The weight of it had torn the draw-bar away, and it had ended up on its side next to the tractor. Munitions boxes had scattered out of the Centaur's load space.

'How did you get down there?'

Sagen looked up and pointed to a bushy overspill of gnarled scrub growing out of the gulley lip. 'That took my weight,' he said.

Varco holstered his pistol and, gingerly, struggled down the gulley side. The woody fronds of the scrub cracked and frayed under his weight, and grazed his palms. He jumped the last metre or so.

'Bad piece of driving,' Sagen said sardonically, nodding to the Centaur.

'Or panic,' Varco replied. 'They came under fire, steered in panic – bang.'

'Poor bastard,' Sagen replied.

Varco realised there was a body on the ground beside the Centaur's buckled nose. The driver had been thrown clear in the fall.

It was hard to tell how long he'd been dead. Varco guessed no more than a day or two, but the harsh climate had already begun its work. The driver had been just a boy, a slender youth. His junior PDF fatigues, stiff with dried mud, clung to his shrunken limbs and seemed several sizes too big.

'Do you think these were the youngsters manning the post?' Sagen asked.

Varco shrugged. 'I hope not,' he said. In his mind, the boys at the post had packed up and fled to safety. That idea seemed comforting. The thought that they'd got no more than half a kilometre and perished here felt bitterly unfair.

The Centaur was unsalvageable. There was absolutely no way to get it up out of the ditch, not without an Atlas. Even if they had, magically, been able to conjure up a recovery vehicle, the Centaur's trans-axle had sheared, and the port-side treads had torn off, looping like a giant's belt across the gulley bed. Varco noted with disappointment that the head-first plunge had also bent the barrel of the Centaur's pintle weapon, a heavy stubber. There were several heavy magazine clips for the stubber in a mesh sling in the cockpit. He sniffed. Ammunition, and no weapon to fire it with.

Sagen thumped the side of the Centaur with his hand. There was a dull echo.

'The tanks are at least half full,' he said. 'If we could siphon some off–'

'And get it back to the post,' said Varco.

'And get it back to the post,' Sagen agreed.

'We'd need a drum.'

'The water reclaimer?' Sagen suggested.

'We need that for water,' said Varco.

Sagen sighed. 'Weren't there some jerry cans in the garage annexe?'

'I don't remember,' said Varco.

He checked the munitions boxes. There were half a dozen, each one nesting four hefty mortar shells for the quad. Working together, Varco reckoned he and Sagen could lift and carry one of the boxes. Getting it out of the gulley and back to the post would be another challenge entirely.

They improvised a sling out of their jackets, and spent twenty minutes hoisting four shells, one at a time, up into the side of the ditch, with Varco leaning out over the rim and Sagen lifting from below. It was slow, uncomfortable work, punctuated by one heart-stopping moment when Sagen slipped and a mortar shell fell out of the sling onto the gulley bed. Once the four shells had been raised, Sagen tossed the empty box up to Varco, and then scrambled up after it.

They put the four shells back into the box, secured the lid and began to walk it back towards the post, supporting a handle loop each. The mist hung around them. They travelled short, quick steps, putting the box down to rest every couple of minutes.

It seemed to take forever.

By the time the vague outline of the post became visible ahead of them, they were breathing hard, and their hands were painfully sore.

Thirty metres from the post, they put the box down again.

'Listen,' said Varco.

'I don't–' Sagen began.

'Exactly. The generator's not running. Stay here with the box. Keep down.'

Sagen knelt down beside the munitions box. Varco took out his weapon and jogged towards the post. It was ominously quiet. The previous night, the post had seemed safe, a reprieve, even though Varco had been fully aware that it was temporary. In the misty glare of day, the illusion was shattered. This wasn't a safe place at all. The poor PDF boys who'd been manning the post had known that. The sooner Varco and his stragglers could get away, the better, unless it was already too late.

Varco tucked his hand into his pocket and clenched the medallion in his sore palm.

He edged around the post, passing the empty garage annexe where the Centaur sat in the shadow of the low, armoured roof. There was still no sound coming from the main block house.

He moved on, nervously, his throat dry. Beyond the post, the scrubby, flat earth vanished away into the occluding mist, a white, opaque veil that now seemed sinister and capable of hiding anything or everything.

He rounded the side of the rockcrete post and came face to face with an aimed laspistol.

'Shit!' he gasped.

Hekton lowered the pistol and put a finger to his lips. Then he gestured for Varco to follow him.

Hekton led him into the gloom of the post. Leopald was in the doorway, holding the carbine. He looked worried.

Inside the block room, Trask sat watching Koder. The

enginseer was perched in front of the post's auspex, and the machine was active, even though the generator was silent.

'What's going on?' Varco whispered.

'There's something out there,' Hekton whispered back. He nodded at Koder. 'He got the auspex up.'

Varco crossed to his enginseer and studied the small, cowled display of the auspex.

'Two or possibly three contacts, east of us,' Koder said quietly. 'The weather conditions and the function-quality of the unit are impairing solid returns.'

'Last night you had your doubts about the auspex.'

'My diagnosis was premature. It turned out that the vox is beyond repair. The main and sub-amps have been deliberately fused, perhaps with a heat-torch. Accepting that the vox was junk, I cannibalised parts to mend the auspex. Its performance is poor, but it's something.'

'What are you running it off?' whispered Varco.

'My integral power source,' Koder replied. Both of his hands were inside the guts of the auspex, his array of mechadendrites extended and intermeshed with the circuitry.

'You can't support that for long,' said Varco. 'The power drain–'

'I will diligently monitor my power levels,' replied the enginseer.

'Koder got the first contact about half an hour ago,' said Hekton, 'pretty much the moment he test-started the auspex. We turned off the generator, because of the noise.'

'You seen anything?' Varco asked.

'No,' Hekton replied.

'However, I have inloaded small snippets of scrapcode,' said Koder. 'Whatever's out there, it is not ours.'

'We can't stay here,' said Varco.

'That much is certain,' remarked Koder.

Varco turned to Trask. 'Sagen's waiting out back with a box of mortar shells we found. Go and help him bring it in, quietly.'

Trask nodded, and slipped out of the door.

'Keep watching the mist,' Varco told Leopald. The gunner nodded.

Varco turned back to Hekton and the enginseer. 'There's a wreck in a gulley about half a kilometre west of us. A Centaur. It's holding stubber ammo, more boxes of mortar shells and fuel in its tanks. Were there any jerry cans or drums in the annexe?'

Hekton shrugged.

They went to look, leaving Koder at the auspex. As they reached the block room door, Leopald held up his hand to stay them.

'Wait,' he said.

They waited.

'I thought I heard something,' he added. Varco looked back at the enginseer. 'Anything?'

'Nothing appears to have moved any closer, captain,' the enginseer replied.

Varco and Hekton left the block room, and hurried around to the garage. The Centaur had two medium-sized jerry cans lashed behind its left sponson. Under one of the rear benches, in a stowage locker, Varco found a length of dirty plastek tubing that, from the smell of it, had clearly been used for ad hoc siphoning before. Hekton rifled the Centaur's basic tool bin for a couple of multi-purpose tools and picked up a length of metal fence post from a pile of entrenching materials in the corner of the garage.

'The cans will be heavy once they're full. We can use this as a yoke.'

Varco nodded. 'Any rope there? Getting things out of the gulley isn't a picnic.'

Hekton rummaged around. 'No.' He stood up and looked around the garage area. 'How about that?'

There was a chain block and tackle lashed up out of the way around one of the roof joists, simple lifting gear for raising engine blocks. They got up into the back of the Centaur again and carefully pulled the oily chain free from the block.

'That'll do,' said Varco. He took a final look into the Centaur's tool bin. There was nothing in it they could use to open the post's store.

'Come on,' he said.

By the time they had returned to the block room, Sagen and Trask had carried the munitions box in out of the mist. They set it down in the corner of the room.

'We're going to have to drain fuel out of that wreck,' Varco told them. 'It's going to be slow work, and it'll take several trips.'

'Why don't we bring one load back?' Sagen suggested. 'Then we can start the Centaur up, ride it over to the gulley, and transfer the rest. It'd be a lot more efficient than struggling to and fro with cans.'

Hekton shook his head. 'The moment we turn that engine over, they'll hear us. We have to do this quietly.'

'My thoughts exactly,' added Varco. 'When we start that Centaur up, we'd better be ready to get going and keep going.'

Hekton made the first fuel run with Leopald to give Varco and Sagen time to rest. Trask took over watch at the door with the carbine.

'Gather stuff together,' Varco told Sagen quietly, 'anything you think we can use, and fill all the water bottles.' Sagen nodded and set to work.

'Anything new?' Varco asked Koder.

'Be confident I would tell you, captain,' Koder replied.

Varco smiled. He looked at the box of shells in the corner of the room.

It took fifty minutes for Hekton and Leopald to return. They reappeared, trudging under the weight of the two cans swinging from the yoke between them. They were both tired and dirty. Hekton had stuffed his coat pockets with stubber clips.

'Just in case we find a gun,' he said.

They siphoned the cans into the Centaur's tanks. It was noxious, multi-fuel fluid: a crude, dirty mixture of recycled chemicals and oils that the goat-like constitutions of the tractors were built to work on. A Centaur's vulcanor eight plant could pretty much run on anything, and the PDF hadn't been issued with clean, quality fuel.

Trask and Sagen made the next run. Varco and Hekton checked the Centaur over, and stowed the stubber clips and the bedrolls from the post on board. Varco thought about unhooking the towed quad. It was a dead weight, and they only had four loads for it. It would probably be a wasted effort to try and bring back any more.

He thought about the box of shells again.

The phantoms on the auspex came no closer, but the bright white mist seemed, to Varco at least, to be beginning to clear.

Leaving Hekton to get the Centaur ready, he went back into the block room and took one of the heavy mortar shells out of the box, turning it over thoughtfully. He removed the back pin and slowly unscrewed the fins.

'On a note of personal safety,' said Koder, watching what he was doing, 'could you do that somewhere else or not at all?'

'Relax,' said Varco. 'I know what I'm doing.'

'You really don't look like you do,' hissed Leopald from the doorway. 'It's pretty inert, but if you drop it the wrong way up…'

'Adjacent to that box of shells,' Koder added.

Varco stopped what he was doing and wiped the sweat off his face. 'You know this stuff better than I do,' he said to Leopald. 'You do it.'

The *Merciless's* gunner leaned the carbine against the wall inside the door and came over. There was a dubious look on his face.

'What exactly are you trying to do, sir?' he asked.

'Remove the core charge,' Varco replied.

'Daft question, I know,' said Leopald, 'but–'

'Why? Because I want to try and blow the door off the post store.'

Leopald whistled softly. 'You don't want much.'

'Can it be done?'

'It can be tried,' said Leopald. 'Give that here.' The gunner took the shell from Varco and sat down with it, nursing it as if it were a newborn.

'If it doesn't work, I won't blame you,' said Varco.

'Given the various ways it's likely not to work, sir, you won't be in a position to.'

By the time Trask and Sagen returned with the second fuel load, Leopald had dismantled the shell and was busy beside the storeroom hatch.

'There's not much left in the wreck,' said Sagen as they siphoned the cans empty. 'One more load, and that'll probably be your lot.'

Hekton and Trask went off to make the final run. With

Sagen's help, Varco carried the box with the three remaining shells around to the annexe and stood it on the ground outside the mouth of the garage.

'You've got a plan, I take it?' Sagen asked.

Varco nodded. 'When we get the last of the fuel on board, we clear the post and blow the store.'

'If we can.'

'If we can. Then we clean out whatever we can find, fast as we can, get into the Centaur, and go hell for leather.'

'You want me to unlimber the quad?'

Varco shook his head. 'No, we'll unlimber it once it's clear of the garage.'

'Why?' asked Sagen.

Varco looked east, into the bright mist. It was beginning to thin quite rapidly, turning a pinchbeck yellow and burning off as the sun reached its zenith. Varco could see traces of hard, blue sky, and visibility had increased to several hundred metres. The lonely scrubland around them was still empty.

'We might need it,' he said.

He left Sagen in the annexe to wait for Hekton and Trask, and returned to the block room. His pulse was really racing, and there was an acid-metal taste in his throat. There was so little time left. Their luck had held this far, but it wouldn't last much longer.

They were about to need an awful lot of it in a very short space of time.

Leopald appeared, wiping his hands on a rag.

'Well?' Varco asked.

'It's not the most precise job I've ever done, but...' he shrugged.

'How do we set it off?'

'I've been thinking about that. We've got no det-tape.'

'So?'

'I've got the core charge snuggled in against the door, and I've stripped out the firing pin to make a detonator. All that's missing is a current source and a safe distance. So I need wire, and the generator.'

'Can Leopald help himself to cabling from the vox?' Varco asked Koder.

'Yes, sir.'

'Go for it,' said Varco.

Leopald got down under the voxcaster and began to unceremoniously yank out sheafs of electrical cable. He pulled strings of it back into the room, and began to strip and cut lengths with a pocket tool.

'Sir,' said Koder quietly.

On the auspex screen, a shape had begun to move in their direction from the east.

'How far away?'

'Three kilometres maximum.'

A second contact appeared behind the first.

'They're not moving directly towards us,' said Koder. 'I believe it's a patrol or raid party sweeping in this general heading.'

'Hurry up, Leopald,' Varco ordered.

'Yeah, 'cause this is a job it's always good to rush,' Leopald grumbled back.

Varco picked up the carbine and went outside. Though the mist was continuing to clear, turning the day into one of harsh, glorious sunlight, there was still no sign of visual contact.

Hekton and Trask returned with a can and a half of fuel. Sagen emptied it into the Centaur's tanks.

'All right, we're as good as we're going to get,' said Varco.

He ordered Sagen into the driving seat. 'Get ready to open her up on my order.'

The rest of them hurried back around to the block room. On the way, Hekton paused.

'What?' asked Varco.

'Flash. Sunlight on metal out there in the mist.'

'You sure?'

'I don't want to be.'

Leopald was playing a long, patchwork length of electrical wiring out from the chambers adjoining the block room. He took the free end and connected it to the generator.

'If we're doing this,' said Varco, 'we're doing this now.'

'One contact has definitely turned this way,' reported Koder.

'Disconnect yourself and get clear,' said Varco.

Koder gently withdrew his mechadendrites from the auspex and its screen went dark. He looked pale and unsteady.

'Are you all right?' Varco asked him.

'Drained,' Koder replied. 'A little movement and sunlight will boost my bio-electrical response.'

'Let's go!' called Hekton.

'Tell Sagen to start up and roll out of the annexe!' Varco called back. 'Everybody else out.' He looked at Leopald. 'How does it work?'

'Someone leans in through the doorway and throws the light switch,' said Leopald. 'Then they lean out again quickly. I'll do it, if you like.'

Varco shook his head. 'It was my bad idea.'

The others cleared out of the block room into the sunlight. Varco noticed that Trask was having to support Koder.

Varco placed himself against the heavy rockcrete seal of the block house door, and reached his arm in until his hand found the light switch.

'Ready?' he hissed.

'The Centaur's not starting,' replied Hekton.

'What?'

'Give it a minute.'

Varco waited, sweating. The rest of them had moved away from the blockhouse and got down in the dirt, except Hekton, who was standing by the corner of the post, looking towards the garage.

'Come on!' Varco urged.

'It's not turning over,' Hekton called back.

'Oh, come on!'

There was a stuttering grumble as the Centaur's engines turned over and then died. Another splutter, and the engines died again.

'I'm not kidding!' Varco yelled.

From around the other side of the post, the Centaur's engines finally lit. There was a throaty turbine roar, followed by a clank of gearshift and the sudden clatter of treads.

'It's clear! It's clear!' Hekton yelled.

'Ease!' shouted Varco. He threw the light switch and pulled his arm clear.

Nothing happened.

'I said it wasn't an exact science–' Leopald began.

'Wait,' said Varco. When they'd arrived the night before, the generator had taken a moment to wake up. He heard a wheeze and a splutter.

A terrible, dull thump shook the ground. Dust and smoke sprayed out of the post's window slots and doorway. Trapped by the armoured rockcrete shell of the post, the blast wash found any exit it could. Varco was thrown off his feet.

He stood up, ears ringing. They ran into the post, into the roiling smoke, and clambered through the debris into the rear chamber. It was hard to see, and harder to breathe.

The store-room hatch was caked in soot. In the adjoining wardroom, the bunks had been demolished.

'It's still shut!' Trask yelled, coughing.

Varco and Hekton pulled at the hatch. It was shut, simply because it had been forced back into its frame by the blast. The lock had been sheared clean off.

The hatch opened. Choking and half-blind, they stumbled into the small store-room. Varco tried to take stock. For all their efforts, there wasn't much there. Two chests of mortar shells stood against one wall, alongside some basic parts and spares, and some cleaning kits.

'Det-tape,' noted Leopald mordantly.

'Leave it,' said Varco. Ration packs, two small drums of cooking oil, two medical field kits, a dozen rebreather masks, six entrenching tools and a perfectly folded PDF flag were neatly stowed on shelves along the other wall. Below the shelves stood an empty rack for small arms, six drums of stubber ammunition and a long crate with a dust shroud over it.

'Take the food and the medical kits and get them into the transport,' coughed Varco.

'We could pour the cooking oil into the tanks,' Hekton suggested. 'Multi-fuel?'

'Forget it! No time! Someone take the stubber ammo!'

Varco ripped the dust shroud off the crate and opened it. The long, bulky shape of a heavy stubber lay inside, along with its collapsed stand.

'Help me with this!' Varco yelled to Hekton. 'Forget the crate, just grab the gun.'

They picked it up between them.

'That's it. Get moving!'

Outside, the sunlight was especially hard and dazzling.

They came out spluttering and spitting sooty phlegm. They could hear the Centaur's engine growling.

'Here they come!' Hekton shouted.

Varco looked over his shoulder. Out in the thinning mist, barely half a kilometre away, steel shapes glinted as they advanced. He thought he could make out two weaponised servitors, scurrying hard, the sunlight flashing off their racing legs.

'They're sweeping for target lock,' said Koder, feeling it.

Carrying the gear, they ran towards the Centaur. Hekton and Varco brought up the rear, heaving the cannon between them.

Sagen had pulled the Centaur clear of the garage, and then dismounted to unpin the draw-bar lock on the quad. They threw the gear into the Centaur, and then helped Sagen lift the lunette of the quad's trails off the Centaur's tow hook. It took all six of them to roll the heavy piece around until it was facing east.

'Get the shells!' Varco yelled as they levered the trails into position and rocked the carriage back onto its spades so that they dug in.

'This is a waste of time,' Hekton exclaimed.

They heard a crack. Heavy lasbolts whined in and hit the front of the post in a shower of grit.

'Still think so?' Varco replied. 'Prep one barrel! Just one!'

Trask and Leopald slid a shell into the hop of one of the quad's four guns and then hand-cranked the breach back to take it. As the breach slammed forwards into ready, they added a second shell to the hop.

'Won't have time for a third,' said Leopald. He wound the elevating hand wheel and lowered the quad's angle of fire. 'Nice and low, yeah?' he asked.

'That would be my choice,' said Varco.

Sustained lasfire peppered the front of the post. They could hear the thump and clatter of the advancing servitors. Several las-shots zipped overhead.

'That's good enough,' Varco cried. 'Get aboard!'

Leopald had hold of the firing lanyard.

'Get on, *now*,' Varco told him. Leopald passed him the lanyard and ran towards the revving Centaur.

Varco took a look over the quad's right wheel. They were partly shielded by the post, but he could see right out towards the advancing enemy machines. They were firing indiscriminately. A thick yellow haze of dust was being lifted by the impacts.

Aiming was a luxury that Varco didn't have. He opened his mouth, closed his eyes, and jerked on the lanyard.

The quad thundered and lurched. Varco felt the volatile air-blast shake his innards. He was temporarily deafened. The shell hit a few dozen metres behind the advancing servitors and kicked up a spray of dirt. The breach automatically seized the second shell from the hop and slammed it home. Varco adjusted the hand-wheel slightly, then yanked the lanyard again.

The second shell thumped away with a visceral punch, and exploded between the advancing servitors, showering them with clods and pebbles, and causing them to break stride slightly.

'Let's go!' Hekton bellowed from the Centaur. His voice was muzzy. Varco was still half-deaf from the mortar punch.

Varco was about to turn and run when the third servitor appeared. Its approach had been screened from them by the post, but it was much closer than the other two. It clattered into view around the side of the block house wall, just thirty metres away.

It clattered into view and paused, cleaning its mandibles. Its weapon mounts were raised and hunting.

Varco howled a curse. The men were screaming at him from the back of the Centaur to come.

'Go,' he yelled. 'Go!' He dived headlong for the shell box and grappled with it to dig out the last round. The Centaur was drawing away, start-stop, as if both frantic to go, and reluctant to leave him. He caught a snatch of raised voices.

Lurching back to the quad, Varco dropped the heavy shell into the hop and cranked the breach. The metal was still hot. The shell wedged in place and he had to slap it to make it drop. The breach slammed ready.

The servitor scuttled towards him, a mass of ugly spiked armour and raised laser mounts. Varco heard the piping squeal of scrapcode. A flurry of lasfire streaked past him, and one shot fractured the iron tyre of the quad's right wheel. Varco wound the elevating hand-wheel furiously, bringing the quad barrels right down until they were horizontal.

This was not what a field mortar was designed to do. He hardly cared any more. The servitor was right in front of him.

He pulled the lanyard for the final time.

The screeching shell missed the main body of the servitor. It struck one of its laser mounts, but that was enough to detonate it.

The blast stunned him, and the concussion felled him. Debris, rocks, fragments of armour, pieces of tubing and spatters of lubricant rained down on him.

Hekton grabbed him and hauled him to his feet.

'Come on, you idiot!' Hekton shouted into his deaf face, and dragged him towards the Centaur. Reaching hands pulled him into the back-bay.

Sagen opened the throttle, and the powerful utility tractor

lurched violently, nose up, and then tail up, as the tracks engaged.

Then it was off and running, waking up dust behind it, as fast as its powerful plant could carry it.

>

Cally Samstag didn't have much of a plan, but she was sticking to it.

She was leading the survivors of Activated Twenty-Six south, away from Fidelis Highway, away from what seemed to her to be the heaviest zones of fighting. As she did so, she tried not to dwell on the fact that *she* was leading anyone. Cally wasn't quite sure how that had happened.

A secret part of her was glad that they were leaving all the decisions to her. She was in charge, and had the freedom to act. This made her feel more connected to Stef, somehow. It was a comfort to imagine that, any time she wanted, she could simply decide to turn around and head home to find him.

She was less happy about the responsibility.

She had decided on a southward route. The logic was simple. Without a chart to consult, the choice had to be based on the most basic merits. To the east, north and west, they were hemmed in by open warfare and skies painted black with smoke. Long-distance artillery duels rocked the horizon, and they heard, now and then, the distant weapon-scream of a war engine. It didn't take a genius to realise that the east, north and west would all eat up a mob of inexperienced, under-equipped ground troops like Activated Twenty-Six.

To the south lay hope and the prospect of survival. The smoky pink contours of the lonely Astrobleme rose above a silent landscape of abandoned ore dumps and the shanty towns of sub-habbers, utility gangs and satellite communities. The south promised safer ground. With viable targets like the Gynex finishing silos, the Lexal refineries, and the yards up at the Mount, no enemy engine was likely to come ploughing into the southern belt to chalk up kills on derelict ore splitters, waste plants and scrap dumps.

Maybe in the south they could find a friendly unit, or a functioning vox.

She tried to remember the names of the little vassal townships that filled the dry southern plain on the doorstep of the Astrobleme, all corroded together in a rusty mass. She recalled the maps she'd been made to review prior to every Astrobleme exercise in the old days. The townships had names like Longdrift, Saint Vital, Staggerhouses and Outberg. The names had made Stef laugh. Most were unofficial. The vassal towns stood outside Mechanicus control, like the notorious black slums on the northern edge of the Principal subsids, and they weren't strictly Imperial either. They simply *were*. They subsisted on the traffic that passed through them: scrap metal, food waste and black market produce seeping out of the hives, and junk-load and harvested minerals seeping in. It was a limnal border between hive and wilderness, where people lived a hard, grafting life or died, with no other options.

The roads were a mix of hardpan and scuffed rockcrete. The forge had mined all it wanted out of the southern belt centuries before, but it had left the marks of its industry behind. What passed for towns were a mix of crumbling modulars, hand-built shacks, and old stone and 'crete buildings converted for habitation. Trash littered the empty streets, and stray dogs barked. Cally saw fenced yards and open barns piled high with what, to her eyes, was detritus. Yet it had been put there deliberately. In the vassal towns, everything had a use or a value.

It was sobering how quickly the landscape changed. They were only five or six kilometres away from Fidelis Highway and the vast, lucrative fields of the refineries and processors. In an hour's walk, they had crossed over into a back-ditch realm of sub-wilderness poverty and parasitic living.

There was no one around. Cally wondered if the shanty dwellers had fled, or hidden. She favoured the former.

Activated Twenty-Six came to a halt and broke for a five minute water-and-rest halt at a crossroads. They were in a shanty that had declared itself to be Gorge Orewelt on a flaking sign. A few of them spread out to search nearby dwellings for water or comms. Dogs were barking plaintively in back alleys. Pink sand swirled in the sighing wind and smelled of graphite.

Gorge Orewelt was a few cross streets' worth of shanty dwellings clustered around three large, ex-Mechanicus tithe houses, five-storey hulks that rose up amid the tin-roofed sprawl like monuments. Their windows were patched and boarded, and the roofs had long since been reduced to fish-bone rafters. Centuries of wind-blown sand had abraded the carvings and reliefs on their grand facades into dull, untrustworthy blurs. Loose, scrap-metal weather-boarding swung in the breeze. A row of bulk ore hoppers stood beyond the tithe houses, structures of such magnificence they suggested that Gorge Orewelt had once been a prosperous and significant subsid. They were huge metal drums, rising taller than the mighty barns, but they had rusted to death years before. The hoppers were dark brown with corrosion, the colour of spoilt meat, except for patches of verdigris on their tubular frames. Flocks of tiny zephyrids fluttered and darted around their rusted eaves in quick, tight formations. The plangent horns of Gynex sounded, far away, as if in someone else's dream.

Behind the hoppers, Cally could see the distant pink horizon of the Astrobleme, and she could smell the peach sand blowing in across neglected wind levees.

She touched the gold medal around her neck.

'It means "star wound",' said Binderman.

'I'm sorry?' Cally replied, becoming aware of him.

'*Astrobleme*. It means "star wound",' he repeated.

'Yes, I knew that, Mister Binderman,' she said.

'Of course you did, educated girl like you. I probably should be calling you ma'am.'

'I don't want to be in charge,' she told him.

'I think you need to be. I think they need you to be,' he replied quietly.

She slung her carbine over her shoulder, wiped her mouth, and took a sip of tepid water from her flask. Behind them, most of Twenty-Six had sat down, or were leaning in the shade. They could hear Lars Vulk bickering with Antic.

'He needs sorting out,' said Binderman.

'Which one?' she asked.

He smiled. Cally watched the others. Janny Wirmac, the posh girl from Summittown, stood away from the main group, staring north in the direction of her home. From Gorge Orewelt, Orestes Principal was a vague blue bump on the horizon.

Janny Wirmac hadn't spoken to anyone in hours.

Lasco, the skinny weaver's mate from Gynex, was re-lacing his boots. Ranag Zelumin, an ore-panner from Antium, had lost two fingers in the attack on the highway, and Reiss was re-dressing his wound. Cally had always known Zelumin to be a cheery, affable sort. Since his injury, he had become haggard and staring. Cally guessed it was shock, rather than blood loss. Another one to worry about.

She tried to remember the names of the faces new to her. The portly, bearded man in the shade, smoking a lho-stick as if it were his last was Zhakarnov, something like that. He didn't say much. Cally understood that he was a loom supervisor from Capetok Subsids who took his PDF service seriously. He was a tertiary veteran, apparently. Cally wondered why he'd never achieved rank; a fitness issue, probably. The middle-aged man nearby was called Braniff. He kept talking about his children and showing the others picts. Cally wished he'd stop, because it was freaking them out. Braniff was simply managing to remind them all that they had loved ones and dependants, except, perhaps for Reiss.

A red-haired, freckled woman called Sasha slouched on the other side of the street. Cally had never caught her last name. She was talking to a dark-skinned Mechanicus menial called Robor, who was serving with tertiary as part of his forge apprenticeship. The forge required most of their menial labourers to serve out a term or two in the PDF. It was supposed to tie the Imperial and Mechanicus halves of Orestes together, but everyone knew the halves would always stay apart, just as everyone knew that the halves weren't halves.

Down from Sasha and Robor was a ratty little underwhelm called Fiersteen who had the worst teeth Cally had ever seen, and smoked stinking black cheroots that undoubtedly explained it. Golla said that Fiersteen was on tertiary as part of a punishment warrant handed down by the Magistratum for trafficking. With him, trying one of the malevolent cheroots, was a nung named Wolper, a thick-necked oaf who worked the handling sheds at Argentum.

There were two others whose names she couldn't remember. How many was that? Eighteen, including herself? Activated Twenty-Six had been reduced to eighteen. Still, it was a lot of responsibility.

Golla wandered over with Iconis.

'Bohn and I took a look around, Cally-girl,' Golla said. 'We didn't find any sign of a vox, no sign of food, no sign of standpipes or running water. Bohn and I looked pretty thoroughly.'

'They must have water,' said Cally. 'A community this size.'

Bohn Iconis shook his head. 'We've looked. There's no water system, no ground pipes, no drains. They must guard and store water as preciously as everything else. They took it with them.'

'They took it with them?' Binderman asked.

'There's no one here,' replied Iconis.

'Then why do I get the feeling we're being watched?' Binderman asked, glancing around. Cally looked up too. In the hard sunlight, the twittering flocks of zephyrids zagged between the hopper tops. Janny Wirmac was still staring at nothing.

'Cally-girl?' Golla prompted.

'We move on,' said Cally emphatically. 'We find water, and we take shelter when night comes. A vox is the third wish. Bohn, Mister Binderman, would you encourage the others to get ready to move, please?'

She walked away, and Golla caught up with her.

'Where are you going, little sister?'

'I need to talk to Janny,' Cally said quietly. 'She's on her thread-ends.'

'Uh huh,' Golla replied.

'So, Bohn Iconis?'

'What?'

'"Bohn and I" this, "Bohn and I" that...'

'You shut up!'

'You like him. You want him to be your special friend.'

'You shut up, now,' Golla hissed, chortling.

Cally stopped walking and turned to look at her friend. She grinned. 'Tell me you don't,' she whispered.

'I don't!'

'Liar.'

Golla Uldana blushed.

'Oh, you've got it bad,' said Cally, 'lethally bad.'

'Is it that obvious?'

'As obvious as him being gorgeous.'

'You're married, Samstag!'

'Just because I'm not shopping for ploins doesn't mean I can't recognise a juicy one.'

Golla giggled. 'He's gorgeous, all right. Am I really being too obvious?'

Cally shook her head. 'Yes, you are.'

'Shut up!'

'Go and get the rest on their feet. You can make kissy eyes at gorgeous Bohn.'

Golla pursed her lips. 'Do I look all right?' she asked.

'You're in the middle of a warzone, Uldana. Get on with you!'

Golla sniggered and ran back to join the group.

Cally reached Janny Wirmac.

'Your friend,' Janny said, without looking at Cally. 'She's a good person.'

'My friend?'

'The big woman. Low-hive, I presume, but very warm.'

'Golla's all heart,' said Cally. 'Are you all right?'

'I want... I want to go home,' said Janny Wirmac.

'We're working on that,' Cally assured her.

'I want to be in the hive, where it's safe. I want to be inside. My papa wants me to come home.'

'Your papa does?'

Janny nodded. Cally could see that tears were welling in her eyes. 'My papa told me to join tertiary. He said it would be an experience, and afford me exercise. He said it would help me meet people and understand the strata of the hive. He never thought I'd be sent to war. He must be horrified. He's probably got his men out right now, searching for me, but they won't find me, because I'm not where I'm supposed to be.'

If you were where you were supposed to be, Janny Wirmac, you'd be dead, Cally thought, but she refrained from saying it.

Janny turned her gaze away from the distant hint of Orestes Principal and looked at Cally Samstag for the first time. 'Can I go home, please? I hate it out here. My heart is thumping so hard it feels like the earth is shaking.'

The tears came. Cally embraced her. Janny Wirmac was a good deal taller than Cally, but she took the embrace as if it was maternal, and rested her cheek on Cally's right shoulder, her arms tight around Cally's back.

'It's all right,' Cally shushed.

Cally could feel the girl's heart pounding furiously against her breasts. Janny had been right, the poor thing. It felt like the earth was shaking with every beat.

Cally looked up over Janny's shoulder. She saw the rusty tops of the ore hoppers against the hot, blue sky. She felt a massive tremor and watched as the zephyrid flocks burst into the air from the hopper rooftops and scattered at the shock.

'Janny?'

'What?'

'Run.'

Cally broke away from the girl and unshipped her carbine. 'Run!' she shouted, still gazing at the rusting hoppers. She turned and yelled at the group at the crossroads behind her. 'Run! Get cover!'

They looked at her, puzzled.

'Do it!' she screamed.

She felt the ground tremble under her feet, no heartbeat this time. It did it again. The others stood where they were, baffled.

'Oh, Throne,' Cally moaned, backing away.

The war engine cleared the row of hoppers and stepped into view.

Cally forgot to swallow, although she really, really needed to.

It was immense. Somehow, in the stark, unforgiving sunlight, it seemed bigger than was even possible. It took another world-shuddering step and turned to face her. There was nothing between her and it, except for the long, straight dusty track that ran through the dilapidated heart of Gorge Orewelt.

Cally found that she couldn't move. Two hundred metres away, it took another step towards her. A Warlord, it was a *Warlord*. She recognised the basic design. Stef had been fascinated by the Titan legions, and once they'd relocated to Orestes, he had taken her to see several public parades on the Field of Mars, where the Legio Tempestus had exhibited their grand engines. Cally recognised the pattern, the shape of it, and the colour-scheme: Legio Tempestus, the legion of Orestes.

It took another massive step. Finally understanding what it was they were seeing, Activated Twenty-Six broke in terror and scattered in all directions. Dropping kit and weapons, they ran to ground in the buildings of the township and cowered in the shadows.

Cally stayed right where she was.

The engine's reactor rumbled. Metal scraped against metal as it took another step. Cally took a pace back in response, still gazing up at it, entirely alone on the street.

The engine looked wounded. It seemed stooped and care-worn. There were scorch holes in its left flank, and faint blue smoke guttered out of its heat exchangers. It stopped and slowly leaned back, its head rising up out of the slouch. It gently traversed its torso from the waist, to the left, to the right, weapon limbs and carapace mounts open and ready. She heard the rattle of well-oiled gears and the hum of refined sub-motors.

Cally took another step backwards.

She felt her eardrums shudder and her eyeballs vibrate. The Warlord was pinging its auspex along the street. It was hunting for something. She was just part of the terrain. Although it had seemed to step out and confront her, she understood that it hadn't noticed her at all.

She raised her hand anyway. 'Please–' she began.

She didn't get any further. The facade of one of the monumental tithe houses exploded as a second engine burst through it, scattering plaster and brick. It was moving fast, its rear-jointed legs loping it forwards aggressively. The Warlord began to swing around to face it, but the smaller machine, a Warhound if Stef had taught her anything, was already thrusting in at its flank with its weapon limbs firing.

Cally flinched at the noise of the weapons. She smelled the stink of ozone as high-yield laser fire spattered against convulsing void shields. The Warhound, fast and dogged, was an ugly little beast, if anything that towered above the rooftops could be described as 'little'. It was hunched and belligerent, boldly driving in at the massive Warlord like an angry, hopping crow trying to scare away an eagle.

The Warlord, towering and ponderous by comparison, continued to turn. The Warhound darted back and then bounded sideways, smashing through shanty dwellings in an effort to stay out of the Warlord's field of fire. It was daubed dirty black, gold and crimson, and its eusuchian hull was poorly riveted, like flesh badly sutured. The crude emblems on its plating made Cally feel nauseous. Moving with a bouncing, sure-footed stride, it fired again, tenaciously harrying the giant's hindquarters.

The Warlord seemed to lose patience with its impudent little assailant. It swung around with astonishing vigour and bore down on the smaller engine. Without warning, its main armaments commenced a blitz.

The huge concussion jolted Cally hard, and she crossed her hands in front of her face to block the dazzling flashes. A line of shanty habs disintegrated in clouds of flying debris.

The Warhound bounded away from the destruction following it, taking hits on its shields, and loped towards the giant hoppers, trampling the pitiful residences of Gorge Orewelt underfoot. The Warlord strode after it. Its chasing firepower shredded two of the hoppers in quick succession, crumbling the weak, corroded drums as though they were made of spun sugar. The hoppers folded and slumped in on themselves with brittle squeals of tearing metal.

The Warhound turned in the billowing orange dust that

gouted from the hoppers' collapse, and came straight back at its massive opponent. Its weapon mounts lit up with vivid muzzle flashes as it charged. Some shots smashed into the Warlord's shields, others went wide, streaking across the township over Cally's head like stray comets. A turbo shot punched clean through the Warlord's ribs, puffing a mist of atomised plating and vaporised lubricant out through the exit wound in its back. In response, the Warlord simply fired its volcano cannon.

The flash seemed to split the heavens like a thunder crack. The blast knocked the baiting engine sideways, its shields fizzling and shimmering as they attempted to repair and compensate.

The Warhound tried to regain its footing, but the giant was on it. Void shields wailed and crackled as they brushed against each other. Cally's teeth tingled. She smelled blood in her nose. The Warlord calmly extended its close-combat flail and lashed it down across the Warhound's hull, like a man beating a stubborn dog. The Warhound roared, bleating noise out of its sirens. It strode backwards hastily. The Warlord's horns boomed in reply and it back-ripped the flail across the Warhound's snarling snout.

Full contact. The ground shivered. One of the Warhound's clawed feet slipped on rubble as it tried to right itself. It continued to back away. The flail, moaning as it cut through the air, came around again and smashed the braying Warhound backwards into another of the ancient, rusting hoppers. The hopper collapsed tumultuously down on top of it.

Silence. Dust. The lingering stench of ozone.

The Warlord paused, staring at the blooming dust. Then it turned away, retracting the close combat weapon. Its horns blared. It began to limp slowly back in Cally's direction.

'Cally! Cally-girl!'

Golla broke out of cover and ran across the street to where Cally Samstag was standing, out in the open sunlight. Golla grabbed her and tried to wrestle her backwards.

'No! I need to–' Cally barked.

'Get into cover, you mad woman!' Golla cried.

As Golla tried to manhandle her backwards, they both felt the jelly in their eyeballs pulse. The Warlord was hunting again.

'Let me go!' Cally yelled.

Directly to the left of them, tin roofs and makeshift shingles were thrown high into the air.

The second Warhound revealed itself. It had been right there, all the time, all the while they'd been sipping water and smoking malevolent cheroots. It had been crouching in wait right beside them, amid the low-rise shanty huts and habs, no more than fifty metres from the crossroads. It stood up, its muscular, hydraulic limbs grating as they raised it up to its full height.

Bricks and tile fragments rained down. Sections of tin roofing crashed onto the street. Golla squealed and tried to pull Cally into cover. A large, tumbling chunk of rafters and tiles missed them by a fraction.

The shadow of the second Warhound fell across them. Cally stared up at it, resisting Golla's frantic efforts. She'd never been so close to an engine. It was side-on to her, confronting the Warlord. She could see up under its jutting limbs, into the shadows between the thick plating, along the underside of the short, segmented tail it held out behind it like a counterweight. The proximity seemed uncompromisingly intimate.

The Warhound was crimson, black and gold like its twin.

They could hear hydraulics rasping and venting, scrapcode crackling like a dirty chuckle, sub-motors whining as they juiced up to power. Cally caught the scent of dry blood and rancid meat. Awful tally banners hung from its wrists and flapped in the dry wind. The tail clanked as it thrashed from side to side.

The Warlord boomed its horns as it came on. The Warhound lifted its snout and chattered back insolent machine code abuse.

Golla slapped Cally across the face. 'Move, you crazy bitch! This is no place to be! Will you please move?'

Cally blinked. Everything had suddenly become very real, especially her fear. She realised that the sight of the Titans had simply frozen her in mortal fascination, like prey before a predator.

'Oh God-Emperor,' she whispered and began to run with Golla, as fast as she could, across the street and away from the monster, the *monsters*. The two women crashed through a door into a filthy dwelling, stumbled through the ramshackle interior, and burst out into a narrow back path lined with rotting prefab walls.

'Get down!' Golla yelled.

'Keep running!' Cally shouted back.

With a piston hiss, the Warhound began to advance, ploughing a path through the township with its plated legs. Its dreadful tally banners dragged backwards across roofs and gutters as it forged along.

It began to burn shots at the Warlord. The shuddering air blasts shook the narrow back path and knocked Golla and Cally against a fence of plyboard planks.

The second Warhound greeted the Warlord with sustained fire as it advanced. Deflected energy blossomed like hot, white flowers across the crackling surface of the Warlord's voids. The Warlord stoically walked into the bothersome onslaught.

Then it returned fire.

The entire street block around the little crossroads came apart in a blizzard of explosions and sub-munition detonations. The dwellings, by-yards and alley paths where Activated Twenty-Six had taken cover crumpled and disintegrated as the Warlord's guns demolished them. Cally and Golla were blown clean off their feet. The plyboard planks around them blew into flying shreds and fibre splinters. Something struck the side of Cally's head painfully, and everything went dark red.

She blinked, and awoke. She'd been out for only a couple of seconds. She was on her side on the path, half-covered by strips of smouldering plyboard. The dwelling behind her was ruptured and burning. The dwelling in front of her was entirely gone.

Cally shoved the debris off her body and struggled to her feet. Golla was sitting nearby, her head bowed in her hands. Cally grabbed her arm and tried to pull her up.

'Come on!'

Golla blinked at her. She was too dazed to respond. She barely recognised her good friend Cally. All around them, the northern quarter of Gorge Orewelt had been laid to waste. Few buildings remained upright, and none intact. There was so much scattered, burning rubble and debris that it was hard to discern the wall plan of levelled dwellings or even the course of the cross-streets.

The thunder of engine gunfire had not abated. Head down, tail up and swishing, the Warhound was menacing the soaring Warlord. Barrages of lasbolts flitted between them, and cannon fire streaked the air like luminous rain. The void shields around the engines blotched and rippled under the impacts. Thick bars of gun smoke and discharge vapour were rolling out from the duel.

Then the duel became a brawl. The first Warhound wrenched itself up out of the ruined hopper and began to advance on the engaged Warlord from behind. One of its weapon limbs hung limp and mangled, like a broken wing, but the other began to retch neon-bright pulses of las into the Warlord's hind shields.

The Warhounds, baying and yapping like dogs, harried the giant from both sides. The Warlord blasted out a defiant note from its horns, but it was beginning to take serious damage. Fragments of plating spalled off its carapace casing, and its hull plate began to dent and puncture. Something ruptured under its left weapon limb and a shower of sparks drizzled out. What was left of its shields had turned an unhealthy colour.

The Warlord rocked and began to turn. It was trying to break off and move clear, but the gleeful Warhounds weren't about to let it go. They moved in closer, emptying their magazines and power reservoirs in frenzied delight.

The Warlord made a final effort to disengage and stride free. Smoke was pouring from its back plates. The jabbing, darting Warhounds fell in behind it. It broke away in the only direction available.

Cally wrapped her arms under Golla's armpits and heaved her up. The Warlord was staggering straight for them, clumsily crushing its way through frail shelters and meagre habs like a stumbling drunk.

'Golla! Come on! Come on!'

Golla was limp, her legs slack and trailing. Cally began to

heave her backwards through the debris, cursing and struggling. The ground was trembling violently. The giant was looming over them, so very close, and the vicious, blasting killers were at its heels.

Cally couldn't drag Golla any further. She wept and screamed with fear and frustration as she sank down with Golla between her legs. She wrapped her friend's lolling head in her arms and pulled it against her chest. Their last and only hope was that the massive engines would stride right over them, ignorant of their existence.

Mid-stride, towering above them, the Warlord lurched as an internal shockwave rippled through it. Fierce yellow fireballs boiled up out of its torso and throat. Cally heard a primordial utterance, part groan, part sigh. The Warlord's limbs locked up, freezing it like a burning metal statue.

The yapping Warhounds halted and enthusiastically raked the noble ruin with rapid fire. Thousands of shots punched and tore clean through the vast engine, perforating its outer plating like a colander. It shuddered and swayed, riddled with gunfire and weeping smoke. A turbo shot knocked its head to the left. Arterial pipe work in its throat tore and vented.

There was a long, slow, groaning, grinding rumble as the Warlord toppled over.

Cally saw it coming down. It was falling on its face, falling like a dead man falls.

'Oh no no no!' she screamed.

It was falling on her and Golla, its vast shadow rushing down to flatten them.

She held Golla so tight.

The Warlord lay where it had fallen, face down in the ragged wreckage of Gorge Orewelt.

The Archenemy Warhounds chattered code to each other and blared their sirens in triumph. They swayed to and fro jubilantly on their hips, and randomly fired point-blank shots into the huge smoking carcass at their feet.

Then they turned together, side by side, and loped away towards the hives.

>

Feist didn't like Adept Kalien much. She was from archives, one of Tolemy's juniors. Wherever she walked, her noosphere jazzed about her twin sister, Fairika, who had just landed a famulous spot on a Warlord. Magos Tolemy was personally opposed to the Analyticae gaining access to the sequestered coils, but even the magi of the archives couldn't overrule the Adept Seniorus. *Knowledge is power*, so ran one of the Mechanicus's oldest proverbs, and the magi of the archives guarded that power jealously.

Tolemy had sent thirty adepts from archives to assist the Analyticae with the work. This was meant to be seen as a benevolent act, a demonstration of the branches of the forge pulling together in a time of crisis. Feist knew the adepts, like Kalien, had been sent to monitor.

'Have you got a transliteral for dossier 618 yet?' Kalien asked him.

'Not yet,' Feist replied.

Kalien smiled. 'May I ask, adept, what is taking so long?'

Feist looked up at her. The atmosphere in the outer Analyticae was hot and oppressive. Servitor teams had annexed ten chambers around the Analyticae, fitting in new doors and connecting new walkways to expand its territory and accommodate the influx of personnel. The tithe factor departments that had previously occupied the areas had withdrawn and the space had been reconfigured around the Analyticae's needs. In some of the new rooms, steel tables had been erected in long lines, and the dossiers, tractates, off-prints, datascripts and trays of storage slates and tiles brought up from the archive had been laid out along them for processing. Feist had been alarmed at how much material was in non-cantable form, and how much was so corrupted or obsolete it needed to be printed out onto paper – *paper!* – just so it could be read.

Feist had withdrawn to one of the outer layers, a private room with a private table where he could review a heap of files. The air was muggy, because servitor teams were still connecting the circulence systems together.

Now Kalien had found him with her smug questions.

'What?' he asked.

'The transliteral?'

'That batch of material is somehow encoded in a bastardised idiolect form of Plural Cognata that the systems refuse to read. I am required to recode it, block by block, via transfercode. The operation will take another half an hour.'

Kalien smiled. 'I see. Transfercode. Ingenious. I had been wondering why Egan selected you as section leader.'

'Magos Egan has faith in my abilities.'

'And as section leader, how do you propose to run this operation?'

Feist looked up at her. The burden Egan had set on him, grateful though he was, felt heavy.

'I intend to run it robustly, Adept Kalien. I intend to run it efficiently. Your persistent questions are getting in the way of that efficiency.'

Kalien scowled. She sent a noospheric shrug at Feist, who bounced it carelessly with a simple but abusive rebuke.

'I think I will tell Tolemy about that insult,' she said.

'Do what you like. Nothing was intended. I'm busy.'

'We are supposed to be working in harmony.'

'Kalien–' he began. Feist switched to binaric. A two second blurt contained everything he needed to say. *Obey me, you stupid cow. Respect me, for cog's sake. There's a war on. We're trying to win. Tolemy is an old fart. Orestes Principal is dying and we have to find a way to stop that. The old data is slow to process, you can't expect miracles. Ask your magos where we're dredging this up from. I can't transliterate half of it. I'm working blind, the data is so old. People are dying out there, engines too. It's a damned warzone. We're at the brink. Don't talk to me. You silly bitch. Don't talk to me. Who cares if your twin sister made famulous on a walking engine. Whoop-de-doo! She can kiss my modified arse! Get back to work, you pompous twank and get some results to me! Now! Now! Now!*

'All right then,' Kalien said. 'If that's how you feel, I'll get back to my console.'

She turned and left the room.

There's too much work, Feist thought, looking down at the ancient dossiers. Far too few able processors. Magos Egan had known what he was doing when he handed this job over, the crafty old devil. *Responsibility*. Egan had palmed the labour off on Feist.

They'd been at it for days solid, and nothing had been turned up. Most of the sequestered material was so archaic, so out of context, it was difficult to comprehend it, let alone isolate proper data for comparison tests.

The hatch reopened and a young man walked in. A delicate, female noospheric-modified lingual servitor escorted him. 'Hello? Adept Feist?' the young man asked.

'What is it now?' Feist began, and then stood up. He

recognised the young man. It was Executor Crusius's famulous. 'I apologise. You're Sonne.'

The famulous nodded and made the Icon Mechanicus. 'I'm sorry to bother you, I can see you're busy. The executor fetial sent me to...'

'See how things were going?'

'I wasn't going to put it like that,' said Sonne, 'it makes the executor sound impatient.'

'This is war, Famulous Sonne. I imagine the executor is perfectly permitted to be impatient, Lord Gearhart too. But I understood the executor fetial had gone out into the sub-sids. Please don't tell me he sent you back here just to check up on me?'

Sonne smiled and shook his head. 'No. There were a number of matters the executor wished me to deal with in the hive on his behalf. I will be returning to his side tomorrow.'

'Then please extend my apologies to him,' said Feist. 'Though we are proceeding diligently, we have not yet isolated a single item of any worth.'

Sonne paused to glance over the dossiers spread out on Feist's work table. 'I had assumed your bold idea to open the sequestered coils might have yielded something,' he commented.

'It has,' Feist replied, 'an unimaginable morass of virtually garbled material. I had no idea of the corruption or the antiquity of the old records. It is like being handed a small net and asked to dredge an entire ocean for a single pearl that may or may not be there.'

'Rumination: any task may be ultimately accomplished if enough minds and hours are directed at it.'

Feist smiled. 'Far be it for me to contradict the venerable wisdom of the Mechanicus, famulous, but I fear that by the time we have found something, the war will be over, one way, or another.'

Sonne bade a respectful farewell to the struggling adept and walked back through the teeming industry of the Analyticae towards the outer exit. He told his escorting servitor to open a canting link to the executor.

'Obligana? Connect me to Crusius, please.'

'Yes, famulous. Link enabled.'

'Thank you. Message begins.'

<*[exloaded from] Sonne, famulous, Legio Invicta (11110001101, code compression te) [begins]*

Sir, I presented myself at the Analyticae as ordered, and I am unhappy to report that no data has yet been identified. It is my contention that Legio Invicta must proceed on the assumption that no tactical advantage will be made using the forge archives.>

Sonne reached the outer hatch, and was about to begin the second paragraph of his report when he heard a cry from the central workstations behind him. He turned. Staff were hurrying over to a particular console where a young adept was canting excitedly.

Sonne retraced his steps to watch.

The adept, a young junior named Sinan, was communicating excitedly about a code match. As a crowd of adepts gathered, Egan and several senior magi appeared on an upper walkway to observe the commotion. Feist appeared, hurrying, and pushed his way to Sinan's side.

'Show me, Sinan.'

'Comparative match,' the adept said, conjuring graphic panels side by side that he then overlaid. 'The remains of a serial number and mark identified on the carapace of an enemy engine recorded on gun camera yesterday in the Jeromihah Subsid. I have found a corresponding code derived from the sequestered archive.'

Feist looked at the data. 'Was the enemy engine named?'

'During combat, it announced itself as *Danse Makabre*, Warlord-class. It harried a column of skitarii and then fell back.'

'And the correspondence?'

Sinan enlarged a panel. 'What appears to be a manifest of engines shipped from Mars, from the Mechanicum, I should say, to Terra, eighteen years before the Great War. Ten engines, reported as a gift of tribute to the Lord Emperor.'

Feist stared at the panel display. 'Code identity?'

'The serial number and mark was borne by *Phobos Castigatus*, adept.'

'What else is there?'

'I've barely begun to look at the dossier blocks this manifest was contained in. Comparative match scans identified it automatically during a first sweep.'

'Root this directly to my main station,' said Feist. <Everybody get back to work!> he canted quickly. <I'm going to sub-divide this dossier block and distribute it between a dozen of you. Go through your section node by node and cross-refer it with the fetial database. Look for any comparisons. Addition: catalogue all background information, and identify all the transcript codes and file markers so we can look for other dossiers made by the same operator or station-source. I want this done by the end of the shift.>

The adepts and magi almost ran back to their stations and codifiers. There was a buzz of agitated noospherics and a warm, pheromonal flush of floodstreams engaging.

Feist nodded to Sinan. 'Well done. You may have found a key. A way in, at last.'

Feist began to stride towards his main station. He saw the famulous nearby.

'Any task may be ultimately accomplished if enough minds and hours are directed at it,' said Sonne.

'Let us hope so, famulous,' replied Adept Feist.

1000

Wounded and trailing smoke, he headed for home. His power reserves were low and his solid munitions were all but spent. He had been eight days in the field since his last resupply, moving from skirmish to skirmish and enduring two long engine duels that had hurt him gravely, even though he had ended both as the victor.

Adrift in the stagnating fluid of his casket, Valen Lustig twitched his wasted limbs in time with the ponderous strides of his great engine. The princeps shared its weariness, the hollow ache of extreme fatigue that seeped into its systems from the hard-plugged crew. No one had slept since the last reload halt at Gynex eight days before. Their bodies, like the amniotic fluid in his casket and bloodstream, were drowning in toxins and the waste by-products of the stimms, mood elevators and anti-fatigue boosters they had been forced to ingest from the engine's clinical bio-support, or gland from their modified bodies.

They were sick, all of them: his steersman, his sensori, his moderati, his servitors. They were chemically poisoned, awash with concentrations of synthetic hormones, their reflexes, attention rates and perceptive faculties dulled and distorted to dangerous levels by the demands of over-extended consciousness. Lustig knew his tech-priest was experiencing hypnagogic hallucinations, and Lustig kept suffering hypnic jerks as he teetered on the brink of involuntary slumber. His body was covered in psychostigmatic sores. He felt nauseous, zombified, his acuity stretched into a hideous state of awareness where nothing registered as real any more. He was so tired, he'd given up maintaining the execution log.

The burning tracts of the Shaltar Refineries, south of Argentum, lay around him like a dream. He was walking *Nicomach Ignix*, mighty Warlord of Legio Tempestus, along an eastern route into Gox, hoping to make the assembly yards at Mount Sigilite before nightfall. Every step was an effort. His swinging feet stirred the dark grume of biological waste that had accumulated in the bottom of the casket. His fingers twitched and trembled.

All communication with the hive and the legio had been curtailed days before. Malign and corruptive, the Archenemy's pernicious scrapcode had begun to invade all channels, and Lustig had been forced to deactivate his vox, his pict-stream and all other transmission/reception devices. He wondered if *Nicomach Ignix* was the last engine of Tempestus still walking. With no evidence to the contrary, it seemed entirely possible. Lustig had left *Dominus Ajax* blazing on its back in a refinery compound close to the Argentum manufactum. He had left *Aquilus Aggressor*, shot through the torso and brutally exoculated, sitting with its back against a high culvert wall, its legs stretched out in front of it, like a dying infantryman propped up in a foxhole. Rancid smoke had been fuming out of *Aggressor's* neck and punctured sternum. He had seen the noble Reaver *Amphiton* face-down in a dry river bed, burned out and blackened as if it had passed through a sun. He had seen the redoubtable Warhound *Canarius* blown onto its side behind the marble facade of a subsid temple house, its legs and one weapon limb missing, chewed off, as if it had been torn apart and half-devoured in some grisly feeding frenzy. He had seen the scorched torso of a Reaver, unnamed and unidentifiable, on top of a mound of rubble and then, half a kilometre further on, its severed head glaring blindly at the sky in a fractured subsid street. From the head, he had made a grieving identification: *Diligens Eroditus*, the princepture of his old friend and regicide opponent Dorcas Veimul.

He had seen too much. If he made it back alive, he was certain he would face fierce animadversion from the masters of the forge. How could he have left so many to die? How could so many have been lost? How dare he live when others were dead?

For the last few hours, he had been aware of a low, animal moaning that echoed out of the MIU. *Nicomach Ignix* was in pain, and it too was mourning. It had seen the hopeless losses and the catalogue of the fallen, and it groaned its despair. He could feel it thinking. It was tugging at his mind, fitful and anguished, wanting to turn back and savagely avenge the losses, yet knowing it had reached its operational limits.

Refit, reload, he promised it, trying to soothe its misery, Refit, reload, and then we will visit reparations on the callous foe.

In a chin-seat in front of the amniotic casket, Dolf Gentrian, *Nicomach Ignix's* moderati, fought against the glazing stupefaction that was close to overwhelming him, and tried to keep his mind on his duties. He maintained a watch over the engine's critical systems, especially those that were dropping past their recommended thresholds. Hydraulic pressure was falling, and he kept having to cancel out the warning notices. The reactor was fluttering badly, like an arrhythmic heart, and there seemed little that the addled tech-priest could do to nurse it back out of its tremulous beat. There was nothing left to stimulate in the engine's bio-support, no more hormonal boosts or glucose/adrenal shots, and none of the crew would have been able to cope with additional stimulation even if there had been anything left to take. Gentrian felt the hunger pangs of the empty magazines and shell hops.

Above all, he watched the Manifold for code-patterns and hard returns.

Gentrian stretched his arms and shook out his neck. The Manifold estimated that, at current stride, *Nicomach Ignix* would take 5.3 hours to reach the outer defence batteries of the Mount and what they all hoped would be safe ground.

He allowed the Manifold to pan his vision three sixty degrees. Several dozen square kilometres of refinery complex stretched out to port, ruined and mangled from the daily visitation of heavy shelling. In places, vast and rapid plumes of burning gas and promethium jetted into the sky from ruptured pipelines or broken tanks. A hydrocarbon smog washed in across the plodding engine.

The heavy sheds and manufactory complexes that marked the outskirts of the Gox Subsid lay to starboard, a broad belt of industrial subhive enclaves. They were passing through a boundary ward called Undergox Edge. The buildings, many of them damaged and scarred, were massive structures of grey ouslite and marble: machine shops, factory barns, fabrication mills, warehouses, work-line plants. Tall stone chimneys rose like blunt fingers. The engine was following a partially clear path along a broad arterial where the rockcrete was covered in a glittering layer of broken glass and silicate shards. A deep crater on one side of the arterial cupped the upside-down wreck of an Arvus lighter, its wings buckled, like a specimen beetle pinned in a circular frame. Three Conquerors sat further on, as if deliberately parked in a row, their turrets and tracks gone, their hulls caked with soot. One wing and part of the tail assembly of a Thunderbolt protruded, high up, from the front elevation of a fabrication mill.

The Manifold sensed far-away carnage. Ten kilometres north-west of them, the sky went wild with a huge, sustained barrage of tracer fire as ground batteries began shooting at some unseen target. The twisting, vermicular streamers of dazzling shots writhed and whipped in the numinous smoke like liquid drizzle, and stopped as rapidly as they had begun. Twenty seconds later, they started up their frenzy again.

Gentrian looked elsewhere. Far behind them, the light flash of heavy detonations underlit the clouds. He tracked eight dozen aircraft, away to port, heading into the west, low and fast.

A deck alarm suddenly sounded, followed by two proximity sirens, which were echoed in turn by a series of dull thumps from below and the rattle of blast scatter bouncing off the hull.

Lustig canted for full stop and back pace.

<What is it?> he blurted.

Gentrian checked the close scopes. 'Mines, princeps. We've just crossed into a mined area. Spring munitions have detonated underfoot.'

<Damage?>

'Minimal, some plate scoring. They were anti-personnel devices.' Gentrian increased resolution on the auspex. Beyond the zone of scattered, half-buried munitions, a long row of heavier, anti-armour mines had been set on posts, raised three metres off the ground. The mines and their thick posts had been straggled with barbed wire.

Lustig had read the scans. <We don't risk that. Not the condition we're in. Reverse motivation. Back pace by turn, rotate south. Sensori, plot me a route around.>

'Engines full reverse, aye. Back pace, rotating south.'

Gentrian had been expecting a rebuke. He knew he should have scoped the jumping mines long before they walked into them. He'd been distracted, and he'd missed the indicators: a beginner's mistake that deserved censure. It occurred to him that the princeps was too tired to raise his cant in angry address.

The Manifold lit up as a large-yield energy bolt shrieked in and exploded the front off a building twenty metres to port. Two more bolts came in, from another source, and chewed deep gouges out of the roadway to starboard.

'Shields to full!' Gentrian yelled. They'd had them held at low to conserve power. The voids struggled and shorted as they tried to rebuild and cohere at main strength. 'Come on. Come on!' the moderati urged.

From his armoured cell behind the cockpit, the tech-priest angrily canted that he was trying. Gentrian could hear him attempting to mollify the machine spirits and coax their cooperation.

More shots rained in, refining their range. A blast licked at their heels and scattered rockcrete debris out across the arterial. Gentrian assessed the energy profile: high-gain, heavyweight quality, undoubtedly from platform mounts or engine weapons.

Nicomach Ignix swung south, chased by the harrowing bolts. It wedged itself into the mouth of a narrow service road between two stone-built manufactories that were almost as tall as the engine, and Gentrian felt his princeps slew the gyro-stabilisers slightly to one side so that *Ignix* leaned its weight hard into the left-hand structure. The manufactory wall cracked under the engine's weight, and came down in a torrent of stone. *Ignix* had widened the service road and cleared a path for itself.

The shields were still failing to light properly. Gentrian cued the Manifold's stochastic modelling to estimate and predict the pattern of enemy fire: two fire sources, both at a distance of at least two kilometres. *Ignix* was being bracketed by long-range bombardment from a brace of enemy engines.

With only hull armour to protect them, they rammed their way through into the space behind the tall manufactories, using the buildings as partial cover. Massive las salvos tore into the structures, blowing giant holes in the walls and caving in the roofs. The sensori fixed a plot on one of the bombardment sources.

<Engine, engine, 2.7 kilometres, bearing 1106 kappa nine.>

'Firing solution supplied!' Gentrian sang out. 'Return fire?'

<Negative, we don't have the power to range it,> Lustig blurted back through his casket augmitters.

As they pushed into a silo yard to the rear of the manufactories, engine fire continuing to punish the ancient buildings behind them, they came under secondary fire across their forwards starboard quarter. It was a mix of field artillery, rocket-propelled munitions and medium laser, and it rattled them hard.

Gentrian rapidly adjusted his scopes and identified a mass of contacts. Weaponised servitors, and the guntraks and cannon-carriages of enemy skitarii, were advancing on them through the sub-streets of Undergox Edge to their right, lobbing shells and spitting las as they came. The Manifold fizzled with their hissing scrapcode.

Lustig turned them east, attempting to move *Ignix* out of the silo yard. The Titan's sub-motors and actuators were wailing and protesting. Damage markers began to stack up on the Manifold display, glowing red. There were still no damn shields to speak of.

'Full stop!' Gentrian yelled out. Beyond the silo yard, another row of post-mounted mines blocked their passage.

<Come about! South-eastern rotation! Engage!> Lustig's command cant sounded strong and confident, but Gentrian knew they were in a bad place. They were being hunted, methodically and expertly, like a wild animal. The distant engines were driving them into a trap where the skitarii could box them in. They had about ten seconds' sustained fire left in the mega-bolter, juice for a couple of low-power shots from the destructor, and a whisper of half-cohered shields.

Nicomach Ignix splintered through a row of iron-beamed storage sheds and tried to break free of the closing noose. The skitarii were pouring out of the sub-streets, approaching like swarming insects. Ugly, spiked warriors raced towards them, hauling gun-carriages or firing their integral weapons. Self-propelled guns rumbled out into the silo yard, barrels elevating. Heavy weapon-servitors scuttled forwards, weapon pods slamming like pistons as they fired. The skitarii force was a feral horde, decorated in flaking, thorned armour, tribal beads and grisly trophies. Gentrian blanched at the sight of horned carapaces, ugly banners, tusked snouts and howling skull faces.

<Alert!> the sensori canted.

Additional servitors and skitarii had surged up through the buildings around them and were appearing on the flat roofs of store-sheds and manufactories. Lithe, powerful skitarii leapt from roof level to roof level, keeping pace with the Mechanicus engine as it attempted to push clear, their beads and chains and ragged cloaks flying out behind them. Hurled missiles, hard rounds and grenades thumped off the hull. Gentrian saw puffs of smoke as grappling cables were launched up towards them.

'They're trying to get lines on us!' he cried.

Weaponised servitors were snapping at *Ignix's* ankles. They too were firing lines, trying to hobble *Ignix* with heavy cables. With a snarl that allowed bubbles to escape his lips into the amniotic suspension, Lustig thrust *Ignix* forwards and began to drag the servitors trammelling them. Straining at the taut lines, the servitors' metal claws scraped across the ground as they tried to dig in and hold the huge engine back. Lustig abruptly engaged a full reverse and crushed the slithering machines underfoot. More scurried forwards to take their places, launching another flurry of hooked cables.

'There are too many!' the sensori yelled. More than a dozen cables draped them from the surrounding roofs, and thick hawsers dragged from their legs.

'Permission to fire!' demanded Gentrian.

<Granted. Bolter, two-second burst.>

Gentrian aimed and triggered the mega-bolter, raking the rooftops to their port side. The burst was brief, but the destruction formidable. Servitors, skitarii and roof sections vaporised in a withering row of blasts.

Unwilling to waste any more of their meagre munition load, Lustig engaged the Titan's close combat weapon – a powerfist with three long, curved claws, mounted on the engine's starboard weapon limb. He hauled *Ignix* around and swung the spiked limb into the upper section of the manufactory to their right. The claws ripped a deep, ten metre-long tear through the building's masonry. The juddering blow demolished the upper storeys and roof. Stone dust billowed up as they fell in, and Gentrian saw cables snapping, sheared off, or spooling away with shrieking skitarii still attached to them.

They were free for a moment. Trailing loose cables and dragging several servitors that were still anchored by lines to their shin plating, they strode on. Detonations and impacts continued to rain against the hull. *Ignix* fought its way into another silo yard, but the path ahead was blocked. To one side of them was a massive finishing platform, a flat-topped oblong structure the size of a large manufactory that rose two storeys high; to the other lay a cyclopean smeltery and adjoining smoke stack. Lustig built a little stride across the yard and tried to ram the smeltery and smash a path through, but he managed only superficial damage despite the powerfist and the thunderous bulk of *Ignix*. He backed off three paces, trampling into the mobbing ranks of skitarii ground forces rushing up behind them.

<Commit remaining weapon reserves to the desructor.>

'Aye!' Gentrian replied. 'Princeps, you have capacity for two shots at sixty per cent yield.'

<Nothing more?>

'Not without compromising the basic motivation and system requirements. The reactor cannot keep pace.'

<Brace for firing.>

The destructor roared twice, and its sizzling bolts slammed into the smeltery, tearing down heavy stonework. *Ignix* engaged its drive and strode towards the breach. Half a dozen more cables had been hooked to its back and legs, and it yanked the servitors attached to them after it like a train.

A warning sigil flashed on the Manifold. Gentrian identified a seismic profile, a series of heavy, ground-shaking impacts.

'Spoor. Engine pace. There's an engine closing, full stride!'

<Triangulate!>

The enemy Warhound, blood-red with a grimacing gold snout, came for them along the top of the finishing platform. It bounded across the platform surface, crumpling machine derricks and metal railings, and then ran along the edge of the platform to peer down at them.

<Come about!> Lustig commanded.

Ignix swung around. The Warhound, issuing a squealing scrapcode challenge, leapt off the platform lip and landed in the yard. The ground fractured under its impact. It righted itself, squealed again, and began to stride towards the cornered Warlord, fast and aggressive, each footfall thumping the rockcrete. The ranks of the skitarii scattered in front of it, greeting its arrival with a massed roar. It crushed many underfoot, indifferent to their plight, and engaged its close combat weapon, a vicious bident of dirty steel that extended and locked out of its right limb.

<You have permission to fire the bolter,> Lustig blurted.

'Princeps, we have eight seconds of fire remaining. How much do I–'

<Whatever it takes.>

Gentrian opened fire. The mega-bolter screamed as it blitzed a super-rapid stream of shells at the oncoming engine.

Thousands of small, individual explosions peppered the Warhound's snout and hull. It recoiled, staggering under the sustained fire. Its shields seemed to shred, and slivers of metal stripped off its painted red plate, revealing bright silver gashes of exposed metal.

Five seconds remaining, 4, 3, 2, 1...

The autoloaders completed their count. The bolter fell silent.

'Count zero. Munitions out,' Gentrian announced.

The yard was veiled in blue fycelene smoke from the bolter's discharge. Recovering its balance, its paint-work scraped and fuming, its hull leaking oil like blood from a hundred perforations, the Warhound broadcast a guttural hiss and resumed its charge.

'Brace!' Gentrian yelled.

The twin points of the ugly bident cracked in through the Warlord's abdominal wall. *Nicomach Ignix* shuddered, and warning sirens screeched. In his casket, Lustig cried out and clutched his belly.

The Warhound wrenched the bident out and immediately thrust it again, aiming it high at the belly and chest of the larger engine. The second blow screeched off the plating, leaving long, scored claw marks in the ceramite surface.

Ignix stepped back, and blocked the third strike with its powerfist, knocking the bident aside with a resounding metal clang. All around them, in the yard and up on rooftops, the skitarii bellowed and bayed, urging on the engine duel.

Single combat, Gentrian thought, one on one, like pit fighters, like gladiators in the circus arena.

The Warhound skipped from side to side in front of the wounded Warlord, jabbing with its weapon, goading and squealing. Blood from deep psychostigmata was staining the tank water around Lustig's belly, and a dilute pink thread trailed from his half-open mouth. He threw a sudden punch with his right arm, almost striking the wall of his casket, and *Ignix* swung for the Warhound. It yelped and tried to dart backwards, but the blow was too fast. *Ignix's* claws hacked into the Warhound's carapace.

Lustig tore them free, advanced a step, and swung again, deflecting the stabbing bident with *Ignix's* left weapon arm. With heavy, weary steps, the Warlord drove the smaller, prancing engine backwards across the yard. Its claws tore away part of the Warhound's gold-and-brass jaw plating, slicing its gleeful smile in half. The Warhound butted forwards and put one tine of the bident through the Warlord's left thigh.

Subsystems erupted and motor-trains severed. Gentrian felt the pain of it, just as he'd felt the pain of the chest wound. He didn't suffer as acutely as his princeps, but the hurt chased up his thigh like fire.

The Warhound plucked the bident out and brandished it again. Half-dragging its damaged leg, *Ignix* slapped the close combat weapon aside with its claws, and then caught the Warhound across the snout with a massive back-handed slap that sounded like two Baneblades colliding head-on at full speed.

The Warhound reeled and almost fell. It struggled drunkenly to regain its footing, steam and smoke squirting out of joint seals and torn hydraulics. As it tried to back clear, Lustig brought the clawed powerfist down into its back.

All three blades fractured down through the carapace. The Warhound quivered and uttered a scrapcode scream. It twisted and bucked, trying to tear free, but the talons had wedged in place. Even Lustig couldn't rip them out of the buckled plate. The two engines were locked, fighting at each other to disengage.

The Warhound lunged forwards instead, into *Ignix's* embrace. With its claws caught in the Warhound's thickly plated back, *Ignix* could neither wield them nor swat the smaller engine with its right limb. Braying, the Warhound came in under the forcibly extended weapon limb and plunged the bident up into the Warlord's chest.

The cockpit shook. Several consoles blew out in gouts of flame and showers of dial glass. A major systems failure was in progress, but the entire crew was too stricken with empathic pain to react. Still hooked to the talons, the Warhound jerked the bident out and then stabbed again. It repeated the upwards stab half a dozen times, the bident punching in and out like a pile driver until the chest plating was shredded and the rib stanchions buckled.

Ruptured lubricants gushed out of the Warlord as if it had been eviscerated. Vital subsystems caught fire. In his casket, Lustig went into a violent, thrashing seizure, his limbs and skull cracking repeatedly against the glass.

The Warhound, whooping through its sirens, stabbed for the final time. One tine of the bident broke off and remained lodged through *Ignix's* pelvic assembly. The Warhound finally tore free and lurched back from the leaning, guttering Warlord. It left part of its carapace dangling from the talons.

Ignix swayed, immobilised.

The Warhound strutted clear of its opponent in reverse, and settled back on its haunches in the centre of the yard, glaring back at *Ignix*.

Copious quantities of oil trickled from the Warhound's multiple combat injuries like gore, and blackened its red coat and its golden half-grin. The skitarii let out a huge scream of approval, shaking their weapons and slamming their blades and pole-staves against their shields and plate. The Warhound raised its weapon limbs and tipped its snout in a mocking bow to its ancient enemy. A fluttering, consumptive gurgle of bastardised code rumbled in its throat.

Whooping and jeering, the skitarii host surged forwards around the doomed Warlord, festooning it with lash-lines and hooked cables. Teams of servitors held thick anchor tethers taut, securing the burning engine as the skitarii warriors began to clamber up ropes and boarding lines.

Gentrian unlocked his harness and shunted the chin-seat back on its guide rails. The cockpit was filling with smoke. He shook the sensori by the shoulder. 'Wake up! Get fire suppression activated!'

Gentrian winced as he pulled out his hard-plugs. There was a nasty crunch of withdrawal, and the Manifold vanished. He hurt all over. He clambered up the tilted deck of the cockpit towards the weapons locker, yelling at the others to make ready.

Lustig drifted in the amniotic casket, slack and limp. The fluid in the casket had turned crimson.

Gentrian triggered the biometric key of the weapons locker and began to pull out the side arms: short-frame lascarbines and pump shotguns designed for companionway clearance. They would be coming in through the hatches and up the leg frames and access shafts. He could hear them thumping and slamming against the outer hull.

'Come on,' he yelled to the others. 'Get unplugged and on your feet. They're coming in. Load up and get ready to protect the princeps for as long as we can!'

'There's no chance,' whispered the steersman as he gazed at the scopes. 'We don't stand a chance.'

Gentrian thrust a shotgun against the steersman's chest and forced him to hold it.

'We keep them at bay for as long as we can, is that clear?'

'Yes, moderati.'

More thumps, more impacts from outside. *Nicomach Ignix* rocked slightly as cables tugged at it and figures swarmed up over it.

Gentrian felt the cockpit's tilted deck shudder as a hatch was blown down below. The sounds of jeering scrapcode and clambering feet drifted up to them.

'They're in,' he said. He racked his shotgun and went over to the hatch at the top of the spinal shaft. Jiggling beams of stablight speared up from far below, casting odd shadows off the rungs of the shaft wall-ladder.

'Deus Mechanicus protect us all,' he whispered.

'What the hell was that?' the sensori called out.

Gentrian looked around. 'What?' The sensori was staring at the auspex grid. It had suddenly lit up with broad columns of red binary code that scrolled rapidly across the display.

'Code!' the sensori exclaimed. 'A mass of exloaded code.' The sensori hadn't unpinned his hard plugs yet. Behind the tinted lenses of his blast goggles, his modified eyes were staring into the Manifold, a realm invisible to Gentrian. 'I'm getting shield noise too. Oh holy forge!'

Lustig stirred in his blood-stained casket. He uttered a single word through his augmitters, 'Invicta.'

An awful noise rose outside the Warlord, like a sudden, breaking storm. The ground shook, and a mighty boom of warhorns drowned out the baying exultation of the enemy skitarii. Gentrian heard weapons fire: multiple, rapid, massed weapons fire. He scrambled towards the cockpit ports and stared out.

The skitarii of Legio Invicta swept into the yard like a flash flood. Gaudy giants in plumed and jewelled armour led the way, sprinting headlong, axe-bills raised and integrated weapons firing. Thick ranks of charging hypaspists followed the screaming elite, blades locked and stave weapons lowered in unified fans and pike lines. Bright banners trailed above them, both cloth flags and hololithic emblems projected from emitter poles. Amongst the surging ranks, Gentrian saw the four- and six-legged construct bodies of weapons servitors moving at full stride. The scarred Warhound that had crippled *Nicomach Ignix* retreated across the yard as servitor weapons bruised and harried it.

The crashing tide of Mechanicus tech guard met the folds of the enemy skitarii at *Nicomach Ignix's* feet. The concussive impact flattened the first few rows of enemy warriors and rolled into the densely packed formations behind them. Mechanicus tribunes and praetorians hacked and blasted their way into the screaming, recoiling host of the Archenemy, piling the ground with dead and dismembered victims. Servitors exploded or were smashed into parts. Sub-munitions sprayed through the air like scatter shot and landed amongst the enemy with a ripple of separate detonations. The entire silo yard became a sea of milling, clashing bodies.

Divorced from it, as if perched on top of a vertical island, Gentrian gazed down into the vast melee. Without Manifold support, he could only estimate the numbers he was seeing: two thousand on each side, three? The enemy skitarii were turning to engage the Mechanicus brigades, leaving the lines they'd hooked to *Ignix* slack. Gentrian's crippled Warlord shook with the turmoil of the brutal fight. He had once been told that no infantry combat, not even the Guard or the vaunted Astartes, could match a skitarii versus skitarii war for frenzy and fury. Bionically enhanced, augmetically accelerated, the onslaught was berserk and savage on both sides. It was like the ancient dark epoch wars of Old Terra, the stuff he'd read about in the almagests and tracts of his youth. It was, he imagined, like a snapshot of the epic contests on the fields of Mars, not the ceremonial Field of Mars up in the high hive, but the fields of Mars themselves, ten thousand years in the past, when the schism of the Great and Terrible Heresy had riven the Mechanicum on the Holy Red Planet.

Blades flashed and ripped. Las-weapons barked and spat. Polycarbon and ceramite burst and shredded. Bio-electrical systems exploded and burned out. Shrapnel flew, skinning and perforating those caught in its path. Quad lasers on servitor mounts pulsed and pumped, burning swathes through the tightly packed, fighting mass. Bodies fell, dead, dying, no longer intact, and heaped up on the blood-stained rockcrete.

Gentrian had been trained for engine war. He had been born to the calling. He was modified and inloaded to participate in the calculated, distance war of engines. The bloody, physical spectacle below him was another breed of combat altogether.

Lau had been built for it. For him, close war was true war.

Lau, the master of the Invicta skitarii, was in the thick of it, flanked by a fighting team of eight praetorian huscarls. He did not shrink from personal combat and, despite the admonitions of his princeps maximus, he often put himself directly in the frontline. He told Gearhart that it served to keep him grounded, and prevented him from ever becoming complacent about the lot of the skitarii who obeyed his commands.

Gearhart privately believed that Lau was simply addicted

to the adrenal high of close combat. After all, Lau, like every skitarii, had been drawn from genic programmes that deliberately developed traits of aggression and strength.

His integrated weapon limb flared, cremating the death-masked enemies hurling themselves at him. His left hand swung its axe-bill, lopping off heads and severing limbs. Blood and floodstream fluid spattered him. Where his swinging axe and stinging lasgun failed, Lau used his surgically inset canines and modified jaw to bite out throats. His huscarls took their toll too. They had learned their business from Lau.

<Into them, for the Omnissiah!> he blurted. Glanded hormones had propelled him into a stimm-fuelled rage, but the strategic centre of his brain, delicately modified to remain intensely calm and focused, even in the pitch of battle, maintained a progressive assessment of the field.

The combat was evenly matched. Despite the shock attack the Mechanicus had unleashed, the enemy skitarii were holding, and holding ruthlessly. Accessing his noospheric links, Lau estimated four thousand enemy components against his force of three and a half thousand. He factored in his numerically superior servitor cadre, the backbone of his strength, and confidently anticipated victory, but it would be bloody.

A huscarl to his left toppled backwards, his head fused and burning. Lau smashed his broad, ornate blade through an elbow and an axe-haft, and gutted two enemy skitarii with snap-blasts from his augmetic weapon. Others scrambled back to avoid his wrath.

Lau's appearance was designed to terrify, just as his physicality was designed to kill. He was resplendent in hawked threat-armour, his feather-edged cloak whipping out behind him. Ivory chevrons were inlaid on either side of the Icon

Mechanicus on his blood-gold breastplate. A dappled panther pelt dressed his massive shoulders over the feathered cape, and tusk-spikes rose from the wings of the crimson steel half-mask that framed the hololithic yellow slits of his eyes. He had raised the iridescent fan of quilled skin around the back of his skull to accentuate his menace. His personal body-void crackled and seethed as shots and impacts struck it.

<Drive the scrapshunts out!> he blurted.

The enemy was far from breaking, but it was being forced backwards by the pressure of the Mechanicus attack. In an attempt to regroup and consolidate, enemy warriors spilled back along the rubble-strewn service streets, away from the silo yard and onto the Undergox Edge arterial.

Lau's cataphractii were waiting for them with three-dozen sentient gun platforms, twenty mobile batteries and eighteen modified Malcador-pattern tanks, all dressed in the livery of the Legio Invicta and all aligned to target solutions on the arterial. As the enemy skitarii came into view, Dorentine, the gun magos, squirted Lau for permission to fire.

Lau considered the noospheric data carefully as he continued to murder his way across the silo yard.

<Wait,> he advised Dorentine. <Wait… wait… my master of guns, you may fire when ready.>

Dorentine's cataphractii opened up and turned the stretch of arterial roadway into a primordial maelstrom of ash, flame, dirt and overpressure. The barrage caught and shredded the enemy host coming out of the service streets. Pounding shells and heavy lasfire took vast bites out of the road surface and tossed lumps of rockcrete and bodies into the air.

In less than a hundred seconds, hundreds were dead.

Like a fast-turning estuary tide, the enemy ground formations surged back into the service streets and yards, fleeing the horrific death offered by the bombarding cataphractii, but Lau's skitarii had locked the manufactory yards solid. A second round of surging infantry clashes broke out in the narrow throats of the service streets and byways. With nowhere to flee to, and no choice but to fight, the enemy forces went up against Lau's ground troop ranks with renewed, desperate vigour. Ferocious hand-to-hand brawls boiled through the narrow streets, the vast, drab manufactories rising like the walls of black canyons above them.

Then the engines appeared. *Divinitus Monstrum*, Bohrman's machine, came striding in through the ruins of the smeltery that *Ignix* had cut down. The Reaver *Philopos Manix*, commanded by Stent Racine, advanced from the south. *Invictus Antagonistes*, the engine of the Red Fury, walked in along *Manix's* flank.

Gearhart signalled Lau to pull his warriors back. At Lau's command, the skitarii Invicta broke off, firing heavy suppression cover as they dropped back across the yards.

There was a hush, broken only by the grumble of three titanic reactors. Cowering in the derelict manufactories and service streets, the enemy host realised that it was finished. Some individuals tried to run. Others sank to their knees and held up clamouring hands to the towering engines as if repenting or begging absolution from what were, quite clearly, god-machines.

The three giants were not in a forgiving mood. *Invictus Antagonistes* let out a deep blast from its warhorn, and held it as the horns of *Divinitus Monstrum* and *Philopos Manix* joined in. The deafening chorus provoked blind terror in the bunched and huddled enemy forces. They broke in rushing, milling thickets, fighting each other for an avenue of escape.

The slaughter was sudden and immense. Lau's forces

flinched and shielded their eyes as the three Titans unleashed cones of jetting fire, spears of searing las, and hurricanes of hard rounds. Trapped, the invaders perished, and the manufactories sheltering them toppled onto their burning corpses.

The blackened Warhound with the broken bident sprang from cover on the far side of the finishing platform and tried to bolt. A salvo from *Invictus Antagonistes* lamed it and threw it against a wall. It staggered upright, gouting flames from its underside, and hobbled on another few steps. *Divinitus Monstrum* and *Philopos Manix* locked it up between them and shredded it with sustained cannon bursts.

The Warhound's half-grinning skull blew loose as the hammering crossfire disintegrated its chassis and crashed across the yard.

Divinitus Monstrum and *Philopos Manix* turned from the blazing devastation they had helped to make, and began to chase down the few gangs of survivors fleeing into the backstreets of Undergox Edge.

'Signal from Lord Gearhart, moderati,' Gentrian's sensori said, one hand raised to his plugs. 'He's hailing *Nicomach Ignix*.'

Gentrian glanced at the amniotic casket. Princeps Lustig was floating face-down in blood-browned water. Gentrian slithered down the sloping deck to the chin consoles and took up the dangling knot of his hard plugs. 'Give me a moment, and then route the hail to me, sensori.'

Gentrian replugged himself. It was as if he was sawing a blunt bayonet through his spinal column at the base of his skull. The seamless omniscience of the Manifold was restored, but the cost was sharing the excruciating agonies of a dying Titan and its mortally wounded princeps.

Gentrian shuddered, a wash of reflux spilling up his throat

into his mouth. He rocked, unsteady, swaying the way the dead, creaking Titan was swaying, and felt phantom traces of blood/oil weeping out of his ruined chest and belly. His heart stopped, for a moment. The pain was dismal and total.

<I repeat, do you hear me, *Nicomach Ignix*? This is *Invictus Antagonistes.* We are here, *Ignix*, and we will protect you. Please respond.>

'I h-hear you,' Gentrian coughed, blood coming up.

<Blurt it, sir!> The sensori urged.

Gentrian nodded. <My lord Gearhart, this is *Nicomach Ignix* responding.>

<Am I canting to Princeps Lustig?>

<No, my lord. Princeps Lustig is indisposed at this time. This is Moderati Gentrian. My lord, we are dead on our feet. We appreciate Invicta's glorious efforts, but our walk is done.>

<Trust in the reassembly yards and the refitter compounds, moderati!> Gearhart canted back. <You're not dead until I say you are. Mighty *Nicomach Ignix* will walk again, and so will Princeps Lustig.>

Gentrian smiled. <Worthy lord, we thank you for your support, but we are crippled and burning. I... I believe my princeps is dead. Bless us by mortifying the enemy.>

There was a brief scramble of code patterns. <*Nicomach Ignix*, this is *Invictus Antagonistes*. We will mortify the enemy, but you must not, must not give up. Nurse your engine systems and keep them alive as long as you can. Relief parties are moving in towards you right now.>

<We will stand by to receive them, my lord,> Gentrian replied. He turned to the other members of the bridge crew. 'Get ready to–'

The sensori's head exploded, showering the cockpit lights

with blood and brain matter. The sensori toppled forwards across the main consoles. Gentrian turned to see spiked, bestial skitarii emerging from the hatch at the top of the spinal shaft.

With a cry of horror, the steersman raised his carbine, but he never got to use it. The first skitarii through the hatch shot him as casually as it had shot the sensori. A metal splinter-shell tore out the steersman's hip and another exploded his throat. He thumped sideways against a bulkhead and sagged, eyes wide, trying to speak as he bled out through his ragged neck.

Gentrian blasted the skitarii. The shotgun load was a wad of fine filament wire and ceramite shot, and it splattered the skitarii across the rear bulkhead of the cockpit. Gentrian pumped the slide of his shotgun and blasted again. A second skitarii exploded from the waist up in a shower of meat, bone and metal.

The third skitarii, rising from the collar of the spinal shaft hatchway, fired its integral lasweapon. The first bolt punctured Gentrian's torso and came out through his back, cauterising its passage. The second bolt blew the plugs out of his neck.

Gentrian blacked out. The sudden trauma of violent disconnection cancelled out even the pain of the gunshots. He sank away into the darkness, drowning in the midnight of some unplumbed lake. Light flickered down at him from high above. It seemed to be bars of binaric code, but it was fading too fast to inload.

His body fell backwards across the cockpit displays. The shotgun clattered from his hands. He closed his modified eyes and felt nothing except nothingness.

1001

Enhort, executor fetial of Legio Tempestus, entered the muted blue gloom of the private residence. Adept Seniorus Solohman Imanual dwelt in the very heart of the forge, in secure but modest surroundings. The chamber was lit as if by stars at twilight, and the air was cool.

The noosphere automatically announced Enhort as he walked in. He was an imposing man with a thoughtful manner. He wore black-trimmed red robes, and his eyes had been extensively modified for data-capture.

The adepts attending Imanual swept out of the chamber as he approached, quickly and fluidly, whirring softly like clockwork ghosts.

The Adept Seniorus was sitting at a wire lectern, reading from a large, leather-bound object filled with paper leaves.

<Enhort.> The Adept Seniorus acknowledged him without looking up.

'Honoured lord of the forge, I–' Enhort paused. 'Is that a book?'

Solomahn Imanual sighed and turned to consider Enhort. He had been using gentle manipulator fields from his coiled mechadendrites to turn the fragile leaves without physically touching them. 'Yes, it's a book,' he replied.

'I thought all our data was stored digitally. Books are such an anachronism.'

Imanual closed the ancient tome with his fields and patted the cover with his hand. 'We forget to remember,' he said.

'My lord?'

The Adept Seniorus nodded his wizened head towards the book on the lectern. 'It was in the archives, one of many artefacts stored in the sequestration vaults. Egan brought it to me. Much of the component data stored in the old stacks is contained in antique forms, as the Analyticae is discovering to its frustration. Books, printed sheets, handwritten–'

'Handwritten?'

'Handwritten records. They were different ages, Enhort. The Mechanicus was once more concerned with knowledge than with the method of its transmission. When we came to Orestes, we brought treasures with us – palimpsests and old hand-copied volumes, manuscripts, voice recordings, objects our forebears thought would be of value. We locked them away in sterile vaults. When this war is done with, executor, I will have all the non-digital archives annotated and transferred for open use in a current format. Knowledge is power, Enhort. How often do we say that? How often do we also forget what we already know?'

'My lord, may I ask what this old... book... has taught you?'

The Adept Seniorus sighed. 'That in ten thousand years,

we have forgotten more than we can remember. That knowledge may be power, but a dogmatic faith in accepted data is a form of ignorance. There is always something more to know. Ignorance has no limits, memories are filtered by time, forgetting is a sin. Knowledge is the only thing that ever has a definable boundary. Have I shocked you?'

Enhort shrugged. 'If you have, I wouldn't know it,' he said, smiling.

'You deflect my question gently, Enhort, and you keep the mood light. That is welcome. If I were to dwell on this, I would grow quite morose. We are so sure of ourselves, aren't we? The knowledge of the Mechanicus towers over all other species and creeds, even the inscrutable eldar, I believe. We can refine the cosmos into its tiniest parts, atom and cell, electron and molecule, and manipulate them. The Deus Mechanicus has gifted us the power to understand these vital mechanisms. Proud of our art, we have become complacent. We forget to remember. I believe, that there is always more to know than is known.'

He rose, and Enhort stepped forwards to take him by the arm and steady him.

'The couch, please, Enhort,' Imanual requested. The Executor Fetial Tempestus led the old man towards a nearby couch. Imanual's mechadendrites rippled wearily in the twilit air as he walked. The cavitic chambers of his plastek heart beat slowly, and his breathing was shallow.

'I suppose you've come to tell me about the war?' the Adept Seniorus remarked as he sank onto the couch and settled himself. 'More bad news, I presume?'

The relationship between Imanual and Enhort was old and warm. In decades past, Enhort had been Imanual's famulous, destined for high status in the forge until Imanual had recognised Enhort's talents and recommended him for service with the legion of engines. Like Crusius, Enhort was subtly modified, and he was one of the few magi that Imanual honoured by using his fleshvoice.

'No, not bad news this time, Imanual,' Enhort said softly, taking out a data-slate. He opened it and the Adept Seniorus inloaded its contents as they spilled into the air as holo-lithic phantoms.

'This was at Undergox Edge?'

'Just this afternoon. The data compression is of a miserable quality, but they were transmitting from a battlezone lousy with random scrapcode.'

'But its provenance is secure?'

'I spoke with Lord Gearhart. Over four thousand enemy foot troops extinguished, along with an engine, and *Nicomach Ignix* barely saved from destruction.'

'Poor *Ignix*. One of my favourites. Query: Lustig?'

'No information, lord.'

Imanual nodded. 'This is heartening news, and timely. The hive should know.'

'I thought so, my lord. I have prepared an advisory bulletin.'

'Wait, wait,' the Adept Seniorus said, gesturing with a manipulator. He conjured a noospheric link and waited for it to connect.

The face of Lord Governor Aleuton materialised in the green wash of the noosphere. Aleuton's image was being processed by a picting device on his stateroom desk.

'My lord adept?'

'My Lord Governor. I bear glad tidings. Data is being fed to you, via encrypted channels.'

'I see it now,' Aleuton replied.

'I thought you should be the first to know of this,' said the

Adept Seniorus. 'This afternoon, the Legio Invicta secured a crushing victory over the invading enemy at Undergox Edge. Four thousand kills. We have taken a long step towards planetary victory.'

'This is worthy news indeed, my good friend,' said Aleuton. 'Praise be the Omnissiah.'

'And hallowed be the God-Emperor. I believe, for the good of morale, that the evidence of this victory should be rapidly circulated throughout the hive. I have bulletins ready.'

'Release them, adept. I will support them with commentaries. I believe we may have turned a corner.'

The Adept Seniorus smiled. 'I agree, Lord Governor. Be sure to remark upon the survival of *Nicomach Ignix*. It was holding the line alone when Invicta came to its aid. *Ignix* is a very popular engine with the masses. They will be uplifted at news of its valour and survival.'

'Be assured I will,' Aleuton replied, his image pixellating against the green wash of the field. 'Thank you for bringing this to me personally.'

Imanual nodded, and the image folded up and vanished.

'So generous,' Enhort said.

'I do what I can. We live in balance with the Emperor's bastard offspring here on Orestes. They are in this war as much as we are, and they rely upon us. Go and release your bulletins, Enhort.'

Enhort rose and bowed. As he turned to leave, Imanual tugged at his shoulder with a manipulation limb. Enhort looked back.

'This is a good day, isn't it, Enhort?' Imanual asked.

'A bright day, lord, a very bright day. Victory is ours.'

The Adept Seniorus nodded and released his manip. 'Go on, then. Off you go.'

Once Enhort had left the chamber, the Adept Seniorus summoned a servitor.

<That book on the stand there.>

<Yes, my lord.>

<Take it away.>

<What should I do with it, my lord?>

<Burn it.>

The servitor trotted over to the wire lectern and collected the book.

I hope to all the numeric gods that volume doesn't have a digital copy, thought the Adept Seniorus as the servitor carried the ancient tome away.

>

In his residence at the summit of Orestes Principal, Poul Elic Aleuton cancelled the link with the Adept Seniorus and sat back in his chair. He looked across at the other picting monitor on his desk.

'I'm sorry, Etta,' he said. 'I had to take that. You were saying?'

On screen, Etta Severin's face was blotched by feed decay. 'The Adept Seniorus confirms what I'm telling you, sir, a crushing victory at Undergox Edge. Crusius speaks of up to five thousand enemy warriors slaughtered.'

'And Executor Crusius is?'

'A niggardly bastard when it comes to facts,' Etta replied, her voice shaved by the bad signal. 'He's exaggerating for effect, but you should release the data all the same.'

'It's done, Etta,' Aleuton replied. 'What about this valiant engine, *Ignix*?'

'*Nicomach Ignix*? A wreck when we came to it. Burned out

and every crew member dead. Imanual's exaggerating for effect too, sir.'

'Adept Seniorus Imanual is feeding the propaganda mill, my dear, and who am I to argue?'

'I understand, sir, but you have to realise that this war isn't even halfway done yet. A slaughter of the enemy, that's good, but the victory at Undergox Edge was just a step along the way. There's a lot of enemy still out there. The last thing we need is to be overconfident.'

'Is this Crusius's opinion?'

'It's my comment to you, sir. The executor is rather more concerned with the reputation of his legio.'

'I understand, Etta. Keep me informed.'

The pict feed blinked out. Aleuton looked up at his waiting aide. 'Prepare the hive generators for shield defence,' he said.

>

A mood of manic jubilation bordering on disorder swept through Orestes Principal as night fell. Public display plates throughout the hive imaged the announcement for everyone to see. A massive victory at Undergox Edge. Thousands of the benighted enemy slain. Invicta unleashed. A securement of future hope. *Nicomach Ignix* saved at the brink. The steadfast valour of *Nicomach Ignix*.

Immense crowds gathered in Kiodrus Square and the Field of Mars, on Perpendicular and Congress, on Franz Homulk Place and Titan Walk. Shift workers congregated in large rowdy masses around the public plates in Leadmarket and Transom, and filled the taverns and dining halls in the Bulwarks and Hammerhab. By the light of the naphtha street lamps, the devout mingled with the thankful and formed long processions that snaked the understreets of Counterpoint and Tangent on their way to the great temples of the hive for services of thanks. Some carried emblems and votive icons of the God-Emperor Undying, others, effigies of the Omnissiah. Drums beat and horns blew. Fireworks were let off over the Field of Mars. The population of Orestes Principal had not turned out to make such a public show since the night Invicta arrived.

In several quarters, the low-hab depths of Layman's Corner most particularly, the public gatherings turned into disordered festivals and lawlessness. The Magistratum sent in enforcement patrols to quiet down the street drinking, brawling and looting. Generally, the Magistratum was stretched to provide crowd control in almost every level of the hive.

Aleuton was kept appraised of the public dynamic. It was relief, he understood that, an expression of relief after weeks of tension and fear. The citizens of Orestes Principal needed the outlet, which was why he had allowed the news from Undergox Edge to be broadcast. He needed his city to be content, to believe that things were changing for the better. His strategic analysts, the PDF and the officers of the Orestean regiments had all concurred with Etta Severin's assessment.

The war was far from won. It wasn't even balanced. Orestes was heading towards a long, dark night before dawn and deliverance could come. Though they had been driven off this time, the forces of the enemy had come in as far as Gox. That put them less than ten hours from the Great South Gate.

The version of events at Undergox Edge prepared for mass consumption had been supplemented with archive footage of *Nicomach Ignix* on routine manoeuvres in the Eastern Provinces, along with the oft-repeated images of the Invicta engines at their deployment staging. Every time the sequences of *Ignix* replayed, lusty, epic cheers lifted up out of the crowded civic centres of the hive.

In the dusty back room of *Anatometa* in the level eighty-eight commercia, Manfred Zember chuckled as he lifted the lid off a fresh pot of heraldic ochre with the blade of a screwdriver. His tea kettle began to whistle on the little back-room stove. He carried the pot of paint to his bench, and then went over to lift the kettle off the heat with a folded cloth. Khulan leaf tea, expensive and imported. Zember hadn't been able to afford such luxury in decades.

A small pict-player sat on his workbench, its projection paused. Zember had back-recorded the footage from the public feeds and stalled various frames to copy the colouration and detail of the famous engines. He took a sip of his tea, put the cup down, took up his slender brush and, with a careful hand, began to painstakingly add specific insignia details to his latest batch of wind-up toys.

They stood on the workbench in front of him. They'd been bare metal when they'd arrived from the machinist that morning in their straw-packed crates. He'd spent the day, between customers, spraying them with layers of lacquer and undercoat, and then applying the base colours: crimson and brass for bold Invicta, blue and silver for valiant Tempestus.

Now he had the makings of ten *Divinitus Monstrums*, Bohrman's machine, ten Reavers that would all be *Philopos Manix*, princepture of the dashing and handsome Stent Racine, a dozen copies of *Invictus Antagonistes*, the infamous engine of the Red Fury, and twenty proud miniatures of *Nicomach Ignix*, hero of Undergox Edge. He was reasonably certain that they would sell the best.

Zember applied expensive gold leaf with a feather brush

to the underpainted talons of a *Nicomach Ignix*, just to make it perfect. It was all about the details.

When he opened his shop in the morning, the crowds would flood in. As it was, through the evening, there had been knocks at his door. He'd taken down the key and opened his premises, 'Just for you, you understand, an exception.'

'Monstrous! Monstrous!' Zember cackled as he wound up a half-painted *Nicomach Ignix* and let it walk along the bench.

The pale dolls gazed down at him from the shelves, forgotten, blank-eyed and unimpressed.

>

In the Worthies Garden beneath the Chancery, once-moderati Zink looked up at the pale grey sky. Shoals of twittering zephyrids fled into the twilight. Deep down in his famished bones, Zink was unsettled. Another night of uproar in the great hive? Was it Candlemas again? How many times did Candlemas come around in a year? He couldn't remember. Perhaps it was Forge Day, or the Festival of Mineral Harvest. Whatever the reason, the streets of the precinct below were crowded with bleating fools. There was music, cheering and fireworks. Zink flinched every time one of the fireworks lofted and burst with a bang and a flower of colours. They reminded him... they reminded him of...

Something that had hurt him, a long time ago.

He couldn't remember what.

Just over the top of the garden's west wall, Zink could see the upper part of the glowing public plate on Lentement Row. It was flashing and scrolling, blazing with light. He wiped his mouth. He made a decision.

Zink hobbled over to his hut at the best full stride his old legs could manage. He took out the worn step ladder that he used for pruning the boughs of the ploin trees, and carried it back to the west wall. This execution took the best part of half an hour, and Zink had to stop and catch his breath twice. More than twice, he forgot what he was about and began to carry the ladder back to the hut. When he reached the wall, he came about, two points, low stride, west rotation, and dragged the ladder into the wet flowerbeds. He set the ladder against the wall and then rocked back on his heels, gazing at it.

A ladder; it had to have a purpose. He looked around at the empty gardens, the long shadows merging into darkness. There was no one around to tell him what to do: no casket, no princeps, no humming Manifold.

Zink remembered his purpose. He gripped the sides of the ladder with shaking hands, snuggled it down into the soft soil and began to climb.

Advance, moderati! Flank pace!

The command puzzled him. He paused, two rungs up. Who was a moderati? What was flank pace?

He climbed up until he was looking over the old wall. He blinked. He could see the public plate now. Bright columns of language were sliding up it, amber and luminous. Zink couldn't read them. Eighty years earlier, he'd lost the ability to read, cant or inload anything.

But there was a voice too, a booming commentary, and pictures. Pictures of…

Zink stared. His thin-lipped mouth moved silently.

Nicomach Ignix strides to war! Do not fear, folk of Principal, engines like *Ignix* will see us through! Full stride, there she goes! With armour like that walking us to glory, let's pity the wretches who side against us! Subduing the Archenemy, that's all in a day's work for the likes of *Nicomach Ignix*!

'Zink? Tendant Zink?'

Zink looked down. His supervisor, Plemil of the Chancery Echelon, was hurrying down the garden walk towards him. Plemil clutched his red robes around his body against the evening cold.

'I brought your supper, Zink. It's in the hut. It's getting cold. Soup, Zink? Soup? You remember soup?'

Zink gazed down at his supervisor for a moment, and then turned back to look at the plate.

'Deus sake, Zink, get down from there!' Plemil called out. 'You'll fall and hurt yourself! There's soup. Mmm, warm soup.'

Plemil mimed sipping from a spoon and rubbed his belly.

Zink ignored him and spoke a word. Two syllables.

'What? Zink? What did you say?'

Zink stared at the images on the public plate. Slowly, and very carefully, he repeated what he'd said.

Two syllables.

'En-gine.'

>

Stefan Samstag finished what was in his glass and smacked it down onto the counter.

'That's me. Goodnight, boys.'

'Stay!' his workmates chorused.

Stefan shook his head. 'I'm done,' he told them. He'd taken the first amasec because Reinhart had bought it for him, and Reinhart was the only reason he'd come along in the first place. 'Do you good to get out, Stef,' Reinhart had said. 'Come on, lose your troubles.'

The second and third amasecs had come easily. After that, he'd lost count.

'See you on shift,' he said, and got up off the barstool. Reinhart rose and came over to him. 'Stay with us, Stef,' he said, his hand on Stefan's shoulder. His breath smelled of neat sacra and lho-sticks. 'Come on. The boys are in the mood.'

'I have to sleep,' Stefan replied.

'We all need sleep,' his supervisor agreed. 'I've been told that Invicta fleet will be sending down its next delivery of munitions tomorrow. Resupply. We'll be hefting payloads for hours. I expect overtime and danger money.'

'So I should sleep.'

'Stef? Come on, today of all days. We killed them at Undergox Edge. Everyone's celebrating.'

'I don't feel much like celebrating. I feel drunk,' Stefan Samstag replied.

Reinhart rubbed his mouth with the back of his hand and lit a lho-stick. 'Friend to a friend, you heard from her?'

'No.'

'Poor girl. It's a bad business. She'll be all right, though. Tertiary, they get the crappy end of the stick, if you don't mind me saying. I had a cousin served in tertiary nineteen years, man and boy. They get to load and lift, label parcels, sort munitions if they're lucky, that sort of thing. Trust me, she's nowhere near the front line.'

'I suppose.'

'Damn straight. Another amasec for my friend here.'

Stefan smiled a vague smile. 'One more then, for the way home.'

'That's the spirit, Stef. The boys are all with you, you know that? Lipple's got a nephew on tertiary.'

'Really?'

'PDF all the way,' Reinhart grinned, perching the lho-stick between his teeth as he paid for the drinks.

'PDF – Fething amateurs,' said the man at the bar behind Stefan.

Stefan looked around.

'Leave it, Stef,' Reinhart muttered, taking his change.

The man was a Tanith émigré, a big brute covered in purple tats. His arms were heavy and corded with muscle. He wore the loop of a licensed longshoreman. Tanith had burned to ash years before, and this man was one of the last of a dead breed. He was sipping from a shot glass.

'What did you say?' Stefan asked him.

'Stef, leave it,' said Reinhart.

'I said,' the Tanith slurred, staring down into his glass, 'that the PDF on Orestes was a fething joke. If they'd done their job properly, we wouldn't be in this mess. Planetary Defence Force, that's what PDF stands for. Did they defend us, no, they fething didn't. Are we in the shit because of them? Yes, we fething are. Do I care if they live or die, no I fething don't.'

'My wife is PDF,' Stefan said.

'Stef, come on now,' Reinhart said.

'Well, then she's partly to blame, isn't she?' the Tanith longshoreman suggested, looking up at Stefan. 'Fething incompetents.'

The boys from the dock dragged him outside. His hands were slippery with blood. He raged at them to let him go.

'You killed him. I think you killed him!' Benkis cried.

'You silly bastard, Stef,' Reinhart muttered as they pulled him into the gutter.

'The glass. Right into his face!' Benkis whooped.

'Shut Benkis up, someone,' Reinhart said. 'Stef? Stef?'

Reinhart slapped Stefan Samstag's cheek.

'What?'

'Stef, you did a bad thing. I think I covered for you, but the magistrates are coming in. Don't come into work tomorrow.'

'All right. Mmh. Why?'

'Get home. Can you get home?'

'Yeah.'

'Go home, Stef, clean yourself up. Me and the boys, we haven't seen you. It was some other bastard.'

They drew Stef to his feet. He glowered at them.

'Did I kill him?' he asked.

Reinhart nodded. 'Pretty much. Go home.'

'All right. Thanks.'

Stefan turned and trudged away towards the nearest maglev station, Happen Hill, second hop on the hoop from Perpendicular. The front of his shirt and his trousers were lank with blood.

'Cally,' he muttered as he limped along, the maglev token Reinhart had handed him heavy in his palm.

Cally...

>

Dawn over Antium. Tarses buckled his belt, slid on his leather coat, and buttoned it up. He looked at himself in the dirty mirror.

A moderati. He still looked the part. He adjusted the Invicta pin on his lapel. Could he still do the job? That was the question.

Two raps at the door.

He nodded it open. Fairika was standing to attention behind it, dressed in tight, black leather field kit.

'Ready?' she asked.

'You're coming with us?' Tarses asked.

'Of course. I am his famulous.'

'I'll discuss it with Prinzhorn.'

'There is nothing to discuss, with Princeps Prinzhorn or anyone else,' she declared.

'Oh, shut up,' said Tarses.

He walked onto the bridgeway connecting the silo to the restored *Dominatus Victrix*, shaking hands and chatting with the new crew, Anil, the steersman, and Kalder, the sensori. Both were reservists from the Invicta fleet pool. Narler, despite an augmetic graft to his missing limb, had not been pronounced fit for the execution tour. Tarses would miss him, though Kalder seemed a bright fellow, and came on high recommendation. He was on the reserve list for Bohrman's engine.

'We stand ready to walk, moderati,' Kalder said.

'Good, good, I thank you for that. Is the princeps installed?'

'His casket was locked in an hour ago, sir,' Anil, said. 'All links and sub-relays fitted and connected.'

Tarses nodded. 'Go, take your places.'

They both made the cog and turned.

'One thing,' Tarses added.

'Yes, moderati?' they chorused.

'You both know what I did? The incident?'

Kalder and Anil glanced awkwardly at each other.

'We do, moderati,' said Anil.

'It was a terrible, terrible thing. I regret it more than I can say. I just need to know that it won't affect our work together. If there's any chance it will, speak up now and I'll have myself rescinded.'

A hot wind blew up from the silo basin below and stirred the long tails of their coats.

'It's not a problem to me, moderati,' said Anil.

'If I might speak frankly?' requested Kalder.

Tarses nodded.

'It was a forgivable crime,' said Kalder, 'an act of passion. It showed immense loyalty to Princeps Skaugen, and I take that as the mark of an honest and devoted plug-man. I don't have a problem either.'

'*Victrix* needs you, moderati,' said Anil. 'You know her better than any of us.'

'Thank you, both, for your candour and support. Take your places. I'll join you shortly.'

The steersman and the sensori walked away and boarded. Alone on the high bridgeway, Tarses gazed down at the mighty bulk of *Dominatus Victrix*, repaired and reforged, her hull repainted in red and gold. He relished the formidable bulk of her foreplating, the brooding weight of the carapace and the weapons set into it, the sleek lines of the immense destructor. Far below, in the base of the silo pit, servitors were detaching anchor lines and lock grapples, and disconnecting the lubricant feeds and telemetry reset cables. Small teams of them busily unhooked and wound in the lines that had been holding steady the huge victory pennants and tally banners depending from *Victrix's* limbs. The ancient, gaudy pennants began to belly and flap in the wind.

The huge gates of the silo had been opened, and the way down onto the vast, illuminated exit ramp was clear. Beyond the ramp, in the murky dawn light, lay the long walk through the finishing silos to the gates of Antium, and beyond that, the realm of war.

The massive blue and silver form of *Tantamount Stridex* stood in the neighbouring silo. She was the Tempestus Warlord that would be walking out with them that morning. Auto scaffolds and support frames were being withdrawn from her upper hull. *Tantamount* had come back alive from the subsids three days before, one of the few Tempestus engines to have made it back from the first phase of the war for refit and reload.

Beyond her, in another gigantic rockcrete pit, the air sparked and shimmered with welding beams and hull cutters. The forge crews had begun repair work on *Nicomach Ignix*, whose ruined corpse had been carried home by heavy lifters the night before.

'It will be a long time before *Ignix* walks again,' said a voice behind him.

Tarses turned and found himself face to face with a tall man wearing the leather uniform of a Tempestus moderati.

'Braydel,' the man said, offering his hand, 'moderati, *Tantamount Stridex*. I thought we should introduce ourselves.'

Tarses shook his hand. 'Zane Tarses. I look forwards to the walk, Braydel. I hope we can do some good.'

'Two Warlords? We'll shake the foundations of hell, given half a chance. I just hope you can keep up.'

Tarses smiled. 'We'll manage. Invicta has experience.'

Braydel grinned back. 'Invicta? With Prinzhorn in your casket socket, you're pretty much honorary Tempestus now.'

Tarses heaved his shoulders. 'Perhaps. So, you made it back intact? All crew?'

'My princeps, Theron, brought us home safe. We were lucky. We made a few decent kills, and then turned for reload.'

'What's it like out there?'

Braydel shrugged. 'Miserable, and much worse now, I would imagine. I've been inloading the battle feeds. It's firefight alley all the way from Gynex to Old Silo.'

'It's a mess, all right, but I'm itching to get out there. We need to bury this and make Orestes safe.'

'Agreed, no argument,' said Braydel. 'The Omnissiah will watch over us.'

'The Emperor protects,' responded Tarses automatically.

Braydel shrugged. 'Him too.'

As the pre-dawn wind tugged at them, they stared across at *Nicomach Ignix* in its silo berth, the white glow of welding pulsing huge shadows against the dank silo wall.

'All dead, you know?' said Braydel. 'All dead when they got to her, apart from the moderati. He's critical in medicae one. They say he may never recover his sanity.'

'Brain damage?'

'The bastards shot the plugs clean out of his head,' said Braydel.

Tarses was uncomfortably aware of the soreness surrounding his new, top-spine plugs. They were still healing in, despite rapid-take tissue grafting and synthetic membrane sleeves.

Tarses turned to Braydel. 'I think we should begin, don't you? Thank you for making the effort to introduce yourself. I appreciate the gesture.'

Braydel nodded. 'Moderati are the human go-betweens. If we don't make the effort, who does?'

They shook hands again, and made the Icon Mechanicus to one another.

'Good hunting, moderati,' said Braydel.

'And to you, moderati,' Tarses returned.

Braydel walked away across the bridge and Tarses turned to face *Dominatus Victrix*. He took one last lungful of fresh air and walked to the hatch.

'Bolt it shut and withdraw the bridgeway,' he told the waiting servitor teams.

'At once. Walk well, moderati,' the crew leader replied.

Ducking his head, Tarses clambered into the cockpit space. It had been cleaned and repaired. The consoles and wall panels were lit up with bright, healthy system activity. Anil and Kalder were strapped into their seats, running through pre-walk checklists. In the cell-like aft compartment adjoining the cockpit, Timon, their new tech-priest, was conducting the last few rituals of appeasement and duress. The air stank of blessed oils and incense. Tarses noted the freshly refitted auspex system, bright and clean compared to the more worn components of the bridge instruments.

Prinzhorn's amniotic casket was installed at the heart of the cockpit, and the young princeps was reviewing and rechecking inload, adrift in his tiny sea of nutrient fluid. Fairika, grim and solemn, stood beside the casket, hands clasped behind her back.

<You grace us with your presence at last, Tarses,> Prinzhorn 'casted through his casket augmitters.

'The moderati is always last to take his seat, princeps,' Tarses replied, refusing to be baited. 'The moderati makes the final once-over, the last eyes-on checks.'

<Are you satisfied?>

'Perfectly, sir.'

<Then take your seat, please.>

Tarses climbed into his chin-seat. He found he didn't have to adjust it. The settings had been preserved just as he had left them. He slid the seat forwards to lock position, and strapped on his restraints. The final bolts were being power-screwed in around the rear hatch. Tarses heard the job finish, and the cockpit bumped as the bridgeway withdrew.

He took up his sheaf of plugs, and inserted them.

Light and information flooded his brain. He felt whole

again. He hadn't realised how incomplete he'd been without the link. The MIU murmured in his hind-brain. It seemed to welcome him.

'I am installed and hard-plugged,' he instructed. The Manifold flared in front of him, lazily appraising and practice-targeting the mouth and walls of the silo.

'Manifold established. Do I have steersman?'

'Aye, moderati,' replied Anil.

'Sensori?'

'Aye, moderati,' replied Kalder.

'Reactor and systems?'

<Aye!> canted the tech-priest behind him and the enginseer in the belly below simultaneously.

'Weapon servitors?'

The servitors chattered their binaric reply.

'Princeps, *Dominatus Victrix* stands ready and eager to walk. What is your word?'

<Begin execution log.>

<active...>

<Guido Pernall Jaxiul Prinzhorn, princeps, Legio Tempestus.>

'Invicta,' Tarses corrected.

<I stand reproved. Invicta, of course. I am linked to the mind impulse unit of the Warlord *Dominatus Victrix*. Is my authority recognised?'

<recognised...>

Tarses manually entered the date, time and location using the punch-keys on behalf of his princeps. 'We are commencing Execution K494103. Begin log recording.'

<recording...>

Tarses waited. He could feel Prinzhorn's mind through the plugs, adjusting to the data flow, to the sudden and immense weight of being a Warlord Titan. Tarses could taste fear and wonder in equal measures. He could feel Prinzhorn's alarm and worry about the burden handed to him.

<Moderati?>

'Princeps?'

<Do I have the Manifold?>

'The Manifold is yours, princeps,' Tarses confirmed.

<Thank you. Open and clear in series the gearings and the power couplings to the limbs. Engage the motor-trains. Condition green?>

'I see green, princeps,' Tarses replied, his hands darting across the dials of his console. He still couldn't bring himself to address Prinzhorn as 'my princeps'.

<Initiate main reactor sequence. Drive start.>

'Drive start, aye, in three, two, one…'

There was a huge, volcanic rumble of unleashed power. The hull frame shivered.

'Drive start, drive start,' Tarses called out.

'Power to all gressorial systems,' Anil reported.

'Full gain on all detection elements,' Kalder remarked.

'We have main traction available at this time,' said Tarses, flipping switches. 'Princeps? What say you?'

Behind him, in the casket, Prinzhorn placed his hands flat against the glass and stared ahead.

<Walk!>

1010

She came round in pitch blackness, sat up sharply, and banged her head.

The atmosphere was airless and she could smell burning. Blind, she reached around and felt a sheet of metal pressing down on her. There was very little space underneath, which was why she'd banged her head against it trying to sit up.

Panicked by both the claustrophobia and the fear of being trapped and burned, she pressed her hands against the metal and shoved hard.

The metal sheet slithered away with a clatter and stale daylight shone in on her. There was smoke in the air.

She pulled herself out of the hole, digging her way out from under a mountain of tangled metal and machine parts. Unsteady, she rose to her feet and staggered away across the strewn debris. Gorge Orewelt's heart had been crushed flat by the falling giant. Even though it was lying flat on its face, the smoking wreck of the engine towered over her. Columns of dirty black smoke spewed lazily from the ruptured heat exchangers on the rear of its hull.

Coughing, Cally retraced her steps and began to search the area where she'd been half-buried. Golla Uldana, her face painted with blood, was curled up in the churned earth under a broken sheet of flakboard. She blinked up into the pale light as Cally lifted the sheet away.

'You saved me,' she whispered.

Cally shook her head. 'I didn't. I don't know how this thing missed us.'

She helped Golla up.

'You cut your head,' said Golla.

'So did you.'

Golla tried to touch Cally's scalp.

'Leave it. Leave it alone.'

'It's nasty.'

'Something hit me. Leave it.'

'Are we the only ones alive?' asked Golla.

'I think so.'

'We should look.'

Cally nodded.

They clambered through the fuming wreckage for a while, moving pieces of fused debris and hoping they wouldn't find anything underneath, but they did.

They found Ranag Zelumin, or at least the top half of him. Something hot, heavy and metallic had severed him below the sternum. They couldn't look at him for long.

'Oh Deus,' muttered Golla.

'Golla! Over here!'

Golla scrambled over to join her. Janny Wirmac was curled up in a ball at the foot of a ruined wall. She was miraculously intact.

'Janny?'

'Is it over?' asked Janny Wirmac.

'For now, yes,' Cally told her.

'Samstag? Samstag? Is that you?' Voices echoed through the smoky air. Golla and Cally looked up, and saw figures picking their way across the debris field towards them.

Reiss had made it, Iconis too.

'Mister Binderman?' Cally asked.

Bohn Iconis shook his head.

Lasco appeared, his nose broken and blood trickling from his shattered teeth. Zhakarnov clambered into view, sucking on a lho-stick. Lars Vulk and Antic followed him.

'What the frig was that like?' Antic asked.

'Oh, shut up,' moaned Vulk.

Braniff, it turned out, was gone, lost under a roof collapse along with his damn picts. Wolper had been mashed under the falling engine. Vulk had also seen the red-haired woman, Sasha, killed, virtually evaporated by a las blitz. Robor and Fiersteen had survived. The two members of Activated Twenty-Six whose names she'd never known had died too. Cally felt even more guilty about not knowing their names.

'Someone else can do it,' she said.

'What?' asked Iconis.

'I'm no leader. This is stupid. Someone else can do it.'

Fiersteen nodded. 'Good thinking, Samstag,' he said.

'What's that supposed to mean?' asked Iconis.

Fiersteen bared his bad teeth in an unfriendly grin. 'Samstag led us into this. Great idea that was. I say she's out. No one could get us more killed.'

'You shut your mouth!' Golla told him.

'I say it as I see it, missus,' Fiersteen replied, lighting a cheroot.

'Samstag didn't do this,' said Lars Vulk. 'This wasn't her fault. She was just trying to look out for us.'

'I don't want to be leader any more,' Cally told them.

'Someone has to be,' said Reiss.

'Cally's all right. I think she's all right. Isn't she?' asked Antic.

'As I see it,' Zhakarnov began, clearing his throat, 'we should appoint experienced command personnel in–'

'You mean, you, don't you? No one's going to follow you,' said Reiss.

'Oh, and why not?' asked the older man. 'It's about time someone–'

'The Mechanicus should take charge,' said Robor. There was silence.

'I hear that,' said Fiersteen.

'No, we–' Golla began.

'This is a Mechanicus war, and I am Mechanicus,' said Robor. 'It is right that I should assume command responsibilities. I should have done so at the start, rather than leave it to Cally.'

'Yeah,' said Fiersteen. 'I bet you wouldn't have dragged us into this backwater to die.'

'Fiersteen, you little piece of–' Reiss began.

'Please! We need some order!' Iconis cried.

'Cally?'

Cally turned. Janny Wirmac was standing several metres away, looking out into the debris field. She beckoned.

Cally Samstag clambered over the wreckage to reach Janny's side. 'What is it, Janny?'

'Is he dead, do you think?' asked Janny Wirmac.

'Oh, Throne,' whispered Cally Samstag.

* * *

The body was hanging like the corpse of an executed criminal from the underside of the engine's vast carapace plating. It seemed to have been caught up in the cables and trunking that had burst like spilt intestines from the rent hull.

It swung limply in the breeze.

It wasn't any member of Activated Twenty-Six. At first, Cally thought it had to be one of the locals, but as she approached she revised that notion.

His skin was whorled and shrunk as if he'd stayed too long in a bath. Tatters of electronic dreadlocks trailed from his head, some of them shorn off, others stretched taut up into the guts of the engine's overhanging hull. Further augmetic implants sprouted from his forearms and spine. His head was slack, and he was naked except for a shredded bodyglove. Cally realised that the man was hanging by the wires and tubes of his implants. Some were pulling out, or fraying, or tearing skin and flesh with them as they slowly uncoupled under the weight.

'He's dead,' said Fiersteen.

Cally reached up. On tiptoe, she could just touch the man's throat. His skin felt like oiled plastic.

'No, he's not,' she called. 'We have to get him down from there.' Golla, Reiss and Iconis hurried forwards to help her.

'Lars. Give us a hand!' Cally called. 'Come and take his weight while we unhook him!'

The big labourer from the Bulwarks came over and took hold of the man's legs, hoisting him a little. 'He's all wet,' he complained.

'There're so many cables,' said Golla. 'Do we just unplug them or–'

'Stop that! Stop that!'

Robor, the Mechanicus menial, pushed in amongst them.

He was staring up at the body in wonder and alarm. 'You idiots! Don't unplug anything,' he cried.

'We can't just leave him there,' said Iconis.

'It's the princeps,' said Robor. 'Don't you understand? This man is the engine's princeps!'

Cally looked at him. 'I'd worked that out for myself, actually. Whoever he is, we've got to get him down and comfortable.'

'He's still plugged in,' said Robor. 'His amniotic casket's been shattered, but he's still plugged in. Disconnection is an extremely complex ritual. A princeps can suffer huge trauma if it's not performed correctly.'

'Do you know how it's done?' asked Cally.

'Of course not! I am a very junior menial. I'm barely modified. I–'

'Well,' said Cally, 'I think the noble princeps has already gone way past huge trauma. Uncouple the feeds.'

Iconis, Reiss and Golla set to work with Cally. Robor turned his back and refused to watch.

As the last tangling cable came away, Vulk and Iconis carried the body clear and laid it on the ground.

'Someone get me a med kit,' said Golla.

'Uh, he's not actually breathing,' said Reiss.

Golla tried to clear the man's airway. A great deal of fetid, gluey liquid welled out of his mouth.

'He's been in the amniotics for years, most likely,' said Robor. 'He's modified to breathe liquid.'

'He's drowning,' said Reiss.

Golla shook her head. 'He's being born,' she said. She pumped the man's chest firmly, forcing the amniotic fluid out of his lungs. There was a great deal of it. Cally helped to wipe it away, and clear it out of the man's mouth. Golla grinned at her. 'Usually, a good slap on the arse is all that's needed,' she said. She leaned in, pressed her mouth against the man's lips and began to exhale air into his lungs. She alternated this with the pumping motion against the ribs.

'Come on,' said Cally.

Golla wiped her mouth. 'Babies usually pick the idea up faster.' She tried again. After another five minutes, she sat back on her heels and shook her head.

'I don't think it's going to work,' she said.

Cally touched her arm and pointed. Almost imperceptibly, the man's chest was rising and falling.

'I always said I was a good kisser, Cally-girl,' said Golla.

They made a makeshift stretcher from spars of debris. Iconis and Robor climbed into the wreck of the engine to check for other survivors, but came out with grim looks on their faces.

'There was a fire in there,' said Iconis, and left it at that.

In the last hours of daylight, they left the ruins of Gorge Orewelt. They headed south again. Cally didn't tell them to, but no one suggested differently. Even Fiersteen followed along without complaint.

They'd lost a lot of their kit, but they'd salvaged bits and pieces from the wreckage. Progress was slow, hampered by the stretcher, but they all took turns carrying it.

They trudged through unnamed vassal bergs and empty shanty hamlets. The evening sky had turned a deep pink, and visibility was dropping. Cally could smell sand in the air. There was a wind storm rising in the wilds of the Astrobleme.

It means 'star wound'.

She looked around, hoping to see Binderman at her side, but knowing he wouldn't be there.

* * *

By the time they had reached a cluster of derelict habs and storebarns called Beaten Track, the dust in the wind was so thick that they'd had to drop their goggles and tie scarves around their noses and mouths.

Thick eddies of pink dust blew across the ground like foam breakers. Scraps of litter and lumps of plastek waste fluttered around, and the old sign announcing Beaten Track to a uninterested world squeaked on its rusted fastenings as the wind swung from it.

Overhead, the sky had gone a disquieting dark blue, but huge, shimmering feathers of russet dust fanned across it.

'We need shelter,' Iconis shouted to Cally, holding his scarf against his face.

'No question about it,' she replied.

They got the stretcher into the partial cover of a lean-to. Then Cally took Iconis, Lasco and Antic to sweep the town's structures. Zhakarnov joined them, unbidden, and Cally didn't send him away.

It was Zhakarnov, his bandana jutting out around his beard, who found the best location, a three-room modular hab beside a tin-and-post store barn. The modular was old and its fabric rotting in places, but it seemed like the most secure space. They forced the door and brought the others in.

Inside, the modular was drab and dark. It smelled of rot, bad water and lichen. The entire structure shuddered on its foundations in the rising gale, and the wind made curious gurgling, wailing noises as it forced its way in through splits, chinks and holes.

It was sparsely furnished, but whoever had lived there had been an avid collector of junk. There were shelves and crates full of metal scrap, and a few usable tools. Lasco found a tray of taper candles and Reiss got a pair of antique fusion lanterns going. She hung them from the rafters overhead.

The sand blitzed against the walls and dirt-caked windows of the modular like rain, and the wind rattled the door violently as if it wanted to come in. Cally wedged a crate of scrap metal against the door to keep it shut.

'Everybody rest,' she said. 'We're going to be in here for a while, so make use of it.'

Cally walked down the length of the modular to the room at the far end where they'd put the stretcher. It seemed likely to her that the modular had seen a long service of hard use before it had been scrapped. Someone had reclaimed it from a metal yard and set it up in Beaten Track. Most of the interior doors were reclaim too, and none of them fitted properly.

Golla was sitting with the princeps. Robor stood at her side. The princeps had shown no sign of waking, or even moving, apart from the shallow rise and fall of his chest.

'His blood pressure is low,' Golla said. 'The pulse is very thready.'

'If there's anything left of his mind,' said the menial, 'it will be in distress. The withdrawal pain of severance is said to be extreme.'

'Because we disconnected him?' asked Cally.

Robor shrugged. 'Before that. He probably felt his MIU die.'

'Meaning?'

'He experienced the death of his engine.'

'Is there anything we can do?' asked Golla.

Robor didn't reply. The wind banged at the roof.

'Is there anything you can do?' Cally asked him.

'I'm just a menial,' Robor said. He looked at her. 'It's imperative we get him back to the forge.'

Both women laughed.

'I'm serious. A princeps is a priceless commodity: his skills, his knowledge, his experience. If there's any chance at all that this man can be saved, it's our duty to get to the forge to–'

'I understand,' said Cally, 'but we're not going anywhere in this.'

'But–'

'Robor, think for a moment. There's nothing we can do.'

The menial sniffed. He made an adjustment to his right wrist, and a small, slender data-drite extended. Cally and Golla watched him with slight unease. It was the first time Robor had used any of his modifications in front of them.

'I have received very little augmetic work,' he said. 'I'm still waiting to be certified for general modification. I have a simple data-plug and inload port. Perhaps, with your permission, I–'

He halted and looked at them. 'I don't need your permission, do I?' he asked.

Cally shook her head.

Robor pulled up a stool and sat down beside the stretcher. He examined the body carefully, methodically, studying all the hard-plugs, the upper spinals, the cranials, and the limnals.

'Such a ruin,' he whispered. Many of the plugs were damaged and torn, matted with blood or oozing amniotic fluid. He finally selected one on the princeps's left shoulder.

He turned to regard the women. 'Please, whatever happens, don't disconnect us. It would probably kill us both.'

'What if–' Golla began.

'Just don't.'

Robor connected his data-drite to the shoulder plug. Nothing seemed to happen. Cally and Golla stared at the princeps in his deathly state, expecting some response.

'Oh shit!' Golla exclaimed. Cally realised that they should have been looking at Robor, not the body on the stretcher. Robor's head was tilted down, his eyes clenched shut. His fists were tightly balled, and his mouth was straining wide open in a silent scream.

'Pull it out,' Golla urged.

'No! No, you heard what he said!'

'Look at his face, Cally-girl. He's in agony!'

'Leave the plug alone!'

Golla glared at her. 'All right, but if he comes to me asking why we let him die, I'm blaming you, Samstag.'

They waited. Robor did not move. He sat frozen in his hunched, screaming pose like the statue of some tormented saint.

Minutes passed. Time seemed unbearably slow. Cally wondered how anyone could remain fixed in such a rictus for so long. The gale shivered the modular and knocked repeatedly at the shutters. Maybe he's already dead. Wouldn't that be another highlight on Cally Samstag's list of command decisions?

'I'm going to unplug him,' Golla announced. Cally grabbed her and pulled her backwards.

'No!'

'Cally, please!'

They scuffled ridiculously for a moment, and Golla called on the extensive reserves of anti-personnel insults that years of service in the busy public wards of a Principal infirmary had armed her with.

Reiss burst in behind them and pulled them apart with surprising ease.

'Stop it. What on earth do you two think you're doing?' Reiss asked, holding them away from one another.

'She–' Golla began. 'Throne, Reiss, you're really strong!'

'I won't let her unplug Robor,' Cally said. 'Let me go, please.'

Reiss released them both. She walked over to the seated menial, peering at him in faint horror. 'What's he done? You let him jack into the dead guy?'

'He's not dead,' said Golla.

'It was Robor's idea. He thought he could help,' said Cally.

Reiss hunched down and gazed into Robor's frozen grimace. She didn't touch him.

'Robor? Robor? It's Liv Reiss. You in there, mister?'

Reiss rose and looked at Cally. 'I think Uldana's right. I think we should unplug him.'

'Robor made one request of us, and that was that we wouldn't disconnect him, no matter what happens.'

'I wonder if he was expecting this?' asked Reiss, dubiously.

'I don't know, but Robor knows more about this kind of thing than we do,' said Cally.

Reiss nodded. 'If that's how you see it, fair enough. He stays plugged.' She looked at Golla and then at Cally. 'Let us know if anything happens,' she said, and walked out of the room.

The wind howled against the modular's shell and the tapers flickered.

'Getting nasty out there,' murmured Golla.

Cally nodded.

'In here too,' Golla added. 'Sorry about that.'

'I'm sorry too.'

'No need.'

They stood in silence for a moment.

'I'll go and check on the others,' said Cally.

Despite the fact that the modular was rocking and shaking like a ship at sea, most of the others had gone to sleep. Janny Wirmac sat alone in a corner. She was toying with a little silver signet ring she wore, and seemed to be praying. Cally decided not to disturb her.

'Cally?' Look at this,' said Reiss. 'Bohn found it.'

Amongst the junk of one of the shelves was a battered field voxcaster, an old PDF-issue unit.

'Does it work?' Cally asked.

Reiss shrugged. 'No way to tell. Its power cells are dead.'

'And there are no spares?'

'What do you think the answer to that is?' asked Reiss with a hard smile.

'You could spike it,' said a voice behind them.

They looked around. Fiersteen was watching them. He was perched on the end of a busted mattress, toying with a cheroot that, in some show of courtesy to the rest of them, he had not lit.

'What did you say?' asked Cally.

'You could spike it,' Fiersteen repeated, grinning and exposing the lunar wasteland of his dentition. 'We used to do that sometimes when we couldn't afford fresh cells.'

'Who's "we"?' asked Reiss.

'Business associates,' Fiersteen replied, 'back in the hive, the old days. My line of work, resources were limited. Sometimes you'd need a vox or something all of a sudden, and there weren't no fresh cells. So we'd spike some.'

'Meaning?'

'You take the dead cells and mate them with the power clip off a sidearm. Laspistol is best. Not for long, mind 'cos the cells blow if there's too much charge. Blow right up in your sweet face. And yours, Reiss.'

Reiss ignored the sly insult. 'How many times can you do that?'

Fiersteen shrugged, 'Oh, it's a one-shot deal. Energy exchange like that pretty much screws the cells to shit, but you get enough juice for a short transmission or two. I could show you, if you want.'

'Does a spiked cell hold its charge?' Cally asked.

Fiersteen shook his head.

'Then show us when the storm's blown out. There's no point trying to send anything with this going on.'

Fiersteen nodded. 'You got a point there, Samstag.' He settled back.

'Mister Fiersteen?'

'Yes, Samstag?'

'Thank you.'

Cally turned to go back to Golla.

'You and Uldana all right now?' Reiss asked her.

'Yes. It was just a thing. I thought I'd leave her on her own for a bit. Show her I trust her.'

Reiss nodded.

Outside, the wind had become so strong it was starting to shriek like an animal. Cally could feel thin, fierce jets of cold air stabbing into the modular through the chinks and gaps around the doors and window frames. The air smelled sharply of graphite, of the Astrobleme sand.

It means 'star wound'.

She thought of Binderman, and the others, dead at Gorge Orewelt. She thought of Mister Sarosh and the ones they'd left behind on Fidelis Highway.

She thought of Stefan, and tears came up in her eyes. She wiped them away with the back of her dusty cuff, and touched the gold medal around her neck.

'That's just good luck in another language,' Mister Sarosh had told her that day aboard the hab wagon. If it was a lucky charm, it hadn't brought them much luck yet.

Unless it has, she thought. Unless this is the good version of things.

She went back to Golla. Her friend was still watching over Robor intently, jumping every time a wind surge smacked a shutter or threw a piece of desert flotsam against the wall outside.

'Go and get some sleep,' Cally told her.

Golla shook her head. 'I'll be all right for a bit,' she said.

Robor opened his eyes.

Cally started and Golla jumped back so hard that she almost fell off her stool.

'Robor? Can you hear me?' Cally asked.

Robor's awful, screaming mouth slowly closed. His eyes stared blank, unfocused, like a victim of massive concussion. His fists remained tightly clenched.

'Robor?'

He swayed slightly, and trembled, as if he was directly exposed to the desert gale.

'Robor?'

'Patent foramen ovale,' he whispered.

'What?' They bent closer trying to hear him.

'Patent foramen ovale,' he repeated, his voice as dry and fine as the sand blowing in off the Astrobleme.

'What are you saying?' asked Cally.

'I've heard gynecaes talk about that,' said Golla. 'It's a hole. A hole in the heart, in a baby's heart.'

'It's a small hole in the wall between the upper chambers of the heart,' said Robor. 'In the womb, a patent foramen ovale is a natural short circuit that allows a developing child's circulation to bypass the lungs, because the lungs are unexpanded and full of amniotic fluid. It is a pre-natal cardiac function artificially re-set in all princeps who are modified for casket operation.'

'Is that why his blood pressure is so low?' Golla asked.

'Yes. Some blood is still bypassing the lungs,' said Robor. 'The ovale is being closed, but until it has been sealed, blood pressure will remain weak.'

'Robor? How do you know this?' Cally asked.

Robor blinked, but his eyes still refused to focus on her. 'He told me.'

'The princeps told you?'

'The princeps told me.'

'Robor, what else can you tell me? Can you tell me anything else? What is it like?'

Robor swallowed hard. 'It hurts,' he said.

1011

A soft chime sounded through the noosphere, and a ripple of gratification and approval rang around the Analyticae. Another name had been formally identified and added to the list.

Feist called it the Hostile Catalogue, and it was on permanent hololithic display over the central console of the chamber. So far, there were twenty-two names on it, each one marked in blood-red type, each name followed by a block of code describing links, additionals and supplementary data.

Twenty-two names. Adept Lolisk had just added the twenty-second, and Feist exloaded a sincere message of congratulation. There was momentum at last. The names were coming faster, and that was encouraging Feist's data crews to work harder.

It was, Feist considered, a little like unpicking a vast tapestry. You had to spend a long while looking to find just the right loose thread, but once you'd found it and started pulling…

Adept Sinan's breakthrough, hours before, had been the loose end of the thread. It had allowed Feist's teams to focus and interlink specific eras of the vast archive, specifying code-type, operation, origin and date. Once they'd found one Mechanicum manifest, they knew what to look for. Like seams of precious ore, certain obscure language codes running through the strata of the archives yielded precious reserves. They began to identify and learn to recognise the engine-specific data bands within the bulk-data as a whole. One discovery often led to another.

They had the names of twenty-two pre-Heresy gross engines currently listed on the Hostile Catalogue as confirmed comparative matches with Archenemy engines recorded on Orestes. This wasn't just a nominal comparison. For all twenty-two, the Analyticae could provide detailed Mechanicum listing for the original spec, fittings and performance character, records that had not been studied in ten thousand years. Feist had a pending list of five more confirmed- match engines that had not made it onto the Hostile Catalogue yet because the archive spec had not yet been sifted out.

He had sixteen of his best code-lingual adepts improvising new, shortcut code versions to accelerate the transliteration of particularly obscure or archaic data forms. He had twenty-eight adepts subbing the translated data blocks down into concise rapid-blurt blocks, so that any princeps in the field could inload and access target data as fast as possible. He had forty multi-limb augmented adepts, who had transferred in from the forge fabricatories, all master craftsmen with extremely high multi-motor function skills, and he had put them to work speed-sorting solid data, such as manuscripts and scrolls. Anything digital was being translated and compared. Anything printed was being optically recognised, converted and reformatted.

He had a sense of satisfaction at last. He had a headache, but it would pass.

Adept Lunos was standing at his console.

'Can it wait?'

'I want to show you something, adept,' she said. She was a pale girl, well-skilled but lacking in confidence, and she often came to him for advice.

'I'm right in this now, Lunos. Can't you get one of the other deck supervisors to–'

'I'm asking you. I think it needs to be you,' she said. There was a strange look on her face.

Feist stalled and saved his workplate, and then rose to his feet. 'Just a minute then,' he said.

'I appreciate it, adept,' she replied.

As they walked across the jostling Analyticae, there was another chime and another chatter of approval. A twenty-third name had just been added to the Hostile Catalogue. Feist blinked noospheric and saw that the exload had come from Adept Zerees, making it Zerees's third confirmation.

<Good work, Zerees.>

<Thank you, adept.>

<All confirmed?>

<I even found its first run weapons test performance reports and the names of its original crew at incept.>

<Make everything available.>

Lunos was working at a station in one of the outer rooms. At the edge of the main Analyticae chamber, Adept Kalien appeared from somewhere and fell into step with them.

'I think we're getting somewhere with the Chryse Annals,' Kalien remarked brightly.

'That's good, Kalien,' he said.

'I was hoping to get your opinion on some formatting discrepancies,' she said.

No you don't, he thought, you want to know what I'm doing. 'I'll be happy to take a look in a second, Kalien,' he said. 'I just need to help Adept Lunos with something first.'

Kalien followed them as they left the main chamber and passed through the new rooms where the adepts from the fabricatories were speed-sorting the solid and non-cantable data.

'I was wondering,' Kalien remarked as they walked. 'Why fabricatory adepts? Why not data specialists?'

'It's a matter of choosing the most relevant skill pools. Those adepts may not be high-yield data processors like most Analyticae conscripts, but they are supremely skilled at manipulating physical objects at speed. Query: could you unseal a manuscript, run it across the optical examination plates, commit it to memory storage and reseal the original manuscript that fast?'

'No, adept.'

'And without damaging the original manuscript?'

'No, adept.'

'That's why they are doing it and you are not.'

'I see.'

'Perhaps you could get back to work, Kalien? I'll stop by your station shortly and review your formatting discrepancies.'

'Thank you, adept,' said Kalien. She turned and walked off the way they'd come.

Feist and Lunos arrived at the girl's station. She used her haptics to unsecure it and wake its stored workplate from memory.

She left it locked while she was away from it, Feist thought.

What an odd thing to do in a secure division like this. Then again, Lunos has always been the neurotic type. Perhaps she's being over-careful.

With a little hunched bow, Lunos suggested he should sit at her console. Feist did so, and interfaced.

<What am I looking at?> he canted as he began to search/scroll the data. It was the oldest, most digitally corrupt file he'd yet seen. The data was a decayed brown on a stained tan field.

<Was this optically scanned in from a manuscript?> he added.

<No, adept,> she canted back quickly. <It's transliterated from a data tile. The header tabs said it was a data copy of an older realbook, but the realbook doesn't seem to exist any more, even though the archive manifest says it should be in the same stow crate.>

Feist continued to scan. <I can't really decipher any of this. You say it's engine-related?>

'No,' said Lunos.

He glanced up at her. 'Oh, Lunos! This may be very old and interesting, but we've no time for–'

'Please. I've highlighted a section.'

He re-entered the data. <I'm not getting anything. This is so primitive. Is this Subcognatix?>

<It's an early form. I suggest you apply pattern 1101001 digital enhancement.>

<Applying… Yes, that's better. Yes, and you can damp back some of the magnetic dirt too. Much better.>

He started to read, rapidly at first, his eyes skipping down the old code. Then he slowed down and reread.

Then he scrolled and slowly read some more.

Lunos stood next to him for ten minutes, waiting in silence as he read.

Feist looked up at her. His face was pale. 'How much more of this is there?'

'A great deal.'

'Lunos, this...' words failed him for a moment.

'That's why I came to get you,' she said.

>

Several centuries of skilfully applied warfare had earned him the name the Red Fury, and he was one of the most feared and respected princeps maximi in the Mechanicus host, but he was afraid.

When the great assembly yards at Mount Sigilite came under heavy assault just after the stroke of hivewatch, Lord Gearhart had been meditating on death.

The steep western end of the mighty installation, a factory-fortress the size of a subhive built into the very rock of the massif, had been under assault for three days. Pressing east through the Shaltar Refineries, large numbers of Archenemy ground forces and artillery units had gathered to bombard Mount Sigilite's western bulwark.

Gearhart had pondered the data. The Archenemy, in his long experience, often ignored tactical logic or strategic merit, but this was an odd choice even by the Archenemy's perverse standards. The western bulwark was by far the stoutest and thickest part of the Assembly Yard defences. It was amply supplied with heavy batteries, laser grids and void shielding. The rock was a curtain ninety metres thick, and the cliff face was virtually unscalable by climbing forces. Still, the enemy persisted, despite several airstrikes by the hive's ground-attack fliers.

What did they know, he had asked himself? What was

their thinking beyond blind aggression? Unable to ignore it any longer, he had sent Bohrman in, commanding *Divinitus Monstrum* at the head of a four-engine deployment. Just before the stroke of hivewatch, Bohrman reported that his formation was at full stride and less than thirty minutes away from engaging the enemy at the western bulwark. Bohrman cheerfully anticipated a repeat of the engine-on-ground-force slaughter at Undergox Edge.

Then the heavy assault began. Side by side, three enemy Reavers came at the northern gates of the assembly yards, at a place known as the Titan Steps.

The night was cold and clear. The engines came out of the Gox Subsid at attack pace and lit up the blackness. The gigantic missile boxes on their beetle-backs shot constant, whizzing streams of rockets at the northern gates as they made their purposeful advance.

Watching the Manifold from his casket, Gearhart finally understood the Archenemy's tactics. The massed attack on the western bulwark was a distraction, an attempt to pull forces away from the far more vulnerable Titan Steps.

It was a crude, clumsy attempt at misdirection, a child's ploy. It was precisely what Gearhart, after careful consideration of the western bulwark attack, had anticipated.

That, in turn, was why *Invictus Antagonistes* was waiting at the Titan Steps to meet them.

The Titan Steps were essentially a vast series of broad, stepped platforms cut out of the side of Mount Sigilite. The platforms ran down from the northern gates up in the cliff face to the vast through-arterial that ran west to Argentum, and they had been specifically cut to allow engines to descend, platform to platform, from the assembly yards, as a human being might descend a broad flight of stairs. Every few hundred metres, the slim milled creases of human-scaled rock-stairs ran down between the giant treads. The Titan Steps were one of the most impressive and famous landmarks on Orestes, second only to the Field of Mars. At times of festival, huge crowds gathered there to see new-fit or rebuilt engines walk down in triumph from the mighty yards. Such events were carried live on all the public plates.

Invictus Antagonistes had ponderously climbed the first few steps, in the late afternoon light, and then reversed in against the towering overhang of the curtain cliff to one side of the vast stepped stage, like a sentry standing with his back to a wall.

Gearhart had ordered a fifteen-minute power down.

'Fluid and food,' he'd augmitted to his moderati, Bernal. 'Everyone unstrap and limb-flex. Personally check the autoloaders, moderati.'

'Yes, my princeps.'

Pietor Gearhart was an ancient being, by any human standards. His body was sixty-eight per cent bionic, and the rest of the flesh was heavily regrafted. He had been bonded to the mind impulse unit of *Invictus Antagonistes* for three hundred and thirteen years sidereal, and princeps maximus of the legio for two hundred and eighty-three. Prior to his princepture, he had been moderati on the *Augustus Terminatus* for eighteen years under Lucius Karing, and prior to that, famulous to the cantankerous engine-master Ervin Hekate for six, aboard the indomitable *Imperius Dictatio*.

It had been a long life, a full one too. There was only one thing Gearhart feared, and that was the final submergence of his humanity.

The gradual loss and replacement of his physicality he could tolerate. Apart from the usual replenishments, medical exams and occasional treatment for injuries, he'd been in an amniotic casket for over three hundred years. Flesh and bone withered and decayed under such circumstances, no matter how thorough the biological maintenance.

A slow decomposition was to be expected, and few princeps feared it. What was there to regret about the loss of motor function or muscle density in a foot or a hand when you could make the earth quake with your stride, see for a thousand kilometres, and demolish cities with a cursory flick of your mind?

No, what Gearhart feared was the loss of his personality. He knew that it would come, eventually. As the body atrophied, the mind increasingly withdrew into the dense matrix of the MIU and personality was debraded.

Gearhart had begun to fight back against the inexorable slide by trying to retain his sense of self. He had attempted to establish a human relationship with his crew and his fellow princeps, by using their names, and making a point of acknowledging their physical requirements and limits. He had begun to speak to them directly, whenever possible, and tried to use his augmitters rather than blurted cant. He struggled to interact with them as a human being would, rather than a commanding machine. He fought to stay human, despite the fact that he had become little more than a powerful brain, held in helpless, vital suspension, because it was all going.

A muffling darkness had begun to swallow the peripheries of his mind, in recent years, as if the outer, human, layers of Pietor Gearhart were rusting away: rusting away, or no longer needed.

Gearhart hated the shadow of encroaching darkness. He didn't want to become lost in it. He didn't want to die, or at least cease to be Pietor Gearhart, alone.

He knew what that was like. He'd seen old Karing at the end of it, raving in his tank, before they'd had to disconnect him.

As the afternoon sun had swung low, they had waited on the Titan Steps. Bernal and the able crew had moved freely around the bridge, sucking down nutrient wash as they flexed their legs and hand-checked the instrumentation. Venk, the tech-priest, had emerged from his cell to hold a service of grace.

Through the Manifold, Gearhart had been watching the sky blush pink and the sun slowly sink and become rinds of light on the horizon. Realising, with a start, that an inner nightfall had, for a moment, begun to settle on him too, he had woken himself up with brisk conversation.

'So, it's going to be cold tonight, moderati,' he had augmitted.

Bernal had hesitated, unsure of how to reply. Lately, his princeps had started to surprise him with attempts at simple conversation. How was one supposed to talk to a princeps about what the weather was going to do? Of course Gearhart knew in advance. There were temperature monitors in the hull skin, ambient air pressure sensors, wind vanes and the predictive meteorological plotting via the Manifold. Gearhart wasn't properly human. One did not idly speculate on the weather with him as one would with a comrade or a friend.

'Really, my princeps?' is all that he had managed.

'Oh yes, Bernal. We're due a storm,' Gearhart had said, 'out of the south, the Astrobleme.'

'Indeed. Climate feed from Principal doesn't show it, my princeps,' Bernal had said.

'Mark my words. Sand particulates in the air,' Gearhart

had replied. 'Pink sand. Smells of graphite. I'm reading it now, very fine.'

'I stand corrected, my princeps.'

'It's going to be a big one.'

When it came, the storm had nothing to do with the Astrobleme, and nothing to do with sand, but it was a big one nevertheless.

'System live, shields up!' Gearhart cried.

'System live, shields up, aye!' Bernal responded.

There was a mounting whine of power climbing and a clatter of gear trains whirring to engage.

'Shields lit,' the sensori reported. 'Multiple incoming missile fire, wide spread. Significant damage to Titan Steps. Significant damage to northern gates, assembly yards. Northern gate batteries are replying.'

Gearhart could see that for himself. In the glass-clear twilight, scores of missiles were streaking in to strike against the ancient walls of the northern gates. In response, Hydra batteries and turbo laser towers built into the wall line were spurting dense shoals of tiny comets into the blue-black spread of the Gox Subsids below the Mount.

'Do we advance, princeps?' asked the steersman.

'Negative, negative, Steersman Zophal. We don't want to spoil the surprise, now, do we?'

The bridge crew laughed, but Gearhart could feel their nerves. No wonder, as they shared one big neural gestalt.

'Arm all weapons components,' he instructed.

'All guns, go live!' Bernal ordered.

Once again, my princeps uses the vocal augmitters for cockpit orders instead of canting, Bernal thought. Why this new habit?

Gearhart felt the satisfying clatter of the massive autoloaders, the building pressure of super-heated plasma and the warmth of radiating laser energetics. He sighed as the missile platform opened its shutters like eyelids. Behind it, he felt Bernal's unease. Perhaps, once the fight was done, he should unburden himself, and tell Bernal about his fears. Would the moderati understand, or would it serve only to deepen the man's unease? Could they talk, man to man, friend to friend, or would it just be man to atrophied-thing-in-a-casket?

'Bernal? Targets, if you please.'

'Trace reading on two contacts, my princeps,' said the sensori. 'Warlords!'

Gearhart tutted. 'Examine the trace again, please, Sensori Vekkers. It's a cold night, and the void patterns are coalescing into a bigger bounce than usual. Adjust for transmitted distortion.'

'We stand corrected, my princeps,' said Bernal. 'Three smaller contacts now painted. Reavers, bearing 101, coming on full stride.'

Gearhart smiled. Karing had taught him that. He replayed the memory, remembering the comfort of his past, an incident against gargants on Oktobris Alpha, another sneak attack at night.

'Cold air magnifies auspex return, and blurs it, Moderati Gearhart! Separate those tracks!'

Gearhart's fingers flexed. The MIU was itching to deliver pain and woe. He held it back. They should wait. It urged him, voraciously hungry. Damn you, he replied, I am still in command here!

The Archenemy's assault was as flawed as it was clumsy. Quite apart from the idiotic presumption of misdirection, the chilly night air made anything out in the open sing with shield noise. Gearhart could manifoldly see all three Reavers, marching in, hot white against the dull blue wash of the subsid.

Nevertheless, they were doing damage. All three of them had fat, multi-loader missile pods on their backs, and two of them had additional missile packs slung as limb mounts. The combined onslaught would have levelled most small towns. Missile after missile, burning darts of fire, whipped in out of the subsid darkness and punched into the Yard's walls and raised voids. Boiling, billowing hurricanes of combustion belched back from the shields and wall surfaces. The vox was squealing with scrapcode.

The gates were holding.

It was time to respond.

'Stand by to stride by two, Steersman Zophal. As we pull clear of the wall, Bernal, I want a clean fix on at least one of those brutes.'

'Aye, my princeps.'

'Infeed data on the attack vehicles?'

'Routing it to you, my princeps.'

Gearhart flash-examined the data feed. There was nothing useful. He opened a link to Orestes Principal via *Invictus Antagonistes's* powerful comm-system.

'Analyticae! Calling Analyticae! This is *Antagonistes*. Have you anything on the following patterns?' Gearhart speed-fed the data at a high-pulse rate.

'My lord,' the vox crackled, 'this is Adept Sinan at the Analyticae. Stand by for comparison match.'

'I await your reply, Sinan,' said Gearhart.

It was a few moments coming.

'Please stand by, *Antagonistes*.'

'We've got all the time you need, Principal,' Gearhart mocked, and his bridge crew laughed again.

'Match identified. Feeding to you.'

The data rolled up across the Manifold view, text accompanied by feed-capture picts for detail clarification.

<Reaver: unknown/untitled, previously identified in Orestean battle footage via partial serial etching on carapace. Confirmed as *Pugnus Alterkate* at inception/launch. Pre-Heresy era Mars-pattern Reaver. Original engine specs follow as dense-packet data-blurt.>

Gearhart accepted the data-blurt and reviewed it in under a second. '*Alterkate* was reported as showing a shield misalignment around the lower motivators. She used to be literally weak at the knees, a bad shield seam. Moderati Bernal, I'm blurting you detail for target solution.'

'Receiving it now. We have a viable solution, my princeps.'

'Target destructor. Stand by and hold.'

'Second match identified, Lord Gearhart,' the link from the Analyticae announced. 'Feeding to you.'

More data spilled across the Manifold. <Reaver: now calling itself *Phantom Magnus*, identified via–>

'We don't have time for details, Principal!' Gearhart snarled.

<As you wish. *Phantom Magnus* confirmed as *Titanus Briarus* at inception/launch. Pre-Heresy Mars-pattern Reaver. *Briarus* originally displayed a shield point weakness along her carapace at the following squirted vectors.>

'Vectors received, Principal,' Gearhart replied. 'Bernal?'

'Target solution on the second engine, my princeps. Destructor limb aimed.'

'Stand by, moderati. Analyticae! Calling Analyticae! Anything on the third engine?'

'Negative comparison match at this time, *Antagonistes*.'

'Thank you, Principal. We'll do the rest.'

'Good hunting, my lord.'

Gearhart swam forwards in his casket. 'Stride by two, Steersman Zophal! Bernal, you have your firing solutions?'

'Aye, my princeps.'

Invictus Antagonistes lurched forwards away from the sheltering wall. The advancing Reavers saw its shield noise the moment it stepped clear and squealed in scrapcode alarm, but they didn't break stride. Though smaller than the massive Warlord, they were faster, they were heavily armed, and there were three of them.

Missile volleys blitzed the steps and the northern gates, and spattered across *Antagonistes's* voids. The mighty Warlord shuddered as its engaged energy walls absorbed the furious hits.

'Bernal?'

'Yes, my princeps?'

'Now, if you please.'

Thumping down the vast Titan Steps to greet them, *Invictus Antagonistes* opened fire.

The pumping salvoes of its destructor struck the Reaver that, ten thousand years before, had been called *Pugnus Alterkate*.

The tearing plasma blasts of *Invictus Antagonistes's* powerful destructor ripped into the Reaver that had once been known as *Titanus Briarus*.

Confronted by an Imperial Warlord Titan, descending upon them in full fury, all three Reavers multiplied their fire rate. Washed in flames and impacts, *Invictus Antagonistes* came down to meet them.

The intelligence from the Analyticae proved to be priceless.

Gearhart's destructor penetrated the suspected shield weakness along *Pugnus Alterkate's* knee-line. Compromised, its shields began to cycle and attempted to re-cohere, but the savage shots had already knee-capped the vile machine. With a shriek of deformed and torn metal, the Reaver's legs gave out and it toppled forwards. Its faltering shields popped violently. Its collapsing upper hull smashed, face down, onto the lower steps with an impact like a thunderclap, its legs buckled and broken backwards behind it.

Seconds later, the remainder of the ancient, mourned *Pugnus Alterkate's* missile magazine cooked off in the blaze, enveloping its carapace, and it blew out in a vast, dirty fireball.

Simultaneously, *Invictus Antagonistes's* plasma blasts found the specific ancient weakness on the shoulder of *Titanus Briarus*. It was a small thing, a mild defect, point zero-zero-one of a discrepancy, atomically speaking. The Mechanicum had always been very precise.

The port side of *Titanus Briarus*, now a daemon engine wearing the name *Phantom Magnus*, blew out in a shower of debris and super-heated gas. Its left weapon limb, entirely severed, dropped away onto the steps in a spray of flames, and bounced, burning. *Titanus Briarus* tilted on the steps, gears straining, metal grinding, and tried to right itself. Fire erupted up through its lower chassis.

Ruthlessly, *Antagonistes* hit it again: two missiles from the box. The first shattered *Briarus's* waning shields. The second smacked it in the face and blew out its cockpit and the back of its mantle.

Titanus Briarus reeled, swayed, and then tumbled back down the steps in a series of heavy, crunching impacts. It hit the arterial down below on its back and went up like a torch.

'Do you still want to play?' Gearhart asked the remaining Reaver. His crew laughed again. The princeps maximus was on form, and he was in a spirited mood.

The remaining Reaver began to back away, retreating down the lower steps.

<*Kharnus Kollidus*!> it blurted up at them in a scrapcode torrent.

<You are not *Kharnus Kollidus*,> Gearhart replied calmly. <You were once something else, something majestic, something transcendent. I pity you. Tell me, before I kill you, what was your name, long ago?>

<*Kharnus Kollidus*!> it screamed back.

It resumed its missile fire, shooting streams of armour-piercing projectiles up at the mighty Imperial Warlord. A halo of fire surrounded *Invictus Antagonistes* as its shields blew back the detonations. Gearhart took another step down the famous Titan Steps.

'Bernal?'

'Yes, my princeps?'

'This is going to go down the hard way, the old way.'

'Yes, my princeps.'

'Bolters, Bernal, destructor, missiles, everything we have. I won't suffer this sick creature to live a moment longer. I want it freed from its misery and its shame.'

'Yes, my princeps.'

Vast, ponderous *Invictus Antagonistes* trod down the steps and unleashed its full arsenal at the retreating Reaver. The enemy engine lashed back with every shot it could make, its multiple missile pods streaming projectiles up at its nemesis at maximum load-rate.

For a brief moment, the Titan Steps lit up as if a noon day sun had come out, and then gone supernova. Barely one hundred metres separated the duelling engines, and they doggedly spent the entire arsenal of several minor wars against one another, point-blank, engine to engine. Ten cubic tonnes of fast-load, high-explosive munitions were expended in the face-off.

The Reaver's shields failed first.

Its voids shattered under *Invictus Antagonistes*'s onslaught. Shuddering, shield-less, it started to quake and rattle, to bruise and lose skin, to abrade and shred. It began to come apart in a welter of plate scraps, metal flying off it. Then something hit its core and it went up.

'Die, you sick animal!' Gearhart hissed, still firing.

The Reaver blew apart. Broken scraps of it went winnowing away into the night. Its death was as bright as a star's heart.

'Full stop!' Gearhart commanded.

'Full stop, aye, my princeps!'

'Let's breathe for a moment,' Gearhart said. His vitals were pushing at their safety limits. His heart hurt. His mind was fuddled. Darkness crept in.

'Moderati Bernal?'

'Yes, my princeps?'

The more he fought, the more he lost himself.

'Cold night, eh?'

'Yes, my princeps.'

'Please signal the Analyticae and thank them for their labour. They won us this victory.'

'I will, my princeps.'

Gearhart heard his moderati turn to the vox. The voice became a dull chatter, a blur. His vision swam. He was very weary suddenly. Combat tension weakened him very quickly these days. He relaxed for a second, and everything went dark and muffled.

It got especially dark when he was tired.

With a shiver, Gearhart forced the darkness back.

I'm not done yet. You hear me? I'm not done yet.

* * *

>

Many kilometres south of Mount Sigilite, *Dominatus Victrix* walked out of the Antium silos into the other storm of the night.

This one was meteorological in nature. It had boiled up days before in the vast, empty quarters of the Astrobleme, and then spilled north in a fury, across the beleaguered vassal states and right up into the hive zone. It was the same elemental monster that rattled the modular sheltering Activated Twenty-Six in faraway Beaten Track.

By the time it had reached the Gynex subs, it had lost a little of its tooth and venom, but its wind's shear force still put a lot of strain on the engine's inertial dampers and gyro stabilisers. The night was blinded by swirling billows of pink sand. Though *Tantamount Stridex* was walking only a short distance off its port flank, they could only see her by hard return and via the Manifold.

It was a less than auspicious start. Tarses would have preferred better conditions to put the refitted engine through her paces, especially with a new crew and a princeps who was not yet familiar with her foibles.

Or war, Tarses reminded himself. A princeps who was not yet familiar with actual war.

Nevertheless, he was enjoying himself. To be back in the old chin-seat, to feel *Victrix* walking again, potent and indomitable, these were things to savour. Re-plugging, after so long away, had been like coming home, or being reunited with a long lost love. Tarses had forgotten how comfortably his mind fitted to the unique contours of the engine's MIU. Or perhaps it was the other way around? Whatever the truth, he let his mind drift in the impulse tides, carried by the rhythm of the engine mechanisms. Away from *Victrix*, his memories quickly lapsed, leaving only a sense of loss and isolation. He forgot so rapidly, so thoroughly, how distinctive and subtle the MIU was. It had its own flavours, its own character, quite different from any other engine. He let the sheer bulk of the Warlord hang on his mind for a while, deliciously heavy, and then thrilled to her buttoned-down power.

As far as he could tell, there was no sense of resentment in *Victrix* at the new princepture enforced upon her, though if any did exist, it would most likely show itself during the stress of combat. Faintly, like a taste at the back of the throat, Tarses could detect something that felt like sadness, as if *Dominatus Victrix* was aware of the death of Skaugen and the others.

Somehow, that reassured him.

'Passing waymarker eighty-eight,' the sensori announced. 'We are joining arterial 797, Fidelis Highway, and entering the Lexal Refinery Zone.'

'So noted, Sensori Kalder,' Tarses replied.

<Thank you, sensori,> canted Prinzhorn from his casket.

A heavy gust trembled them slightly, and Tarses heard the hiss of sand particles spattering against the hull.

<I could do without this sandstorm,> Prinzhorn blurted. <Instruments-only is an inefficient way to operate. And the sand abrasion will be ruining the hull finish.>

Tarses shook his head. The idiot's worried about the paintwork. 'It's regrettable, princeps, but I imagine we'll cope.'

'My princeps was not suggesting we wouldn't, moderati,' said Fairika, standing at the casket's side.

You can hold your tongue too, thought Tarses.

Prinzhorn's comment had been telling. He craved the visual scoping that the sandstorm was denying him, because, by his own admission, running by instruments alone was inefficient.

Tarses knew that the reverse was true, and he knew that any half-decent princeps of experience would back him on the point. A princeps didn't need to see, and the grimy ports and fuzzy pict-feeds of an engine hardly equipped them well for the task anyway. In engine war, more often than not, given the range and power of a Titan's arsenal, your opponent was likely to be beyond visual acquisition anyway. Most engine fights took place at a distance of five kilometres plus. Throne help you if you got up close. That was a mutual kill-kill scenario, unless you happened to be a Warhound on a snap-ambush attack or, as a datafeed from Mount Sigilite earlier that night had informed them, Lord Gearhart. The details had been scrappy, but apparently the Red Fury had taken down three enemy Reavers on the Titan Steps at dusk in a fast, furious, point-blank confrontation.

The news had roused them. Only Gearhart had the ceramite balls to risk a showdown like that.

In dismissing the instruments, Prinzhorn had betrayed his singular inexperience. A good princeps lived and fought through his instruments, and read the world only through the Manifold, even under distance-clear conditions. Skaugen had often cancelled out pict-feed, optics and, on occasion, closed the cockpit shutters so that he could focus on the instrumentation data. Tarses hoped Prinzhorn would learn.

Tarses hoped Prinzhorn would learn fast.

When Prinzhorn made his 'instruments-only' remark, Tarses had happened to catch Steersman Anil's eyes. They had grinned at one another darkly. They had both been thinking the same thing.

Tarses kept his eye on the auspex, as was his job, processing the fluctuating, updating stream of return patterns. As per Prinzhorn's orders, *Dominatus Victrix's* entire auspex system, including remote feeds sensors and peripherals, had been stripped out and replaced, new for old. It was a fine new system, an Orestes-pattern unit far superior to the old Proximus model, with eizonic capacitors, its own slaved sub-servitor flesh brain, and options for free-sweep, field-retain and multiple target vectoring. Tarses noticed, with some amusement, that it was still given to ghosting.

I did tell him.

They advanced purposefully at medium stride through the broiling dust into the ruined landscape of Lexal. A few of the refinery complexes were still operational, and their blooming gas burners, white-hot cones on the Manifold, added to the instrument confusion. Tarses had been in situations like this before, and he sorted the infeed diligently and cleverly.

<A target!> Prinzhorn declared suddenly, and the engine tensed, autoloaders clacking.

'Negative, princeps,' Tarses replied. 'That was an echo return on the gas jet at Parnold Refinum, bearing 251, bounced back by the sand in the air.'

<The auspex is still ghosting?> Prinzhorn asked, aghast.

Of course it is, you silly fool. That's the way *Victrix* likes it.

'It's just the atmospherics, princeps,' Tarses lied, not wanting to get into it. 'Damn those atmospherics.'

<My sentiments precisely, moderati,> Prinzhorn responded.

Oh, Throne, he's scared, thought Tarses. And, oh Throne, I still can't bring myself to call him 'my princeps'. What's the matter with me?

The return pattern abruptly shifted again. This time, Tarses paid it more attention. Something was off, something was wrong. Something had just shifted.

He leaned forwards, frowning, and gently manipulated the gain settings.

'Where did *Stridex* go?' Kalder muttered.

'Just what I was thinking,' Tarses replied. It had been right there, a huge and hard return off their port flank. Suddenly, all bounce and trace of the Warlord *Tantamount Stridex* had vanished.

'How is that possible?' Kalder began.

<What's going on?> Prinzhorn demanded.

'One moment please, princeps,' Tarses said, holding up a hand. 'We have an anomaly. Sensori?'

'Aye, moderati?'

'Check the vox-log immediately. In this hell-storm, we may have missed a manoeuvre signal from *Stridex*.'

'Checking now, moderati.'

<I won't ask you again, Tarses,> Prinzhorn blurted.

Tarses could feel Prinzhorn's rising tension through the link. All of the engine's flow rates were spiking in sympathy with the princeps's agitation. *See for yourself,* Tarses wanted to snap. *Look into the damn Manifold and see for yourself. I'm not hiding anything. It's there, bold and plain, for you to see.*

<Moderati!>

'We've lost contact with *Tantamount Stridex,* princeps.'

<She's right beside us. It must be a vox glitch.>

'I'm not talking about comms contact, princeps. We've lost return contact. She's just not there any more.'

<Impossible.>

'And yet,' said Tarses. He felt the uncanny flavour of it too. How did one lose something as big as an Orestes-pattern Warlord, even in a sandstorm?

<She must be there!>

'Hailing her now,' said Tarses.

'I've checked the vox log,' said Kalder. 'Absolutely nothing, no signal, but there is a little knot of code noise timed at about forty-three seconds ago.'

'Wash it and run it through the modifiers,' Tarses ordered, 'quickly, please. Look for any signal pointers, call markers or data identifiers.'

'On it, moderati,' replied Kalder, turning to his station with expert, nimble fingers.

Tarses opened the hard-band vox. '*Stridex*, *Stridex*, *Stridex*, this is *Victrix*. Report your position, respond?'

He set the vox to repeat hail, and coded it as binaric squirt too: belt and braces.

<Repeat the hail!>

'I am doing so, princeps,' said Tarses. 'Nothing. Zero response.' As he worked his console, Tarses watched the auspex. Was it just ghosting? Was *Victrix* toying with them, as she was often wont to do? *Dominatus Victrix* was sometimes wilful and mercurial. She liked to play games with her human collaborators.

This is not the time, lady, he thought.

'Moderati?' Kalder called from his chin-station.

'Go,' replied Tarses.

'I've washed the code noise. Very indistinct. Playback to you.'

'Ready.'

Tarses cocked his head and cupped his hands to his 'phones.

——175665 twelve twelve twelzzzzzssshhhhh! Klk klk tssssssss! there! Right there! Tzzznnkkk! For the love of tshhhhhhhhhhhh! Hard port, hard port! we have— zzzzrrwwww tssshhhhhh!——

The signal blanked out.

'Need it again, moderati?' Kalder asked.

'No, I don't,' Tarses replied. 'Shields. Now.'

'Shields aye,' responded Kalder.

<Shields? That is my command to give! How dare you go below me, moderati!>

'How dare you!' Fairika agreed.

'For Throne's sake, shut up!' Tarses said. 'Do we have shields?'

'Full shields, moderati,' Kalder replied.

'Princeps,' Tarses called out. He hesitated. What the hell? 'My princeps. I suggest you go weapons live immediately.'

<Famulous, get Tarses out of that seat and remove him from authority! He is wilfully–>

'Prinzhorn! Will you look? Look!' Tarses yelled.

Prinzhorn paused. <I have acquired hard return data. No ghosting. I have a clear view of the Warlord. *Tantamount Stridex* is back on the scope, although I have no idea how it came to be ahead of us. Hail her, please and–>

'That's not *Tantamount Stridex*,' said Tarses.

In his casket, Prinzhorn baulked. He reviewed the data-feed. He half-blurted, but all that came out was stammered code mess.

<How–?> he began.

'Weapons live *now*!' Tarses screamed.

The Archenemy Warlord ploughed out of the night and the shrieking, blinding dust storm, and strode towards them, its weapon mounts crackling as it released shot after shot right into them.

1100

Adept Kalien sat back in her seat and gazed across the Analyticae.

To an unmodified eye, the main chamber was a dim cave, with toiling adepts hunched over the dark pulpits of their stations while servitors and menials scurried between them, running errands and serving their needs. The central hub glowed like a dying grate in the heart of the room. There was a soft and constant background hum of power feeds, code chatter, mechanical operation and beeping data.

To a noospheric view, the dark, spare physicality of the chamber was transformed into a dazzling vista of realised data blocks, flickering communication tracks and drifting, multi-coloured shoals of code that swam around them all like gaudy reef fish, darting from one operator to the next to feed on and excrete coral-bright packets of information. Haptically guided streams of intelligence zipped back and forth like green tracer fire, exloaded from one adept, inloaded by another. In places, streams had converged in mid-air, creating data matrices as complex as fractal patterns, glowing Mandelbrot crystals where algorithmic programs tied information streams together and compared them. Sometimes, the matrices were fed by streams from three or more diligent operators.

Kalien liked to watch the noosphere. She read it particularly well, even by the standards of the Inner Forge. Her line supervisors had already recognised in her a particular aptitude for mass data differentiation and high-end code work, and had earmarked her for specialist enhancement and promotion into the most rarefied disciplines of the Logis. Like her twin, Kalien was destined for greatness.

Magos Tolemy had asked her to monitor the Analyticae as a personal favour. Of all the adepts sent over from the archives, she was the most significant spy. Kalien had understood from the outset that the likes of Egan and Feist expected her and her ilk to operate as spies, so she had cleverly masked some of her ability statistics and aptitude scores, and adopted a deliberately spiky, irritating manner. It had worked. Feist, an overly dutiful and unimaginative fool if she'd ever met one, had already dismissed her as tiresome, arrogant and intellectually weak. Unable to hide the fact that she was a spy, Kalien had simply presented herself as a bad one.

She watched the constantly moving radiance of the noosphere, and felt reassured by it. To her, it was the life-glow of the Mechanicus. She remembered, vividly, when she had first been modified to appreciate it. She pitied any who could not perceive it, and understood why unmodified Imperials generally regarded the Mechanicus with such wariness and contempt. To an Imperial subject, the devotees of the Mechanicus were dull, hard-plugged, bionically dependent wretches, canting their strange code-tongue and physically subsumed by the technology grafted into their bodies. The Imperials could not see the brighter, bigger and more explicated universe that the Mechanicus shared. Their flesh-minds had no grasp, no grasp whatsoever, of the rapturous, enlightening information-rich medium in which the Mechanicus lived and worked, and learned.

Kalien paused in her rumination. Apart from the massed code activity of the main Analyticae and its adjoining subchambers, thousands of separate transmissions were pouring in from the combat zones, a steady feed, constantly updating and renewing. One small, fleeting nugget of data had caught her attention.

Leaning forwards attentively, she used retrocognition to relocate it.

Lexal/Fidelis [time/locale code incanted via Manifold]; Dominatus Victrix *reports direct engagement.*

No other data was available, though she expertly block-searched and code referred.

She looked around. The entire workforce was concentrating on the processing tasks. Feist was not at his station. He was still off somewhere with the dreary Adept Lunos.

If there was any more detailed information, it would have been routed directly to the banks of the senior magi. Kalien's station was not adjusted for infeed clearance of that level. Encrypted battle-data came top-down through the senior ranks.

She made several surreptitious gestures and empowered the clandestine link-tools Tolemy had secretly provided her with. They could do little with the muzzled operational facilities of her station, but she reached out, sheathing her efforts in cloaked code. Feist had left his console unsecured. She let herself into his open workplate, and began to haptically sift through his inload buffers. If she hadn't been so concerned about her twin, it would have amused her enormously to remotely rifle through her senior's desk with such ease.

She was not rewarded. Feist's station had no supplementary information regarding *Dominatus Victrix*. She began to cancel out the links and cover her trail.

One of the last workplate items was an archive file open in read mode. She was about to mark it pending when she realised it was in use. Feist was studying the file at another station while simultaneously exloading it back to his own console for further study. The load track was coming from Adept Lunos's workstation.

What are you up to, Kalien wondered? It was too good an opportunity to waste. Using the powerful, covert link-tools Tolomy had equipped her with, Kalien took a speed copy of the file and brought it across to her station with a deft haptic gesture. Feist would have no idea that his work had been manipulated and copied.

She began to read. Within sixty seconds, she realised that Feist was going to find out his work had been copied.

He was going to know, because there was no way she could keep what she was reading to herself.

>

'Full stride!' Tarses roared. 'Full stride now or we're dead!'

The cockpit shook. Another damage alert lit up and an alarm sounded. The target capture detector was mewing like a frightened kitten.

<Who is in command of this engine, moderati?> Prinzhorn blurted.

'I'd be interested to hear your thoughts on that, *my princeps*,' Tarses replied, 'but I doubt either of us will live that long.'

<Full stride!> Prinzhorn ordered.

'Heading, my princeps?' asked the steersman.

There was a moment's hesitation. Two more impacts shuddered across the anterior port shields. Scrapcode came at them on all channels, chattering, menacing, amused.

'The princeps orders left, left and full motivation!' Tarses called out, covering fast. 'Isn't that correct, sir?'

<Uh, I… Yes. Left, left, full.>

'Left, left, full, aye!' agreed the steersman.

Dominatus Victrix surged forwards into the dust-storm, and turned to port around the side of a towering energy grid station. Powerful shots chased it and struck against the grid station's thick walls.

They had bought a moment's grace. The engine moved with great thumping steps along the broad pavement behind the station. Tarses hunted with the auspex. *Where was it? Where was it? Coming in behind them, or circling the station complex to meet them?*

As he worked, Tarses opened a private link to Prinzhorn.

<Princeps, it is not my intention to undermine your authority, and I stand ready and eager to follow your orders, but those orders must be processed rapidly or we will suffer the consequences.>

<Don't lecture me, Tarses.>

<It is a moderati's job to ensure that his princeps is informed, empowered, and fit for purpose. I am doing that job. You need to become proactive and affirmative. I understand this is an overwhelming experience, your first taste of combat–>

<My record is–> Prinzhorn interrupted with a snarl.

<Simulated. I *know*, my princeps. It's all been simulated until now. Let me help you. *Please*, let me help you.>

There was silence between them.

<My princeps?>

<Find that engine for me, Tarses.>

<My pleasure, princeps.>

Dominatus Victrix advanced through the grid station complex, cutting between a row of blockhouses and two tall vox masts that were swaying like reeds in the storm. The particulate haze in the gusting air was dense, and heavy static was building on all exposed metal. Little twists of bright blue light writhed like maggots around the vox masts.

There was suddenly no sign of the enemy stalking them, not even a whiff of scrapcode.

<Ahead twenty, low stride,> Prinzhorn augmitted.

'Ahead twenty low, aye,' responded the steersman.

Tarses and Kalder watched the scopes. Tension in the cockpit space was palpable. The air was close. The only words exchanged were the back and forth of standard commands. They were surrounded by the noises of the moving engine that contained them: the rumble of gears, the dull growl of the reactor, the chime and ping of instruments, the creak of metal, and the steady thump/shock of low stride.

Then the shields started to sing.

'What the cog is that?' Fairika started, unnerved.

'The voids are scouring heavy, famulous,' said Kalder.

'What does that mean?' she snapped back. During the walk out from the finishing silos, Tarses had realised that Famulous Fairika didn't like it when the veteran crewmen used engine slang, as if she supposed she was being excluded from some engineman's club by dint of her gender and youth.

'It means we're in a dry, high-static environment,' said Tarses. 'It charges dust on the shield auras and makes them squeal.'

The noise was indeed dismaying. It sounded as if numberless lost souls were clinging like limpets to their engine frame and bemoaning their plight, while their cold, numb fingernails furtively scratched at the hull to get in.

'Always a bad portent when the voids sing so, isn't that right, moderati?' murmured Kalder ominously, winking at Tarses.

'Stop it,' said Tarses.

Kalder grinned and shrugged. Goading Fairika was too easy a game.

They advanced a little further. Though they could rationalise the eerie shield noise, it began to play on their nerves. Strange hoots, trills, whines and stutters came in, muffled, through the armoured hull: odd squeals, long dry groans, timorous whispers that sounded uncannily like voices.

Tarses kept watching the scopes, noticing how Kalder expertly fine-tuned the dials and kept the patterns steady and clean. This is a good crew, he thought, a good crew, except for one weak link.

<If the enemy has voids raised, won't they be singing too?> asked Prinzhorn softly.

Tarses turned in his seat. In his amniotic tank, Prinzhorn was staring right at him.

'Sir?'

<If the enemy is using its shields, moderati, surely they will be audible like ours?>

Tarses slowly nodded his head in respect. It was an extraordinarily canny remark, and so logical that Tarses had overlooked it. 'An excellent observation, my princeps,' he replied. 'With your permission?'

A half-smile flashed across Prinzhorn's face and a few

bubbles escaped the corner of his mouth into the suspension fluid. <At your discretion, moderati.>

Tarses turned back to his console. 'Steersman?'

'Moderati?'

'Ahead ten, then full stop and cut power to minimum turnover. Sensori?'

'Moderati?'

'Stand by to run a three-sixty locator sweep, acoustics only.'

'Aye,' said Kalder, throwing a series of switches and re-plugging several connections.

'Weapon servitor six?'

The upper starboard carapace servitor stirred in its web of plugging and acknowledged Tarses with a binaric chuckle.

'Open the missile pod, load and arm four AP warheads, code them for heat, and await my solution.'

<100101001 1100101 1000101.>

'Thank you, six. Standing by to drop shields.'

'Drop shields?' queried Anil, his hands clamped to the steering rods. 'Have you taken leave of your senses?'

'My princeps?' asked Tarses.

<Permission granted to drop shields at the moderati's command,> Prinzhorn canted.

'Thank you, sir,' said Tarses. 'Stand by.'

'Full stop!' Anil reported. His gloved hands fluttered over the drive console, throwing switches and pulling levers. 'Power to systems cut to turnover only.'

'Kill the vox,' Tarses ordered. 'Silence, all crew! Dropping shields on three, two, one…'

Tarses deactivated the voids. The awful scratching, singing noise abated. They could hear the wind hissing around them, and the cargo of sand it carried softly grating against the bare hull.

'Sensori? Run sweep, please.'

'Aye, moderati.'

Kalder activated the sweep. The aural phones began to cycle around through three hundred and sixty degrees in their geared sockets up on the heavy mantle, and secondary phone arrays rotated in the shin armour and the thick ceramite cuffs of the weapon limbs.

On the second rotation, they got the bounce.

'I have it, moderati,' announced Kalder, listening intently to his headphones. 'One point one kilometres south-south-east. Triangulation places it near the cooling towers to the rear of the grid station.'

'Playback?' Tarses requested.

Kalder put the sound-burp on speaker. It was just a five-second garble of shield noise.

Tarses nodded. 'Turn that into a firing solution, please.'

Kalder already had. 'On your port repeater, moderati.'

Tarses squirted it to weapon servitor six.

The servitor greeted the data hungrily. It chortled code. The cockpit crew heard the missile magazine whine and clatter as warhead rounds elevated into the pod.

'Satisfied, my princeps?' Tarses asked.

<I am.>

'Sensori?'

Kalder held up a hand. 'Allow me another pass, please. It's shield song, but I'd hate for it to belong to *Tantamount Stridex*.'

<Well cautioned, Sensori Kalder,> canted Prinzhorn.

Kalder nodded. He adjusted his instruments and listened. The process seemed to take an unnecessarily long time. 'It's not *Stridex*,' he announced at length. 'The signature's quite distinct.'

'Stand by,' said Tarses. 'As soon as we have weapon launch, we'll raise shields and advance ahead fifty at full stride. All crew be advised, we may wound them, but we probably won't kill them. As we follow the strike in, stand ready for an engine duel. Autoload all weapons.'

All the weapon servitors responded smartly.

'Prepare to route all available and non-assigned power to the front voids.'

'Aye.'

'We're ready. At your command, my princeps?' said Tarses.

<My word is given.>

'Launch!' Tarses ordered.

Dominatus Victrix lurched slightly as the four warheads banged off, one by one, into the dust storm. The crew watched the streaking, curling heat washes trail away across the Manifold.

'Missiles running. Raise shields!' Tarses cried. 'Advance, full stride!'

'Full stride, aye!'

'Voids engaged, aye!'

They were moving again, their shields clamouring and squealing. It seemed to take an eternity for the inbound missiles to reach their target.

Tarses watched the scopes. He saw a series of four abrupt flashes, squalls of heat that showed up as hot pink blooms on the graduated darkness of the Manifold.

'Impact, impact!' he called out. 'Four hits directly on target!'

'Advancing at full stride,' the steersman observed.

<Assess target, sensori,> Prinzhorn requested.

'It's still standing, my princeps,' replied Kalder, 'but I'm detecting reduced volume on its shield noise. I believe we've hurt it.'

<Excellent! Drive in to front quarter and–>

'My princeps,' Kalder yelped, 'the target has engaged drive and is advancing to meet us!'

'Give me a clean visual!' Tarses ordered. Leaning forwards in his chin-seat, he gazed into the vista of the Manifold, trying to separate cold, clear fact from dust-storm distortion. Kalder expertly washed the imaging for him, and Tarses abruptly resolved the enemy engine coming at them, accelerating to full stride. Its chilling daemonic code bursts were starting to impinge upon their vox systems and acoustics. Tarses saw a swirl of collapsing energy dragging around the enemy machine like a torn cloak.

Its shields had failed and were shredding apart.

The enemy engine began firing. Mega-bolter rounds streaked like burning hail through the air around them, smacking into their shields, into the ground, into the grid station, into the lonely night. They severed one of the swaying vox-masts fifteen metres below its summit. The vox mast hinged over in a welter of static and sparks.

'Its shields are ruined, my princeps,' Tarses said.

<Destructor,> Prinzhorn told him curtly.

'Power to destructor, aye!' Tarses yelled. The reservoirs surged. 'Target!'

Hololithic crosshairs floated in front of Tarses. He took control of the fluid gunnery system, adjusted for wind shear and distance, and centred the pippers on the blackened beast ploughing eagerly through the dust storm to meet them.

<Now, if you're doing it, moderati,> urged Prinzhorn.

'Let it close,' Tarses replied calmly.

<How tight?> Prinzhorn asked in alarm.

'Just let it close.'

<Moderati Tarses, how tight do you intend to let it get?>

'*Killing* close, sir,' replied Tarses.

The crosshairs were throbbing arterial purple, pulsing like a panicked heart.

'Firing,' said Tarses, and triggered the gunnery system with his mind.

The massive destructor began to discharge. The first two scalding shots smashed against the hostile engine's torso plating with enough force to bring it to a shuddering halt. The plating glowed like a neon sore and superheated flakes of spalled ceramite billowed off it like burning leaves.

The third shot disembowelled it. The enemy engine exploded above the hips in a vivid star of blue-tinged flame. Its thoracic frame buckled, and its entire upper section – carapace, weapon limbs and cockpit – fell backwards off the chassis waist-mount. It landed with an impact so jarringly heavy, they all felt it through *Victrix's* dynamic hydraulics.

The severed legs remained upright, locked and smouldering. Fire rapidly engulfed the fallen wreckage.

'Engine kill,' Tarses announced.

<I find that satisfactory,> agreed Prinzhorn.

Tarses looked up from his station, a grin beginning to split his face. He punched knuckles with the delighted Anil and Kalder.

The flames were starting to lick off munitions in the fallen wreck. They spat and popped, and crackled out showers of sparks like mismanaged fireworks. Tarses signalled to Anil, and the steersman backed *Dominatus Victrix* off to a safe distance.

Tarses turned in his seat and looked around at the casket. Prinzhorn nodded back at him. His eyes were bright.

'My princeps,' Tarses smiled.

<My moderati,> Prinzhorn replied.

* * *

>

Erik Varco woke up a million kilometres from anywhere. It was cold, and the slow dawn was too feeble to thaw him out.

Everything ached. He'd billeted down in a scoop in the sand, huddled in his bedroll in the lee of the Centaur. There'd been a storm in the night, a bad one. It had spilled out of the south, out of the Astrobleme far away, and it had lost most of its fury by the time it had reached the Western Prospection. Still, his nostrils stank of graphite, and the early morning air was hung with dust.

They had run west from the PDF post, pushing the Centaur hard across the scrubland and silt dunes, and kept going until nightfall. Then, as the storm overtook them, they'd dug in under canvas to weather it out.

West felt like entirely the wrong way to go. It was counter-intuitive. Everything they cared about – the subhives, the subsids, Principal – everything lay to the east behind them. But the weaponised servitors at the post and, before that, the skitarii forces in the refinery belt, had proved without question that east meant death. They had been cut off by the invading forces. They had no choice but to head out into the scrub and fens, and waste tracts beyond the hive zone. The vast territory known as the Western Prospection lay before them, a realm of blunt crags, calderas, sump valleys and rockspine, where lonely mining outposts and metaltrade camps lurked in the dank pockets of dreary hills, eking out a living from mineral ores and semi-precious motherlodes.

The Western Prospection was a lawless place, considered bandit country by most civilised hive-folk. In Orestes Principal and Argentum, it was commonly referred to as the Deadlands. Like the vassal town borderlands that fringed the northern extremities of the Astrobleme, the Western Prospection was the home of migrants, sub-habbers, indigent crawler tribes, fugitive criminals and anyone else who had fallen, slipped, jumped or been pushed off the edge of Imperial society.

Over the years, Varco had visited both the Prospection and the 'Bleme on Pride Armour exercises. The bleak wastelands of both regions were ideal for mechanised manoeuvres and live firing. In his experience, one defining characteristic marked them apart. Both were wildernesses outside the hive zone, but where the Astrobleme had a rugged beauty to recommend it, a romantic spectacle of sculptural pink cliffs and russet sands, of pale blue daylight skies and endless starfields at night, the Western Prospection was a dire, grey, dusty waste. Its soil had become impoverished from thousands of years living in the climatic and electromagnetic shadow of the vast hives, and it had been mined out by the Mechanicus pioneers who had first claimed Orestes. Many of the valley pockets were the relics of old quarries, and many of the hills were heaps of neutered slag or rock waste dug up by the massive tillers of the early era geo-harvester machines and terraforming engines. The rusted wrecks of those antique giants could still be discovered out in the Prospection, like the fossilised remains of primordial monsters; machine cadavers the size of starships, half-buried in the bottoms of man-made canyons. Varco had once spent an afternoon, years before, taking test shots at one of them with *Queen Bitch's* main piece, quietly marvelling at the size of it. The Western Prospection had been robbed out and plundered by such monstrosities so that the hives could be built.

The Western Prospection was where they were going. There were no alternatives left.

Besides, he had consulted the Omnissiah. Whether he faced north or south, every time he put his hands in his pockets, the medallion was in the pocket closest to the west. He had even, out of sight of the others, drawn a crude compass cross on the dirt and flicked the medallion in the air over it. It had landed squarely on the tip of the western arrow. Something, perhaps the machine spirit of *Queen Bitch* herself, was firmly guiding them. Who was he to argue?

Varco stood up and stretched his stiff joints in the bruised light. Leopald had been standing the last watch, but he'd fallen asleep over the stubber in the ride seat of the Centaur. Varco shook him awake.

'Sorry, sorry, sir,' Leopald muttered, swimming back to life. 'I didn't mean–'

'Don't let it happen again,' Varco smiled. 'Let's get some of the ration packs and share them out.'

'Yes, sir,' said Leopald.

The graphite residue of the storm draped around them, making the light soft. The place was almost unbearably quiet. Stretching his legs, Varco found Koder standing a few hundred metres from the Centaur, his head back, his arms outstretched, as if he were taking a summons from some deity. Koder was turning slowly on the spot.

As Varco approached the enginseer, he saw that Koder had opened and extended small, slatted receptors from the flesh around his throat and chin, and behind his ears. They reminded Varco of the threat-frills of hissing desert lizards.

Koder closed the frills the moment he was aware of Varco's proximity.

'You carry on,' Varco said.

The frills were solar receptors. Koder was trying to replenish his internal power source.

Koder glanced uncertainly at his captain. 'The non-modified often find such displays of augmentation unsettling, sir,' he said.

'I may be unmodified, Koder,' Varco replied, 'but I am a servant of the Mechanicus. You carry on. I need you healthy and fit.'

'Thank you,' Koder replied. There was a noise like a paper fan flipping open, and Koder extended his solar arrays again. 'It is wasted effort, however,' he remarked. 'There is so little light. The dust, you see?'

Varco nodded.

'Rumination: are we going to die out here, captain?'

'I hope not, Koder,' Varco replied.

'Can you be certain?'

Varco smiled and shook his head. 'Of course not. But we've lived this long, haven't we?'

'Contemplation: if I was in the mood, there are so many logic gaps in that statement, I could take issue.'

'But you're not in the mood?'

'I am tired, captain.'

'Me too.'

They ate a share of the ration packs, sitting in and around the Centaur. A thin sun began to poke holes in the dust cover, and breezes stirred in the west.

'Where do we go?' asked Hekton, scraping at the disposable tray of his ration pack with a cardply fork.

'We keep going,' Varco replied.

'To do what, begging you pardon, captain?' Sagen asked.

Varco shrugged and took a swig of water from his flask. 'No idea. Choices have been made for us. If we turn back, we die, so I'd say that's a no. It's not a case of what *are* we going to do. It's a case of what are we *not* going to do. We're not going to die if I can help it. However, you all should know that I believe our part in this war is over. Survival is our only concern from here.'

Nobody liked the thought of that.

'Feels like we're giving up, Erik,' said Hekton.

'I know.'

'You can live with that, can you?'

'What do you propose instead, Gram?' Varco asked, sliding off the footwell of the Centaur and balling up his empty ration tray.

Gram Hekton shrugged. 'A run back towards Argentum? Maybe we can hook up with a PDF or Pride force and add to their numbers. Maybe if we don't make it, we can at least take some of the bastards down with us on the way.'

Gram Hekton had always been a courageous soul. 'Anyone else up for that?' Varco asked. No one wanted to make eye contact.

'Then we keep moving west,' Varco said. He thought of telling them about the medallion, but he didn't want them to start doubting his sanity. Belief in machine spirits was one thing, and no one questioned that because it was rational, but flipping a medal over a cross in the dirt to decide their fate smacked of crawler tribe superstition or worse. Varco stuck to the survival theme in a bid to sound reasonable. 'We run out into the Prospection as far as this tractor can take us,' he said, 'and maybe find a mining town or something like that to take us in. In a few days, a week or two perhaps, depending on how this war swings, maybe we can make a run back into the hives. We're all skilled and experienced mechanised crew, a valuable commodity. We keep ourselves intact and ready until such a time as we can be put back to good use where it counts.'

'So... not get ourselves killed until then, you mean?' asked Hekton.

'Yeah, let's not do that,' said Trask.

Leopald and Sagen snorted.

'Are we all fine with this?' Varco asked. 'Koder?'

The enginseer was looking pale and wan. He had barely touched his rations. 'You expect me to disagree with you, captain?' Koder asked.

'I thought you might be the one to dissent,' said Varco. 'No burning need in you to get back and fight for the forge?'

Koder shivered. 'Captain Varco, I have no burning need in me at all.'

Varco caught Hekton's eye. Hekton shook his head sadly. Koder was dying. He'd expended too much power. They all knew it. No one would say it.

'Prospection it is, then,' said Varco.

The Centaur churned north-west. The day was as pale and empty as the landscape. The sun nervously showed its face. The sky was grey, and looked as if it had been sanded down ready for re-painting.

Bracing against the roll and tilt of the rocking, fast-moving tractor, Varco clambered over into the back-bay and sat down next to Koder.

Koder was staring up at the meagre sky.

'Feel any better?'

'A little, captain,' Koder replied.

'Don't you go dying on me, Koder,' Varco said.

Koder looked at him. 'I will do my best not to, captain,' he replied.

'Is there anything we can do for you?'

Koder shrugged.

'You used too much power on that auspex, Koder,' Varco said quietly. 'You put your neck on the line.'

'I did what I had to do,' said Koder.

'What you have to do now is stay alive. That's an order.'

'Yes, sir.'

The Centaur was bouncing and bucking over the landscape. Sagen was driving it as if it was a main battle tank, rejoicing in the power and acceleration. On several occasions, they had to hang on as they were bounced off the deck by a deep berm.

Koder reached out his hand and Varco took it, surprised by the intimacy.

'What is it?'

'There's something wrong with the sky,' Koder said.

'Something wrong? Like what?'

Koder shook his head. 'I don't know. It's blank, somehow. Unreadable.'

'I don't understand.'

Koder shrugged. 'I have been sensing it for a while. I thought it was a symptom of my fatigue, but it is not. It feels like something is masking the sky from us, captain.'

'Can you explain that to me?'

'I will, as soon as I understand it.'

Varco nodded.

'Hey, captain!' Sagen yelled from the wheel. 'I see dust!'

The wall of dust flumed across the horizon like smoke. Something big was moving towards them out of the west.

At Varco's orders, Sagen drove the Centaur up into a small range of hills, a residual slope of ancient slag heaps. They pulled up and dug in, hull-down, behind the ridge line, then everyone got out and bellied up to the rise.

A wide valley of scrub, gorse and talon-fig lay below them. A few straggly pepper-thorn trees twitched in the intermittent breeze.

'I don't see what–' Trask began.

'Hush and wait,' said Hekton.

They lay low for ten minutes. The dusty slag beneath them had been warmed by the sun. Huddled close, Varco could smell his comrades and himself. It wasn't simply dirt and unwashed bodies. There was a sweeter odour, sickly like corruption, the residue of days of peaked adrenaline, acrid fear and a lousy diet sweating out of them.

This is how our corpses will smell, Varco thought. Koder smelled different. The enginseer smelled of burnt plastics and charred ceramics.

They all watched the veil of dust approaching from the west.

'What is it? Another storm?' asked Sagen.

Varco shook his head. Pebbles in the scree around them started to shake loose and dribble. The earth was quivering.

The stampede came into view.

It was a moment before they appreciated what they were seeing. Varco heard several members of his mongrel crew gasp in disbelief. He might have let out a gasp of his own.

A river of indigents was rushing past in the valley below, coming out of the west in a broad, tidal surge, like a badly regimented cavalry charge. Outriders and foot runners came first, racing ahead of the main flood on uni-lopers, bikes, mono-traks and frightened steed animals. Through the dust, Varco glimpsed galloping hippines, bounding daku-maku, sickly struthids and mangy saddle-cats. Caravansaries of crawlers and tug-habs, carts, wagons, mech-teams and walkers came after them, en masse. A huge migration of vassal souls was pouring out of the Western Prospection.

There were thousands of them: miners on growling tractors, gem-finders on low rigs, heavy prospection trains struggling to keep the rapid pace, hab crawlers with canvas dust sheets flapping, unlashed, in the wind, indigent carts, carriages, coaches, clans running together in family groups, nunk-brain twists dragging caboose habs, wildernauts, outsiders, prospection derelicts on old, clanking mechanised striders, bikers grunting out black exhaust, stake-makers riding cargo-8s, nugget farmers on big-trak freighters, and mineral prospectors aboard utility drives.

They were lifting up a vast dust wake behind them. It was like a frantic land claim or a gold rush.

No, thought Varco, they're running. It's not a gold rush, it's a fear rush.

'What are they doing?' asked Trask, agitated. 'What the frig are they–'

'Shut up!' Hekton snapped.

'Stay down. Stay quiet!' Varco told them.

'Stay quiet?' Hekton replied. 'Over this racket?'

Koder mumbled something.

'Koder? What did you say?' Varco hissed.

The enginseer rolled over onto his back. 'The sky… the sky has…' he said, his mouth gnawing, his voice dry and empty.

'What about the sky?' Varco urged. 'Koder? What about the sky?'

'The sky has gone out,' said Koder. His eyes flipped back into his head until they showed only whites and the trace evidence of modification. He went into spasm, his limbs twitching.

'Shit!' gasped Varco. 'Hold him steady. Gram. Hold him steady!'

Varco tore the cuff off his coat and forced it in between

Koder's clenching teeth. Blood was welling up between Koder's grimacing lips. Hekton and Leopald tried to brace the enginseer's seizing frame.

'Sacred Omnissiah!' Sagen stammered.

Down in the valley, the source of the fear rush had appeared.

The indigent tide below them was still thick and teeming. Heavier elements were passing by now: big mobile homesteads; mobile mineheads thumping along on their tortoise legs; sled-wagons with teams of grox pulling them, and trains of tied hippines braying along behind; gross mineral shredders clanking on heavy treads; tracked dozers and rock-splitters, burping soot from their upraised pipes. Others were fleeing airborne: scout drogues, their worn props chopping hard; battered omnithopters with cracked wings, sawing through the air like fledgling birds; grav-lifted survey plates and the odd, whipping lift-buggy coming in low over the stampede; flocks of buzzing cybernetic drones, and ore-finders, dark and wheeling like carrion birds, and behind them... *behind them*.

Three black-as-black enemy Warhounds bounded into view over the western skyline. They were striding at full pace, worrying the laggers and the slow-behinds. Bird-like, the trio of Warhounds hopped in behind the tail hem of the fleeing indigent mass, taking random shots and crushing unfortunate stragglers underfoot. Varco blanched. The Warhounds were driving the host like a body of livestock, turning them, coaxing them, herding them, slaughtering them.

As they ran, the Warhounds pumped off shots or loosed the occasional missile. Lasbolts tore through the rear echelons of the stampede, cutting vehicles and bodies apart. Dirty blasts of soil and fire thumped up out of the fleeing ranks, tossing mangled engine frames, wheels and track segments into the dry air and strewing them wide. Varco saw a cargo-8 explode from a direct hit, and one of its heavy axles, a spinning wheel still attached, hurtle out of the blast and pole-axe a speeding low rider, causing the light, fast-moving machine to cartwheel and disintegrate. A haphazard gout of mega-bolter fire hamstrung the starboard legs of a heavy minehead unit and it toppled over, crushing two racing hab-crawlers under its rusting, sooty bulk. A zipping missile ripped into the heart of a mineral shredder and turned its monumental iron structure into a volcanic storm of flame and whizzing debris. Three omnithopters, caught by the expanding envelope of the fire wash, fell out of the sky like burning moths.

'We have to get out of here,' Leopald urged.

'Stay down and wait,' Hekton told him.

'For what, sir?'

'They'll pass us,' said Varco. 'They'll pass us by.' He glanced at Koder. The enginseer had gone stiff and dead. Blood leaked out through the shred of cloth clamped in his mouth. Varco closed his hand around the medallion in his pocket.

Heads down, they lay still and waited. The ground gradually shook less and less, and the deafening roar of flight and destruction moved away from them.

Varco looked down over the rise. The air was heavy with slow dust. The valley was a trampled ruin. All the vegetation had been shredded flat or snapped over. Dozens of burning wrecks and hundreds of crumpled bodies littered the valley floor.

Looking east, he saw the retreating dust cloud that marked the progress of the exodus. The towering, trotting shapes of the Warhounds were just visible, bringing up the rear. Varco saw the distant blink and flicker of their weapons.

'Now we move,' he told Hekton.

'Which way?' Hekton replied.

'West.'

'Still?'

'Unless you want to go chasing that,' Varco replied, 'we stick with the plan.'

'An awful lot of people just demonstrated their desire to get the hell out of the west,' said Hekton.

'For Throne's sake, Gram, I know. Have you got a better idea?'

Hekton shrugged.

'All right. Get the Centaur prepped and ready to start.'

Sagen and Trask headed for the tractor. Hekton was still staring at Varco.

'What do you want me to say, Gram?' Varco asked. 'Whichever way we turn, there'll be danger. I still believe the emptiness of the Prospection is our best chance to disappear.'

'What did Koder mean?' asked Leopald.

'What?'

'What did Koder mean when he said "The sky has gone out"?' Hekton's gunner looked dubiously at the enginseer's limp body.

'I don't know,' Varco replied.

'He was raving,' said Hekton.

'Get him onto the back-bay and see if there's anything you can do to make him comfortable,' Varco told them.

Hekton and Leopald went over to Koder.

'Where are you going, Erik?' Hekton asked.

'I'll be back in a minute.'

'Where are you going?'

'I saw something.'

Varco slithered down the dry slurry of the valley slope into the wreathing dust. Hot, scorching smoke billowed across him from the various wrecks, and he held his scarf across his mouth and nose. Most of the wrecks were just tangles of metal debris. Spilled oil and lube soaked the dry ground. He tried not to look too closely at the dead. Most of the corpses, thrown clear of exploding vehicles and often stripped of their clothes by the blast-force, had been run over or trampled by other fleeing elements, a final indignity. In places, the heavy feet of the bounding Warhounds had crushed bone, flesh and metal in their deep impressions. In those impacted footprints, true horrors lurked. The slicks of blood and oil, mirror surfaces, were slowly clouding with settling dust.

He trudged past a tug-hab, on its side and burning, a big-trak freighter crushed into the earth by a giant's wanton step, and two daku-maku, eviscerated by lasfire, as dead as their blood-soaked riders. He passed a damaged cybernetic drone that would never fly again. It gazed at him with broken optics and clacked its voiceless jaw.

Pity overtook him. He knelt down, fumbled to find the drone's CPU linkage, and snapped it out. The light in the broken eyes went out.

He rose, and wiped his mouth with his scarf. He'd seen something from the ridge, something *moving*.

Varco walked on a little way, past the flaming pyre of the minehead. Beyond it lay a smashed hab-crawler, overturned, its torn canvas awnings snapping in the wind. Two bodies lay nearby, an older woman and a young man, both dressed in wasteland gear. The young man wore insulated leather jack-armour and a rebreather mask fashioned to resemble a gorgon's screaming face. He was dead. Varco could tell that without examining him. A heavy wheel had crushed an ugly furrow across his torso. The woman was clad in twilight-grey silks, and wore a simple, ancient dust-mask over her face.

There wasn't a mark on her. It was only when he came to check her that Varco felt how cold she was and how loose the pivot of her neck.

A few metres away, a big, crimson duo-trak bike lay in the dust, its thick, front forks twisted around at a crazy angle, its treads split and broken. A man was sprawled beside it on his side. He was wearing dirty jack-armour and a rebreather mask made to look like the head of a desert lizard.

Varco crouched beside him. The man twitched. His left arm was evidently broken, and Varco wasn't sure what other injuries he'd suffered.

'Let me help you,' he said.

The man twitched again, and moaned.

'Sir, I'm Orestes Pride. I can help you, if you'll let me. I have med-kits.' *Two*, he thought. Just two. We can barely spare anything. Why am I doing this?

The man wheezed something. He was clearly in considerable pain.

'I'm going to turn you over, all right? Do you understand? I'm going to turn you over and take a look at your arm.'

Varco turned the man as carefully as he could. The man screamed, a scream that came out through his rebreather as a shrill, glottal burble.

'It's all right. It's all right. I can splint this, and make it more comfortable. Can you tell me if you're hurt anywhere else?'

He heard a hard, ratchetting click and felt a ring of cold metal press into the back of his head.

'You leave him be.'

Varco slowly raised his hands. 'I'm just trying to help him. Do you understand me? I'm just trying to help him.'

The gun muzzle kept pressing into Varco's scalp.

'You leave him be. You leave my da be. He don't need you. We don't need you.'

'Let me turn,' suggested Varco, his hands still raised. 'Can I turn? Is that all right? I'm going to turn around.'

He shifted round on his knees and found himself looking into the wrong end of an old and mighty las-lock rifle. It was an antique piece, its furniture richly carved, its metalwork finely engraved.

It was being aimed at him by a young man in jack-armour. The young man's face was covered by a breather mask designed to resemble a Warlord's cockpit.

The sight of it made Varco laugh, involuntarily.

'What are you supposed to be,' he smiled, 'a war engine?'

The snout of the las-lock butted forwards and split Varco's top lip across his teeth. He yelped and spat blood, his hands moving to his damaged face.

'Keep your hands up! Up, up, up!'

Varco spat blood again. He raised his hands.

'Is this your father?' he asked, nodding his head sideways at the stricken man beside them.

'So what if it is?'

'So... he needs help. Medical attention. Can you splint an arm? His left arm is broken. I can help him.'

'Maybe you can, maybe you can't. Who are you?'

'Erik Varco. Captain, Orestes Pride Armour Six.'

'Means nothing to me.'

'What's your name?' Varco asked.

'The hands. Keep them up!'

'I'm keeping them up. What's your name?'

'I don't give my name to no one. My da neither.'

'Your da needs help. I can help him.'

Engine-face didn't move.

'Are you going to let me help him?' Varco asked, staring down the long barrel of the powerful rifle.

'The Centaur's ready to roll, captain,' said Sagen, trudging back to Hekton and Leopald.

'Good,' said Hekton. 'Help us carry Koder to the back-bay.'

'Where's Captain Varco?' Sagen asked, bending down to take hold of Koder's legs.

'He went down into the valley,' Leopald replied.

'Why?'

Leopald shrugged.

Sagen pulled out his scope and took a look. 'Whereabouts?'

Hekton pointed vaguely. He was busy cleaning the blood from Koder's mouth and chin.

Sagen swore loudly.

'What?'

'Take a look,' Sagen said, passing the scope to Hekton. 'Down there. No, past the minehead. You see?'

'Oh, Throne,' said Hekton. 'Erik, you'll be the death of us all.'

Through the haze of drifting dust and smoke, Hekton could see what Sagen had spotted: Erik Varco, on his knees, hands raised, facing an indigent savage with an energy musket.

'Get me the carbine,' Hekton told Sagen. 'Run, man. Quickly!'

Hekton retrained the scope on his old friend.

'Oh, Varco, you silly bastard.'

Koder stirred.

'Captain!' Leopald called. 'The enginseer's coming around. I think–'

Prostrate on his back, Koder opened his eyes. They were bloodshot, the pupils blown. His cracked lips parted. He emitted a delirious stream of fractured code and passed out again.

It felt as if the wind had changed direction. Hekton rose to his feet and looked east, down the valley.

The trio of Warhounds were distant blobs, dots on the horizon.

One turned. At full stride, it began to plough back up the valley towards them.

'Oh no,' murmured Hekton. 'Oh, Throne, we're in trouble. Now we're *really* in trouble.'

'It heard the code burst,' murmured Leopald.

'Yes, it frigging well heard the code burst!' Hekton replied.

'What do we do?' asked Leopald.

'Sagen. Where's that carbine?' Hekton roared.

'What do we do, sir?' Leopald repeated, looking at Hekton in panic. 'We can't fight that.'

'No, we can't,' Hekton agreed. The Warhound was bounding up the valley towards them, the size of a zephyrid, and then the size of a crow, closing, closing...

Sagen ran back from the Centaur and tossed the carbine to Hekton. Trask was with him.

'Play dead, all of you,' Hekton ordered.

'What?'

'Get into cover and play dead, for Throne's sake, and pray that's enough!'

Hekton began to scramble down the slope into the valley.

Varco felt the ground tremble. Loose rocks skittered. The wounded indigent beside him murmured.

'Something's coming,' he said to the boy with the las-lock. 'We have to hide.'

'I don't trust you.'

'Then trust your own eyes!' Varco spat, risking a glance over his shoulder. Through the dust, he saw the black, diseased shape of the Warhound bounding down the valley towards them. 'For frig's sake, boy!'

'D-do as the man says, Kell!' the wounded indigent groaned. With a shaking right hand, the only one that would work any more, he pulled off his breather mask, revealing the face of an old man, lined and wizened by desert living. His white, walrus moustache was spectacularly bushy.

'I mean it, Kell!' the old man ordered, a sharp thread of pain in his voice.

Engine-face kept the las-lock aimed at Varco's head.

'Da, but it could be a trick. He could be one of them. Don't trust no one, that's what you and muma always taught us.'

'Muma's dead,' the old man sighed, looking over at the body of the older woman in the twilight-grey silks. Tears welled in his eyes. 'Oh, Shenna. And my poor Bekk too.'

Engine-face glanced at the older woman's limp form. The las-lock began to lower.

Behind him, Varco could hear the Warhound pounding ever closer. Pebbles knocked and trickled at every pace. Ripples pulsed across the puddles of oil and blood around them.

'This isn't a trick,' he said carefully. 'We have to run and hide or that engine will–'

'Drop the weapon!' Hekton yelled, running in through the dust, the carbine aimed. 'Drop it. Drop it now!'

Engine-face half-turned to face him, the las-lock swinging around.

'Don't make me take you, sir!' Hekton called, aiming his weapon with military finesse. 'Drop it, I said!'

'Drop it, for muma's sake, Kell,' the old man gasped.

Engine-face hesitated, and then threw the las-lock aside.

'See how I save your arse every time, Erik?' Hekton called out as he ran up, covering Engine-face.

'Every time,' Varco admitted, feeling the ground shuddering under him. He got up and looked at Engine-face. 'Help me carry your da into cover. Move it!'

'There's no time for that!' Hekton cried. 'You have to play dead!'

'What? Gram? Play dead?'

'Play dead, Erik! Please, for Throne's sake! Play dead, all of you, or we won't get out of this alive!'

The striding Warhound was five hundred metres away and closing fast.

'Lie still, sir. Don't move!' Varco told the old man.

The old man obediently curled up on his side.

'You heard. Play dead!' Varco shouted at Engine-face.

'But–'

'Play dead. Kell, is it? Play dead, Kell.'

'No, I–'

Varco threw himself at Engine-face and brought the youth down underneath him. They sprawled in the dust. Varco wrenched off the Warlord mask. He looked down into the terrified face of a girl no more than twenty years old. Varco blinked in surprise.

'Stay down. Stay still,' he told her.

Covering her with his body, Varco looked around at Hekton. 'Gram, you've got to get down too, you fool!'

Gram Hekton glanced back at him and grinned. 'Oh, don't worry. Stay down and don't you dare move.'

The Archenemy Warhound slowed its pounding course up the valley and raised its snout to sniff the air. It had felt a code burst, a trace of the thrice-hated Mechanicus. It surveyed the burning wreckage scattered before it, reading the cooling traces of dead machines and deader organics. It absorbed and studied the heat-waste residue inload, scanning for modified organics, resolving the world as a variegated fuzz of hot red and cold blue blobs.

It began to advance tentatively at low stride, its head hunched down beneath its carapace, crunching wreckage underfoot. Varco heard the squeal of collapsing metal and, far worse, the crack of bone.

The Warhound pinged its auspex, hunting for a source. Varco felt the prickle of the ping-wash, and felt the girl beneath him tremble as she sensed it. He heard the old man nearby stifle a groan as his broken bones vibrated.

Everything suddenly went cold and dark. The Warhound was right over them, its shadow spilling across them. It took another step, crushing a wrecked walker unit. It rocked back and forth on its hips, unsettled and curious.

His face pressed down into the dust, Varco heard a whir and ratchet as its weapon limbs auto-loaded. Time seemed to go into hibernation.

The Warhound took another step. It pinged its auspex again. It dribbled out a tempting invitation of scrapcode.

Please, please, please, Varco willed.

'Over here, you piece of shit!' a voice yelled out.

Varco heard the Warhound crank around and adjust its stance.

'Here I am!' yelled Hekton. 'Here. Over here!' He had broken cover and, at a sprint, was moving away from the wrecked hab-crawler. 'Here I am, you son of a bitch!'

As he ran, Hekton took a pot-shot at the Warhound with his carbine. The round splashed off its voids.

The Warhound shuffled around, trying to track the tiny human leaping and dashing through the wreckage around its feet.

Hekton leaped over a crumpled uni-strider and turned to fire the carbine up at the towering engine again.

'Come on!' he yelled, defiantly.

'Oh, Gram,' Varco choked. 'Gram, please don't do this...'

'Come on, you bastard-son!' Hekton mocked. 'Here I am. You see me? Here I am!'

Hekton set the carbine to full auto and sprayed the legs and lower chassis of the Warhound. The shots ricocheted off its voids. Uttering a jubilant cry, Hekton set off through the wreckage again, ducking and swerving, running as fast as he could.

With a creak of metal, pistons turning, the Warhound swung around and began to pace after him.

Running, jumping, vaulting through the debris field away from Varco and the hab-crawler, Gram Hekton kept yelling insults over his shoulder at the towering monster. He paused occasionally, and shot at it, spanking bolts off its voids, off its cockpit lights, off its carapace.

'Come on, you bastard! You see me, don't you? You see me? Come on!'

The Warhound raised its stride-rate and began to crash through the wrecked vehicles to run him down.

'Here. Here. Here I am. What are you, slow? I'm right here!'

The Warhound answered with a burst of indignant scrap-code. It bore on, kicking wreckage out of its path.

Hekton came to a halt between a burning cargo-10 and a crushed utility drive. He shouldered the carbine and framed its sight on the gigantic engine ploughing after him.

'So, you notice me at last? Well done. Took your time. Here I am!'

Oh, Gram. Oh, Gram...

Hekton aimed his carbine up at the Warhound bearing

down on him and clenched the trigger. A steady stream of lasbolts stripped up through the air and kissed off the lower void shields.

'Come on then, you bastard!' Hekton yelled. 'What are you waiting for?'

The Warhound wasn't waiting for anything.

Its left weapon limb burped a single pulse of las and vaporised Gram Hekton. When the rancid smoke cleared, there was nothing left except a smoking crater and a few steaming long bones.

The Warhound waited, hesitating, clicking and whirring to itself. It was looking for movement.

Reading nothing, it turned and strode away down the valley, loping east after its murderous colleagues.

>

The executor's crawler, trailed by its vast escort, lumbered into the Jeromihah Subsids, following Invicta's mass advance.

'The war is focused in the west now, executor?' Etta asked.

'It is too early to say we have them on the run, but the balance is shifting, mamzel,' Crusius replied. He was studying displays on the bridge. Turning, he called out to Lysenko. 'Ahead full, Lysenko. The engines are out-pacing us. I won't have that!'

'Aye, executor!' Lysenko returned.

Etta felt the crawler's drive throb up a notch.

'Are we looking at victory, sir?' she asked.

Crusius smiled his peerless smile at her. 'Of course.'

At her side, Gotch muttered to himself.

'Something you want to share, major?' Crusius asked.

'Not at all, sir,' Gotch replied.

'My bodyman was simply making a private remark to me, executor,' Etta said.

'I think your bodyman forgets the fine tuning of modified ears, mamzel,' Crusius said. He paused, and augmitted a perfect playback of Gotch's voice: *'The engine-boys are just chasing their own arses all over the sub.'*

Etta glanced at Gotch and he blushed.

'My bodyman–' she began.

Crusius raised a hand. 'No need for comment, Etta.'

'I apologise, sir,' said Gotch gruffly.

'For what exactly?' asked Crusius.

'For... doubting the success ratio of your forces, sir.'

Crusius scratched a finger behind his right ear, frowning. 'I understand,' he said. 'I understand. The expression of this war is governed by two conflicting elements: public morale and actual materiel gain. I won't lie to you, Etta. I may say I never have. Orestes remains on the brink. Invicta has achieved several significant gains... Undergox Edge, the Titan Steps... but this war is far from done. Gotch understands that, don't you, major?'

'I think so, sir,' Gotch replied.

'We have to keep the hives happy, Etta. We have to send them good news. The good news may not be the whole truth.'

'I'm not a fool, executor,' she replied. 'I understand how public relations work.'

'Of course. And the data you send back to your Lord Governor, that has to be more brutally accurate, doesn't it?'

'Yes.'

'I know it does. The Lord Governor has a right to know how things are actually going.'

'Have you been intercepting my messages, executor?' Etta asked.

Crusius paused and smiled. 'Did you, for a moment, believe I wouldn't?'

'No,' she replied, smiling despite her indignation.

Crusius shrugged. 'Here are the clear, cold facts. This is what we're not telling the hive habbers. We've broken them at Undergox, and through Jeromihah. We've made multiple engine kills for few losses. Invicta has robbed them of their momentum.'

'But?'

'Must there be a but, Etta?'

'Always, I think, executor.'

Crusius nodded. 'But… they are marshalling their forces around Argentum, and orbital tracks suggest they are pushing elements in around Gynex and up through the subsids. This war is balanced, but it is not won. I must say I am alarmed by the disingenuity of the orbital tracks. No matter. By dawn tomorrow, the main thrust of Invicta's engines will advance on the subsid beyond Argentum. With the Emperor's grace, we will break their strength there.'

'What alarms you, executor?' Etta asked.

'I'm sorry?'

'I said, executor, what alarms you? What was that about the orbital tracks?'

'Nothing of any importance.'

'Tell me anyway.'

Crusius demurred. 'The fleet is having problems reading the surface tracks here and here.' He indicated the areas on the underlit hololithic table.

'The Western Prospection?' she asked.

'I'm told it's storm residue. There was a big storm last night.'

'Yes, over the Astrobleme. I monitored the meteorological scans myself. But in the north-west?'

'A secondary storm front, so the fleet reckons. It's currently blocking our scans.'

'Is it significant?'

'No.'

'Is it natural, executor?'

'Of course. It must be. Trust me, by dawn, we will have broken the temper out of them and turned them back.'

>

'Where was this material uncovered?' the Adept Seniorus asked.

'My staff came upon it by chance, sir,' said Feist. 'In a basic overview of the encysted data, we–'

'Hush, Feist,' said Egan.

Feist fell silent and waited as the Adept Seniorus finished reviewing the data that was hololithically projected in front of him. Even when he was done, he could not take his eyes from the glowing text on the display.

'Have you any idea of the implications of this?' he asked.

'Yes, my adept, I believe–'

'Again, will you hush, Feist?' Egan said. 'The Adept Seniorus is addressing me. Yes, my lord, I understand the significance but–'

'As a matter of fact, Egan, I was addressing the young man there. Feist, isn't it?'

'Yes, sir.'

The Adept Seniorus shifted his position to look at Feist. 'This data you have brought to my attention, what do you understand of it?'

Feist cleared his throat, aware that Egan was staring at him. 'It is an old document, sir, a very old document…'

'More than ten thousand years old, Feist. Go on.'

'It purports to convey evidence that validates the Orestean view of the Omnissiah, sir.'

The Adept Seniorus smiled at Egan. '"Purports", Egan. Listen to how the young man self-edits.'

'Adept Feist is the very model of restraint, sir,' Egan replied.

The Adept Seniorus turned his attention back to the display. 'This is heresy. Heresy, from a time before such a term mattered. This text denies His sanctity.'

Feist shivered. He had never heard the small word 'his' carry such shocking force.

'This–' Egan began. 'This is enormous.'

'Yes, Egan my old friend,' the Adept Seniorus said, nodding. 'It actually is.'

The Adept Seniorus's private residence felt unbearably warm. Feist realised that he was trembling. He could actually feel the glacial creep of history being made. He adjusted his biologics deftly, and brought his panicked metabolism under control. This was a time for a clear head and a steady heart.

'This text,' he said, 'effectively settles the matter of the Schism at a stroke. It clarifies issues that the Mechanicus has been debating for ten millennia.'

'If it is authentic,' Egan warned.

'Magos,' Feist replied levelly, 'everything we have so far extracted from the sequestered vaults has proven to be painfully authentic. We have tested the data in engine fights, and it has not been found wanting.'

Egan shook his head. 'It is wrong,' he said. 'Even though I want it to be true, to be conclusive, it is wrong.'

The Adept Seniorus shook his ancient head. 'It is simply old, Egan.' He rose to his feet. Feist stepped forwards immediately to steady him. Solomahn Imanual patted Feist's arm gratefully as he rested against it. He sighed.

'We brought this on ourselves,' he reflected. 'We brought this on ourselves when we opened the sequestered vaults.' He looked sidelong at Feist. 'I'm not blaming you, boy. It was a smart suggestion, and one that has benefited the war immeasurably. But the things I've read, these last few days... Egan's brought me several realbooks to look at, haven't you, Egan?'

Feist glanced at his senior. Egan blushed.

'I thought they would amuse you, Adept Seniorus,' said Egan.

'Amuse me, he says.' Imanual laughed. 'You brought them to me because you didn't know what to do with them and you didn't know who to show them to.'

'Is this true, magos?' Feist asked Egan. 'Have you taken material directly from the archive without allowing us to examine it first?'

Egan opened his mouth, and then shrugged instead of speaking.

'Rest assured, Feist, there was nothing in them of tactical value,' the Adept Seniorus said. 'I studied them carefully.'

'What were they, may I ask, sir?' Feist asked.

'Other works like this one,' Imanual replied, gesturing at the display with a dendrite. 'Ancient gospels, unpalatable truths; most of them too uncomfortable to consider.' He paused.

'Where are they now, sir?' Feist asked.

'I had them destroyed. Oh, don't look so shocked, Feist. What would you have done with them?'

Feist blinked. He had no answer.

Imanual's eyes were narrow and sly. 'Exactly correct, adept. Nothing. Silence. I wish to all the machine spirits that I had found this one too, and erased it before... before it came to this.'

'But, with respect, sir,' said Feist, 'this material is vital to our understanding of our place in the galaxy. It defines the Mechanicus. It provides us with the proof we've been searching for. It should never have been sequestered and it should not be censored and destroyed.'

Imanual patted Feist's arm again. 'So headstrong, the young. So determined to uphold the truth, no matter the cost. Have you considered the cost, Feist?'

Feist hesitated. 'There would, of course, be repercussions, sir, but–'

'Repercussions, he says. Repercussions!' Solomahn Imanual augmitted a strange, electronic guffaw. 'We argue over the Schism, we debate and speculate. Some forges, such as ours, believe one thing; other elements of our great empire, such as Invicta, as I understand it, believe others. This speculation, these contrary beliefs, are tolerated for the good of free thought. But Feist, my dear Adept Feist, for better or for worse, the Mechanicus is an integral part of a vast and ancient society. The Mechanicus and the Imperium have grown so far together that we have become entirely reliant on one another, and our union depends upon an implicit understanding that the God-Emperor of Mankind is also the Omnissiah of the Mechanicus. What do you suppose would happen, Adept Feist, if we put the lie to that?'

Feist opened his mouth, and then closed it again.

'The Imperium is old and worn,' said Egan quietly, 'and embattled on all sides by rapacious enemies. A truth like this would drive a chisel through its foundations and collapse it entirely. Mechanicus and Imperium would dissolve their unity.'

'And neither could survive alone,' whispered Feist.

'And neither could survive alone,' echoed Solomahn Imanual. 'Precisely. You understand, Feist. The truth is a beautiful thing, but it will kill us. No wonder, then, that we sequester it. It is too bright to look upon.'

'Assessment: what do we do, sir?' asked Egan.

'Purge this material, Egan.'

'You can't!' Feist exclaimed.

'We must, adept, for the sake of survival.' The Adept Seniorus sat back down at his station. 'Watch, Feist. I am making an encrypted copy. I will send it to Mars. You're right, it is too valuable to erase. Understand, Mars will sequester it. In years to come, perhaps, it will be useful. Now, it is too dangerous for anyone's eyes. Who's seen this?'

'Feist showed it to me,' said Egan.

'Adept Lunos found it in the first place,' said Feist.

'Will she have talked?'

'No, sir.'

'Take this Lunos to one side, Egan. Make her understand. If she appears unwilling, erase her immediate inload and buffers.'

'Yes, my lord.'

Solomahn Imanual looked gravely at the pair of them. 'Egan? Feist? I'm asking you both to forget you ever saw this. I'm going to delete it now and–'

He paused. The three of them had just become aware of a blizzard of traffic suddenly inundating the noosphere.

'Somebody explain this unseemly commotion,' the Adept Seniorus demanded.

Feist was already hunting and scanning, using haptic touches to rake his way through the high-volume data flooding across all noospheric fields. It took him four point three seconds to locate the trigger source. 'It's been published,' he said.

'What?' asked Egan, cold and wary.

'This material is on the noosphere. All pages, all specs. Somebody leaked it.'

'Holy Omnissiah,' murmured the Adept Seniorus. 'We're going to have the mother of all panics on our hands.'

1101

The panic spread. It rolled out through the Hive Principal and beyond like the thumping tremors of a seismic event. Various sections of the High Forge and its noospheric sub-networks shut down or went comm-opaque. Disorder and rioting erupted in the streets, especially in the lower quarters and the sink-levels. The PDF moved in. Cordons of guards were despatched to police all the significant Imperial shrines and temples in the main hive area. In the covered cloisters and inner courtyards of the Great Ministoria itself, the hierophants of the Orestean Ecclesiarchy and their servants gathered in splenetic huddles, demanding audience with, and comment from, Gaspar Luciul. The prelate ecumenic ignored their entreaties and envoys, and kept himself in camera, conferring with his most senior and intimate aides.

In his residence at the summit of Orestes Principal, the Lord Governor rose to his feet and went over to the thick, shielded window. He gazed down at the smoke-hazed bulk of the forge as if it were a child that had unexpectedly and wilfully disappointed him.

'What the Throne is this?' he asked nobody in particular. 'What the holy Throne *is* this? In time of war, the Mechanicus does *this*? Get the old bastard on the link immediately.'

The attending aide nearest to him paused. He could almost feel wrath radiating out of the Lord Governor like heat. 'Uh, pardon me, sir, but by "the old bastard" do you mean the Adept Seniorus?'

Aleuton wheeled, furious. 'Yes, I damn well do. Get him. Get him for me now!'

The aide attempted to obey his master. 'My lord, all links are jammed. The comm-web is frozen with traffic weight.'

'Simple vox?'

'That too, sir.'

'Keep trying, and send a courier to the forge. In fact, send a platoon of our best men, armed. Get them to demand an audience. Tell them not to take no for an answer. I will not have this.'

'Yes, my lord,' replied the aide, hurrying from the chamber and calling for the staff guardsmen.

'Public disturbances reported in the Bulwarks and Transept, my lord,' the chief of staff announced, looking up from his link-enabled slate.

'Contain them. Increase the PDF strength!'

'My lord, we don't have–'

'Mobilise the fourth reserves! Mobilise all Orestes Pride personnel barracked in the hive. Get this quashed!'

Stefan Samstag hadn't gone back to the hab on Makepole. He'd slept rough in an underblock warehouse instead, intending to clear his head and make his way home after daybreak.

When he woke, grey daylight poking in through the warehouse's air bricks and roof lights, he realised that his plans were going to have to change. There was a great commotion in the streets outside. There were magistrates everywhere, PDF squads too, moving from block to block as if they were hunting for something.

He knew they were looking for him. They were out to get him for what he'd done to the longshoreman.

Stefan Samstag moaned quietly. His head throbbed and his gut churned. His mouth was as dry as vac-crate packing. He slipped out of the musty warehouse, kept to the shadows of the undersink walk behind Happen Hill, and quenched his thirst at a public water fountain on the corner of Lumbercut Row where it met the steps down into Sink Hollow. As he cupped his hands to drink, he tried to wash the blood off his knuckles and scrape the dried residue out from around his nails. His clothes were caked in it. The blood didn't show so badly on his dark breeches, but there were incriminating brown smears on his shirt and jacket.

He knew that passers-by were looking at him.

Stefan hurried away down the wide stone steps into the dingy under level streets of Sink Hollow, slipped along the narrow alleys that ran between the backs of the tenement habs, and kept his face down.

His disgust with himself became absolute when he snatched a damp vest and work-shirt off the washing line of a sink hab and ran.

Even the under level streets were busy. He hid behind some rubbish carts as a Magistratum carrier whooped by, and then prised away some of the rotting fibre-plank boarding up the rear of a derelict hab unit and hauled himself inside.

The place smelled of mildew, urine and despair. It had been empty for several years. A few wretched sticks of furniture remained in the dingy living space. Upstairs, in an attic bedroom, there was a rusted cot frame with a bare, stained mattress. He lay down on it, the stolen clothing clutched to his chest.

High up, under the eaves of the little room, he saw the remains of the hab's domestic shrine. Cobwebs hung like a gauze veil over the crude, tarnished aquila. Stefan got up, went over to the shrine and scooped the cobwebs away. They felt like silk. He blew out the dust, and coughed as it billowed.

Then he knelt down on the rough floorboards.

He thought of Castria, of Reinhart and the dock crew, and of the Tanith longshoreman who had driven him over the edge. In his head, he saw the little domestic shrine in his hab in Makepole sink. He remembered the posy of flowers in the tiny, glass offering bottle that Cally had refreshed every day, without fail, until she had gone away.

Not one single, articulate prayer would form, not a word of contrition, not a plea for salvation, not even the Common Prayer of the Throne they had recited every morning at school.

He felt he had nothing to say to the God-Emperor, nothing that would matter.

He'd killed a man, and they were coming for him, and the worst of it was, Cally would never forgive him.

Servants and magi of the Mechanicus were being stoned and abused on the street in the mid-hive. Several low-grade errand servitors had been smashed by rioting crowds. The PDF began to close down street blocks and order crowds to disperse.

Zink decided not to unlock the gates of the Worthies Garden that morning. As the sun began to creep out across the lawns and paths, he stole away to his shed. Angry mobs were boiling up Lentement Row, and people were hurling bottles, cobbles and abuse over the garden wall. Zink was scared, and winced as the missiles damaged the flowerbeds and chipped the busts.

Plemil would come soon, bearing his breakfast. Then things would be better. Plemil would order them all to go away, and then Zink could begin to sweep up the mess.

'Traitor!' the man screamed into Zember's face.

'But, sir, I just–'

'Mechanicus lackey!'

'Sir, I only–'

The man punched him in the mouth and broke one of his teeth. Then he spat on him. Zember backed off, inflamed by pain and outrage. He fended the man off with a broom and bolted the door of *Anatometa*. The man began to hammer furiously on the shop's door. It shook in its frame.

Zember frantically wound the shutters down across the door and front windows. Rocks clanged off the metal shutters as they dropped. Outside, in the level eighty-eight commercia, people were running mad. They had simply lost their minds.

Secure for the moment, Zember tried to steady his old heart. He spat the broken bits of tooth into an enamel cup, and looked down at the little fragments of yellow ivory suspended in pink spittle.

'What in the name of the God-Emperor did I ever do?' he whimpered, feeling at the sore socket with the tip of his tongue.

Rocks and cobbles continued to thud off the shutters sporadically. Ranged along his counter, the brightly painted Titans, spick and span and ready for war, gazed back at him, as if awaiting an order to ignite their drives and walk in defence of the shop.

The open pict-player was receiving the public feed. Data scrolled up the screen. The word 'heresy' was being used repeatedly. His hands shaking with shock, Zember read and re-read the astonishing news.

'This can't be,' he said, his words slurred by his swelling lips. 'This won't do at all. How can this be true?'

Zember looked up at the pale dolls perched on the shelves.

They did not answer him. They seemed to be averting their painted and polished glass eyes, as if finding other things to be interested in.

They seemed to be disapproving.

>

Etta Severin was compiling her latest report when Gotch knocked quietly at her cabin door.

'What is it, Gotch?' she asked, letting him in. 'Has the main advance begun already? Crusius said–'

Gotch closed the cabin door behind him and slid the bolt. That alarmed her. When Gotch drew his sidearm and checked the load, her heart began to flutter.

'Major? What the Throne is going on?'

'Have you not linked to Principal yet today, mamzel?' he asked.

'No. There's some kind of problem with the communication service. I presumed it was atmospherics.'

'It's not,' he replied.

'Gotch? You're scaring me.'

Gotch looked at her. His eyes were hard and dark, like the painted eyes of a porcelain doll. The scar on his right cheek was as horseshoe-shaped as the day it had been made. His lips were flat and tight.

'I'm scaring myself, mamzel,' Gotch replied. He holstered his pistol and crossed to his kit bag, stuffed into a stowage alcove. She watched as he began to unpack two sets of body armour and the ceramite weapon-box that held his hellgun, cased in disconnected sections.

'You're going to be safe, mamzel,' he said as he worked. 'I swear it to you, like I swore it to the Lord Governor. I will keep you safe.'

'From what? Gotch, from what?'

He opened the weapon-box with his biometrics and began to take out the sections of his main weapon. Etta jumped as each part clacked together. Gotch assembled the gun with deft, professional finesse.

'Throne alone knows,' he replied, concentrating on his business. 'The Mechanicus, perhaps? I was up on the bridge with Crusius. The links just went mad. Something's happened in the hive.'

'Something like what?' she asked.

'As far as I can tell,' he replied, locking the hellgun's stock into place, 'the Mechanicus just publicly distributed a text that disavows the Emperor.'

'That...?' She hesitated. 'What did you just say to me?'

'It's all gone off, mamzel. The forge just went public with proof that our Emperor, our Emperor, isn't their Omnissiah after all.'

'Slow down, major. You're not making much sense.'

Gotch redrew his pistol and offered it to her, grip first.

'Can you handle a weapon? Woman like you, I bet you can.'

'Put that away and talk to me!' she snapped.

'No time,' Gotch replied.

'Put it away, major!' she ordered.

Gotch shrugged, and slipped the heavy pistol back into his holster.

'Now, tell me exactly what the hell is going on.'

He blinked, stung by the sound of a high-born female using such a low-sink word. He chose his words carefully.

'A text, an old text, went public in Orestes Principal late last night, source unknown, but, you can bet your pretty face, it came from the forge. It purports to be undeniable proof that our God-Emperor is not the Omnissiah that the Mechanicus worships. *Irrefutable*, that's the word frigging Crusius used, pardon my sink-talk.'

'Excused. Go on.'

'Well, that's it. The entire basis of the Imperial relationship with the Mechanicus is up the spout. They're claiming – *proving*, thank you Throne – that the Emperor isn't divine after all, not to them. Not in their eyes. If this goes the way I think it's going to go, there's going to be a lot of blood lost over it.'

Etta stared at him. He waited for a moment to see if she'd speak, and then set about assembling his weapon with renewed vigour.

'Stop that,' she instructed, holding up her hand. 'Stop it, Gotch. I can't think!'

He stopped, and dropped the semi-formed hellgun onto his lap. 'What is there to think about?' he asked.

She shook her head, wondering. 'A schism. According to the old lore, the Martian forges only joined with us on the simple understanding that we shared the same god. They acknowledged our Emperor as a facet of their own deity. We were divided empires linked by a common belief.'

'Yeah, that was then,' he said. 'It's all gone up the hairy now. Seems they can prove their god isn't our god, and our god isn't a god at all. The forge has gone into meltdown. The hive has gone berserk. There's rioting.'

'I can guess.'

He shrugged. 'And the rest. Faith panic. Public stonings. Adepts are burning effigies of the Emperor in Forge Avenue. Our own frigging people burning effigies of the Omnissiah in Imperial Place. It's a mess, mamzel. But I need you to know that I'll look after you, whatever. That's my job.'

'I appreciate that, major. Look after me despite what? Crusius?'

Gotch shook his head. 'He's all right. I think he's pretty sound, but he's been thrown over the wire by this, like us. He's all messed up. However, he did tell me to come down here and secure your circumstances.'

She stared at him. 'This is you securing my circumstances? I've never had my circumstances secured before.'

Gotch grinned and the horseshoe scar did its ugly curl. 'Get used to it, mamzel,' he said. 'Crusius is worried that certain parties on this crawler won't stand for an Imperial presence aboard.'

'And you think?' she asked.

Gotch clunked the muzzle of his hellgun into place and connected the power feed. There was a slow, rising whine of power.

'I think it's us and them, mamzel,' he replied.

Etta nodded. 'I agree.'

'Good,' said Gotch.

'Zamual, I trust you to look after me.'

He nodded. 'Bet your pretty face.'

'When you say that, are you mocking me? I've had juvenat work done, as I'm sure you must realise. Are you mocking me, major?'

'Not one bit, mamzel.'

Touched, she hid her smile. 'You mentioned that you thought I could handle a weapon. You thought I was *that kind* of woman?'

'Sure. Are you?' he asked.

Etta nodded. In one fluid move, he slid out his pistol and tossed it to her. She caught it, braced it, raised it, and racked the slide to check the load.

'Thought so,' he grinned.

'My father taught me.'

'I didn't think there was any love lost there,' Gotch remarked.

'There wasn't. But he knew how to kill.'

'That's a blessing then, mamzel,' Gotch said. He rose to his feet, the hellgun's power pack strung over his right shoulder, the assembled weapon comfortable in his grip.

Down below, in the lower levels of the crawler, voices had raised. Etta heard shouting, running footsteps and hands banging on compartment doors.

'You and me, then, eh, Zamual?' she said.

'Wouldn't have it any other way, mamzel,' he answered.

>

The sun raised its head slowly, as if its neck were sore. The dust storm abusing Beaten Track had blown out in the small hours.

Cally Samstag shoved open the outer door of the modular.

Sand drift had been driven up against it in the night, and wedged it shut. She stepped outside.

In the dingy modular behind her, the remains of Activated Twenty-Six were waking up. Robor had settled into a restless dream state, a state in which, Cally was certain, the dying princeps had been whispering to him. Golla had sat up, watching over them.

Outside, the light was fuzzy and golden. A residue of dust was settling, smelling of graphite, and the sun beamed through it. It felt as though the world had been gilt-plated. It was calm and quiet.

Cally stretched. She looked at the rising sun and nodded, whispering her morning prayers. For want of a shrine, the sun would do.

Zhakarnov came out of the modular behind her, and gazed up into the sunlight as he lit a lho-stick.

'A fair morning, ma'am,' he remarked, fiddling with his beard. 'Any plans for today?'

'I'm considering several. Want to make a suggestion?'

Zhakarnov shrugged. 'We hold the life of a precious princeps in our care,' he replied. 'I suggest we make for the nearest hive.'

'Noted,' Cally replied.

Coughing like a badly flued furnace, Fiersteen emerged from the modular. Zhakarnov offered him one of his lho-sticks, but all Fiersteen took was a light, igniting one of his noxious cheroots.

'At friggin' last,' he sighed as he took the first suck.

Cally wrinkled her nose as the smoke reached her.

'You did well yesterday, finding this place,' Cally said to Zhakarnov. He seemed surprised.

'Thank you, ma'am,' he replied.

'We're all in this together, Mister Zhakarnov,' she said.

'It's Ludwin.'

'I beg your pardon?'

'My name is Ludwin.'

'Then thank you, Ludwin.' Cally looked at Fiersteen. He was enjoying his smoke with every ounce of his body. He grinned his bad teeth at her. 'Fancy spiking that vox, then?' he asked.

'I've prepared a signal,' Cally replied, holding up her data-slate.

'Very thorough,' Fiersteen remarked. He tossed the butt of his cheroot away and ground it under the heel of his service boot. 'Let's you and me, then.'

Fiersteen sat back from the old voxcaster and sighed.

'What's the matter?' asked Iconis.

'The power cells are fried out,' Fiersteen said.

'Dead, you mean?' Cally replied. 'That's why we're going to spike them.'

Fiersteen shook his head. 'No, I mean fried.'

'But last night–' Cally began.

'Last night they were fine,' said Fiersteen. 'I looked them over. They were fine. Now they're fried.'

'What are you saying?' asked Cally.

'I'm saying somebody already spiked it,' said Fiersteen.

Cally turned to the others. 'Who did this?' she asked. 'Who burned out our only working vox?' Her angry gaze switched from face to face. 'Answer me! Who did it? Who transmitted? What did they transmit?'

'Look here, missus,' Fiersteen muttered. He was still fiddling around. 'Whoever did it, they were in a bit of a hurry. They left something behind.' He had opened the voxcaster's top cover, and found a silver signet ring, locked bezel-first into the data-reader. 'Who does this belong to, I wonder?'

He twisted the ring to disconnect it, and handed it to Cally.

She studied it. 'It's a data ring,' said Fiersteen, 'encrypted with a core of classified content and built to match any standard data-reader port. Expensive piece of kit. Must be someone's.'

No one said anything, but Cally already knew.

'Janny?'

Janny Wirmac, curled up in the corner of the modular space, turned her head in Cally's direction, but refused to make eye contact.

'This is yours, isn't it?'

Janny nodded.

'What did you do, Janny?'

Janny stared at the floor. 'I heard what Mister Fiersteen said last night,' she said quietly, 'about how to spike a vox. I did it when you were all asleep. My papa gave me the ring. He said it would keep me safe. He said I should use it if I was ever in trouble. Now, he knows where I am and his men will be able to find me.'

'You transmitted our location?'

'How long ago, Janny?'

'Three hours ago, maybe?' She started to cry.

Cally put the ring in her pocket and looked back at the rest of the group. 'The fact that the vox is fried is the least of our problems. Three hours ago, we gave our position away.'

'Someone will have heard,' said Iconis.

'Anything could have heard,' Reiss corrected.

Cally nodded. 'We're going to have to move fast,' she said.

Cally went into the back room of the modular where Robor sat, connected to the princeps on the stretcher.

'Robor?' she said softly. 'Can you hear me? Robor, we're going to have to move.'

Robor slowly looked up at her with slightly mystified eyes, as if he didn't recognise her.

'Samstag?'

'That's right, Robor. We have to move. It's morning. Can you walk?'

Robor thought for a moment. 'We are weak,' he replied quietly, 'and the hole in our heart is still healing. There is a great deal of pain. Memory damage, and psycho-stigmatic nerve trauma. We were connected to the link when the MIU died. We may not live. Healing may be too great a task to achieve. We are only living because Robor has joined us as one to share his strength and carry part of the pain.'

'Am I talking to Robor?' Cally asked.

'Of course. We are Robor.'

Cally realised that Golla was standing behind her. 'He's been saying stuff like that all night,' said Golla. 'They've become one being, like conjoined twins. Robor is keeping him alive by taking some of the trauma away.'

'Is that safe?' Cally asked.

'Beyond me, Cally-girl. I do babies. Babies is what I know. Not this...' Golla nodded at Robor and the princeps and trailed off, unable to find words that properly articulated her revulsion.

'Did he ever say his name?'

Golla shook her head. 'Not his name, but a name.'

'What was it?'

'Teratos Titanicus.'

It was a name Cally remembered Stefan using. It was the name of one of the Legio Tempestus's most celebrated engines.

* * *

Searching Beaten Track by daylight, Antic, Lasco and Vulk found an old, four-wheeled barrow in the back of a shed. It was little more than a wooden cart, with rusted iron tyres on the warped wheels, but it was light enough for them to roll it between them, and sturdy enough to carry the stretcher.

Activated Twenty-Six came out of the modular into the hazy sunlight and watched as Vulk, Iconis and Golla settled the stretcher on the cart. Moving stiffly, like a somnambulist, Robor was obliged to walk beside the cart to preserve his plugged link.

'Are we set?' Cally asked. There were a few nods, and a couple of quiet replies. She went back into the modular. Janny Wirmac was still curled up in the corner.

'Janny? Come on,' Cally said.

Janny glanced up. Her eyes were red. 'You want me to come with you?' she asked.

'Of course I do.'

'But, I... I...'

'I'm not leaving anybody behind,' Cally told her firmly. 'Get up and get your things.'

Rejoining the others outside, Cally heard a distant rumble.

'What was that?' asked Antic.

'Thunder,' said Cally.

'You sure?'

'Let's hope so,' she said.

>

Gearhart reviewed the distressing intelligence from Orestes Principal. It beggared belief that anyone would make such scandalous claims public during a planetary crisis.

The pernicious data was everywhere. The entire communication architecture of the hive zone had almost seized up with the weight of traffic. In uncountable numbers, people were attempting to incant the source data and examine it for themselves. They were exloading commentaries, responses, demands for authentication, calls to arms, desperate appeals for common sense to prevail, terrified exclamations of doctrinal anguish, and pleas for guidance and salvation.

From the Forge, the noosphere had become almost uncantable. Magi and adepts, whole departments and specialists were locked in furious and thoroughly undignified noospheric debates. There was no discipline, just warring data flows: a maelstrom of information and opinion, comment and threat, rebuke and abuse. Factions were forming, and Gearhart had registered at least a dozen open threats of violence, but it was hard to pick much out in the blizzard of data-noise.

Gearhart was personally troubled by the disclosures. No servant of the Mechanicus could remain unmoved by the implications contained within the revelations, but his focus was entirely on the execution and its successful prosecution. The pandemonium gripping the hives he was trying to defend was impeding the efficiency of his forces. The hive and its subsids could not be relied upon for effective support, either in terms of materiel supplies or coordinated military responses. Vital sources of strategic data from Principal, including access to the Hostile Catalogue at the Analyticae, had become patchy. Furthermore, the gross overuse of the communication networks and the noosphere was having an effect on the Manifold. Though a discrete system, the Manifold was serviced by the zone's communication architecture, and in less than two hours, its flow speed and response time had been degraded by two per cent.

Unacceptable. Quite unacceptable.

On top of everything else, his crews had been rattled by the news. Word had spread through the legio, through the support echelons and the ranks of the skitarii and auxiliary armour, to the engine crews.

And the day had started so promisingly.

At dawn, *Invictus Antagonistes* had begun a walk on Argentum Hive. Five battlegroups, a total of twenty-eight engines, had formed the advance. Gearhart's engine led the first group, Bohrman's *Divinitus Monstrum* the second, and *Sicarian Faero* the third, with Tempestus Warlords *Orestes Magnificat* and *Cullador Braxas* honoured with command of the fourth and fifth. Sixty-two per cent of Lau's ground forces, reinforced by Tempestus skitarii files, had advanced with them. A second front, led by *Ajax Excelsus*, old Levin's engine, was striding up from Gynex in the south to bolster them on the approach to Argentum.

Gearhart's battlegroups had pushed out of Gox at first light and moved at mid-stride into the deeply contested zones of Jeromihah. After a brief pause while Dorentine's cataphractii engaged in an artillery duel with enemy ground forces, the advance had gained momentum. In the twisted wastes of the Boroma Konstruct mass engineering complex, a fifty hectare site alongside Prospect Highway, the first real blood of the day had been spilled. Stent Racine's *Philopos Manix*, shadowed by the Warhound *Morbius Sire*, had faced down an Archenemy Warlord and blown it to shreds. Less than ten minutes later *Vengesus Gressor* reported an engine kill, and then *Lupus Lux*, Krugmal's princepture, stalking as adroitly and loyally as any good gundog, smoked out a brace of enemy Reavers that had been closeted in the ruins of a plate works near the Shaltar spur of the main highway. *Lupus Lux*, as fast and dogged as any Warhound in the legio, had driven them into the open, ably supported in said enterprise by long-range barrage fire from *Divinitus Monstrum*. The first of the enemy Reavers had gone down under the guns of *Amadeus Phobos* on the main highway, a bloody, thundering death. The second, turning hard west at full stride in an effort to break towards Gox, had run right into Gearhart's field of fire, and he had terminated it without compunction.

The mood was good: four kills in less than forty minutes, and the way to Argentum open.

Then the breaking news had reached them.

The entire advance had slowed to a crawl as they became sensible to the significance and implications.

At best, what had happened overnight in Orestes Principal was a debilitating act of counter-propaganda, designed to derail and divide Imperial and Mechanicus efforts. At worst, it was a crisis of faith in the making, a schism that might result in the separation of Terra and Mars, and, as a consequence, allow the Archenemy of mankind to win not just this war, but *all* wars.

It was a potential heresy as wounding as any that the Imperium and the Mechanicum had weathered together, and the last great heresy had almost destroyed them both. Gearhart knew that only too well. *Invictus Antagonistes* had been there, and memories of that bleak, ignominious age still stained the darkest, furthest corners of the MIU.

Sometimes, Gearhart wondered if those memories were contributing to his own, inescapable nightfall.

Ill at ease, the looming dark was on him now. He felt he were all machine, all oil and alloy, and that the vestigial flesh of... what was his name again? Pietor Gearhart, that was it...

That the vestigial flesh of Pietor Gearhart were being ground up by the meshing black gears.

'Call full stop, all groups,' he augmitted.

'Full stop, all groups, aye,' his moderati replied. *Invictus Antagonistes* thumped to a halt, and the systems went into standby.

In his tank, Gearhart tried to shake the blackness off. He couldn't remember his moderati's name. *He couldn't remember his moderati's name.*

'Zophal?'

'Yes, my princeps?' responded his steersman.

'Good man, Zophal, good man. Stand to.'

Not Zophal, then. Dammit! I don't want to go this way. I don't want to lose myself like this.

'Bernal?'

'Yes, my princeps?'

Thank the Deus. The moderati was named Bernal. Of course he was.

'Come close,' Gearhart augmitted. 'Let us talk, you and me.'

Bernal unlatched his harness and climbed out of his chin-seat. Gearhart saw him exchange quiet shrugs with the steersman and the sensori.

They're worried about me, and my odd ways. They think I'm going mad and I'm simply trying to hang on.

Bernal came up to the casket and stood to attention.

'At ease, man. You can relax around me. How long have we been friends?'

Bernal hesitated. 'I believe I've been your moderati now these eight years, and your steersman for twelve before that, my princeps.'

What you're telling me is your service record, Bernal, Gearhart thought. *What you're not saying is: 'We've never been friends. We never can be friends. I serve you and you are my princeps.' Well, I need you, Bernal. I need your humanity to keep me human. I will not go like Karing. I will not go, screaming like that, not knowing my own name.*

'The crew's uneasy, I suppose?'

Bernal shrugged. 'It's troubling, my princeps.'

'Of course. But I need you to focus for me, all of you. Tell this to the others, and remind them how much I appreciate their skills.'

'I will, my princeps.'

'The news that's broken today, Bernal, it's disturbing stuff, I know. But it's not an engine matter.'

'It's not, my princeps?' replied Bernal, surprised.

Gearhart nodded. 'No, not right now, not while we're walking on an execution. The fight, that's what we're about. We can't let this trouble upset our game. You understand?'

'Yes, my princeps.'

'There may be truth in these declarations, or no truth at all. Not for us to decide, Bernal. We're engine men. We leave that stuff to the scholars and the magi. We just have to concentrate on our job and get it done.'

'Yes, my princeps. But–'

'But what? Speak freely, Bernal.'

Moderati Bernal looked distinctly uncomfortable. 'What if it is true, my princeps? What then?'

Gearhart grinned. 'Then we may have to fight another war when this one's done, my friend. Let's take them one at a time, shall we?'

Bernal smiled and nodded. 'Of course, my princeps.'

'I'm going to consult the battlegroups. While I do, get the crew focused and then squirt me the latest tactical the Manifold can provide. That's all. Good man, Zophal.'

'Bernal, sir. My name's Bernal.'

Gearhart blanched. 'Of course. Slip of the aug. I apologise, Bernal. My mind's on a hundred different things.'

'No need to apologise, my princeps,' said Bernal.

'Very good.'

Bernal returned to his chin-seat.

Damn, damn, damn! Right to his face like that. Damn. I refuse to slip under. I refuse!

Gearhart engaged the Manifold and opened links with practiced haptic gestures, his hands brushing through the warm fluid. In seconds, he had established virtual interfaces with Bohrman, Kung, Crusius, Lau and Kovenicus.

<So, my young devils, what do we make of this?> he canted.

Apart from a slight hololithic tremble, the five men appeared to be standing around his casket.

<There'll be hell to pay,> canted Bohrman.

<Of course.>

<I think this is an Archenemy ploy,> Lau snarled. <Is there any evidence that this is data sabotage designed to undermine our efforts?>

Gearhart shrugged. <Crusius?>

The image of Crusius was grim and wary. <My famulous was in the Analyticae when the outrage occurred, lord. I have urged him to identify the source and origin, by force if necessary. Thus far, there is no indication that this is the work of the enemy. The forge systems and networks were powerfully protected.>

<So noted.>

<Do we suspend this walk, sir?> canted Bohrman.

<Have you ever known me back off from a fight, first princeps?> Gearhart canted back, smiling fiercely.

<No, princeps maximus, I haven't,> Bohrman canted directly, returning the grin.

<Then you've answered your own question. My dear magos navis, what can you report?>

The image of Kovenicus, master of the Fleet Invictus, was being transmitted via the Manifold from his ship in low orbit. Kovenicus was an old, bearded, rotund man with augmetic implants peppering his skull. He was the best fleet master Gearhart had ever known.

<The fleet is at dispersal, lord,> Kovenicus canted back. <I have made the reserves ready. They can deploy, at your order, in two hours. I have taken the precaution of geo-synching our main cruiser squadron above Orestes Principal.>

Gearhart nodded. <You anticipate me, Kovenicus. That is precisely what I was about to ask you to do.>

Kovenicus smiled and bowed obediently.

<Draw in all fleet elements, Kov, you old devil. We may not be the mighty Imperial Navy, but we can deliver hurt. Draw up target solutions on the hive zone, all key locations, and charge the main batteries.>

<Yes, my lord. You are expecting more trouble? From our own side?>

Gearhart sighed. <I don't intend to drive the Legio Invicta through this execution only to find a civil war has broken out behind us. The data that's been released is inflammatory. It is already causing public unrest in the hives, and worse could follow. If the Imperial factions feel threatened by us over this...>

<I understand, sir,> Kovenicus canted.

<Not just the Imperials,> Kung sent quietly.

They all regarded the princeps of *Sicarian Faero*. Kung shrugged diffidently. <I notice that you have linked us all

here, but you have not included the princeps of the Tempestus engines.>

<And why would that be, Vancent?> Gearhart inquired gently.

Kung frowned. <I supposed it was because of our doctrinal differences, lord. The legios of Proximus have always believed in the certain divinity of the God-Emperor as Omnissiah. I am given to understand that the Orestean forge does not agree. They refer, disparagingly, to our beliefs as the *new way*. The forge teaches the notion that the God-Emperor and the Omnissiah are quite separate.>

<I am aware of their ontological stance, Vancent,> Gearhart canted.

<The data released last night, if authentic, proves their standpoint, and justifies their doctrines. If it comes to it, unless we submit and recant our beliefs, we may be considered heretics. And thus, opponents.>

<This point had already occurred to me, lord,> canted Crusius.

<To us all, Crusius,> Gearhart snapped. <We must stand ready to defend our faith. If this data propels us into civil war, we'll see more than Imperial versus Mechanicus. The Mechanicus itself will be bloodily divided. Kovenicus?>

<My lord?>

<Send a summary of this matter with all haste to Mars, under my seal.>

<Lord, I'm sure the situation has already been communicated–>

<Not by us it hasn't. State the facts and state our position. Urgently request that the magi of Mars study this matter in detail at once and report their findings and conclusions to you directly, for my attention.>

<I will do this thing at once, lord,> Kovenicus canted back.

<Executor?>

<My lord?>

<Convey my support to the Lord Governor. Assure Aleuton that the Mechanicus is not about to leave Orestes to its fate.>

<The Mechanicus, lord?>

<I take your point. Legio Invicta, then. And communicate my displeasure to Adept Seniorus Imanual. Tell him I expect him to get his forge in order. This panic must be contained and secured. Tell him that if it isn't, my displeasure will be upgraded to wrath.>

The image of Crusius nodded.

<That's everything, gentlemen. Let us walk.>

The engines resumed their ponderous advance. Almost immediately, *Morbius Sire* made another kill, bringing down a loping enemy Warhound that was trying to escape across a clearance behind two bombed-out manufactories.

Gearhart accessed and replayed *Sire's* gun camera capture via the Manifold. The feed-response was lagging at almost three per cent. Gearhart watched the enemy Warhound come down, first hobbled by *Morbius Sire's* firepower as it attempted to run clear, and then blown apart as it lay writhing on its side, too wounded to get up again. Max Orfuls was a damn fine princeps. No quarter and no wastage in his actions. The pinpoint accuracy of his kill shots was phenomenal.

Gearhart waved up his copy of the heretic data. He had stored it in his buffers. He studied it, puzzling, wondering. It seemed authentic, but he would leave such determinations to scholarly experts.

If it was true, everything he believed in would be overturned, and the cultures of Man and Mechanicus would be overturned with it.

* * *

>

'Order to renew advance has just been given, my princeps!' the sensori sang out.

Rufus Joslin, princeps of the *Orestes Magnificat,* stirred in his amniotic casket and looked up.

<Ordered by whom?> he canted.

'Lord Gearhart, my princeps.'

Joslin accepted the Manifold, haptically folding away the copy of the released data he had been studying. <Acknowledge order. Full ahead.>

'Full ahead, aye.'

Joslin was first princeps of the Legio Tempestus, and since the demise of his princeps maximus, Sorlan Veykot, a week before, he had been acting commander of all that remained of the Orestean forge's Titan complement. A dedicated engine officer, Joslin was a bullish individual, eighty per cent bionic, and staunchly rigid in his faith.

The data that had been released the night before by the forge, it was uplifting, edifying, liberating. The truth at last. No more question of schism, no more debate or argument. Verified, undeniable truth. The galaxy was about to change for the better. It was time for Mars to come into the ascendancy.

Joslin acknowledged that this process would be painful and difficult, but the Mechanicus had lived under the sway of Terra and its impudent Emperor for long enough. The machine spirits would sing at last. The lies would be overturned.

<Moderati Glenik?>

'Yes, my princeps.'

<Be so kind as to prepare target solutions on the Invicta engines as we proceed.>

Glenik hesitated. 'The Invicta engines, my princeps?'

<You heard me, moderati.>

'But why, my princeps?'

<The truth has been disclosed, moderati. The Mechanicus stands at the brink of a new era, and the Legio Invicta, though it pains me to say it, may not embrace that new era without a fight. Let's make sure, quietly, that we're ready to give it to them.>

>

'Why did you do it, Kalien?' Feist asked.

She shrugged. 'It had to be known.'

'Do you have any idea what you've done, adept?' asked Egan.

'Yes, and I care nothing,' Kalien replied. She was sitting in a chair in a private interview chamber, her arms folded tightly across her breasts, not looking at either of them.

<Oh, I think I might make you care yet, adept,> augmitted Solomahn Imanual, entering the chamber.

Adept Kalien went pale at the sight of the Adept Seniorus. She slid out of her seat and knelt on the floor.

<Get up, girl.>

'No!'

'Will your transgressions never cease, you silly little scrap-shunt?' Egan snarled. 'Get up when the Adept Seniorus instructs you!'

<Let her be, Egan,> Imanual ordered, reaching up a manip for quiet. With Feist's dutiful support, the Adept Seniorus bent down beside the terrified girl.

'Kalien?' he whispered, switching to his fleshvoice. 'Kalien, you've done a terrible thing. Deus, I think I understand why you did it, but the *repercussions*. Throne alone knows how deep this will run.'

Kalien did not reply.

Feist carefully raised the infirm Adept Seniorus to his feet. 'Let me talk to her, lord,' he suggested. Imanual nodded, and settled back on the seat that Kalien had vacated.

Feist sat down on the floor beside Kalien's cowering, snivelling form.

'That's enough of that,' Feist said. 'I thought you were strong. You rode me like a bastard in the Analyticae. Feist this, Feist that. I thought you had backbone.'

Kalien swung her face up at him, her eyes wet, her nose running. 'I have! More than you, I think, Feist! You are a coward not to have done it yourself. Don't you understand what you found?'

'Rumination: yes. That's why I took the matter directly to our lord the Adept Seniorus.'

'Why would you bother with consultation?' she sneered.

'With data this sensitive–'

'We are the Mechanicus!' she interrupted. 'There is either data or no-data! Truth or scrapcode! Knowledge is a binary state! There is no in-between on which we should consult and debate. When we find truth, truth must be told!'

'Whose truth, Kalien?' Feist asked. 'What truth? Who decides that?'

'We do!' she hissed.

'You saw the data Lunos had uncovered. You stole it from my workplate.'

'Is that all that matters? That I spied on you and invaded your privacy? The crime pales before your own. You were concealing something that absolutely had to be known!'

'And you broadcast it?'

'What's the matter with you? It's the truth. The affirmed truth! We've lived in the shadow of the Emperor for too long!'

'We're at the pitch of war, Kalien,' said Feist softly. 'Did you not consider that there might be a better time to reveal such inflammatory claims?'

'No, I–'

'Then you are naive. Whether this data is truth, as you claim, or not, its revelation has reopened the wounds of schism within the forge, and between Mechanicus and Imperial. You have weakened and divided us in the face of the Archenemy. We may not prevail. We may not survive.'

'But–'

'It was just an old document, Kalien,' Egan said.

'Additional: it was not verified,' said Imanual. 'Old documents are full of lies. I should know, I've seen my share of them. They're full of lies.'

'*You're* full of lies!' she growled, averting her eyes. 'It was fully authenticated. No lies, just truth!'

'You betrayed my trust,' said Feist.

Kalien looked at him sharply. She blazed with self-righteous confidence, but there was something else, something that was beginning to erode her show of defiance. Feist could see it in her eyes and in the tremble of her lips. 'I don't care about you,' she said. 'I did it for the Deus Mechanicus. I did it for our god.'

Imanual turned to Egan. <I've heard enough, Egan. Suppress the data. Purge it, maximum intensity, if you have to. Instruct the magi probandi to oversee the purge. Clean our house and have the skitarii put down, by force if necessarily, any resistance. I want the forge and the hive settled down within the hour and–>

'She wasn't acting alone,' said Feist quietly.

'What did you just say, adept?' asked Egan.

Feist had gone quiet. He was sitting on the hard metal deck beside Kalien, who had sunk her face into her hands. 'She couldn't have done this alone. Someone must have given her the means to steal it from my workplate. Someone was using her.'

'Adept Feist,' said Egan. 'That's quite an accusation.'

The hatch behind them opened and Magos Tolemy, the master of the archives, entered the chamber. He was escorted by a quartet of fearsome skitarii warriors, led by Enhort, executor fetial of the Legio Tempestus.

<Adept Seniorus, I demand to know what you are doing to my adept,> Tolemy canted briskly, indicating Kalien with a manip. <I will not suffer to see one of my own placed under duress.>

Imanual looked at him wearily. <She's the one, Tolemy. She's the one who triggered this scare. Reflection: how dare you come here, flanked by my skitarii?>

<Your skitarii?> Tolemy smiled unpleasantly, his cant curt and blunt. <Welcome to the truth and the future.>

He made a gesture. The skitarii on either side of him raised their weapons and aimed them at the Adept Seniorus.

'About time, Tolemy,' said Egan.

1110

In the early afternoon of Revelation Day, the weather turned and came to the aid of the beleaguered authorities. Torrential rainstorms hammered the main hive, churning the sky the colour of charcoal, and transforming the upper level streets into waterlogged mirrors.

Rain beat down on every roof-slope, every sink-link, every covered walk and every tower. It choked gutters and iron-work, and caused reflux to wash back up storm drains. It fell on the high hive and the low, and its sheeting fall obscured open spaces like the Field of Mars and Forge Park. It was, remarked one magos, like an expression of grief that this day had come upon Orestes.

The force and persistence of the rainstorms broke up and dissolved many public demonstrations. Crowds dissipated around the temple concourses, or took shelter in colonnades and covered spaces, their agitation dampened. The rain put out oil drum fires, and chased protesters and malcontents indoors or into the lower hive levels. Moving in rain-slickers, the PDF and Magistratum were able to clear many block areas and resume public control, for the time being at least.

The rainstorms had not been predicted by any meteorological scans or climate surveys. The day should have been sunny and clear. The hive's advanced, interdisciplinary climatographic systems were entirely surprised by the rain. When the adepts and magi of the Meteorologi were able to tear themselves from the heated Revelation debate long enough, they concluded that the unseasonable rainstorms were the consequence of freak atmospheric physics and chemistry, generated by an uncharted phenomenon, such as the Astroblemic dust storm the previous night, or the condensation of soot and petrochemical smoke particulates accumulated over the war zone.

They were right about the nature of the rainstorms, but entirely wrong about the cause.

Rain was tipping down across the concourse outside the forge's north-western entrance.

'Wait for me here,' Sonne told his four companions. He hauled his jacket up over his head and ran out across the overcast space into the wet, dodging between the rippling puddles that littered the concourse.

By the time he reached the huge entrance portico, he was soaked to the skin. He entered the shelter, shook out his jacket and wiped the rainwater off his face. A skitarii blocked his way.

Sonne flashed his biometric.

<Access denied,> the warrior blurted.

'Read it again,' said Sonne. 'I am famulous to the executor fetial, Invicta. I request audience with the Adept Seniorus.'

<This one sees who you are,> the skitarii sent back in a quick code burst. <Access denied.>

The skitarii was large, a full head and a half taller than Sonne. His weapon limb was armed and ready. His exotic armour displayed details of colour and flourish that Sonne recognised as belonging to the skitarii Legio Tempestus Orestae.

'I don't think you understand–' Sonne began.

<You are failing to incant my directive, famulous of the executor fetial, Invicta,> the warrior code burst back. <This way is barred to all outsiders.>

'The Analyticae, then? Let me in there. For the attention of Adept Feist or Magos Egan? This is war-work, soldier. You are impeding the legio in its defence of the forge.'

<This way is denied to all outsiders.>

Sonne sighed. He tried his last card. 'What's your designation, skitarii? I want your name. Enhort and the senior magi will hear of this offence.'

<I am designated Kolobe 111010:1101 alpha stroke addition 1101.>

'Noted,' replied Sonne, but he knew he was beaten. He hiked his sodden jacket over his head and ran back through the rain to rejoin his companions under the shelter of a rockcrete overwalk.

'No go,' he told them.

<The unit defied your authority, famulous?> asked Karsh. <Let me kill him for you.>

'Slow down, soldier,' Sonne said to the massive Invicta skitarii that Crusius had loaded to serve as his lead bodyguard.

<But it is disrespectful to you, famulous,> Karsh code-growled. The arming lights on Karsh's modified weapon blinked and his inbuilt loaders clattered.

'Yes, it is,' Sonne admitted. Karsh's two subordinates, Lux 88 and Tephlar, clattered their loaders threateningly in concert.

'That's enough,' Sonne told them. 'Calm down.'

The three skitarii fell silent, rain dripping off their immense shoulder armour and sagging their feathered plumes. Sonne glanced at his fourth companion, the delicate comm-servitor Obligana.

'Famulous?' she augmitted.

'I'm thinking.'

'You looked at me. Did you desire connection?'

'To what, Obligana?'

'Listing options: the vox system; the noosphere; Executor Crusius.'

'Can you patch me through to any of those?'

Obligana searched her buffers for a moment. As she did so, she wiped dew-drops of rain off her high, white forehead with a mechadendrite.

Sonne heard a little shiver of data code.

'No, famulous, I cannot do any of those things.'

'Then why did you ask me?'

'I was trying to serve, famulous,' the servitor replied.

Sonne smiled at her. 'Thank you for that, Obligana. We're all in a bit of a bind right now.'

Sonne knew he should never have left the Analyticae. When the data had gone hot, the comm-systems had jammed with traffic. Sonne had taken himself, his skitarii escort, and his lingual servitor, out of the forge in the hope of getting a decent noospheric signal on the Field of Mars. He'd been successful, and had spoken at length with Crusius. That had been hours earlier. Now he couldn't get a link, and he couldn't get back into the forge.

The rainstorm atmospherics and the crisis explained the

signal block. Nothing, except Sonne's most uneasy ideas, explained the barred entrance.

<We could shoot our way in, famulous,> suggested Lux 88.

<Agreed,> canted Tephlar, <we could shoot our way in, and burn the stubborn skitarii of Tempestus. We could gouge and shoot–>

<I could take many down with me, famulous,> bragged Karsh.

'I'm sure you could, Karsh,' said Sonne. 'Calculate this for me, tactical. How far would you get?'

Karsh computed. His eyes pulsed with a hot, yellow venom. <Between eight point six and eight point nine metres into the entrance way. We would take between twelve and seventeen of the Tempestus skitarii down with us before destruction.>

Sonne sighed. 'Full marks for effort, boys, but do you think I want to get between eight point six and eight point nine metres into the entrance way?'

<You probably want to get further,> blurted Lux 88.

'Right. All the way to the Analyticae or the office of the Adept Seniorus. How far would that be?'

<Analyticae: nine hundred and four point six metres,> reported Lux 88.

<Office of the Seniorus: fifteen hundred and sixty-nine point two metres,> added Tephlar.

'See what I mean? We're falling a little short either way. But thanks for showing such spunk.'

<I have an automatic grenade launcher,> announced Tephlar, proudly.

'Great. How does that change the calculations, Karsh?'

<Calculating: we would get between fifteen point five and seventeen point three metres into the entrance way. We would take between fifty and fifty-five of the Tempestus skitarii down with us before destruction.>

'So, let's round up. Better, but not good enough. Agreed?'

The three skitarii murmured a grudging assent.

Thunder rolled. The rain increased in its intensity. The five of them huddled closer together under the shelter of the rockcrete overwalk. Sonne leaned back against the damp support and watched the collecting rainwater drum down from the overwalk onto the paved ground below. The drops were beating rhythmically.

Tap, tap, tap...

'Obligana?'

'Yes, famulous?'

'What are the haptic levels like?'

'Famulous?'

'The haptics, Obligana! Everyone's so worked up, using the vox, the pict links, the data-direct noosphere. I'll bet no one's using the old haptic channels. No one uses the finger-code these days unless they have to!'

Obligana paused. Her fingers twitched, like a spider's legs, delicate and cautious.

'All lower haptic and push-code channels are reasonably clear, famulous,' she reported.

A grin spread across Sonne's face. 'Copy this to Adept Feist,' he began. Then he paused. 'No, I tell you what... copy this code order to all channels.'

His fingers began to type on an invisible keyboard in the rain. Her fingers precisely echoed the movement of his hands.

'Command control executor fetial, Crusius,' Sonne muttered as he air-typed, cursing the fact that he was so unmodified. 'Are you getting this, Obligana?'

'I am, sir.'

'Override, Crusius twelve maximal nine.'

'Copying override, Crusius twelve maximal nine,' she echoed.

The five of them walked into the north-west entranceway. Kolobe 111010:1101 alpha stroke addition 1101 sniffed Sonne's biometric and waved them through.

'Stay tight,' Sonne told them quietly as they entered the forge. 'Here's where things start to get interesting.'

>

Dominatus Victrix walked north-west with the second front out of Gynex. The Red Fury's main battlegroups were moving on Argentum, and the second front, commanded by Princeps Levin aboard *Ajax Excelsus*, was lagging about two and a half hours behind them as it cleared the southern approach.

The engines and their skitarii support elements were traversing the great, war-broken tracts of the Shaltar Refinery Zone. The engines were moving at broad spacing, no less than a kilometre between any of them and sometimes as much as five, and though the day was fine with excellent visibility, they all had their scopes and auspexes set to maximum. A large number of enemy engines, especially fast hunter-killers and anti-engine specialists, had haunted the Shaltar Wastes since the third week of the war, so no one was taking any chances. The feed of tactical data from the Hive Principal, especially from the Hostile Catalogue, had been unreliable all day.

Tarses knew why. They'd all seen the released data.

The engine kill they'd made during the storm in the night had lifted their collective confidence and when, as the storm faded towards dawn, they'd relocated *Tantamount Stridex*, the mood onboard had verged on ebullient.

Stridex had been circling all night, trying to reacquire them, having been surprised and forced into evasion by the enemy engine that *Victrix* had subsequently killed. Princeps Theron had signalled his compliments to Prinzhorn. *Stridex* had suffered some damage in the clash, but not enough to force its return to the silos. Theron pronounced himself battle-fit, and they had pressed on together.

At dawn, both engines had inloaded orders from *Ajax Excelsus* to join the second front push, and they'd moved to cruise stride through the Lexal Subsid, with the great peak of Mount Sigilite, ice-white in the crimson dawn, turning slowly in the starboard ports until it looked like the edge of a flat blade.

By then, the full ramifications of the data released overnight in the hive had seeped into the crews' consciousness.

Tarses knew that the data was false and divisive, and felt that it had to be part of a scrapcode offensive by the Archenemy, feeding toxic misinformation into the allied data-systems. He kept this opinion to himself. Prinzhorn and his famulous were evidently delighted by the news. They chattered together on a private link, and Tarses could feel their excitement. It was confirmation of the very substance of Orestean belief.

In the chin-seats on either side of him, Anil and Kalder said little. Like Tarses, they had both greeted the data release with dismay. He hoped they had the sense to see it for the pack of lies it was.

The first evidence that the walk to Argentum would not go unopposed presented itself in the compounds of the Shaltar Auxil 18 Refiner. Two enemy engines, Reavers by their brief auspex spoor, were lying in wait in the battered, shell-holed gyro barns of Shaltar Auxil 18, using the metal structures and nearby ore-rich slag heaps to baffle scope-sweeps and auspex paints. They caught the Warhound *Martial Nox* in a surprise attack and crippled it with missile fire as it moved into their kill box.

Two kilometres back, *Victrix* had seen the ambush happen. The rapid, searing missile strikes had shown up on the scope as sharp jags and bright bursts of heat waste. Tarses had actually glimpsed the light flash through the front ports.

'Attack! Attack!' he had reported.

<Tactical specs!> Prinzhorn had returned.

A stream of anguished code was flooding in from the injured Warhound. It was trying to limp clear. Tarses listened hard, trying to untangle the multiple code sources. He stared at the thready, incomplete auspex patterns they were inloading.

'*Martial Nox* has been hit, my princeps,' he reported. 'Data suggests two contacts, bearing 458.'

<Confirm, please, sensori.>

'In work, my princeps,' Kalder called back.

<Raise shields. Attack pace. Ready main weapons.>

'Shields, aye!'

'Attack pace, aye!'

'Main guns at your discretion, my princeps,' said Tarses.

There was another sizzling play of missile fire from up ahead. The stricken Warhound emitted more desperate code.

'Shit,' growled Kalder. '*Nox* is in real trouble.'

<Formal exchanges only in this cockpit, if you please, sensori.>

'Yes, my princeps. Sorry, my princeps.'

<Where's that confirmation?>

Kalder was struggling with the scope. 'It's hard to get a fix, my princeps. Even at full gain, the auspex is being bounced by mineral deposits in the target area.'

<I don't want excuses, sensori!>

'No excuses, my princeps,' Tarses cut in, adjusting the scopes. 'Sensori Kalder is correct. We're dealing with ambush predators, Reaver-patterns, I believe. They are skilled at using any magnetic and mineralogical nodes in the landscape to camouflage their profiles.'

A kilometre to the east of them, *Tantamount Stridex* announced its intention to set up long-range interference fire. Three kilometres to their west, the Tempestus Warlord *Vanquist Solace* announced it would be doing the same.

Both engines lit off, launching streams of heavy fire at the distant gyro barns as they bore on. The distort patterns of the combined broadsides screwed the auspex signals still further.

<Maintain attack pace,> Prinzhorn ordered. <I am informing *Stridex* and *Solace* that we will drive up the centre line in close support of *Nox* while they lay down the suppression bursts.>

'Yes, my princeps. An excellent idea,' replied Tarses. It was a good tactical decision. Prinzhorn, his confidence growing, was beginning to act and think like a real engine fighter, not a simulated one, and Tarses believed it was his place to enthusiastically ratify his commander's choices.

Two and a half kilometres beyond Shaltar Auxil 18, the Invicta Warlord *Cour Valant* had turned to add its own long-range discouragement to the wrath being dished out by *Stridex* and *Solace*. The Reaver *Imperius Crux,* on the *Cour Valant*'s starboard wing, signalled that it was striding in to close along with *Victrix*.

<I'll try to leave something for you, *Crux*,> Prinzhorn jested with *Crux's* princeps, Dendrake.

'Moderati?' Kalder hissed.

'One moment, sensori,' Tarses replied, trying to keep his

attention on the target zone, the aiming systems, and *Victrix's* rate of stride. One of the aft autoloaders seemed to be jamming or running slow. It was like spinning plates.

<Tech-priest! Attention! Aft loader nine!> he augmitted briskly.

<Misfunction detected, moderati,> the tech-priest canted back. <I have a servitor on it now.>

Tarses looked back at Kalder. 'Sorry, what did you need me for?'

'I'd be obliged if you gave your opinion on this signal.'

Tarses switched to full Manifold. 'Inload.'

Kalder sent the data chunk to Tarses. Tarses reviewed it carefully, and asked for two playbacks.

'Well?' asked Kalder.

'In your opinion?' Tarses replied.

'There are three contacts, not two.'

'The ghosting could be due to an auspex bounce off something like aluminium or bauxite.'

Kalder sniffed. 'I washed it, and adjusted for latents.'

'Three, you think?'

Kalder nodded.

'Good enough for me,' Tarses told him. He cut to a live channel. 'This is *Victrix*, be advised, we are painting three, repeat three enemy engines in the target zone.'

<*Victrix, Victrix*, suggest your auspex is faulty,> *Crux* canted back, its signal distorted by scrap-noise. <We're barely painting two.>

<Moderati?>

'My princeps?'

<Is it our damn auspex again? I swear to the Deus, I'll rip it out and replace it with my own hands if it is.>

Tarses looked over his shoulder at Prinzhorn in the casket.

'Sensori Kalder says it's three, my princeps, and I trust his skills.'

Dominatus Victrix entered Shaltar Auxil 18 about two minutes ahead of *Imperius Crux*. As the two Titans came into the refiner plant complex, *Stridex, Solace* and *Valant* suspended their long-range bombardments for fear of hitting a friendly.

The area was a tangled mess of exploded silos, ruptured pipelines and fractured cooling towers. Smoke and code echoes threaded the air. The three engines had pummelled the place, and the place had been dead to begin with. The ground was a matted knot of rubble spill and deep craters.

'Multiple gressorial instability warnings!' Anil shouted out.

<Slow to one-third stride,> Prinzhorn ordered.

'One-third, aye!'

Tarses sat forwards. He could feel the bulk of *Victrix* sliding and scuffing over the loose and broken terrain. Skaugen had told him horror stories of engines that had pushed too fast into treacherous terrain, and exceeded their traction limits. Their ill-advised haste had taken them beyond a point where their gyros and inertial dampers could right them. They had fallen, and been helpless when the enemy came for them.

'You don't ever want to be in that situation,' Skaugen had said.

'Indeed I don't, my princeps,' Tarses had replied.

'Ease off,' Tarses said to Anil. 'Stop fighting with the levers. Keep it slow and soft, and we'll stay stable.'

'Yes, moderati.'

They were walking through ribbons of black oil-smoke. It washed across the cockpit ports. They could hear *Martial Nox* bleeding code from somewhere up ahead.

'Steady,' Tarses advised.

Another step, and another. The auspex was straining at its limits, reading only ruins and the shells of structures.

<Where are they?> asked Prinzhorn.

'They can't have run, my princeps,' said Kalder. 'We'd have seen their tracks. They're still here.'

'Steady,' repeated Tarses.

<We should be able to see them,> blurted Prinzhorn.

They're hunters, stalkers, ambush predators, thought Tarses. Of course we can't see them. This is what they do. They hide in cover, in ruins, and attack, point-blank.

'Steady,' said Tarses. 'Slow by a tenth. Rotate waist mount and track, fluid. Keep the guns live and ready.'

The upper body of the Warlord began to traverse slowly: left, then right, left, then right.

'There's nothing here,' said Fairika. 'We've lost them.'

'No, we haven't, famulous,' Tarses said. He was patiently scrutinising every landscape element ahead of them: the burning store barn twenty metres to port; the long, buckled run of gyro sheds fifty metres to starboard; ahead, the cluster of fire-damaged silos.

'Steady,' he said, feeling *Victrix* slither again. His breathing had slowed right down, his heart rate too. They were approaching ignition point, the moment when everything went insane. He could feel it.

He checked the weapon systems for load and tension, and brought them to the bite. Another step, and another.

'Suggest active ping, my princeps?' said Fairika.

'No,' replied Tarses smartly.

<I believe the suggestion was mine to decide on, moderati,> canted Prinzhorn.

'If you want to be a fool, go ahead, my princeps,' said Tarses. 'Let them know we're right here, if you like.'

<You're like a fussy old wife, my moderati,> said Prinzhorn.

'I'll take that as a compliment, my princeps,' Tarses replied, maintaining his scanning.

'Seventy metres, bearing three-four-three,' Kalder whispered. 'I think that's heat-bleed.'

'I think so too, sensori,' Tarses replied. He flicked in the aiming systems and let them settle across his Manifold view. 'Permission to fire, my princeps?'

<I don't see any kind of target!>

'Kalder does. Permission to fire?'

<Granted.>

Tarses triggered the firing system. The destructor unleashed its fury. The sensory backwash through the MIU was delicious, almost orgasmic. *Victrix* wanted this.

The massive gunfire brought down a ruined barn. As the flames boiled up, a Reaver, dressed in scabby brown enamel, bolted out of the ruined building like a game bird scared out of cover. It was hurt. It was dragging one leg, and showers of sparks were vomiting out of the heat exchangers on its back.

'Clean target!' Kalder yelled.

'Give me missile lock,' Tarses replied.

'Missiles locked, aye!' Kalder confirmed.

<Five spread, launch!> Prinzhorn ordered.

The missiles spat off out of the carapace mount. In the cockpit, they felt the jolts as the solid munitions banged away, and heard the grind of the loader systems sliding fresh rockets up into the pod.

It was overkill. Tarses would have gone for a three spread, but he'd always been conservative.

The first three missiles caught the Archenemy Reaver across the back and killed it, blowing its torso out in a violent exhalation of flame. The fourth took out its cockpit as it turned and fell, unnecessary but satisfying. The fifth went wide and destroyed a silo tower.

Yes, a three spread would have done it, Tarses thought.

Ablaze and disintegrating, the Reaver collapsed. Anil and Fairika whooped.

'Watch your port!' Kalder yelled.

The second Reaver, painted in such a dark, oily substance that it seemed as purple and iridescent as a beetle's wing case, burst out of a gyro barn to their left. It was firing its limb weapons on auto, a sustained salvo that made *Victrix* shudder as her shields soaked it up.

<Traverse! Traverse!> Prinzhorn yelled.

It came right for them... one hundred metres, fifty, still shooting.

'Voids holding!' yelled Kalder.

<Prepare for close combat!> Prinzhorn commanded.

'Close combat weapon engaged!' Tarses yelled back, activating *Victrix's* energy mace. 'But I don't think we'll need it,' he added.

'What are you talking about, moderati?' Fairika squealed.

Tarses fired the destructor again. The first three shots overwhelmed and punctured the charging Reaver's voids, the next three scalped it and shredded its carapace. Its cockpit exploded.

'Hard to port, please, Anil,' Tarses suggested.

The steersman wrenched on the controls.

Victrix lurched aside, slipping slightly. The gyro stabilisers whined as they compensated for the sudden change of direction. Trailing luminous streamers of fire and dead on its feet, the Reaver strode right past their starboard flank and crashed into a gyro barn. It slumped forwards into the barn's sagging roof and blazed like a funeral pyre.

<My compliments, moderati,> Prinzhorn said. <You'll take full credit for that kill.>

'Thank you, my princeps, but the kill should be scored to *Dominatus Victrix*.'

Half a kilometre on, they found *Martial Nox*. It had limped as far as it could go, and then, on fire, it had knelt down to die.

It wasn't going to go without a struggle. As *Victrix* approached, *Nox* attempted to rise. Flames boiled out from under its carapace.

<We're here, and you're safe,> Prinzhorn canted to *Nox*, <but I'm afraid you're done.>

<I will not go like this!> Nox's princeps, Talentine, canted back.

<Then save your crew at least, Talentine,> canted Prinzhorn.

There was a blistering puff of exploding bolts, and the cockpit section of the burning Warhound tore away from the burning carcass. It flew clear for about twenty metres and then grazed across the rubble. Behind it, the main body stuttered and blew out as the reactor caught.

Dominatus Victrix stayed on station until the skitarii support squads had recovered Talentine's crew from the ejected head unit.

<So, sensori, a third engine, you supposed?> Prinzhorn asked as they made way again.

Kalder was listening to the noises coming through his headset. 'I'd have put money on it, my princeps,' he replied, 'and here's my question: *Imperius Crux* was two minutes behind us. Where the hell did it go?'

Victrix advanced at a low, careful stride to the limits of the Shaltar Auxil 18 site, and crossed into the shattered compound of the Allied Conglom Mineral Fabrik. The main area of the Fabrik was dominated by a kilometre-long row of gross processor units, fat rock-splitting machines twice the height of a Warlord and ranged in pairs.

'I'm getting bounce wash and noise echo,' Kalder reported.

<Comm?> Prinzhorn asked.

Kalder shook his head. 'Weapons discharge, my princeps.'

<Slow advance, bearing 231,> Prinzhorn ordered. <Check shield tension. I sense a weakness. That pummelling may have attenuated the thorax cover.>

<Checking, my princeps,> acknowledged the tech-priest.

They came around the far end of the gross processors. *Imperius Crux* had found Kalder's third engine.

Dendrake's Reaver had squared off against an Archenemy Warhound with a thickly spiked carapace. Tonne for tonne, the Reaver outclassed the smaller 'hound, but it had clearly been taken by surprise. Alarming amounts of sickly yellow smoke were pushing out of the Reaver's port limb mount, and Tarses could see that *Crux's* comm-pods and transmission antennae had been shot to pieces. The enemy had rendered *Imperius Crux* dumb so that it could finish it off without interruption.

'That explains why we haven't heard from her,' remarked Kalder. He pulled off his phones and grimaced. The air was full of the Warhound's chaotic, guffawing scrapcode. The enemy machine danced nimbly around the slower, stricken *Crux*, like a wolf playing with a wounded grox, snapping off shots to hobble the noble Reaver.

<End this sport,> Prinzhorn ordered.

'Selecting missiles,' answered Tarses. 'Locking target.'

'It's seen us!' Kalder yelled.

As the Warlord came into view around the processors, the

enemy Warhound froze, like a thug caught in the act of beating its victim to death. It turned, fired two defiant blasts at *Victrix*, and ran.

'Fire!' Tarses cried.

Two missiles streaked off, but the Warhound's shields took their force. It staggered, and then ploughed on, loping away down the central transit-way between the paired rows of gross processors.

'We can't follow it in there!' Anil protested. The central transit-way was just big enough to accommodate the lithe Warhound. No Reaver, and certainly no Warlord, could fit into the space.

<Full stride!> Prinzhorn announced. *Dominatus Victrix* moved back down the line of the processors, glimpsing the fleeing Warhound through the pipework and ducting. Tarses signalled the support units to move in and assist *Imperius Crux*, and then turned his attention to tracking the hostile.

'Sneaky little bastard,' Tarses murmured, following the fleeting profile of the Warhound as it darted back and forth behind the fat iron towers of the processor line.

'Formal exchanges only in this cockpit, moderati,' Fairika told him. 'My princeps's standing orders were clear.'

<I'll allow it, famulous,> canted Prinzhorn. <My moderati is right. It *is* a sneaky little bastard.>

Like a feline hunting for a rodent in a wainscot, *Victrix* moved back and forth along the processor row, catching glimpses of the lithe Warhound as it skittered to and fro along the central transit-way, embracing the cover of the vast splitter towers.

'This is undignified,' remarked Fairika.

'I tell you what, famulous,' said Tarses, 'why don't you hop out and go in after it?'

She glared at him.

'I'm sure the sight of you would scare the living shit out of it,' Tarses added.

<Enough, moderati,> canted Prinzhorn. Glancing back, Tarses was pleased to see that the princeps was smiling.

<I want this engine, Tarses,> Prinzhorn canted. <We will not pass by and leave this thing active. I want a confirmed kill before we move on.>

'Agreed, my princeps, but right now the only way to get at it is to demolish the processors bit by bit, and I fear that would exhaust our munitions.'

'Signals!' Kalder announced. *Tantamount Stridex* and *Vanquist Solace* had both arrived in support.

Tarses quickly appraised the two engines of the situation.

'Three Warlords to take one Warhound?' Moderati Braydel sent to Tarses from *Stridex*. 'That constitutes bullying, doesn't it?'

'It is what it is, my friend,' Tarses replied. 'The enemy has the advantage of location cover. It could wait us out all week, and I doubt that would please Levin or Lord Gearhart.'

'The way ahead is plagued with difficulties,' Braydel sent back. He squirted Tarses a tactical update. They weren't the only engines to have been harried by opportunist hunter-killers in Shaltar. Several engines or engine groups in the second front had reported hot contact with enemy machines during the day. *Valorus Aquila* had been lost to a sneak attack in the Perthenom Refiner, and *Gladius Agon* had been so badly damaged in a fight to the death with an Archenemy Warlord that it had been forced to turn back for the repair silos at Antium. The damned enemy had left the Shaltar zone well defended, lacing it with lone predator engines, or small groups of ambush machines. Levin had also been forced to fight off an ambush. *Ajax Excelsus* had duelled with a screaming, manic Reaver for three minutes before *Guardax Ascension* had intervened and blown the Reaver to scrap.

'Levin is incandescently error shunt abort,' Braydel told Tarses. 'The second front advance has slowed to a crawl, and he hates the idea that he is keeping the Red Fury waiting at Argentum.'

Before Tarses could reply, there was a devastating explosion. The Manifold shivered and almost greyed out for a moment.

<What was that?> Prinzhorn demanded.

Tarses and the bridge crew were working frantically to recover feed.

'*Imperius Crux*!' Kalder cried. '*Imperius Crux* just went up!'

The damage to Dendrake's Reaver had been more serious than they had suspected. Awaiting the promised support/recovery units, *Imperius Crux* suddenly developed a critical reactor event. The drive compartments were engulfed by radioactive fire, torching the tech-priest, who had been trying to facilitate repairs. As the gauges red-lined, Dendrake frantically attempted to eject his crew.

No one had made it. There had been a blink of light, and then, where the proud Reaver had once stood, there was only a deep, black crater and a slowly curling, slowly souring mushroom cloud.

<Enough,> canted Prinzhorn. <Now, we settle this. Now, we kill the sneaky little bastard.>

He exloaded his tactical plan via the Manifold. Princeps Theron of *Tantamount Stridex* and Princeps Shon Ku of the *Vanquist Solace* agreed the plan.

The three Warlords manoeuvred into position around the row of gross processors. *Stridex* covered the west, *Solace* the east. *Victrix* strode to the far end of the processor row until it was facing the entry of the central transit-way.

<Positions?> Prinzhorn called.

'All engines report positioning as per your scheme, my princeps,' replied Tarses.

<Good. Decline stature, on my mark, three, two, one... mark!>

Carefully, expertly, Steersman Anil released the hydraulics, and brought *Victrix* down into what amounted to a crouch. Limb joints locked out, and *Victrix* leaned her heavy carapace forwards. Anil used the weapon limbs to counterbalance the bowing weight of *Victrix*. They were vulnerable now. It would take a minute at least to gather up enough hydraulic pressure to return to upright traction.

The mouth of the central transit-way lay open before them. Somewhere down there, in the shadows of the ducts and pipes, the Warhound lurked.

<Ready all weapons,> canted Prinzhorn.

'Weapons ready, my princeps,' replied Tarses.

It was suddenly cold in the cockpit space. Tarses felt the chill, a clammy chill. They were exposing themselves. It was a terrible risk. If the Warhound decided to come at them, they would be off-balance and their chances of fast, evasive motion seriously limited.

The mouth of the transit-way yawned, gloomy and mysterious.

<Fire,> canted Prinzhorn.

Victrix fired all weapons: both weapon limbs, the megabolter and a flurry of missiles to boot.

The combined salvo rushed up the transit-way, turning it into a firestorm. Ducts fractured and burst. Pipes exploded and tore away. Burning hell ripped up between the rows of processing towers.

'It's running!' Kalder cried.

Attempting to escape the blizzard of energy packets and

hot munitions pouring down the throat of the transit-way, the Archenemy Warhound broke west, emerging at full stride between processors eighteen and twenty.

It got thirty metres before *Tantamount Stridex* slew it. A bracket of eight missiles took out its voids and tore it into burning fragments. The fleeing Warhound's legs kicked out and bicycled as it fell, half its carapace blown away in tatters of flaming debris.

It dropped on its snout, still moving and kicking, and gouged its nose across the rubble before disintegrating in a massive, terminal explosion.

<Engine kill, engine kill,> announced Theron.

<Very good,> Prinzhorn canted. <Steersman? Restore upright traction posture.>

Anil re-engaged the hydraulics and *Victrix* slowly rose out of its crouch, vapour hissing from its pistons.

<We're done here,> Prinzhorn remarked. <Let the second front continue its advance.>

>

The old indigent's name was Ashlag. He sucked in his breath, but made no vocal complaint as Sagen set and dressed his broken arm. His old, faded eyes seemed to be focused on something so far away that it had to be a when rather than a where. His daughter, the engine-face rebreather hooked to her belt, sat in sullen silence on the ground near the Centaur. Varco had taken her las-lock away.

Varco didn't feel much like talking. Gram Hekton's death had been a tragic mixture of courage and futility. The loss filled Varco completely, leaving no room for anything else in his head. He had to force himself to start thinking.

'What were you running from?' he asked Ashlag.

The old man looked at him with dead eyes, a faint sneer curling under the white tails of his splendid moustache.

'You saw what we were running from, soldier,' he replied.

'Engines, yeah. I saw the engines. Tell me the rest.'

Ashlag looked as if he wanted to shrug, but his arm hurt him too much. 'I lost my wife and my boy, soldier. Could you leave me be to grieve?'

Leopald grabbed Ashlag by the front of his jack armour so hard that the old man yowled. 'You old bastard! My captain just got fried saving your miserable arse! Answer the question Captain Varco asked you, or I'll–'

Varco dragged Leopald back. 'Enough of that!' he ordered. He understood the gunner's anguish, but he wouldn't tolerate the abuse of civilians. 'Enough, I said!'

Sagen helped Varco pull Leopald away. Ashlag was cradling his broken arm, his eyes squeezed shut in pain. The daughter had risen to her feet.

'No need for you to get involved,' Varco told her. 'No one's going to hurt your father.'

'I'll kill them if they do,' she replied, matter-of-factly.

'Your name? It's Kell, right?' Varco asked.

'I don't give my name to no one,' she said. It was old indigent community wariness, the trademark lack of cooperation that the closed communities of the Prospection showed to servants of the hive. The folk of the Deadlands often had good reason to be off the grid. They kept their names and business to themselves, and greeted with suspicion anyone from the hive zone who came asking questions. Varco understood that, but he wasn't in the mood to be circumspect.

'Your *da's* already told us his name is Ashlag, girl,' he said. 'Family name Ashlag, which makes you Kell Ashlag, right?'

She opened her mouth to say something, but merely nodded instead.

'I'm sorry about your man,' Ashlag said. 'I really am, soldier. You stopped to help us, and you didn't have to. Brave thing, he did. I'm sorry about him, but my poor wife, and my son...'

His head bowed and he wiped his eyes with the filthy knuckles of his good hand.

'There was engines,' the girl said quietly, 'lots of engines, out in the wild parts where you lot don't go. They came down on some of the townships, smoked them into ash.'

'Go on,' Varco said to her.

'We started to come together for safety as word spread. Even 'spectors and nugget farmers who work out on their own, they all come in. There was a big meeting, at Barter Hill, two nights back. I've never seen so many people in one place before.'

You've never seen a hive, Varco thought.

'Hundreds of people,' she said, shaking her head at the very idea of it. 'There was debate, and then we took a vote, according to Prospection Law.'

'A vote?'

'A community vote,' said Ashlag. 'It was agreed that Swayne, the mayor of Barter Hill, would contact the big hive on behalf of the vassal communities, and make an earnest request for deliverance.'

Varco raised his eyebrows. The indigent nation calling on the hive for help? It was unprecedented.

'The mayor of the big hive, he's got engines of his own, hasn't he?' Ashlag asked.

'He's not a mayor–' Leopald began contemptuously.

'Yes, he has,' said Varco.

'We hoped he would send his engines to help us,' said Ashlag.

'He's a little preoccupied,' said Varco. 'The hive is at war. Orestes has been invaded.'

'Oh,' said Ashlag. 'That would explain a lot.'

'Where's Orestes?' asked the girl.

'It's–' Varco began. He sighed and looked at the old man instead. 'What did you mean, that would explain a lot?'

'Once the vote had been carried, Swayne tried to contact the big hive using the Barter Hill vox mast,' Ashlag said. 'But the channels, they were all dead. Just... bad code. Swayne tried for hours, but he couldn't get through.'

'And then?' asked Sagen.

'Then the engines came,' said Kell Ashlag.

'At dawn, like they'd heard our calls, like they'd been listening to Swayne on the vox.' The old man sniffed. 'They came upon Barter Hill, and they wiped it off the land.'

'And you fled?' asked Varco.

'Yes, soldier, we fled. All that could, ran like the dust-daemons themselves were screaming after us. And they were, I think.'

'The engines came after you?'

'You saw them.'

The dry wind pattered dust against the side of the Centaur. Varco looked east. During the day, a great black bar had slowly been forming across the eastern rim of the horizon. It was a storm, but not a dust storm like the one they'd weathered. It was a mass of thunderstorms, fat with precipitation, accumulating over the hive zone. The wind was getting colder, and Varco could smell the tang of rain.

'How many engines?' Trask asked.

The girl looked at the *Treadfire's* driver.

'You said lots of engines,' said Trask. 'How many is lots?'

'How many is many?' she answered back. She shrugged. 'I don't know. More than I've ever seen.'

'Had you ever seen an engine before?' asked Leopald.

'No,' she said. 'That's not what I meant. It was many engines. There was word coming in from all over.'

Varco thought about it. The Archenemy's main engine strengths had been deployed into the hive zones at the start of the war. He supposed they might have left a reserve echelon behind to clear the Prospection and stand in reserve. How many engines? A dozen at most? That would seem like a lot to a girl who had never seen one before. It would certainly seem like a lot to a girl who had lived such a closed life that a gathering of hundreds of people could feel like an extraordinary multitude.

'Do you know anywhere in this area we can shelter?' he asked.

They buried Ashlag's wife and son, and Hekton's pitiful remains, in shallow graves by the trackway, and then drove north-west into a range of hills that Ashlag called the Topples. Ashlag claimed to know of an old 'spector's halt halfway up the cut.

The Topples were blocky limestone crags threaded with wiry desert scrub. As the sun began to set, the rocks turned cadmium red under a hard, flint-blue sky. The smell of rain was stronger, and though the wind hadn't risen, it had grown considerably colder.

The sky was ominous. The colour of a bruise, it closed in over the red rock, until the crags around them seemed like frozen flames, and the sky resembled their pall of smoke. Varco knew that the rainy season was still months away.

The halt was a longhouse built from scrap metal and wedged under the lip of a cliff overhang. It was worn and decayed, and partly concealed by netting and wire matting. A small, wooden latrine block stood away to the left.

The door of the longhouse wasn't locked. Ashlag explained that the longhouse, and halts like it, were common property, left open to shelter anyone in the indigent community who might pass by.

The place was empty, and didn't seem especially welcoming. Varco and Trask went in first. Varco drew his service pistol, and Trask carried the girl's las-lock. The only other weapon they owned was the stubber mounted on the Centaur. Hekton had taken their one carbine and his own service pistol to his grave.

The patchwork metal floor creaked under them. The ceiling was low, and looked as if it had been formed from reinforced chunks of cargo pod. At one end of the longhouse there were nine metal bunks arranged in stacks of three. The bunks were small and bare. A tatty curtain could be pulled to screen off the bunk area. In the main part of the longhouse was a stove, a water recycler, a metal table, a bench and four wooden stools. One wall was shelved from floor to ceiling, and the shelves were crowded with unwanted items that previous visitors had left behind: small pieces of machinery, jars of preserved rice and less readily identifiable foods, rusted tools, a rebreather mask, ore samples, a prospector's hammer, three dead lamps, shards of polished glass, animal bones, twine, a billhook, wire and shreds of cabling, a pair of gloves, two flasks of mixed spice, the blade of a rotary saw, battered pots and pans, three chipped drinking glasses and a signal flare.

'Offerings,' said Ashlag, entering the longhouse behind

them. 'You use this place, you leave something for the next visitor.'

'What kind of offering is an animal bone?' asked Trask.

'The kind left by someone who has nothing else to give,' Ashlag replied. He opened a door in the back wall of the shelter. The scrap-construction of the longhouse was so jumbled that neither Varco nor Trask had realised the door was there. The door opened into a small alcove space with cupboards to either side and a small generator unit set at the back. Ashlag fiddled with the generator for a while, one-handed, and got it going. It coughed into life, and small glow-globes built into the ceiling of the main room began to throb with yellow light.

'Liquid fuel?' Varco asked Ashlag, nodding to the generator.

Ashlag shook his head. 'Solar. There are collector panels up the hill from here, and they feed down to the accumulator.'

He opened the cupboards in the alcove, revealing stained but dry bedrolls, some basic tools and kitchen utensils, various tin bowls and cups, an old chrome-plated caffeine pot and tin drums of dried provisions. Ashlag opened a few of the drums and shook the contents.

'They haven't left us much,' he said, 'but there's enough. Typical of old Wessman to clean the place out. Always takes more than he leaves.'

'Who's Wessman?' Varco asked.

'The last person to use the halt,' said the old man.

'How do you know that?'

'It's on the wall,' said Ashlag.

Varco looked at the bare wall. He realised that its irregular, mismatched panels were covered in tiny writing, floor to ceiling. Many different hands had made the marks. There were scripts of different sizes and styles, in various colours of ink, some so badly faded with age that they were barely visible. Most of the separate entries were short, just a few lines, and all of them were crammed tightly together. In places, there were sketches of maps or diagrams.

Varco couldn't read any of it.

Ashlag had filled the caffeine pot and set it on the stove. He came over to Varco. 'Anyone uses the halt, see, they write it here. Who they were, when it was, what they used or left. Sometimes they say where they were going, or where they've been. Sometimes they leave news. Halt walls are a marvellous place to hear news of old friends and rivals. See here? Durn Tasler's son wedded, two winters back, at Shortwater. Durn wrote this on his way back from the gathering.'

'You can read that?' Varco asked, squinting.

'Well enough,' said Ashlag. 'It's all here.' He pointed a dirty finger at another small chunk of script. 'See? Says Orgman halted here, seven years back. There's the date. He took a shovel he needed, with thanks, and left a battery that still had work in it. And here, six weeks later, the Zamne brothers halted, driven up by a dust blow. They were here three nights. They took the battery, with thanks, and left a servitor's manip, in good order. They also filled the rice drum, but apologised for taking the last of the salt meat. And they promise to replenish the salt meat next time they pass this way.'

Varco was still struggling to decipher any of the writing. Ashlag tapped a lower part of the wall with his finger.

'The last entry, see? Wessman. Just his name and the date. He was the last one here. Typical of him to take and not leave.'

'What are these sketches?'

'Sometimes a person leaves a map, or a route. Gives notice

of a pass that closed, or a track that's opened, or shows the way to a promising stake or seam they haven't had the time or means to work. Here, see? Albrech has left instructions how to locate a nitre deposit he found, and wasn't bothered with.'

Varco began to make sense of some of the scribblings. The handwriting was dense and compacted, but the real problem was that the wall had been over-written many times. The halt had stood for so long, visitors had filled the wall up over and again. When the last entry filled the bottom right-hand corner, writing began again at the top left. Varco wondered how many years of comings and goings the writing represented, and decided it was probably centuries.

'I must find a stylus and write my name,' said Ashlag. The caffeine pot on the stove began to gurgle.

Sagen brought the Centaur up beside the halt and, with the girl's help, covered it with netting. Trask and Leopald carried Koder into the longhouse, and then unloaded the vehicle. Night was gathering fast and there was thunder in it. The crags turned from deep red to a pale violet, and then to a soft blue.

'What's wrong with your friend, soldier?' Ashlag asked, staring at Koder.

'He's sick.'

'Sick how?'

'He's Mechanicus. He's over-stretched his power reserves. With your permission...'

Varco dragged Koder over to the door of the alcove, and then gently extruded one of the dendritic plugs from the enginseer's left forearm. It was a task he didn't relish. It felt like he was stripping an artery out of Koder's arm. Varco wished that the enginseer was awake enough to perform the task, or at least give him prudent instruction.

Varco pulled the plug line clear. Though flexible, it was oddly warm and organic for a piece of metal trunking. He carefully connected the plug head to one of the generator's power outlets.

The generator note changed slightly as it compensated for the additional drain. Koder did not stir.

'Will that help him?' Sagen asked.

'I don't know,' said Varco. 'It's worth a try.'

They drank caffeine from tin cups. Ashlag's brew was as thick and dark as sump oil, and sour to boot, but its richness and heat was very welcome. Ashlag then set about preparing some food, but his broken arm was too much of a hindrance, so the girl took over, with Ashlag hovering nearby, giving her instructions she obviously didn't need. Every now and then, the girl looked up from the stove and stared at Koder. The enginseer was evidently something of a novelty to her too.

Sagen, Trask and Leopald sipped from their cups and took some rest. Varco could hear them exchanging memories of Hekton. Outside, the first heavy spots of rain *thukked* against the halt's walls.

Varco unhooked a glow-globe and took it over to the wall to study the writing. It was such a mesmerising record. Slowly, painstakingly, he read Albrech's report of the nitre deposit, and then the words of someone called Horkin, who thanked the halt for a good night's rest and said that he'd left dried biscuit in the food drums. The Swetoth clan, a family of eight, said that they had taken two water cans, and had left 'a pick and two good sifting pans, as well as a sun charm, woven by our eldest daughter.'

Varco went over to the shelves. He found the faded charm amongst the bric-a-brac. It had been woven from dried desert grasses. The sun was the defining reality of Deadland life, but this looked more like a wheel of dark gold, or a cog.

Maybe, in the end, we all worship the same thing, thought Erik Varco.

The food was plain, but good. The tankers forked it down with such relish that Kell Ashlag almost smiled. Reconstituted rice, flavoured with spices and rehydrated vegetables, tasted like an up-hive feast. There was a little salt meat too, and dumplings made of crushed cracker-bread, softened and hand-rolled in flour, and then fried. Ashlag made some more caffeine.

'Thank you,' said Varco when he was finished.

'Thank the halt,' replied Kell, dismissively.

'Leopald can clean the pots,' said Varco.

'Yes sir,' said Leopald with a nod. It was amazing how compliant a man became when his belly was full.

The rain was beginning to batter against the longhouse with some force. They all appreciated the little, glow-lit sanctuary of the halt.

Ashlag took a stylus and a glow-globe over to the wall and set about making his mark. His arm was sore, and he found it difficult to reach the lower part of the wall.

'Can I help you?' Varco asked.

Behind the white walrus moustache, Ashlag's mouth frowned. He seemed dubious.

'Will you set it down as I say it, soldier?' he asked.

'Of course, sir,' said Varco. The old man handed him the stylus.

'Orwen Ashlag came here, with his daughter,' the old man began.

Varco started to write. It was tough to keep his writing small enough. His scrawl looked giant and clumsy next to the practiced, miniature script of the indigents. Varco wrote in the date. It reminded him how long he'd been adrift, and how long the war had been raging.

'We have come here after the great flight from Barter Hill,' the old man continued, 'running as we were from the terrible engines. I have this day, to my great pity, lost my good wife, Shenna, and my son Bekk. Does anyone reading these words have other news of the flight from Barter Hill? I am concerned for my brother, Samwen, and also his family, and the families of my good friends Jart Oreman, Ruman Jedder, and also Terk Darshin, all of whom I have not seen since Barter Hill.'

Varco wrote it down, word for word.

'I have come here with soldiers from Big Hive,' Ashlag went on, 'who saved me and my daughter Kell from an engine, at the cost of one of their own. We have taken caffeine, water, and rice and other foods, as well as power from the stack, but this is due and proper payment to the soldiers for their efforts, and I trust that none will begrudge it. I fear the food drums are now knocking empty, worse than they were when Wessman came, but I will try and leave something in return, perhaps a fine las-lock piece that I own.'

Ashlag looked at Varco. 'That's enough for now,' he said. Varco lowered the stylus. Kell's old las-lock was just about the only thing the father and daughter owned any more. Varco was humbled by the old man's determination to observe halt traditions.

'We'll find something else to leave,' he told Ashlag. 'We have things that might be useful.'

'Thank you, soldier, but I'll make my own offering,' the old man said. He took himself away to one of the bunks, and settled down to ease his arm. Trask had fallen asleep on a bunk too. He was snoring. Sagen sat at the table, sipping the last of the caffeine. Leopald was scrubbing the tin bowls and cooking pans in a tub of water he'd drawn off the recycler.

The girl sat in the far corner, nursing a cup of caffeine, watching the unmoving enginseer.

Varco picked up the glow-globe and turned his attention back to the wall. He read that someone called Reydo or Reldo had halted four months back, and left a spool of mining det-tape in return for the food he'd taken. An unnamed wildernaut, six weeks earlier, wrote how he'd taken the lube oil left by another visitor, urgently needed for the gears of his strider, and left 'a pail of assorted screws, nuts and nails'. A hippine driver called Caswester, passing by with his train of animals at the turn of the year, proudly reported that he 'had taken nothing and therefore left nothing'. Someone else, nameless and dateless, had simply written 'thank you for the shelter. I was going to die.' Another entry, made by an individual who signed himself as 'Jindal, twist', blessed the halt for its power and water, and 'most excellent, comfortable craphouse'.

Varco laughed, and shook his head.

'Something funny?'

He glanced up.

The girl was standing behind him.

'No, just reading.'

'That is our lives you laugh at.'

'I know. I'm not laughing.'

The girl pursed her lips.

'Can you help me?' Varco asked.

'How?'

'This entry here, the second to last, above the notorious Wessman's. There's some kind of diagram, but I can't make out the script at all. It's so tiny, so neat. Can you read it?'

'Why do you want to?'

'I'm interested,' said Varco.

She knelt down beside him and peered at the section he had indicated.

'Hanx,' she said. 'A surveyor.'

'You know him?'

The girl shook her head.

'Then how do you know he's a surveyor? Does he say so?'

'No,' she said, and tapped the wall with her fingertips, 'but that's a surveyor's hand, if ever I saw one. Surveyors, they're very meticulous, very precise. Look at the style of that, so very tight and fine. A chart maker's hand.'

'What does he say?'

She frowned and squinted. 'He was forced to land his omnithopter at the Topples because of a storm. This was... eighteen weeks ago.'

'Before the war began,' murmured Varco.

The girl shrugged her shoulders. 'He says the storm was unnatural.'

'Unnatural?'

'That's what he wrote.'

'Read it to me.'

She frowned at him.

'Please?' he added.

She bent down and scrutinised the tiny script carefully. 'Well, it says "Forced to land late afternoon, inclement cross-winds, increasing north-north-west. Unnatural for this time of year. I had intended to survey the structure at Mouth Point again today, but was disabled by the weather. Set in overnight, severe unseasonal storms. I took some dried rations, and left two blocks of solid fuel." Then he made the sketch.'

'What does it show?'

The girl pursed her lips. 'The Topples, here. The dust basin beyond. Barter Hill. The Low Metal Reaches, here, I think. And a cross at Mouth Point.'

'Where's Mouth Point?' he asked.

'About ten kilometres west of here,' said Ashlag, getting up off his bunk and hobbling over to them, a dirty sheet shawled around his shoulders. 'What else is there, daughter?'

'Da, it's just ramblings,' the girl said.

'Too tight and small for my old eyes,' he agreed, 'that's why I passed over them. What else does this Hanx say?'

'He says he intends to zip to Barter Hill once the storm is done, and ask Mayor Swayne if he knows what sort of structure is being raised at Mouth Point. He says he wonders if it has anything to do with the sky lights.'

'"Sky lights"?' asked Varco.

'All this winter, there have been pieces of star falling out of the sky onto the Prospection, soldier,' said Ashlag.

'Oh, shit,' said Varco. 'Is there anything else?' he asked, looking up into the puzzled face of Kell Ashlag.

'Not really,' she replied. 'The surveyor simply says that he woke early, once the storm was blown out, and shut off the generator before leaving. He says that the sky is so clear, he will cross once more to Mouth Point before turning to Barter Hill. And then he initials it.'

Varco got up. 'I need a scope,' he said.

'There's a scope in the cupboards,' said Ashlag. 'What the Orb do you intend to do with a scope at this time of night?'

Varco ignored him. He went over to the cupboards in the

alcove, feeling the warmth of the sputtering generator by his side. He found several pairs of goggles, more bedding, and then a huge service revolver, double-barrelled, under and over, wrapped in dirty vizzy cloth, along with a large ply-board box of bullets. He recognised the trust Orwen Ashlag and his surly daughter had placed in him. They could have drawn this weapon and killed them all.

It was a massively heavy piece. He pushed it aside, and found the scope.

'Where are you going?' asked Ashlag as Varco walked past him, scope in hand, strapping on Ashlag's gorgon-face rebreather.

'Out,' Varco replied.

Out in the dark, the rain was hammering down, and turning the dusty slopes to clay and mud. Soaked to the skin the instant he stepped out of the longhouse, Varco clambered up the slope, the scope tucked into his belt. Hand and foot, he dug his way up the muddy bank, slithering back as the waterlogged ground gave way in places.

Thunder rolled. There were no stars. The sky was a heavy black lid spitting rain.

Clambering up through the gurgling slopes and mini-waterfalls, Varco ascended the rain-swept cliffs. He passed a block of solar panels bolted to a south-facing rock, gleaming with raindrops. By the time he reached the summit, he was caked in wet mud and shivering. The rain beat down on him furiously.

The utter darkness of the Deadlands night enveloped him.

He climbed onto the top of a flat rock five hundred metres above the desert floor, and took out the scope. He could see nothing. Visibility was cut by the rain, and he couldn't keep the scope's lens free of water spots.

He sat down, wearily.

Thunder rolled again. The constant rain soaked his already sodden form.

Then it stopped.

He sat up. The rain had ceased, as if a tap had been screwed shut somewhere in the sky. Weather patterns were curling and moving aside. The heavy clouds parted slowly. He saw the suggestion of stars to the west.

The stink of fresh rain and mud in his nostrils, Varco rose and took out the scope again. He wiped the lens and activated the thermal switch.

Mouth Point. About ten kilometres west of here, Ashlag had said.

Varco looked west, the scope whirring and stuttering.

'What are you doing up here?'

Varco lowered the scope and turned around. The girl climbed up onto the rock shelf behind him. She had followed him up the wet and treacherous slopes.

'Go back, Kell,' he said.

'What are you doing up here?' she repeated.

'I don't know. Trying to find Mouth Point. Throne-cursed scope doesn't want to work in this wet.'

'Give it here,' she told him, taking the scope, and adjusting it. 'There. Look west, by the bearing marker. Keep it steady, slightly away from your eye.'

'I know how to use a scope, Kell,' he said, taking the instrument from her.

'Oh, you do, do you?' she sneered back.

Varco trained the scope west. Kell had aligned it and focused it precisely. He saw the tower at Mouth Point.

'Oh, Throne,' he gasped, trying to keep the scope steady.

Ten kilometres away, three hundred and seventy metres

tall, a throbbing grid of bastard ironwork plunging up at the low sky like a dagger. Corposant, like neon capillaries, sparked off its upper structure into the lank, swollen clouds.

The tower was an Archenemy creation, raised out of the desert dust using the scrap and metal debris left over from Barter Hill and all the other torn-down indigent burgs. Varco realised that it was doing something ugly to the weather. It had to be a shield generator, a massive shield generator. The tower was emitting a vast void field that hid a significant region of the Western Prospection from orbital view, and the field effects were seriously disrupting weather patterns.

There's something wrong with the sky, Koder had said. *It feels like something is masking the sky from us, captain.*

Varco angled the scope down and took in the desert floor around the base of the monstrous tower. He murmured in despair.

'There, you see? There they are,' said Kell, training her own scope. 'All of them.'

'Engines,' whispered Varco.

'Lots,' she agreed.

It *was* lots, not by Kell Ashlag's simple standards, but by *any* standards. Sixty engines, at the very least, had drawn up around the base of the tower, hooting at the thundering sky like feral beasts: sixty engines hidden from any orbit scans by the cloak of the tower's void shields.

It was a second host of Archenemy Titans, a second host that the hives were completely unaware of.

1111

It was as if all four elements had conspired to bring about Argentum's downfall. Rain lashed down, fire roiled through the outer hive levels in uncontrolled fury, the air was a toxic mix of smoke and pollution, and the earth shook.

The Titans were walking. Gearhart's assault on Orestes's second city had begun.

With the second front closing in behind them, Lord Gearhart's five battle groups of Invicta and Tempestus engines had begun their effort to put the great hive to death.

Unable to cut a path through the subsids to the Hive Principal, the Archenemy had drawn its strengths in around Argentum Hive, which it had effectively controlled for over a fortnight. Not that there was much to control. The first battle for Argentum, or Soak Town, as it had become known, had effectively destroyed the ancient hive. Vast sections of its structure had collapsed, or burned out, or were in the process of burning. Archenemy engines had broken into the hive from the north and west, and ravaged it with indiscriminate wrath. The enemy's skitarii forces had smashed through the remains of the PDF and the Orestean regiments, and systematically slaughtered the population. Unconfirmed reports spoke of millions of refugees fleeing into the south-western subsids. Other reports spoke of thirty or forty kilometre-long files of prisoners being marched, under escort, into the Astrobleme and the Western Prospection. The Archenemy, it was said, was procuring a slave workforce. A slave workforce perhaps, others muttered darkly, or the raw materials for some appalling sacrifice to their deranged warp gods.

Lord Gearhart, sweeping all other concerns out of his troubled mind, believed that he had the measure of the enemy. The Archenemy wanted a fight. It wanted to draw the significant engine force protecting the high hive and the forge out of the subsids, and eradicate it in one decisive action. Argentum was their intended killing ground.

The tactic worked both ways, however. To draw the Mechanicus engines to Argentum, the Archenemy had focused its forces there. Eradication of the enemy in one decisive action was now a possibility for *both* sides.

Gearhart was aware that it was a risky gambit. Several of his senior princeps, including Racine and Jekcrow, had advised against it. The enemy strengths were vast and focused, and they committed themselves with mindless fury.

Gearhart knew fury. It had become his name and his reputation, but his fury was not mindless. It was clinical, it was controlled. At its peak, it was so ruthless and methodical that Gearhart was scared of himself. He was scared at his capacity for destruction. When he allowed himself to be engulfed by the Red Fury, he let go to the machine spirit. He let go to the MIU and the sentient rage that blazed inside *Invictus*

Antagonistes's reactors. That sublimation had won him many battles, and had taken him from lowly famulous to princeps maximus. It would win this battle for him.

Gearhart was sure that the years of sublimation were also to blame for the slow erasure of his being. He had a feeling deep down in what had once been his gut, a visceral response, like the thudding purr of a reactor buried in his skinny abdomen, that Argentum would be his last walk.

He examined the faces of his bridge crew through the Manifold, all of them urgently toiling at their stations in preparation for the coming assault. He would miss them. He wondered if they would miss him. He wondered who would take his place in the casket. Would his successor, one day, lose his self to *Invictus Antagonistes* too?

There were other faces on the bridge that evening. They had come, unbidden, and lurked like wraiths in the shadows, watching the crew at work. The crew was oblivious to their presence. There, Lucius Karing, hunched and muttering, tutted at the steersman's sloppy manipulation of the drive train. There, Lodem Banns, Gearhart's first moderati, dead two centuries back during the Genestealer Wars, watched Bernal at work in his chin-seat. There, Ervin Hekate of *Dictatio*, upright and grim, waited for the bloodletting to begin. There, Gaetan Sanktos, Gearhart's predecessor in the principeture of *Antagonistes*, stood stiff and silent. At his side was Taurus Mengs, who had been princeps before Sanktos, and with them, other faces, paler ghosts, some so old and faded they were scarcely visible, like overwritten script fading on a wall.

Gearhart didn't know their names, but he knew them all the same. They were the princeps who had commanded *Antagonistes* down through the ages, an honour roll that dated back ten thousand years to Mars, and the birth of the

Imperium, and the death of innocence. They represented a legacy no man, not even Gearhart, could ever fully measure up to. The MIU had summoned them all forth to witness Gearhart's final action.

'Set and ready, my princeps,' said Lodem Banns.

<Thank you, my moderati,> Gearhart replied.

'Watch for shield noise, young man,' advised Sanktos. 'Down in the hive streets, there'll be echo and ripple-knock. Tell your sensori to keep it clean.'

<I will, sir.>

'Remember, you are the mightiest destroyer in creation,' said Hekate softly. 'Even the great Astartes fear us. Arrogance is not a fault. Pride is not a failing. You are a god, a very specific god.'

<A god of war. I know, sir.>

'Then *be* a god.'

<I will. I am.>

'And don't let them unplug you,' hissed Lucius Karing.

<My princeps?>

'Don't let them do it to you. Not like they did it to me. The bastards. Better that you should die first.'

<Yes, my princeps.>

'Do you understand me, boy? Do you *properly* understand me, oh-so mighty Lord Gearhart?'

<Yes, my princeps.>

The shadows began to draw in around him, closing around the casket, until all he could see was their old, lost faces peering in at him. Their cold, lifeless hands pressed against the casket casing and left no mark.

<I know what I'm doing,> Gearhart canted. <Kindly leave me alone!>

'What did you say, my princeps?' Bernal called.

Gearhart steadied himself in the amniotic suspension. The shadows had gone. <Moderati?>

'You said something, I think, my princeps.'

<Just musing to myself, Bernal. Status?>

'Routing tactical to your Manifold view, my princeps.'

Gearhart surveyed the data swiftly, blink-absorbing over six thousand separate elements of data track.

<We're as ready as we're going to be,> he canted.

'Yes, my princeps,' the moderati replied, locking his chin-seat forwards and nodding to the steersman and sensori.

<Manifold command to all groups,> Gearhart canted, <the order is walk, and the order is given.>

At Lau's roared command, a three kilometre-wide mass of skitarii and cataphractii rushed the outer ditches and boundary walls of Argentum. As they charged, they uttered, en masse, a code scream that shook the heavens and made even Gearhart wince.

The black, rain-drenched air lit up with gunfire, flaming rockets and zipping las beams. In less than forty seconds, the fight closed. Invicta skitarii smashed into the massed ranks of the enemy warriors, shattering them, and pushing them back through the mud and smoke. Massive detonations ripped through the fighting line. One of the main hive gates blew out and collapsed.

Ponderous, magnificent, the engines paced in behind the surging skitarii line. They moved through the rain and the whirling smoke, thousands of tiny shots flashing and bursting off their voids, las tracers whipping past them like bright, careless ribbons in the wind. The engines began to unload their limb weapons and carapace mounts into the hive's walls and gates. Seething clouds of stuttering light and whipping flame ripped through the outer hive levels, scouring firestorms that left nothing in their wake except fused ceramite and shattered rockcrete.

The Warhounds bounded ahead, running in through the skitarii formations – *Morbius Sire, Lupus Lux, Raptus Solemnus* – the cream of Gearhart's loyal attack dogs. Fast and sure, they split their way through the enemy ground troops, and hammered tanks and heavy cataphractii pieces apart.

Amadeus Phobos was the first engine to reach the main east gate of Argentum, and the first to engage with enemy engines. In the tight confines of the gate entry, it slit the air with missiles as two scrapshunt Reavers attempted to defy it. *Philopos Manix* strode in beside *Phobos*, took a heavy hit to its voids, and casually executed one of the Reavers with its cannon. The top structure of the mighty gatehouse, its stonework ages old, toppled in, and chunks of broken masonry crashed and slithered off the engines' voids. The gatehouse, reduced to a pair of shot-cratered piles with no top, was never repaired. In later days, it would be called Manix Gate, and the Mechanicus faithful would make pilgrimage to it, to dress and adorn its wounded, punctured stone with ribbons, icon cogs and placards.

Manix and *Phobos* continued to plough their way through the entry space, crunching weaponised servitors underfoot. The second Reaver died under *Manix's* guns, and crushed a hundred enemy skitarii beneath its burning, toppling frame. A blood-red Warlord, squealing scrapcode, loomed out of the sink levels to take the place of the two fallen Reavers.

Manix and *Phobos* fired together.

Bohrman walked *Divinitus Monstrum* in through Prospect Arch, two kilometres north of the main east gate. *Kalix Avenger* strode in behind him, spitting missiles from its carapace mount, and the street levels ahead of them both were obliterated by swirling detonation backwash.

Oblivious to the gusting fire, three Archenemy Warlords trudged out of the surging inferno to greet them.

Monstrum and *Avenger* engaged their close combat weapons and advanced on the Warlords, firing.

Sicarian Faero entered Argentum by blasting a hole through the skin of its outer wall. Lau's ground forces poured in over the smoking rubble behind it. *Faero* slew an enemy Warhound with an expert gut-shot, and then closed with a Reaver that was pounding it with missiles.

Voids holding, *Faero* walked into the abominable onslaught, blastgun raised and tracking.

Orestes Magnificat led the fourth battle group through Bardolphus Gate into the Sequence Gardens and the outer walks of the hive's rich southern quarters. It despatched an enemy Reaver near the boating lake, and left its carcass burning on the once-perfect lawns. Then it turned north into the upper-class hab zone known as the Symphony.

Eleven minutes into its walk, crunching past the ornate public fountain at Lear's Circus, a marble edifice of the Emperor carried in almost-death by his surviving primarchs and noted in all visitor guides to Argentum, *Orestes Magnificat* died with all hands.

The skitarii supporting the Warlord fell back in terror at the sight of the engine that had killed their leading Warlord.

It screamed its name at them as it advanced out of the sub-streets, a scrapcode noise that burst eardrums and conjured abject fear. As it advanced, burning the fleeing skitarii to ash, it howled again.

It was called *Augmenautus Rex*, and it had once been an Imperator-class Titan.

* * *

>

Crusius followed the progress of the main assault via the Manifold. The crawler, along with its support elements, had halted less than five kilometres from the front line. The crew watched through the dome of the observation bridge as Argentum burned in the hard evening rain.

Crusius wasn't bothered with the apocalyptic scenery. He was more concerned with tracking the individual data feeds and gun-box memories that the Manifold flickered up in front of him. His overview of the Argentum assault was on a par with Lord Gearhart's.

Lysenko came over to join him.

<I've re-transmitted your signals to the Adept Seniorus and the Lord Governor, executor,> Lysenko canted. <Still no response from either.>

<Is it still a comm problem?>

Lysenko shrugged. <I hope so. If it isn't, their continued silence is ominous.>

<Sonne?>

<Nothing from the famulous either, executor.>

Crusius nodded, still staring at the Manifold display. <What's the mood aboard?>

<It's settled, executor,> Lysenko canted. <I was obliged to rebuke several members of the crew for unruly conduct, and for expressing inflammatory anti-Imperial and anti-forge sentiments, but we have good order now. This,> he gestured at the spectacle of the burning hive, <has rather focused everyone's attention.>

Lysenko turned as the bridge hatch opened.

<Mamzel Severin, executor.>

Crusius took his attention away from the Manifold and

moved to greet Etta and her bodyman. He had deemed it safe enough to allow her out of her quarters, but he noticed that Gotch was armed with a hellgun. A cursory trace-scan told him that Etta Severin had a pistol concealed under her jacket.

'Etta,' he said with a gracious nod.

She was looking past him, mesmerised by the view of Argentum. 'Holy Throne,' she murmured.

'As you can see, the assault on Argentum is underway,' Crusius said. 'I thought you would like to observe. I can arrange for Manifold interface, if you wish to review individual data feeds for specifics.'

'There'll be nothing left of the hive,' she said, still staring out through the observation dome. There was no detail to perceive: it was just an impressionistic blur of smoke, rain, fire and darkness moving against the mountainous shadow-bulk of the hive.

'To be fair, the main point is that there'll be nothing left of the enemy,' said Crusius. 'Lord Gearhart is confident that we have drawn the Archenemy's main strengths together here. I share that confidence. You may be witnessing the deliverance of Orestes.'

'Then the deliverance of Orestes is the most appalling thing I have ever seen,' she replied.

'It's war,' said Gotch. 'War has a purpose, war has a point, and war can be just and right, but it's never pretty.'

'Well put, major,' said Crusius. He turned to her. 'Etta, if I can tear your attention away for a moment?'

She looked at him, and allowed him to steer her away across the bridge space. Gotch stayed put, watching her rather than the inferno outside.

'You are aware of the troubling developments in Hive Principal?' Crusius asked her quietly.

'Yes,' she replied. 'I find them very disquieting. They have the potential to make what's happening to Argentum seem trivial.'

'Indeed. May I ask, have you had any correspondence with Lord Governor Aleuton since we last met?'

'Since you admit to monitoring my transmissions, executor, I would expect you to know full well that I have not.'

Crusius smiled. 'I wanted to be sure. It is entirely possible that you have comm devices that are invisible to my scans. Please, Etta, I need to know. This situation is too precarious for us not to be entirely frank with one another. If it comes to choosing sides, you must understand that the Legio Invicta is on yours.'

'Against the forge?'

'If needs be. Invicta will not stand by and allow heretical beliefs to split Imperium and Mechanicus.'

She didn't reply.

'Do you trust me?' he asked.

'I think I trust you enough,' she said. 'No, I haven't had communication with the Lord Governor. I have no devices invisible to your scans.'

'Thank you. At Lord Gearhart's instruction, I have been trying to contact the hive, specifically the Lord Governor and the Adept Seniorus. Lord Gearhart wishes me to assure the Lord Governor that Legio Invicta stands four-square behind him. I have received no response.'

'I see,' she said. 'There could be many reasons–'

'And some of them are bad,' he said. 'Could I ask you to compose a message, and send it to him via the crawler's main vox and the noospheric links? If, for any reason, he is choosing to ignore my signals, a message from you might be a way to get my assurances to him. You must make him understand that we support him and all Imperial interests.'

'Of course,' she said. He led her to a communication console and she began to compose a transmission on the keyboard.

<Executor!>

Crusius left Etta to her work, and hurried over to Lysenko, who had been overseeing the duty servitors that were running the tactical appraisal.

<Report?>

<Gun-box feed from a cataphractii unit in the Symphony district,> canted Lysenko. <Exloading feed marker to your Manifold view.>

<Inloading,> replied Crusius, switching his eyes to Manifold interface. <Oh, Mars! Is that an Imperator?>

<Trace confirmed,> canted Lysenko. <I've linked the feed to the Analyticae for Hostile Catalogue cross-match, but–>

<Let me guess, Lysenko. There's no response?>

<None.>

<Get me Lord Gearhart.>

<Link enabled.>

Crusius took a step back. Through the Manifold, he was suddenly looking into Gearhart's casket aboard the *Invictus Antagonistes*. There were psychostigmatic wounds visible on Gearhart's flesh, and he was hunched and shaking. Crusius knew that the Red Fury was beginning to overtake him. Via appended Manifold sub-feeds, Crusius read that the *Antagonistes* was engaged in a shooting match with two enemy Warlords in Argentum's third largest commercia.

<I'm busy, Hekate,> Gearhart growled. <Please, sir, stop staring in at me.>

<It's Crusius, my lord.>

The image of Gearhart blinked slightly. <Crusius? Yes, it is you, you young devil.>

<You addressed me as Hekate, my lord. Did you mean the great Ervin Hekate?>

<The old dog's been on my mind of late. Look, I'm preoccupied. Bernal! Juice the fore shields! Come about two points and resume destructor fire!>

Crusius heard the echo of the moderati's response.

<I realise you're engaged, sir,> Crusius canted, <but we've just detected an Imperator in the Symphony district. It's already killed *Orestes Magnificat* and *Crusadus Anthrop*, and it's in the process of driving the fourth battle group back to Bardolphus Gate.>

<Dammit! Stand by, executor. Bernal! Missiles, six spread! And turn the bolters on those scrapshunt servitors!>

Crusius waited. Through the Manifold, he could feel the punch and thunder of *Antagonistes's* missile pod firing. He could smell the rancid oil, the hot circuits, the venting exhaust. He could taste the sour sweat of *Antagonistes's* bridge crew, the secretions of adrenaline rush oozing from the hard-pressed weapon servitors and the tang of blood as it leaked into the amniotic suspension.

<Engine kill! Engine kill!> Gearhart cackled.

<My compliments, lord,> canted Crusius.

<We got it square with a six spread. The other engine is trying to run for it. Steersman. Pursuit stride!>

The image of Gearhart turned back to face Crusius.

<You were saying something about an Imperator, Hekate?>

<It's Crusius, lord.>

<I know that, dammit! An Imperator?>

<In the Symphony district, sir. It's already killed *Orestes Magnificat* and *Crusadus Anthrop* and–>

<Yes, *yes*, I'm reading the feed now. I'm too far away to deal with it. Third group is closer. I'm alerting Kung. He'll have

to take his engines against it. If *Magnificat* is gone, who has command of fourth?>

<Gorman Kharzi, on the *Vulcanus Havok*, lord.>

<Not Hekate, then?>

<Princeps Hekate is long dead, my lord,> replied Crusius, stifling his unease.

<I know that! I meant Sanktos!>

<My lord, Gaetan Sanktos was your predecessor on the *Antagonistes*. He too is long dead.>

The Manifold link greyed out for a moment. When it reframed, Gearhart appeared, laughing at Crusius. <Can't you tell when I'm playing the fool with you, Djared? For cog's sake, you young devil, did you think I was losing my mind or something?>

<Of course not, my lord. Although, it seemed an inappropriate moment for levity.>

<Stick your levity up your access-port, executor. We're in the thick of it, if you hadn't noticed. I have an engine in my sights. Tell Levin to bring in the second front to support Kung. The whole cohort, you hear me?>

<Yes, my lord. Consider it done.>

The link blanked away.

Crusius stood for a moment. He raised his head and looked out at the hive burning in the night.

'Lysenko?'

<Yes, executor?>

'I require a link to Levin.'

<Yes, executor.>

'And Bohrman, I think. A secure channel.'

Bohrman. I have to say something, Crusius thought. If Gearhart was joking with me, in the heat of combat, then I'll look like a fool. But it was too strange. I have to say something. I have to confide in the first princeps. He needs to know. He needs to be ready to take over legio command if–

<Princeps Levin on channel 631 for you, executor. First Princeps Bohrman on channel 304.>

'Thank you, Lysenko,' said Crusius. He adjusted his Manifold links. 'Lysenko?'

<Yes, executor?>

'Could you please try to raise Sonne for me?'

<Of course, executor.>

Crusius sighed and enabled channel 631 with a haptic gesture. <Princeps Levin, this is Crusius. Orders from our Lord Gearhart begin...>

>

Sonne paused and waved his escort to a halt. Apart from the odd Tempestus skitarii sentry, the looming halls of the Inner Forge were silent and empty. Comm-servitor Obligana had established that a link blackout had been imposed. The vox and the noosphere weren't just jammed, they had been deliberately embargoed.

The forge was a dense maze. Hidden in gloom, the ceilings rose four or five storeys high. The long halls and vacant chambers were muffled with doubt and bright with echoes.

Sonne felt lost. He also felt very scared.

'Analyticae?'

Karsh consulted a stored noosmap. <One hundred and fifty metres, left turn, fifty-three metres, right turn, ten metres to cross-corridor–>

'Enough. Lead me there.'

* * *

They opened the hatch and entered the Analyticae. The main chamber was empty, the pulpit stations unmanned. The central catalogue hub glowed softly in the heart of the room. Sonne approached it.

He read the data display. There were five hundred and seventy-eight requests for catalogue comparisons pending, all unanswered. Invicta's engines were calling for supportive intelligence, and their cries were being ignored. All work on the Hostile Catalogue had been suspended.

By whom? Why?

'We're going to lose this damned war,' Sonne muttered.

<Invicta never loses,> Karsh canted automatically.

'This time, maybe,' replied Sonne. He turned to Obligana. 'Any chance of opening a link to the executor from here? I'm guessing no.'

<No link at this time, famulous,> she blurted.

'Can you locate the Adept Seniorus for me? Or Adept Feist?'

<In work,> she replied, her eyes flooding with scrolling data. <The Adept Seniorus and Adept Feist are both in interview chamber sixteen, two decks down.>

'Take me there,' Sonne told his skitarii.

>

'I want you to tell me how long you've been planning this,' said Imanual, reverting to his fleshvoice in tired dismay. 'And I need you to understand that I consider this a treasonous crime. I am disappointed in you all. More than disappointed. I am ashamed of you.'

<You are old, adept, you don't understand,> Tolemy replied in cant.

'I understand the threat of weapons well enough, master

of the archives,' Imanual replied. 'These skitarii point their limbguns at me, and at Feist. I understand that. I just don't understand you.'

<Cant, for cog's sake,> blurted Enhort. <I can't stand that slurring fleshvoice of yours!>

Imanual turned to look at the executor fetial, Tempestus. He answered, very deliberately, in his fleshvoice. 'You, Enhort. I am disappointed in you most of all. My famulous, my friend. I trusted you with everything, and you conspire with these fools against me. Against me, against the forge, against the Mechanicus.'

Enhort stiffened. <The cosmos changes, Solomahn. The Mechanicus grows and evolves. Truth empowers us. The galaxy should not, must not, burn with the Imperium's wars forever. The Emperor and his kin will take us down with them into the pit. Yes, I was your famulous. I believe I am still your friend. Why can't you see the worth of what we're doing today? It is time for Mars to ascend again. Join with us.>

'I cast you away, Enhort, as a friend and as a companion,' muttered Imanual. 'You have abused my trust. You have poisoned the forge of Orestes. You have dishonoured the Mechanicus.'

<Shut up, you old fool!> Tolemy canted. The skitarii around him bristled.

'I'm an old fool, am I, Tolemy?' said Imanual. 'Perhaps. I saw this schism in the making, and I tried to divert it. Maybe I should have tried a little harder. Maybe I should have monitored the behavioural diagnostics a little better and realised that idiots like you should be removed from office before you could do any damage. I imagine I will regret not doing so for the rest of my life. And I imagine the rest of my life can be measured in hours.'

<You would not dare harm the person of the Adept Seniorus!> Feist blurted.

One of the skitarii turned and aimed its weapon directly into Feist's face.

<I think it's better if you don't talk, adept,> declared Egan mildly. <Your work is done.>

<My work? To facilitate this blasphemy? You used me, didn't you, Egan?>

Egan shrugged, and his mechadendrites flexed nervously. <Not deliberately. But you were so damn useful, Feist.>

<Kill me,> Feist canted.

Egan and Enhort looked at him sharply. Tolemy laughed.

<Kill me,> Feist repeated. <I want no part of this transgression. Just grant me the satisfaction of explaining your madness before one of your warriors puts a round through my skull.>

<It won't come to that,> canted Egan. He glanced at Tolemy. <Will it? Tolemy? Will it?>

Tolemy did not reply.

<Tell the adept what he wants to know and we'll find out,> canted Enhort.

Egan stepped towards Feist. His modified eyes were furtive, and Feist could smell his over-active floodstream. <Feist, I never meant to draw you into this, I never meant to get you into any kind of–>

<Just tell me,> Feist blurted.

'Yes, tell him, Egan. We're all aurals,' said Imanual.

<Tolemy discovered the texts nine years ago, during a routine catalogue,> Egan canted.

<You've known this secret for nine years?> Feist responded.

<Nine years?> Kalien echoed, incredulous.

<Nine years to decide what to do with them,> canted Enhort. <Nine years to make choices.>

<Let's get one thing clear before I go any further,> canted Tolemy. <The texts are authentic, absolutely authentic. They are not forgeries. They are not hoaxes. I haven't manipulated or changed anything. The texts are exactly as I recovered them from the deep archive, and they prove, beyond a shadow of doubt, that the God-Emperor of Mankind is not our Omnissiah. That fact alone should help you understand the sincerity of our actions.>

'Fact or no fact,' replied Imanual slowly, as if explaining something to a child, 'division with the Imperium would lead to war, to damnation, to the ultimate obliteration of the Mechanicus. It's an unpopular view, I know, but without Terra, we are nothing. Ten thousand years of history have left us in a position of mutual reliance. A symbiosis. Your truth, Tolemy, however true, will kill us all.'

<In your opinion, Solomahn,> replied Enhort.

'Right this minute, my famulous, my opinion is all I have,' said Imanual.

<From the first moment I read the texts and appreciated their worth,> Tolemy canted, <I knew that you wouldn't tolerate their publication, Adept Seniorus. I knew this would be your argument. Enhort thought you might be talked around, so we tested your opinion.>

'You tested me?' repeated the Adept Seniorus.

<Egan would bring you realbooks, from time to time,> Enhort canted. <Realbooks, files, snippets, copy-texts, extracts. He would say he was bringing them for your amusement.>

'I remember.'

<You had them all burned.>

'And from that you knew I would never allow this material to be formally published,' said Imanual.

<We understood your reasons,> canted Egan. <We disagreed

with them. We gave you every chance, but you demurred. The *new way* is not the way of Orestes Forge. You taught us that yourself. Why are you so blinkered?>

'Because, unlike you, Egan, I appreciate the calamity that will befall us if these texts get out.'

Tolemy turned away. <There's no canting to him,> he blurted in disgust.

<Finish your tale, please,> canted Feist.

'I would imagine,' ruminated the Adept Seniorus, with a faraway look in his augmetic eyes, as though he was contemplating some distant, abstract problem, 'that the next part of the tale involves them devising a way to circumvent Mechanicus politics and my authority, without casting themselves in the role of villains. It is so very hard to proselytise when your audience is booing you.'

<We wanted the material to be published, but we knew that to do so without your permission or contrary to your edict would make us rebels in the eyes of the forge,> canted Enhort. <The material had to come to light as if by accidental discovery.>

'Very devious,' murmured Imanual. 'I am impressed by your capacity for subtlety, my famulous. Your only other option was a coup. The master of the archives, the master of the Analyticae, the executor fetial... quite a triumvirate to move against an old and old-fashioned Adept Seniorus. You might have rallied many with you, but it would have been a risk. This war was a gift from the machine spirits for you, wasn't it?'

<I... I don't understand,> canted Feist.

Egan looked at him, his dendrites still waving nervously. <This war was an opportunity. And you, my dear adept, you couldn't have played your part better if we'd rehearsed you.

So clever, so resourceful, suggesting that we open even the sequestered vaults to assist the war effort.>

<Tolemy left the text where you or one of your adepts would find it, Feist,> canted Enhort. <It suited us to have someone else 'locate' the data for us. And Kalien was the final part of our equation. Tolemy placed her beside you in the Analyticae because he knew she was an ambitious little scrapshunt who would do anything to make a name for herself. He read her well. He knew she would not allow you to hide anything you found.>

At Feist's feet, Kalien hugged herself into a tighter, snivelling ball.

<You did our work for us, Feist,> canted Tolemy. <The data is revealed and Enhort, Egan and I are quite blameless.>

<Our thanks to you both,> agreed Enhort, with a sarcastic binaric tone. <The truth is out there now. It cannot be taken back. Once the petty war on Orestes is done, the future will welcome us. A changed future. Mars, ascendant.>

Feist sagged. He gazed down at the deck and shook his head. <What happens now?>

'My dear adept,' said Imanual, taking Feist by the arm with two of his manips, 'where's your imagination? Now the coup begins. In a time of war, with public emotion raised to fever pitch, and general panic just a heartbeat away, it is revealed that Solomahn Imanual, Adept Seniorus and Master of the Forge Orestes, deliberately concealed data that effects the destiny of human culture. What an almighty monster I must be! What a blinkered old fool, too long in authority! The magi of the forge, the common folk, the skitarii and the legios, even the Imperial population of the hive and their grandees and statesmen will bow down in gratitude and understanding when the brave, dutiful masters of the archive and the

Analyticae, along with the handsome and charismatic Executor Fetial Tempestus, step forwards selflessly to wrest power from my feeble manipulators and restore order. That's pretty much how it will go, isn't it, Tolemy? Egan? My dear, trusted famulous? Isn't that pretty much how it will go?'

Tolemy said nothing. Egan fidgeted nervously, unwilling to catch Feist's eyes. Enhort folded his arms. <Pretty much,> he canted.

<But *we* know,> blurted Feist.

'That's why they have to kill us,' replied Imanual. He released his manipulator grip on Feist's arm. The moment before he did, Feist felt the manips give a little haptic tap.

Get ready, dear boy.

'I have one last thing to say,' announced Solomahn Imanual, gathering his robes and turning to face the trio and the skitarii. He opened the augmitters built into the corners of his jawline and exloaded a brief, shrill burst of code.

It was a command signal, an override of the highest authority and clarity. Imanual had been patiently devising it during the conversation. It was the most beautiful and perfect code composition Feist had ever heard, the work of a true Mechanicus genius.

It countermanded, temporarily, Tolemy's high-function authority over the four skitarii, and replaced his codified orders with a new command.

The skitarii turned on one another, and opened fire. At such close range, their powerful limbguns tore them apart, and splattered the chamber with blood, meat and biomechanical ichor. Feist shielded his face, and Kalien screamed at the sudden noise. A stray shot sliced through Egan's left thigh and he sprawled, squealing.

<Run!> Imanual blurted at Feist, phrasing his order in the

most serious and emphatic binary tense. Despite his age and infirmity, he raged forwards, his dendrites whipping and lashing. He threw himself at Tolemy and Enhort.

<You stupid old fool!> Enhort canted, fighting him off. Imanual's manips ripped at him and cut him across the cheek and forehead.

Tolemy tumbled backwards, his throat slit by another of Imanual's flashing manips. Floodstream spurted out of the puncture and he crashed to the floor.

His face and arms speckled with blood and bio-fluid, Feist grabbed Kalien by the hand. <This way!> he exloaded furiously. <Come on!>

He dragged her out of the interview room and into the hallway outside. They ran, hand in hand, frantic and desperate.

'Feist–' Kalien yelled, sprinting to keep up with him. Their footsteps clattered down the huge hallway.

<Shut up and run, adept!>

Though his duties are principally ceremonial and diplomatic, an executor fetial is fully modified for combat. Enhort's body was loaded and enhanced to the standards of any high-ranking skitarii. His jet-black robes flying out, Enhort severed two of Imanual's thrashing mechadendrites with chops of his reinforced hands, and spin-kicked the Adept Seniorus across the interview room.

Imanual hit the far wall hard. The impact broke bones, burst organs and cracked skeletal augmetics. He slid down the wall, with a gasp, and folded over onto the deck. Breathing hard, Enhort stood and gazed down at the Adept Seniorus's crushed body. He wiped the blood from his face.

<You stupid bastard!> he canted.

Tolemy rose to his feet. Egan was still moaning and writhing on the floor, clutching his leg. The front of Tolemy's robes were soaked with blood and stream juice. He pinched the slit in his throat shut with two manips, and diverted his flood-stream via redundant vessels to bypass the ruptured carotids.

<Still with me?> Enhort enquired.

<Feist and the girl. They have to be stopped,> Tolemy canted.

Enhort nodded and headed out into the hallway, summoning skitarii from nearby posts.

Holding his throat shut, Tolemy gazed down at the shuddering, groaning body of the old Adept Seniorus. He walked over to one of the exploded skitarii carcasses, and drew a pistol from its belt webbing. The weapon was slick with blood.

<You're in the way,> Tolemy told the old, fatally injured adept. <You're in the way of the future. The future is us.>

'Then the f-future,' Imanual gasped, chewing the words out one by one with his unaccustomed tongue, 'is something I have n-no wish to s-see.'

Tolemy aimed the pistol and shot the Adept Seniorus six times through the chest. The first shot shattered his spine, the next two exploded the cavitic chambers of his ancient, plastek heart. The other three were simply overkill.

Solomahn Imanual spasmed and slowly sagged into the gleaming, widening lake of blood that surrounded him. Tolemy bent down and closed Imanual's static-fuzzed, dead eyes with his wet fingertips.

'Then look away,' he suggested.

Feist and Kalien ran. Hand in hand still, they raced down the wide hallway of Forge Level 1823, turned at the junction, and sprinted on.

<Why didn't you just leave me?> Kalien screamed at him.

<Go back, girl, if you want any part of that!>

<I don't! I swear! I had no idea!>

<Then come on and help me put this right!>

<How can you trust me after–>

<No one likes being used,> he told her.

They flinched as las-bolts burned down the hallway past them. Enhort had re-established control of the skitarii, and several warriors had burst into the hallway behind them. The skitarii ran forward, halted and aimed their weapons at the fleeing pair, snatching target solutions out of the noosphere that would bring Feist and Kalien down.

Kalien and Feist felt the noospheric crosshairs ghost over them as they ran. There was nowhere to hide.

<We're dead, Feist!> she blurted. <We're so dead!>

Heavy gunfire stripped down the hallway. Enhort's skitarii buckled, twisted and fell, torn apart.

<What the cog?> Feist canted, stumbling to a halt and looking back at the smoking bodies.

Sonne appeared out of the shadows ahead of them, flanked by his warriors. Discharge vapour was threading from the gunlimbs of Karsh, Lux 88 and Tephlar.

'Hello, Feist,' said Sonne. 'You'd better come with me if you want to stay alive.'

>

The first hints of approaching rain hung in the air. Cally could smell it. The distant edge of the Astrobleme had become fuzzy and indistinct. There was a faint scratching sound, like insects or static, just at the edge of hearing, masked by the breeze.

Activated Twenty-Six moved out of Beaten Track quickly, at a jog, rolling the cart with them. Their rate was pretty much determined by how fast Robor could walk alongside the stricken princeps on the cart. Antic, in a moment of inspired disrespect that Cally had neither the time nor inclination to rebuke, had inscribed the words *Teratos Titanicus* on the prow of the cart.

'It's like a joke,' Antic announced.

'Only smaller,' said Golla Uldana.

Despite herself, Cally found it funny. A battered wooden cart, a dying princeps and eleven terrified PDF troopers who had, between them, virtually zero combat skills, and who were all, to a man and woman, yearning to be entirely somewhere else... And the cart was called *Titanicus*.

They passed out of the limits of Beaten Track, into the ruins of Slow Going and Next Town Along. The rain began to fall, and grew harder. They kept the rate up, guiding the cart through the mud.

'Come on, faster,' Cally urged.

'Oh, you try pushing this, Cally-girl!' Golla complained.

Cally noticed that Janny was working extra hard to keep the rickety cart moving.

Good girl.

Thunder rolled down out of the bruise-blue, fulminous sky.

'That *is* thunder, isn't it?' asked Lars Vulk, the weight of the cart pulling on the drag ropes he had lashed over his mighty shoulders.

'Yes, Lars, it's thunder,' Cally said. 'Come on now.'

'It's not thunder, is it?' Liv Reiss whispered to her.

'Of course it is,' Cally replied with a wink.

Inside, she wasn't as confident. The thunder sounded too much like engine tread, as though something was following them, something alerted by Janny Wirmac's signal.

Worse still was the scratching sound. If they'd heard it at

all, the others had dismissed it as the faraway fizzle of lighting. Cally knew better.

It was the noise that weaponised servitors made as they scurried and hunted. It was the trademark noise of Antic's famous shockroaches, seeking them out to kill them.

>

Settled and utterly focused, Vancent Kung strode *Sicarian Faero* through the firestorms of Argentum's southern streets into the Symphony district. The fluid suspending him in the casket felt as cold as meltwater. His mind was set as hard as a cast ingot.

The engines of the third battle group followed *Faero* along the molten streets. Their sweeping suppression fire was bringing down entire tenement stacks in avalanches of rubble. Ceramite walls tore like wet paper. Glass dissolved in drizzling sprays. According to received signals, Princeps Levin was advancing the leading engines of the second front in through Canticle Gate and up the lower ramps of the hiveskirts to converge with them.

Kung read monumental engine fire ahead of them. Eight engines of the fourth group, led by Gorman Kharzi aboard the *Vulcanus Havok,* were engaging the grotesquely large enemy Imperator. The feeds exloading from Kharzi, chopped into fragments by scrapcode interference, bordered on the frantic. The fourth group had been badly mauled, and the defensive options available to them against the cyclopean machine were woefully limited. The Imperator had caught them head-on, and it was levelling city blocks and hive stacks to get at them. Kung winced at the code scream of the *Tempus Ionicus* as it perished in a ball of light hotter than a sun.

The super-heavy Imperator was so massive that the Manifold tracks made it look like part of the hive's vast structure, detached and moving of its own volition. The towers and castellated structures of its colossal upper section loomed through the sheeting flames and heatwash.

<What the hell do we do against that?> canted Moderati Daross.

<Discipline!> Kung warned. <Sensori, I want a full-spectrum shield analysis!>

The sensori rapidly executed the complex task and squirted the results onto the Manifold linkage. Kung examined them, and found that they confirmed what he had already suspected. *Augmenautus Rex* was wrapped in voids of such power and cohesive performance, they could withstand anything *Faero* or any of the other engines fired at it. The only way to break them was sustained, erosive fire. If they all hit the same shield section hard enough, for long enough, they might force a rupture. The necessary coordinated bombardment would take minutes to arrange and accomplish.

The moment they commenced such a bombardment, however, *Augmenautus Rex* would turn on them, and they wouldn't have anything like minutes left of their lives.

The third group was still three kilometres away from the raging giant.

<All engines request permission to begin distance firing, my princeps,> Daross reported.

<Negative. Permission denied,> replied Kung. He was running the numbers and the options in his head, making tactical calculations at an inhuman rate thanks to the enhancing chemistry of his floodstream. He calculated the minimum energetic force required to rupture a single section of the Imperator's voids, and the rapidity with which such

force could be delivered. Perhaps if all the engines locked to a pre-arranged target solution and fired simultaneously? No, the margin for error was too broad. Different engines in different places, each with its own auspex view and firing traits... A vox or cant was too clumsy a tool to ensure full, coordinated fire.

What then? Gearhart had trusted him with this giant-killer action. How would Gearhart handle it?

<Daross! Link me to all third group and second front princeps!> Kung ordered. <And any fourth group princeps still active in the field! Full Manifold congress!>

<Yes, my princeps.>

One by one, in a rapid series of shimmering materialisations, the Manifold images of the summoned princeps appeared around Kung's casket, facing him grimly. The link image of Romulur Cibor, princeps of *Celestus Aristeas* in the fourth group, looked distracted and agitated, and fizzled out into code-noise a second after it appeared as *Aristeas* was slain by the rampaging Imperator.

<Princeps Kung?> old Levin began.

<Listen to me, all of you,> Kung canted. <This isn't up for debate, and there's no time for discussion. Link your MIUs directly to my engine. Slave to me your auspex and fire control systems. Grant me authority over your Titans.>

<Manifold linkage of MIUs is forbidden!> Theron of *Stridex* canted.

<If we open our impulses to the Manifold, we risk scrap-code invasion and corruption!> declared Philostartus of *Atrox Terribilis*.

<I said this wasn't a discussion,> replied Kung. <Do it now.>

The images of the princeps blinked away as fast as they had

appeared. Kung shivered as he felt the links being enabled. He heard the growls and snarls of dozens of other engines, as if he was inside them. He tasted sweaty, unwholesome floodstream secretions, as if all the other princeps were inside his casket with him.

The sensory load was numbing. He moaned in distress at the weight pulling on his mind. To be linked to one engine was to chain a feral beast in your head. To be linked, simultaneously, to many, was to peer over the lip of the abyss into hell.

Kung shuddered, fighting off the rancid tongues of insanity that licked and crisped the edges of his mind. He attained clarity for a second. Existential shockwaves rippled through him. Kung was used to being a giant, but now he was many giants, linked together, a giant giant, bigger than even the howling Imperator that rose before him. He was third group, and the second front, and the remains of fourth group. He was the centre of a whirling, roaring mass of sentience as brilliantly savage as a supernova and as catastrophically heavy as a black hole.

Steeling himself, weeping, he merged the auspex feeds coming to him from the other engines, selected a target solution, and snap-fed it back to the various firing systems. Scrapcode wailed and chattered around the extremities of his mind, gnawing and chirring to get in and run riot.

<Ready all weapons,> he exloaded.

Dozens of engine minds answered him obediently. Dozens of autoloaders clattered, dozens of missile pods opened their receivers to chamber munitions, dozens of massive main-limb and carapace energy weapons came up to charge, guzzling power from their accumulators. Dozens of crosshairs and target reticules overlaid and pinpointed the same small section of the Imperator's void structure, the third lower left anterior lumbar. The overlaid targetters formed a hard, glowing mass on the Manifold view, like an incandescent remnant of cobweb.

<Fire!> canted Vancent Kung.

In a perfect action of simultaneous discharge, the merged engines opened fire. From their scattered positions in and around the Symphony, the engines of Invicta and Tempestus lit off in absolute coordination. Stark beams of energy lashed out through the fire and the rain, missiles spat out into the dark, broadsides boomed: enough combined fury to bring down a city.

All of it struck the same ten metre square section of void shield at the same instant.

The third lower left anterior lumbar distorted like blown, wet glass and popped. A nanosecond later, *Augmenautus Rex* experienced a system-wide, cascade shield failure as the generators blew out, attempting to compensate and underlap the remaining voids.

On the Manifold, the shield halo surrounding the monster vanished like the flame of an extinguished candle.

<Kill it,> snarled Kung.

The massed engines opened fire again. Kung had held on to the merged link long enough to be sure his gambit had worked. As the batteries of Titans commenced individual fire, and visibly scored hits on the towering superstructure of the Imperator, Kung gratefully let the links go, one by one, feeling the terrible weight and the unbearable tension lift off him.

He thanked the Machine-God for the release.

Augmenautus Rex took ten whole minutes to die. Serial bombardment felled its towers and thorned minarets, shattered its black glass windows and exploded its crenellated battlements. Ablaze, a ghastly, staggering behemoth sheeting white-hot flame and noxious black smoke, it kept firing, and took two more forge-loyal engines down with it.

Kung heard its awful, scrapcode shriek as death claimed it. Its gyros failed, and its gigantic legs collapsed. The castle it carried across its enormous shoulders crashed down onto the rubble of Argentum and disintegrated in a holocaust blast.

<Engine kill! Engine kill!> Daross exloaded.

Sinking in his amniotics, his mind smouldering, his limbs weak, Kung nodded.

<Give me a moment, my moderati,> he replied.

>

When Varco and Kell Ashlag, both soaked to the skin, returned to the halt, it was dark and lifeless.

Pistol drawn, Varco entered the longhouse.

'Oh, it's you,' Sagen muttered in relief, lowering the frying pan he'd hefted as a weapon.

'What happened to the lights?' Varco asked.

The glow-globes had gone out and the generator was silent. Someone had set up a few candles in jars to light the halt.

'He sucked all the power dry,' said Leopald.

Varco realised that Koder was standing in the corner of the room, carefully examining the tight script on the halt wall.

'Koder?'

'Yes, my captain?'

'You're alive?'

'Apparently, my captain.'

Koder went stiff as Varco instinctively hugged him.

'I don't do intimacy well, Captain Varco,' Koder said.

'My apologies. It's good to see you.'

'And you, sir.'

'Are you well?'

Koder shrugged. 'A diagnostic evaluation would deem my activity and fitness level at around fifty-eight per cent, but I'm better than I was.'

'He drank everything in the generator,' remarked Ashlag, sipping caffeine from one of the tin cups.

'Yes, I drained the generator's accumulator. I have already apologised to Master Ashlag about that. It was involuntary. I was in need.'

'And properly deserving,' noted Ashlag.

'What did you see out there, captain?' Trask asked. 'You've got one Throne of a look on your face.'

Varco glanced at Kell, went over and poured himself a cup of caffeine, and sat down on one of the stools. Slowly, carefully, he told them about the tower, the engines and the shield.

Sagen rolled his eyes. Leopald, never one to hold back, uttered the bluest oath Varco had ever heard. Trask simply shrugged.

'Seems like you're deep in the nasty, soldier,' Ashlag cackled. He reached for the pot, and banged it back onto the stove when he realised that Varco had taken the last of its contents.

'What do we do, sir?' asked Sagen.

'Alert the hive,' Varco replied quickly.

'That plan would work,' said Koder, 'except for two key points.'

'And they are?'

'We don't have a vox set, or any other means of communication.'

Varco nodded. 'Yeah, I'd already realised that. Your second point?'

'Even if we had a vox, or a noospheric link, the shield is blocking us.'

Varco looked at him. 'The sky's gone out, Koder.'

Koder nodded. 'It really has, captain.'

'Anyone got a suggestion?' Varco asked. 'I'm searching for ideas here.'

No one replied. The rain hammered at the longhouse. There seemed no possibility of dawn ever coming.

'If–' Koder began.

'What?' asked Varco.

'Nothing.'

'Say it.'

'I was just speculating, captain. If the engine host could be exposed to orbital scans, then the threat would be communicated.'

'Of course it would. And how do we do that?' Varco asked. He paused, thinking, realising what Koder was suggesting.

Kell Ashlag got there a second before he did. 'You knock out the tower,' she said.

'We knock out the tower,' said Varco. 'We knock out the frigging tower and kill the shield.'

Leopald began to laugh. He laughed so hard, he dropped his cup. Trask and Sagen started to laugh too, and old Ashlag, caught up in the merriment, sniggered until his arm hurt.

'Good luck with that, captain!' Leopald whooped.

'We knock out the tower,' Varco insisted.

'With what?' asked Sagen, wiping happy tears from his eyes. 'We've got a pistol and a las-lock, a Centaur, a stubber, a few drums of rounds... hell, yes! Let's take on an engine host! We'd clearly win!'

'We'd need explosives,' Koder said, straight-faced.

'How do we get explosives?' snorted Leopald.

Koder pointed at the wall. 'Someone called Albrech has left instruction for the location of a nitre deposit.'

'Nitre?' Leopald shrugged. He quickly sobered up and stopped laughing. 'I suppose that could work.'

'Can you find it? The deposit?' Varco asked Ashlag.

'Of course,' the old man replied. 'I'll use Albrech's map.'

'These hypothetical explosives? What would you pack them in?' Leopald asked.

'The food drums,' replied Koder immediately. 'They have capacity. We could also manufacture grenades using the jars and pots, and make fragmentation devices from the pail of assorted screw, nuts and nails.'

'Whoa, whoa,' said Leopald, rising to his feet. 'You're getting ahead of yourself. Nitre is a fine, basic compound for cladistics, but you'd need a proper precipitant.'

'Like urine?' asked Koder.

'Yeah.'

'Stale urine?'

'Better.'

'There's a latrine right outside,' said Varco.

Leopald hesitated. 'We'd have to build a filter–'

'Stove ash and charcoal!' Ashlag announced, rising to the theme.

'Good,' said Varco. 'Really good. Can you do it?'

'Just find me that nitre deposit,' Leopald said to Ashlag, reaching for his jacket.

'I'll clean and prep the drums,' said Trask.

'I suppose that means I get to dig the slurry out of the latrine,' sighed Sagen.

'I'll love you for it,' smiled Varco.

'I'll help you, Sagen,' said Koder.

'I'll build the filter,' said Kell Ashlag. 'I know how the process works.'

Varco kissed her on the cheek. 'Good girl,' he said. She grinned at him.

'We'll need an ignition source, of course,' said Leopald, pulling on his jacket.

'There's mining det-tape on the shelves somewhere,' Varco remembered, 'left by a Reydo or a Reldo, I forget which.'

Koder held up the spool of det-tape. 'It was Reldo, captain,' he said.

'Let's get to work,' said Varco.

10000

Assisted by two surgical servitors, the magos organos operated rapidly to repair the wound in Tolemy's throat and regraft the skin.

<Work faster,> Tolemy canted impatiently.

The magos acknowledged the order with a binaric assent, but his progress did not seem to accelerate. He applied the delicate spinnerets of micro-surgical dermal weavers, and slowly drew the lips of the wound together.

Egan fretted nearby. Another magos organos had just finished the repairs to his leg wound. Agitation flickered through his body.

<Get hold of yourself,> Tolemy canted to him on a direct link that the magi organos could not hear.

Egan looked at the master of the archives sharply. He rose to his feet and gingerly tested his patched leg. <This is sliding out of our control, Tolemy,> he replied.

<Get hold of yourself.>

<You never said anything about killing. You never said anything about murder. You–>

<Shut up, Egan. Did you really suppose we could change the course of human history without spilling blood? No one can manage such a feat. Not even the vaunted God-Emperor.>

<But *Feist*. Feist will–>

<Shut up.>

Enhort marched into the chamber with all the self-possession of a Warlord at full stride. Three dozen Tempestus skitarii followed at his heels. The executor fetial had already taken it upon himself to adopt the role of figurehead, and a commanding presence he made. Tolemy approved. Enhort had the noble bearing, diplomatic grace and dashing manner to make a perfect leader. The forge would rally around him. Tolemy also reflected that Enhort was less intelligent than he pretended to be, and that made him malleable and controllable. Enhort, like any leader, was nothing without an arsenal of data to empower him, and the master of the archive controlled all knowledge. Enhort would be utterly reliant on Tolemy, and Tolemy could manipulate him any way he wanted to.

<The forge and all Mechanicus facilities are locked down at situation one,> he canted to Tolemy and Egan on a private link. Situation one was the most draconian status that could be imposed on the forge.

<Have you found Feist?> Tolemy asked.

<Not yet, but he simply cannot get very far. The skitarii have all the gates and exits in the central forge complex covered, and they are flushing the internal systems deck by deck to locate his biometrics.>

<We need to find him and silence him before–>

<I am fully aware of the urgency,> Enhort canted.

The magos organos finished his work on Tolemy's throat and he dismissed him with a curt augmitted order.

<The senior magi are assembled and waiting for us,> canted Enhort. Tolemy got up and followed the executor fetial towards the Audience. Egan hesitated, and then hobbled after them. The skitarii formed a V-shaped phalanx around the trio.

Huge shutters peeled back with a squeal of metal and the rumble of sub-deck motors. The immense space of the Audience lay before them, and the senior magi of the Orestean forge were gathered in the centre of the vast floor between the hololithic threads of data-light rising from the deck projectors like temple smoke. Their chatter and noospheric muttering ceased and they turned as one to face the approaching seniors.

Enhort greeted them with a solemn code blurt.

<Make account of this situation immediately,> Keito demanded in an aggressive code form. Other magi echoed the demand.

<I have called situation one,> Enhort responded, facing the crowd levelly with Tolemy and Egan on either side of him. <The following data is for your consumption only. It is not, I emphasise not, for broadcast or dissemination. We face an internal crisis, and until it is properly remedied and contained, any communication will be deemed a crime punishable by termination.>

<Termination?> Talin blurted. <Preposterous! On what legal basis can you possibly–>

<Code Belli,> Enhort canted, cutting Talin off. <I have determined it necessary to impose Code Belli. Legio Tempestus has taken control of the Orestean facilities for the duration of the crisis.>

The assembled magi reacted in consternation and outrage.

<The Adept Seniorus will not allow this usurpation! Only he can order the imposition of martial law!> Lorek augmitted furiously.

<Where is the Adept Seniorus?> Keito coded. <He must rule on this immediately.>

<'Under extraordinary circumstances, Code Belli can be declared by the ranking officer of the legio',> Tolemy recited from a buffer-stored extract of the Codex Probandi. <I aver that this situation entirely merits such an action and, as most senior member of the Legio Tempestus, Executor Enhort is entirely justified and within his rights to apply it. Shame on you, brothers and sisters. You should be thanking him for taking wise and sober charge of this situation.>

<But the Adept Seniorus–> Talin began.

<The Adept Seniorus is dead,> Enhort augmitted.

There was a stunned silence.

<His death must be considered an act of war,> Enhort canted, <and as such Code Belli must be enforced. There is no time to elect a successor during the current emergency. I have assumed authority.>

<How did this death occur?> canted Keito.

Enhort looked directly at the master of fabrication. <You are all aware of the data that has been revealed to the Mechanicus. It was accidentally discovered by the magi of the Analyticae during archive sweeps undertaken in support of the war effort. Its release was not sanctioned. The data was broadcast by a junior adept. My brothers and sisters, I can confirm that the data is the authoritative truth. None of you can be in any doubt as to the staggering ramifications of that. It is the proof we have always wanted, and our lives are about to change.>

<It is the truth?> Lorek asked Tolemy.

<It has been verified and authenticated, brother,> canted Tolemy.

A mantra of *Praise be the Omnissiah, Deus Mechanicus* began to loop and pulse in the noosphere linking the magi.

<Brothers Tolemy, Egan and I went directly to the Adept Seniorus immediately to see what action he intended to take,> Enhort canted. <Our discussion proved to be disturbing.>

<Explain!> Keito blurted.

Tolemy fingered the almost invisible seam across the flesh of his throat. <We discovered that the Adept Seniorus had known about this material for nine years and had been deliberately keeping it from the magi.>

Tolemy phrased his code expertly to elicit the maximum outrage and disgust from the gathered seniors.

<Inevitably, this revelation led to a heated argument,> Enhort canted, raising a hand to quiet the agitation. <It was at that point that violence broke out. The junior adept who had released the data for public access became very distressed at the Adept Seniorus's continued insistence that the material be kept secret. The adept grabbed a weapon and assassinated the Adept Seniorus.>

The senior magi expressed their horror at the crime.

<I agree, it is intolerable. Whatever Solohamn Imanual's faults at concealing the data, and I am certain they would have led to charges of dereliction and his removal from office, he did not deserve such a fate.> Enhort studied their expressions. <Once apprehended, the junior adept will face the full censure of Mechanicus law.>

<The assassin is at large?> asked Keito in alarm.

<The junior adept effected an escape,> canted Tolemy. <The skitarii have mounted a full search. Imanual's killer will not

escape the forge precinct. Adept Feist will be arrested and brought to justice.>

<Feist?> Egan blurted, shock etched on his face.

Tolemy glanced at Egan. <You have a comment to make, Brother Egan?>

Egan tried to recover his composure. <I… no, of course… Forgive me. I am still in distress over the killing.>

<Brothers and sisters, please make allowances for Magos Egan,> canted Tolemy. <The killer was an adept from Magos Egan's department. It is unbearable to be betrayed by a trusted member of one's staff.>

Egan glared at Tolemy.

<Lord executor,> Keito canted, <would you tell us what your intentions are for the immediate future?>

<A restoration of order, master of fabrication, that is my priority,> Enhort canted back smoothly. <We are at war, and Argentum is burning as we speak. The revelations may well trigger challenging situations in the days and weeks ahead. There is already considerable unrest and disquiet. Let us work to contain and control public uproar until the war is concluded and more active measures can be brought into play.>

<The revelations were made generally,> canted Talin. <The hive is already aware of the claims. The Imperium is already aware of the claims.>

Enhort nodded. <Regrettable, but unavoidable. I will enter into discourse with the Lord Governor. However, be advised that Imperial reaction will be unpleasant. The security of the forge is paramount. Enforce full security in your departments and areas of supervision. Open the arsenal. All general use or non-assigned servitors must report to fabrication for weapons fitting and combat protocol inloads. Magos Keito?>

Keito bowed. <I will prepare fabrication immediately.>

<You think we may be about to go to war with the hive?> canted Lorek.

<I think it is highly likely, brother,> Enhort canted back. <We have just declared their Emperor's divinity to be a lie.>

>

Skitarii warriors, badged in Tempestus colours, clattered down the companionway, weapons hunting, optics scanning. Sonne waited until they were out of sight.

'Come on,' he said.

'I don't understand why they didn't see us,' said Feist, following the famulous out of hiding.

'I'm using Executor Crusius's command codes to obscure our biometrics from the forge data-sphere.'

'But security conditions have been imposed,' said Feist. 'Enhort had even overridden the Adept Seniorus's codes. Imanual only broke Enhort's control by the most extraordinary feat of code-work, and then only briefly and locally.'

'Executor Crusius was granted full and free access to the forge data-sphere when the execution was ratified,' said Kalien quietly. She looked at Sonne. 'That's correct, isn't it, famulous? As a mark of respect for his status and a display of cooperation with the Legio Invicta.'

'This one's clever and quick,' Sonne said, smiling at Feist.

'Too clever for her own good,' Feist replied. Kalien scowled at him. 'Rumination: surely Enhort would have cancelled your executor's clearance?'

'Tell him, Kalien,' said Sonne.

Kalien pouted. 'It is likely that the consideration has not occurred to Executor Enhort. Executor Crusius is outside the forge, and all lines of comm and feed to the noosphere are suspended. Executor Crusius cannot gain access, and therefore there is no reason to cancel his clearance. Executor Enhort has no way of knowing that there is an individual inside the forge equipped with Executor Crusius's codes.'

'Nor should there be,' said Sonne. He grinned impishly, 'but you keep company with a master officer long enough, you can't help accidentally memorising their command codes.'

'I am surrounded by traitors and miscreants,' muttered Feist, shaking his head.

<Traitors and miscreants that are keeping you alive in your skin, adept,> snarled Karsh.

Feist recoiled. 'Leave him alone, Karsh,' Sonne told the big skitarii. 'Our friend Feist has had a bad day.'

They began to hurry down the companionway, and turned left into the echoing length of West/sublink/1101/11. They could hear the drumming footsteps of skitarii patrols on other levels, and the code readers built into the wall panelling every twenty metres were emitting the rolling, pink light beams of trace-scans. None of the code readers reacted to their presence.

'Do you have a plan, famulous?' Feist asked.

'Yes, to get out of here,' replied Sonne. They ducked around a corner bulkhead as a patrol clattered past the T-junction ahead. Sonne's three skitarii held their limbguns ready until the danger had passed. Karsh beckoned the group on.

'I need to get clear enough to establish a link with Executor Crusius,' Sonne told Feist. 'I think the hive is my best bet. There should be active comms there, or at least a chance to get Obligana linked. I need to talk to him. I need to tell him what's happening.'

'Because Invicta will side against the revelations,' sneered Kalien. 'You of the *new way*...'

Sonne turned to face her and the party stopped in its tracks. 'Actually, adept, I believe Invicta will side with the Mechanicus, because it is of the Mechanicus and it has been unswervingly loyal to the Mechanicus for millennia. If your revelations prove to be authentic–'

'They are.'

'*If* they prove to be authentic, Invicta will not betray Mars. Data is data. We will revise our beliefs and face the future… whatever the future brings.'

'Damnation and destruction for us all,' muttered Feist.

Sonne shrugged. He kept staring at Kalien. 'The thing is, adept, I'm wondering if it's occurred to you what's really happening here on Orestes? It's not about the truth. It's not about the divinity of the God-Emperor. From what you and Feist have told me, it's about men like Tolemy and Enhort grabbing power. We're in the middle of a revolution, and your precious truth, my dear adept, is merely a weapon of revolt.'

'Enhort believes in the data,' Kalien objected. 'Enhort is only doing this because of the truth of the data.'

'Maybe,' Sonne shrugged.

'Tolemy isn't,' said Feist. 'For Tolemy, this is about power.'

Kalien didn't disagree. She gazed down at the deck.

'You know him, Kalien,' said Feist. 'He's your master, and he groomed you for this. He's known for nine years. Why didn't he act sooner? He's used you, me, the war, the Legio Invicta and Enhort to effect this revolt. Tell me I'm wrong.'

Kalien clenched her jaw. She wiped a tear from her left eye with an angry, balled up fist. 'Twice he has been overlooked for advancement. He was Imanual's chief rival when the office of Adept Seniorus became vacant. Imanual was master of noospheric processing. Tolemy was archives. Archives! It was an injustice. The synod of magi must have been insane to choose Imanual over Tolemy. He told me personally that he had been rejected when he applied for the Seniorus office at Hensher Forge. He said he suspected that Imanual had blocked his candidacy because he didn't want to lose such an experienced record keeper.'

'And now he's on his way to getting exactly what he wants,' said Feist.

'Executor Enhort has been declared acting authority in extremis,' said Sonne. 'The imposition of Code Belli has put him in charge for the duration.'

Feist raised his eyebrows at the famulous sardonically. 'Enhort's the public face. Tolemy is the real power. And when the election of the next Adept Seniorus is held, you can wager who the synod will back.'

They left West/sublink/1101/11 and followed the 1101 spinal through to Forge Plaza Nineteen. The skitarii patrols were thicker there, so they used Karsh's noosmap to navigate a secondary route through the storage capacitors and machine bays of Technical/Pre-fabrication. The situation on lock down had left the bays and lathe shops empty of personnel. Half-finished items of work and product lay on the work beds of deactivated fab-systems. The glows were set to quarter-lumin.

<If we follow exit 1101110 and go down a deck, we can gain access to one of the western sublinks,> Karsh advised. <That will bring us out through Forge Gate West and onto the transit-way beside the Field of Mars.>

Sonne nodded. 'Let's go,' he said.

They found the exit and descended to the sublink access. The patrol discovered them as they were crossing the marble atrium towards the mouth of the sublink tunnel.

'Run!' Sonne yelled.

The Tempestus skitarii came howling down the steps from a suspended crossway, and screamed orders to stop and desist. Though Crusius's command codes were concealing their biometrics, the face-scans of Feist and Kalien were embedded and flash-tagged in the pattern-memory of the forge skitarii, and they had made an instant visual identification.

<Halt. Go no further,> they blurted. <We are coded to employ terminal force!>

<So am I,> Karsh blurted back. He turned and fired his limbgun. The cannon reduced the nearest skitarii to meat debris. Karsh reviewed his aim and fired again. Red mist swirled as two more warriors of the forge crashed over onto their backs. Momentarily astonished by Karsh's defiance, the Tempestus skitarii began to return fire.

<Keep moving!> Lux 88 roared. Without hesitation, Lux 88 and Tephlar turned to support Karsh. As Sonne, Kalien and Feist raced into the mouth of the sublink tunnel, the first of the returning fire began to chew into the atrium's old marble floor and pepper the walls around the tunnel entrance.

Tephlar reached Karsh's side, braced his feet and triggered the automatic grenade launcher he was modified to carry. Packet munitions detonated amongst the forge warriors swarming towards them. Many were shredded by micro-shrapnel or knocked over by blast-shock. Tephlar kept his launcher pumping. Another volley of grenades brought down the suspended crossway in a welter of flame and threw skitarii headlong off the steps. Lux 88 took up position on the other side of Karsh and added his considerable firepower to the desperate resistance.

Sonne, Feist and Kalien ran down the sublink tunnel, hell breaking loose behind them. Obligana followed them as rapidly as her delicate gressorial systems would allow. Klaxons began to whoop, and amber hazard lights flashed along the tunnel walls. Slowly, the tunnel's heavy blast doors began to shut.

'Move! Move! Move!' Sonne shouted.

It felt as if the entire forge were closing in to prevent their escape. Karsh, Lux 88 and Tephlar stood side by side at the mouth of the sublink and blazed away at the Tempestus skitarii pouring into the atrium from all sides.

It was a heroic last stand. Tephlar tallied eighteen body kills before a las-bolt exploded his head and felled him like a sack of engine scrap. Lux 88 lost an arm and part of his face, but kept firing until two centre-line gut-shots dropped him to his knees. Stricken and bleeding out from his mortal wounds, Lux 88 took a headshot that spun him off his knees and down onto his back.

Firing with his limbgun and a heavy sidearm, Karsh backed away down the sublink tunnel, keeping the skitarii of his fellow legio at bay. He tallied thirty-one body kills in defence of his master, the famulous. It took one hundred and nine separate hits to overcome his glanded rage and reinforced constitution. He fell half way along the tunnel, almost disarticulated by damage.

The Tempestus skitarii trampled over his mangled remains in their fervour to apprehend the fugitives. They had countermanded the blast door closure so as not to be shut off from their targets.

Feist and Kalien came out of the tunnel into the open, running at fall stretch under the huge arch of Forge Gate West. It was raining torrentially. They were both panting hard. Through the sleeting rain, they could see the great expanse of the Field of Mars before them, and the bulk of Hive Principal rising on the far side like a sombre mountain range. Sonne followed them out into the rain, supporting Obligana, who had been winged by a stray shot and was leaking floodstream.

'Come on!' Sonne yelled. He could hear the pounding feet of the skitarii coming up the sublink tunnel behind them. Additional patrols, summoned by the klaxons, were clattering down walkways on the outer face of the forge, rushing to intercept them on the gate approach. Shots whined down, puncturing the rockcrete surface of the approach.

'Come on, what's the matter with you?' Sonne shouted. Feist and Kalien had come to a halt.

'I mean it, what–' Sonne suddenly fell silent and stopped in his tracks beside them. Behind them, the massed sections of skitarii were closing in, shouting, yelling.

As they came out into the open, into the rain, or scurried down the external walkways, the skitarii came to a halt too, weapons raised. Their officers called for clarification and advice.

A detachment of Imperial Guardsman, three hundred strong, supported by main battle tanks and weapon platforms, was drawn up on the approach facing the gate. Every single rifle, every single main gun, cannon and launcher, was aimed at the skitarii and the forge.

An officer – a major – stepped forwards, squarely aiming a pistol at the forge skitarii. He wore a glinting beak helmet with a huge crinière of white feathers, a crimson coat and a silver cuirass. His face was utterly unforgiving.

'Major Tashik,' he shouted through the rain, 'gubernatorial lifeguard, Orestes Pride, on the authority of Senior Frenz. I extend the cordial greetings of Lord Governor Aleuton. The forge is cordoned. Mechanicus, you may not exit into the Imperial byways of this hive, under penalty of death. Do you understand me?'

<Your declaration is understood, major,> canted the commanding skitarii.

'In frigging mouth-talk, mech, if you don't mind!' Tashik roared.

There was a pause. The rain belted down.

'Your declaration is understood, major,' the skitarii said in halting speech-function. 'The four individuals before us are, however, fugitives from Mechanicus law. We insist on our right to secure them before withdrawing.'

Tashik kept the pistol aimed at shoulder height. Rain streamed down his face and dripped off the beak of his gleaming helmet. 'Looks to me,' he yelled, 'like you want to kill them pretty bad. That makes them interesting to us. Back off.'

'The Mechanicus insists on this, major,' the skitarii officer declared.

Caught in the open at the centre of the stand-off, Feist felt utterly vulnerable. Imperial guns were trained on his face, Mechanicus guns on his back. Kalien clung to him in the rain and sobbed. Sonne was holding Obligana upright, his eyes wide in alarm.

'They're ours,' Tashik shouted at the skitarii. 'Back off. Do you really want to make something of this, right here and now? Do you really frigging want that?'

The rain seemed to hammer even more heavily. Thunder rolled.

'I'm waiting,' Tashik shouted.

>

The rain was as heavy as any Varco had known. He had stopped jumping at the thunderclaps, even though they were ear-splitting and directly overhead.

Sagen had driven the Centaur down from the Topples, and, following a route Ashlag had given them, they had edged their way up through the slippery ravines and rock-forks to Mouth Point. It had been slow going. Leopald had advised Sagen to take it 'extra easy' over the rough terrain because of the payload they were lugging.

There was no longer any telling where day and night began or ended. In Koder's immortal words, *the sky had gone out.* Varco checked his chron, but only out of habit. The actual time was superfluous. Orestes had become a black, rain-thick, never-ending nightmare.

Varco had insisted that Ashlag couldn't join them. The old man had been eager to do so. There had been genuine disappointment in his faded eyes when Varco had told him he'd be staying at the halt.

'Then, just… just do it right,' Ashlag had said.

'Orestes Pride, sir,' Varco had replied. 'We always do it right.'

Kell Ashlag had been a different proposition altogether.

'I'm coming with you,' she had insisted.

'You're staying here.'

'You'll need the las-lock. The las-lock is mine. I'm coming with you.'

That was the kind of circuitous female logic Varco had joined the Pride to escape. Yes, he needed the las-lock. He could have taken it from her, but there'd have been a fight. He was tired. They had been labouring for hours. He hadn't been able to construct a decent rebuttal.

'Fine,' he had said.

'I'll look after your daughter, old man,' he'd told Ashlag, 'but I'm not a miracle worker. We're going to be running into the maw of hell.'

'Kell's life is her own,' the old man had replied. 'She'll use it up as she needs to use it up, and whatever happens, I'll be proud of her.'

The Centaur rolled up a deep rock cut in the streaming rain. They'd had to come the long way round to avoid being spotted by the enemy gathered at the tower, and they were all sore and frozen from hours of grinding progress through the storm.

The payload, packed into the food drums, was lashed together on the Centaur's back-bay. Varco had his pistol, Kell the las-lock, and Leopald was armed with the heavy double-barrelled revolver from the halt's cupboards. Trask was manning the pintle-mounted stubber.

'What if they hear us, captain?' Sagen asked.

'In this?'

Thunder boomed again.

'Again, I say, in this?'

Varco looked up. He could see the tower rising into the sky beyond the jagged ridge of the rock cut. They had swung around to the west of it, and it was less than a kilometre away. Worms of blue electrical discharge writhed around its ugly black ironwork, and the storm itself, a twenty kilometre-wide cartwheel of churning grey cloud, turned cyclonically above the apex of the tower like an ink-stained whirlpool. Lightning sparked and crackled in the folds of the storm. Over the reek of mud and wet rock, Varco could smell ozone.

'Scrapcode,' noted Koder quietly, listening. 'Also, seismic vibration.'

'Seismic vibration?' asked Varco.

'The earth is shaking, captain,' said Koder.

Sagen halted the tractor, and shifted the transmission into neutral. Varco and Trask dismounted, and scrambled up the steep, muddy ridge. They huddled down on their bellies at the rim. Varco aimed his scope.

Through the torrential rain, he could see the tower in its entirety. They were so close to it, the sheer scale of the scrap-fashioned monstrosity took his breath away.

'This isn't going to work,' said Trask.

'Show a little faith,' Varco replied, but his confidence was leaking away with every passing second. The tower was huge and, though they could make out very little detail in the rain, it had to be well guarded. The ground shook. They both felt the earth quiver beneath them. Water popped and splashed in puddles and mud holes.

'What's going on?' asked Trask. 'What's doing that?'

'The engines are walking,' replied Varco, staring through the scope. 'They've gone to drive start. They're starting to walk away east en masse.'

Engine tread shook the ground again.

'East,' Trask murmured. East was Argentum, Antium, Gynex, the Hive Principal. Varco knew what Trask was thinking. Orestes had no idea what was coming for it.

Varco stared through the scope. He watched the rain-blurred shapes of the engines as they moved away, like a herd of grazing giants, turning one by one from the base of the tower to trudge east in the deluge. He heard them baying and hooting, blasting their sirens. He could feel their scrapcode itch across his skin. So many of them, so very many, Warlord patterns, massive and ponderous; Reaver patterns, hunched and murderous; Warhounds barking like hunting dogs around the edges of the fold.

Enough engines to take a world down. Orestes had to know.

'We'd better get on,' he remarked matter-of-factly.

Trask smiled at him. 'Save the world, eh, captain?'

'Exactly, Trask. Let's scout forwards a little way and check out the best route to the tower from here.'

They scrambled up over the lip of the ridge and ran forwards a short distance, heads down. At the next mud bank, they crouched again. About half a kilometre of broken mire, dotted with rocks and pools of water, was all that stood between them and the base of the huge tower. It seemed, simultaneously, so close and yet so far.

'We can make that, can't we?' Trask asked.

'No doubt about it,' Varco replied.

Trask was about to say something else when he died. A hard round entered his skull from the back and destroyed it, showering Varco in gore. The slug bounced off the back of Trask's teeth and hit Varco in the left cheek with decayed force, knocking him over into the mud.

Varco blinked, trying to assemble his thoughts, trying to work out what had just happened. He sat up, gripping his service pistol.

'Trask! Oh Deus! Trask!' he gasped. 'No!'

Gunlimb aimed, snarling, an Archenemy skitarii slithered down the bank towards him. Awful symbols jangled on the chain around its neck. Varco fired at it twice, and missed both times. Whooping, the skitarii tried to impale Varco with the cluster of rusted bayonet blades fixed to the snout of its limbgun.

A las shot hit it just behind the left ear and blew its cranium out like a glass bulb. Left with only a face, like the facade of a demolished building, the skitarii frowned and keeled over.

Her las-lock reloaded and re-aimed, Kell Ashlag ran up.

'Are you all right?' she asked Varco.

'Yeah, probably.'

'Trask?'

'Dead,' he said.

The girl looked down at Trask's twisted corpse and sucked in her breath. Varco got up and put his hand on her shoulder.

'He's dead,' she said.

'You saved me.'

'He's dead.'

'Yeah, he is. We have to move. Fast. That skit probably got a squirt out to its pack, and even if it didn't, the control patterns will soon realise it's missing.'

Varco took her hand and they ran back to the ridge overlooking the waiting Centaur.

'Where's Trask?' Sagen called, standing up in the drive cabin.

Varco looked back down the slope and shook his head.

'Oh no!' Sagen exclaimed, sitting down again.

Varco scrambled down alongside the tractor. Koder and Leopald stared down at him.

'It's on foot from here,' Varco said.

'Holy Throne,' groaned Leopald.

'The Centaur will be too visible,' Varco told him.

'Eight drums, and only four of us,' Leopald complained.

'Five,' Kell corrected, clambering down to join them.

'You're staying with the Centaur,' Varco told her.

'I refuse!'

'The drums are too heavy, Kell,' he said. 'Each one will need two people to carry it. There's no one to pair up with you. I need you to stay here and cover us with that las-lock.'

She looked doubtful.

'No arguments.' He looked at the others.

'We're going to have to make four runs per team,' said Leopald.

'If that's what it takes,' Varco replied.

They lifted the first two drums out of the Centaur's back-bay gingerly. Varco and Koder took one of them and manhandled it up the slope.

'No sign of movement,' Koder reported. They set out across the mud-waste to the base of the tower, struggling to keep the packed drum steady. Leopald had warned them how volatile the improvised charges were. Sagen and Leopald followed them, hauling the second drum.

Thunder shook the sky. It was murderously hard going. The mire came up to their shins in places, and sucked at their legs. They slipped and slithered. Sagen lost a boot to the sucking ooze. Varco knew a bad slip could twist or break an ankle.

Koder was finding it especially tough.

'A moment, captain,' he implored. They set the drum down while Koder got his breath back. The enginseer was a great deal weaker than he had admitted, and the tower was still two hundred metres away.

'Can you go on?' Varco asked.

'Of course,' Koder panted. 'Just a second.'

Leopald and Sagen, hobbling and bowed, overtook them. Varco watched as they reached the tower's base and bedded the first drum under the overhanging girderwork.

'Come on,' Varco said to Koder. They lifted the drum again and began to struggle on. Koder's face was pale and his grip was shaking. Varco knew the enginseer was barely going to make one run, let alone four.

Sagen and Leopald were running back towards them. 'Help me with this one!' Varco called to Leopald. 'Sagen, take Koder back to the tractor. You'll have to use Kell to help you with the next drum.'

Sagen nodded. He took Koder by the arm. It was obvious

that the enginseer was unhappy about the decision, though he couldn't argue with the logic. Sagen and Koder began to battle their way back towards the Centaur. Leopald and Varco lifted the drum and, grunting and gasping, carried it the rest of the way to the tower. Leopald secured it beside the one he and Sagen had brought over. Varco looked up at the huge, dank structure of the tower above them. Sheet lightning convulsed the sky, back-lighting the cold metal-work. Rain streamed down off the cross-beams and girders. The smell of ozone was overpoweringly strong.

'Done!' declared Leopald.

Varco and Leopald began to run back to the Centaur, heads down in the driving rain. Kell and Sagen appeared through the downpour, struggling towards them with the third drum.

'Keep it steady!' Leopald called.

Still running, Varco glanced back at the tower. He saw something moving in the rain behind him. He saw a flash. The first las round hit him in the right shoulder and knocked him down. Other rounds struck the mire around them and kicked up spatters of steaming mud. He heard Leopald cursing. He tried to rise, but his shoulder was a white-hot tangle of pain. Leopald dropped down beside him, rain streaming off his face, firing the heavy service revolver. Its huge flash and boom sounded like the storm overhead.

'Stay down. They've found us, captain!' he yelled.

Despite the pain, Varco did not stay down. He grimaced in agony as he pulled himself up. Forty metres away, enemy skitarii were advancing out of the pelting night, firing as they came. Varco fumbled to draw his pistol left-handed, and started to shoot back alongside Leopald. His aim was hopeless, but he saw one of Leopald's large calibre rounds smash a skitarii off its feet.

Varco's right arm was useless and his shoulder was a shattered mess. He fought against the awful pain and looked behind him. The incoming fire had forced Kell and Sagen to crouch down, the third drum in the mud between them. There was no way anyone was going to reach the tower on foot now. *Idiots! We were idiots to think we could pull this off!*

Leopald was trying to reload, an almost impossible task in the lashing rain. The *Merciless's* gunner kept losing his grip on the heavy, wet bullets. Varco cracked off a few more frantic shots with his pistol. A las-round struck Sagen in the ribs and sent him sprawling into the mud. Leopald finally got shooting again, but it was nothing like enough. The skitarii were on them.

Heavy cannon fire ripped into the skitarii lines. A big gun, firing on full auto, chewed across their charging ranks. Dark, bestial, modified bodies exploded, or were dismembered, or simply fell. Varco heard a roaring engine.

The Centaur was lurching and churning across the mire towards them. Koder was at the controls. The pintle-mounted stubber they had liberated from the PDF listening post was streaming tracer rounds into the hellish night. Somehow Koder was driving and manning the gun. Its punishing rate of fire was driving the skitarii backwards.

Leopald and Sagen seized their chance. They grabbed the third drum and started off towards the tower again. Sagen was flinching from the pain of the flesh wound in his side.

'No!' Varco yelled. 'Sagen! Lee! Come back!'

'Get our captain on the Centaur, girl!' Leopald bellowed over his shoulder. Kell snaked an arm around Varco and began to heft him towards the rapidly approaching tractor. Koder was still firing the stubber, mowing down skitarii and keeping them at bay.

Varco was close to blacking out. The girl was the only thing keeping him upright. He looked back at Leopald and Sagen in time to see his loyal driver hit. This time Sagen wasn't going to be getting up again. Varco howled. Leopald had fallen beside Sagen's body, pulled over by the man's dead weight, but he hadn't been struck. As Varco watched, Leopald rose again. He hefted up the drum single-handed, clutching its weight against his belly, and staggered on. He was only thirty metres from the base of the tower.

Leopald made ten of them before enemy gunfire dropped him. He got up on his hands and knees, swaying, and began to crawl through the mud, dragging the drum after him. He managed another five metres. They hit him again. Leopald fell on his side in the mud and stopped moving.

Kell fought to keep Varco upright. The Centaur bounced towards them, kicking up showers of muddy spray. Varco could see Koder at the controls. The enginseer's face was as pale as death. He was operating the stubber with his mechadendrites, multi-tasking as expertly as any servant of the Mechanicus.

The tractor lurched closer. From its engine-note alone, Varco realised that it wasn't going to slow down.

'Koder!' he hollered as the Centaur roared right past them and churned on towards the tower.

'He isn't coming back,' said Kell. 'Come on, soldier!' Clinging together, they half-staggered, half-ran towards the ridge.

The Centaur thrashed towards the base of the tower. Skitarii weapons fire pelted it. Many of the rounds punctured the tractor's bodywork and skin-armour. Gripping the controls tightly, Koder stopped counting the number of times he'd been hit.

The solid reality of the black tower filled his vision. Throttle down as far as it would go, Koder detached an extended mechadendrite from the stubber and snaked it back into the tractor's back-bay. The enginseer connected the dendrite to the det-tape that Leopald had carefully woven into one of the drums. He triggered an electric spark.

The Centaur met the base of the tower at full speed. The tower did not give. The Centaur was torn to pieces.

Then the world was torn to pieces too.

Scouring yellow flames rushed up the tower as if they were using it as a conduit to launch themselves at the stars. The corposant at the tower's apex became a torrid frill of thrashing neon thorns. The vile energies channelled by the tower's structure broke loose and exploded outwards in a series of blinding pulses that hurled whirling spars and broken girders out into the Deadlands.

Varco and Kell, hopelessly running for cover, were knocked flat by the concussion.

Uttering a long, drawn-out shriek of rending, buckling scrap metal, the tower began to topple.

10001

The first, heartbreaking feeds were coming in from Argentum. In his residence at the summit of the main hive, Governor Aleuton shook his head sadly as he watched the track-feed images of firestorm and devastation that the Imperial systems had intercepted.

'Is that a victory, do you think?' he asked quietly.

At his side, Senior Commander Frenz of the lifeguard considered the question carefully. 'It doesn't look like much of one to me, sir. But then, I don't know what an engine war is supposed to look like when it's been won.'

In his gleaming white battle plate, Frenz turned and accepted the data-slate that an aide was holding out to him. 'According to the reports, my lord,' he said, studying the slate, 'Lord Gearhart is claiming dominance of Argentum. He announces that a pivotal number of Archenemy engines have been destroyed, and that his forces are pursuing the small remainder still active out of the hive into the western subs.'

'One hive burns, and we stand ready to tear our own apart as we watch,' mused Aleuton. 'Do you suppose that future generations will forgive us, Frenz?'

'For Argentum, my lord?'

'Yes, for Argentum. And for whatever now unfolds in Orestes Principal.'

After long hours of unrest and disobedience, the stacks, streets and concourses of the Hive Principal had at last been brought to some semblance of order. It was, however, an uneasy quiet. The news of Imperial forces surrounding the forge in a cordon had appeased those sections of the public that had risen in indignant protest at the Mechanicus's heretical revelations, but for most hive dwellers, the news was bleak. The blunt truth was that the hive had risen against the forge in a show of arms. Mechanicus and Imperium were drawn face to face. Orestes appeared to be teetering on the brink of an era of bloodshed, disorder and schism. That was precisely what they had all feared the revelations would bring about, the moment they were disseminated.

Aleuton had taken the decision to cordon the forge after long consultation. He recognised how confrontational the action would seem. He knew that, potentially, he was napping flints in a powder keg. The Adept Seniorus had refused to respond to his signals, however, and divisions of skitarii and armed servitors had blocked all forge access to his messengers and troops. When his aides confirmed that the forge had gone into a situation one security lock-down, Aleuton had finally signed the order. The Mechanicus had always held the balance of power on Orestes, but he was Lord Governor, proxy of the Council of Terra, and voice of the Imperium. Aleuton had decided that he was not going to stand by and watch Imanual and his modified servants turn the world on its head.

The question is, he thought to himself, what is my next move? And now the engine war is apparently done, and the forces of the Archenemy driven to rout, what will the legios do? Will they side with the forge or the Throne?

Aleuton had a bitter feeling it would be the former. 'In which case,' he murmured to himself, 'we don't stand a chance.'

'My lord?' asked Frenz.

'Just talking to myself, Frenz,' the governor replied.

'There's been a development, my lord,' said one of the aides.

'What sort of development?' asked Aleuton.

The tall nalwood doors of the inner office opened, and Major Tashik entered. Behind him, four lifeguards escorted a trio of Mechanicus personnel. All three of them were soaked to the skin.

Tashik took off his silver helm, saluted the Lord Governor and Senior Commander Frenz, and handed Frenz a slate. Aleuton lifted the slate out of the senior commander's hands before Frenz could examine it, and studied it for himself.

'Famulous Sonne?' he said.

Sonne stepped forwards and made the sign of the aquila.

'Yes,' said Aleuton, 'I recognise you. Says here you were apprehended outside Forge Gate West.'

'Apprehended isn't the word I'd use, my lord. Rescued by your forces would be a more accurate summary.'

'Rescued? From your own kind?'

'The skitarii were hell-bent on frigging well killing the three of them,' said Tashik.

'Major Tashik!' Frenz cautioned.

'My humble apologies for speaking out of turn,' said Tashik.

'The skitarii were hell-bent on frigging well killing the three of them, *my lord*.'

'Who are these people with you?' Aleuton asked Sonne.

'Adept Feist of the Analyticae. Adept Kalien of the archives. My lord, I request access to a communication grid so that I can contact Executor Crusius as soon as–'

'Why were they trying to kill you, famulous?' Aleuton asked.

'The skitarii were under orders to prevent us from leaving the forge. The three of us are privy to information and circumstances that the senior magi do not want to see conveyed to the outside world. To you, in particular.'

'This is why you so boldly demanded an audience with me, is it, famulous?' asked Aleuton.

'Yes, my lord.'

'Then speak.' Aleuton sighed. 'I can imagine what you're going to tell me, but speak anyway. The forge is about to turn against us, isn't it?'

'Adept Seniorus Solomahn Imanual has been assassinated, my lord. Executor Enhort has seized power and declared Code Belli. It is insurrection, my lord.'

Aleuton listened patiently as first Sonne, and then Feist, made their account. Senior Commander Frenz interrupted them on several occasions to challenge details, but Aleuton remained silent and pensive. He thought of the stack of transmissions and requests for acknowledgement that he had received in the previous hours, requests that had come from Executor Crusius to begin with, and then from Etta Severin. He had not replied to any of them. Crusius's messages had seemed too ingratiating and eager to please, and Etta's had smacked of the executor's coercion. Aleuton had resolved not to answer until he had obtained solid intelligence from the forge.

Etta's last message, received just a few minutes before the first feeds from Argentum started to come in, had been the most direct and perfunctory:

<*[exloaded from] the grid of Crusius, magos executor fetial, Legio Invicta (110011001101, code compression zy) [active correspondent: Severin, Henrietta] [begins]*

My lord, further to my previous messages, I request you respond with all urgency to the executor's signals. Please, my lord, trust him.>

Sonne gave a small shrug. 'We have told you, candidly, everything, my lord. Will you grant my request for a link to the executor?'

Please, my lord, trust him.

Aleuton glanced at Frenz, and made a curt nod. A secure channel was prepared.

Hololithic emitters in the centre of the office space fizzed, and a life-sized image of Crusius materialised, so solid and real that it was as if he had entered the room in person.

'Sonne! For cog's sake, boy! Where have you been? I've been–' Crusius stopped short, noticing the other figures. He turned on his smile and bowed. 'My apologies, Lord Governor. I did not expect to find you standing at my famulous's side.'

'Crusius,' said Aleuton, 'this boy of yours has just communicated grave news to me that I imagine will disarm you too. I trust we will find a way to deal with it together.'

'I trust so too, Lord Governor. As my repeated messages to you have tried to indicate, Legio Invicta is fully supportive of the hive.'

'Against the interests of the forge?' asked Aleuton.

'My Lord Gearhart was quite emphatic about it, sir. Invicta serves the God-Emperor above all, for the God-Emperor is the Omnissiah. The revelations made by the forge are pernicious and divisive. They are, for whatever reason, an attempt to reignite the age-old schism between the branches of man. They simply cannot be tolerated.'

'Even if they're true?' asked Aleuton.

Crusius began to reply, but caught himself. It was too hard a question for an easy answer.

'We know the reason,' said Sonne.

'The reason?' asked Crusius.

'The reason behind the revelations,' said Sonne.

>

One step at a time, *Titanicus* advanced through the empty, broken towns, along water-logged trackways, past rusting ore-plants and chemical mills caked in caustic dust. The rain that had been threatening all morning finally began to come down as *Titanicus* entered a small, malodorous place called Somewhere Else.

The sky turned the colour of wet plaster and big raindrops began to fall around them.

'Can we shelter, Cally-girl?' Golla asked.

'No,' Cally replied.

'Oh, come on, it's raining.'

'No. Keep going.'

The heavens really began to open. Antic let out a curse, and Fiersteen shook his head as the rain put out his cheroot.

'Cally?' called Iconis, pulling his jacket up over his head.

'We've got to keep going!' Cally shouted back. 'Move!'

'This thing's going to wedge in the mud!' Lars Vulk shouted, gesturing to the cart he was dragging.

'It's going to wedge in the mud whether it's raining or not!' Cally replied. 'Come on!'

The others looked at her, miserable and weary, the rain running off their faces. Zhakarnov's beard looked like wet thatch.

'Have a heart, Cally,' said Liv Reiss. 'Just ten minutes, until this passes?'

'Come on, little sister,' said Golla.

Cally could see how weary her friend was. They'd been moving without a proper break for hours. They were all tired. Cally was tired. She was bone-tired, and the rain was hiding her tears. Was there a point, she wondered, when it all just ceased to matter any more? Could you go so far and no further? Was there a place where you just gave up and waited for death to overtake you?

Cally sighed. She had a feeling that Somewhere Else was going to be that place.

'If Cally says we keep going, we keep going,' said Janny Wirmac, her voice a whisper in the rain.

'What did you say?' asked Lasco.

'I said,' Janny repeated, raising her voice, 'that if Cally Samstag says we should keep going, we should keep going.'

'Oh, shut up, you silly little bitch,' said Antic. 'We're only running because of you and your silly bitch games!'

Cally took three steps towards Antic. He didn't see the fist coming. It caught the end of his jaw and laid him out flat in the mud.

'Whoa! Whoa! Cally!' Iconis yelled.

'Cally! That's not helping!' Reiss cried, holding Cally back.

'Easy! Easy!' shouted Golla.

'Let go of me!' Cally screamed, fighting them off.

'Just calm down!' Reiss told her.

'Calm down? Calm down?' Cally tore herself free of their

hands. She backed away from them, glaring at them. 'Calm down? I'm trying to keep us all alive! You look to me for leadership! For instructions! I don't know why! I never asked to be in charge of this idiot's outing!'

Some of them looked aside, embarrassed, awkward.

'Why me?' Cally yelled at them. 'Why me? Why pick on me for this?'

'Because you always seem like you know what you're doing,' said Janny.

Cally began to laugh. Her laughter rose into the sheeting rain and made them uncomfortable. 'I don't have a clue!' she shouted. 'I'm making this up as I go along. I'm trying to make whatever seem like the best decisions, because I want to go home. I want to see my husband again! And I don't want any more of you to die!'

Golla Uldana stepped towards Cally, her arms outstretched. 'Come on, Cally-girl. Take a breath. We'll keep going, if that's what you want. Won't we?'

Nobody spoke.

'Won't we?' Golla hissed back at them.

'Sure,' said Reiss.

'Oh, of course,' said Lasco.

'We can get moving in this, no problem,' said Lars Vulk. 'Just a shower.'

'It'll be fine,' said Iconis.

'See?' said Golla. 'So come on, little sister. What do you say? Take a breath.'

Cally shook her head. When she spoke, her voice was softer. 'Sorry, I didn't mean to lose it. I didn't mean to hit Antic. Is he all right?'

Vulk nodded, helping Antic to his feet. 'Probably knocked some sense into the little ninker,' he said.

'You've got to understand,' said Cally. 'I've been trying to keep us moving because–'

'Because what?' Iconis asked.

'None of you seem to have heard it, but it's there. All the time. The scratching.'

'What scratching?' asked Zhakarnov, cocking his head.

'Well, it's raining now. You can't hear it. But I heard it. It's been following us. Hunting for us. I didn't want to say anything because I didn't want to scare you.'.

'You're scaring me now,' said Antic.

'Something heard Janny's transmission, just like we feared. Don't blame her, it's not her fault. But something heard it. I think enemy ground forces are hunting for us. That's why I wanted us to keep going.'

'Oh, shit,' said Fiersteen.

'I want out of this unit,' murmured Antic.

'Janny,' said Liv Reiss, 'could you tell me exactly what you sent?'

Janny Wirmac shrank away from the stern, hard-faced woman. She shrugged. 'I told my papa where I was, and I told him I really wanted his help to get home. I said there was a bunch of us, and we were trying to help some engine princeps who was really hurt.'

Fiersteen groaned. 'We're pretty much dead in our boots, then,' he said.

'Way to paint the biggest possible target on our heads, Wirmac!' Antic snarled. He glanced quickly at Cally to make sure she wasn't about to hit him again.

She had ignored his comment. 'Shall we get moving?' she asked what little remained of Activated Twenty-Six.

'Samstag?'

She looked around. Beside the battered cart named *Titanicus*,

Robor was staring intently at her. At his side, the sickly body on the stretcher twitched and trembled in the rain.

'We can hear code, Samstag,' said Robor.

Cally felt her guts cramp with anxiety. Everyone looked at her.

'Move!' she cried. 'Everyone move. Find cover!'

They scattered in every direction. Golla and Cally helped Vulk roll *Titanicus* through the mud towards a nearby stow barn. Robor plodded along beside the cart.

The barn's doors were locked. Vulk threw the cart's drag ropes off his mighty shoulders and kicked the doors in. It took two heavy slams of his boot to break the lock. Golla dragged the wooden doors open, and Cally and Vulk hauled the cart inside. Rain beat on the roof and streamed down through holes in the tiles.

'Stay here. Keep an eye on them,' Cally told Golla.

'Where are you going? Cally-girl?'

'Stay here, Golla, and keep an eye on them. Look after them.'

Cally slipped back out of the barn, and pulled the doors shut behind her.

There was no one in sight. Cally ran through the heavy rain, hunched down, crossing from cover to cover, hugging doorways and corners. She unshipped her MK2-sk lasrifle, and armed it. It had taken a Throne of a lot of knocks since she'd been issued with it at the place of muster, what seemed like forever ago.

She hoped it still worked.

Something whirred in the rain. She ducked into cover. An aircraft slid overhead, hovering low in the downpour. She only got a glimpse of it, but enough to see that it was armoured and studded with weapon-pods.

As soon as it had passed out of sight, she got up again and ran through the rain, clutching her weapon. She darted between two rickety habs, and out through the back into the alley behind.

How many can I take down before they finish me, she wondered? Five? Two? One? One, if I'm lucky.

She crouched, weapon aimed. She felt her skin creep. Slowly, ever so slowly, she turned, the rain pouring off her face. A skitarii stood over her. It was a most massive, fearsome thing. Its inbuilt gunlimb, a weapon of huge calibre, was aimed at her. Feathered plumes decorated the skitarii's modified skull in a crest, and votive talismans dangled on chains around its neck. Its eye-slits were phosphorescent yellow. It curled its lips back in a lethal smile and exposed a row of massive metal fangs.

Cally sank to her knees in front of it. *This was going to be that place. This was going to be that place.*

The skitarii uttered a burst of code.

'I don't understand!' she yelped.

It coded again, and leaned down, pushing the muzzle of its cannon into her cheek.

'I don't know. I don't understand you!'

The skitarii licked its lips and slowly curled out malformed vocals through a fang-enhanced mouth not designed for speech.

'Where – is – the prin – ceps?' it asked.

She heard its weapon arm itself.

>

At Argentum, the rain had stopped. It had ceased suddenly, just after dawn. The massive storm front raging over the

Western Prospection had suddenly and inexplicably blown out.

Its cessation was a mixed blessing. The sky was clearing, to the colour of mildewed whitewash, and visibility had improved, but without the rain to douse them, the firestorms in the hive ran unchecked. Entire hab blocks and sinks blazed, pushing rank black smoke into the sky. Richelon District, a massive sub-spire buttressed out from the northern waist of the hive, was so undermined by raging backdraft that it slid away like a launching ocean liner into the outer hive belt.

Virtually nothing in the old hive had survived intact. The engines of Tempestus and Invicta picked their way through acres of smouldering rubble, through the ruins of foundered spires, across seas of broken glass and screes of shattered stone, past burning sinks and flaming habs, and down demolished avenues that had, in ancient times, been lined with jubilant and loyal masses.

Argentum was dead. The massed engine assault had slain it. Inner squares and streets were littered with enemy dead, charred beyond recognition. Every few blocks, the remains of an enemy engine lay twisted and blackened, threading sooty vapour into the sky.

Gearhart nodded. <I am satisfied,> he told his moderati. <Signal to Crusius that victory at Argentum has been achieved. The Archenemy has been broken. Do so with all haste.>

Gearhart sank back in his casket. Fatigue wrapped him like a shroud and distant, thundercloud dreams loomed along the horizon of his mindscape. He could not accurately recall where he was or why he was fighting, but victory was a sweet enough taste all by itself.

The enemy was running. Their assets broken, they were fleeing from the dead hive into the west. A battle group led by Bohrman was chasing them down. Numerous death duels between fleeing machines and Imperial engines were reported on the western slopes. Gearhart had ordered *full purge*. No scrap of the enemy should survive. Bohrman would not let him down.

'Bohrman. He will succeed me,' Gearhart murmured.

'My princeps?' Bernal asked.

'Bohrman. Tell him. Tell him, Ervin.'

'It's Bernal, sir.'

Gearhart turned to look out at the moderati. 'Of course it is. What can I do for you, Bernal?'

'There's a reply signal, my princeps. From Executor Crusius.'

'Put it on, there's a good man.'

The image of Crusius appeared.

<Crusius,> canted Gearhart. <Come to celebrate the victory with me?>

Crusius's image looked grim. <My lord, I need to send data to you for review, via a confidential channel. It is of the highest urgency.>

<Send it,> Gearhart canted, shrugging off the fatigue.

<Exloading now.>

<Inloading.> The data flooded across Gearhart's Manifold view. He scanned it at maximum incant speed, and then straightened up and rested one hand against the casket glass. <When did this happen?>

<During the fight for Argentum.>

<It's confirmed?>

<By several separate sources,> Crusius canted. <My famulous, Sonne was a first-hand witness, and he has with him an adept called Feist, a trustworthy sort, who was able to

decant a great deal of pict-feed from his memory buffers. Much of what you've just seen came directly from his eyes.>

<Where are Sonne and the adept now?>

<In the protective custody of the Lord Governor. Aleuton is rather anxious to discover which way this will turn.>

<Have you given him my assurances?>

<Of course, my lord.>

Gearhart's old mind whirred. The reactors of *Invictus Antagonistes* grumbled angrily in sympathetic response. <Oh, Crusius. The revelations troubled me when they were made. I knew they'd lead to blood, but I thought the conflict would arise from whether or not the data was genuine. I never dreamed they would lead to this. Stand by, please.>

Gearhart haptically suspended his link to the executor, and opened a direct, priority channel to the forge using his formidable levels of clearance.

Enhort appeared. <My Lord Gearhart, may I commend you on the success of your action at Argentum. The forge will–>

<Don't talk to me, you little shit. I know what you've done. Now this is what you're going to do. Cancel situation one, disarm the forge, and surrender yourself and your fellow conspirators to the governor's forces.>

Enhort didn't even blink. <I'm not entirely sure why you're speaking to me like this. The forge is in crisis. I have taken authority, and imposed Code Belli. I expect you and your engines to support me unequivocally.>

<I am princeps maximus, vermin. I don't take orders from a jumped-up pretender like you.>

<You forget your place, Gearhart. I am the acting Adept Seniorus of Orestes Forge. Invicta has sworn to execute on behalf of this forge. You will obey me.>

The reactors of *Invictus Antagonistes* rumbled more furiously.

<You've usurped the place of Solomahn Imanual. This is nothing more than a grubby little power play. You've used the state of war as a distraction, you've played on fears and insecurities, and then you've released pernicious filth to make yourself look like a brave and selfless saviour stepping in to rescue us from ourselves!>

Enhort glowered. <The *pernicious filth* you refer to is authenticated truth. It is the greatest revelation of the age. You should be rejoicing, you senile old bastard! The Mechanicus can at last throw off the shackles that have bound us to Terra for millennia!>

<Some of us don't mind those shackles,> blurted Gearhart. <Show me a servant of the Mechanicus who objects to being bound to the Omnissiah, and I'll show you a damnable heretic!>

<The data refutes that old lie! It is authentic! It–>

<Who told you that? Tolemy? What possible reason could he have to lie, you idiot?>

Enhort held up his hand and turned his face aside. <I don't have to listen to your ramblings, Gearhart. Your engines will stand in support of the forge or you will be deprived of command.>

<I've seen the footage, you stupid shit. *I've seen the footage!*>

Enhort paused. He looked back at Gearhart.

<What footage?>

<I've seen through Feist's eyes,> canted Gearhart. <You tried to silence him, but he got out, and I've been allowed to see through his eyes.>

Enhort shook his head. <Is that what this is about? Is that why you link to me and spit your bile? My lord Gearhart, you have been duped. Feist is a craven assassin, and a partner in Imanual's criminal attempts to deprive the

Mechanicus of revelatory knowledge. He would claim anything to undermine our unity. You have seen through the eyes of a mendacious traitor.>

<The footage–>

<Gearhart, for cog's sake! Feist worked in the Analyticae! Data can be manipulated!>

Gearhart chuckled. <Ah, now you admit it. Yes, Enhort, data can be manipulated. It can be altered and yet still appear authentic, if that should serve a purpose.>

Enhort faltered slightly.

<You've got one hour,> canted Gearhart. <Disarm the forge and surrender to Governor Aleuton, or I'll come for you.>

<You've got one hour,> Enhort canted back. <Declare your engines in full and unqualified support of the forge, and I will erase this unpleasant conversation from my memory buffers. Failure to do so will result in your removal from both command and your engine.>

<I'm *Invictus Antagonistes*, you little fool. Who exactly is going to do that?>

Enhort did not reply. The link closed. Gearhart brooded in silence for a moment, and then resumed the link to Crusius.

<You were listening?>

<Of course, my lord.>

<Observations?>

Crusius looked solemn. <I don't think Enhort is going to back down. Tolemy may be motivated by self-interest, but I honestly believe Enhort is acting out of principle. He truly believes he is doing the right thing.>

<And you don't believe that a man acting out of principle would ever give in?>

<Would you, my lord?> asked Crusius.

* * *

>

On his observation bridge, Crusius turned thoughtfully and found Etta Severin watching him.

'Has it really come to this?' she asked.

'Possibly,' he replied.

'Everything's about to go to hell in a paper hat,' Gotch sniffed.

'That's a possibility too, major,' the executor said. 'We may be about to witness the outbreak of schismatic war inside the Mechanicus. We have a saying, you know? A *Mechanicus* saying: "knowledge is power". Of all the terrifying weapons the Mechanicus is able to wield, knowledge is by far the most dangerous. And all too often, I think, we forget how badly we can damage ourselves with it.'

'Lord Gearhart won't submit to Enhort, will he?' Etta asked.

'Never. Nor should he.'

'Then, if I may ask, how will Enhort enforce his demands?'

'He has the power of Orestes Forge at his command.'

'Against Legio Invicta?' she asked.

Crusius paused.

'He's got the Tempestus engines too,' said Gotch quietly.

Crusius looked at the bodyman and nodded. 'The Tempestus engines are bound to side with Enhort. They are loyal to the forge, of course, and they all share the forge's old belief in the distinction between Omnissiah and Emperor.'

'But the Legio Tempestus was under strength when this war began, and the losses it has taken since have depleted it still further,' said Etta. 'Surely–'

'The Legio Tempestus has nine engines operational in the field,' said Crusius.

'Against... how many Invicta engines?'

'Invicta has thirty-six operational engines.'

'Then, it's hardly a fair fight.'

The executor fetial looked at her. His eyes flashed electric green for a second. 'That's not the point, Etta. Even one engine would be enough. If a Titan fired upon another Titan, it would be the first shot in a Mechanicus civil war.'

She pursed her lips, thoughtfully.

'Like I said,' said Gotch. 'All the way to hell. In a fancy paper hat.'

Crusius crossed to the main communication station. 'Link analysis,' he told the station's servitor. 'Source all active Tempestus engines. Analyse Manifold traffic. How many of the Tempestus machines are in contact with, or have recently been in contact with, the forge?'

<All nine Tempestus engines are currently shown as linked to the forge on secure transmission feeds, executor.>

'He's already briefing them,' Crusius growled. 'That scrap-shunt Enhort is already whispering in their ears. All of them, you say?'

<In total, executor, ten engines are currently linked to the forge on secure transmission feeds.>

'Ten? Show me.'

<Routing engine specifics to your Manifold view, executor.>

'Oh,' breathed Crusius unhappily as he incanted the data in front of his eyes. 'Of course. You too.'

>

Supply and repair vehicles had moved into Argentum's shattered heart. In Oldmagi Square, a once-stately plaza that had been tragically scarred by sustained bolter fire, *Morbius Sire* stood hunched and impatient as enginseers worked to realign a shield emitter that had been distorted by a missile hit. On the far side of the square, *Ajax Excelsus* waited as a pair of heavy munitions crawlers used umbilical docks to feed fresh payloads into the engine's magazine.

Dominatus Victrix came into the square at low stride and moved towards another pair of munitions carriers. Tarses signalled the other Titans, and then positioned *Victrix* so that the crawlers could service the magazine hatches. Sitting in his chin-seat, he watched the climbing in-feed rate of bolter rounds and missiles. He heard the soft chant of the tech-priest as he blessed and purified the hard munitions loading aboard.

'He's quiet,' said Anil, nodding sidelong at the casket behind them.

'He's talking to the forge,' said Kalder.

Tarses glanced at the sensori. 'He's been on a secure link to the forge for the last eight minutes,' Kalder said.

'Let's hope he's getting clarification,' said Anil, running a quick control check.

'Clarification?' asked Tarses.

'About this business,' replied the steersman, looking over at him. 'The revelations.'

Tarses nodded. 'Let's hope.'

A receptor chimed. Kalder punched some keys. 'Notification from *Antagonistes*, moderati,' he said. 'All engines are to stand by. Lord Gearhart is going to address the legio in ten minutes.'

>

Gearhart opened a general band. <To all engines, Tempestus and Invicta, this is Gearhart. Acknowledge my exload.>

Manifold signals rapidly fired back to him from all quarters.

<Thank you, princeps. First, allow me to applaud your efforts. Argentum is ours. The battle for Orestes is won.>

There was a chorus of emphatic code blurts from the engine ranks.

<Indeed, indeed. First Princeps Bohrman, continue to push west with your battle group and finish up the dregs of the enemy. Make them all burn, please. *Full purge,* as ordered. Let not one scrap-engine escape.>

More emphatic bursts of code echoed from the engine ranks.

<Your orders are understood, princeps maximus,> Bohrman canted back.

<Thank you, first princeps,> canted Gearhart. <Engines, there is a further matter I wish to decant. I know that you are all aware of the provocative data that has recently been put into circulation. Furthermore, I imagine you are cognisant of the fact that Orestes Forge is currently held at situation one. The release of the data has plunged the forge into crisis, and generated friction with the Hive Principal. This requires our urgent attention. In the next twelve-hour period, all engines not engaged with First Princeps Bohrman's purge effort must complete their final sweeps of Argentum, and prepare to withdraw from this theatre with me. At sunrise tomorrow, we will begin the walk back to Hive Principal.>

Gearhart fell silent and waited, watching the audience of small, white, code-blurred faces gazing back at him through the Manifold. Each one was a princeps, accessing the Manifold link from his casket or command seat. A noospheric tag beside each face identified the engine and princeps in code.

Who will be first, I wonder, Gearhart thought?

<We are to return as a military force, my lord?>

Ah, Rhapson, of *Mercurius Beati*. A Tempestus engine. How did I know a Tempestus engine would be the first to speak?

<As a moderating influence, Princeps Rhapson,> Gearhart canted. <As a stabilising influence.>

<To intervene, then, my lord?> canted Levin of *Ajax Excelsus.*

Dear old Levin, always so keen to get things 'just so' in his mind.

<As necessary, my old devil,> Gearhart returned.

<In support of the forge, lord?> Theron canted from *Tantamount Stridex*.

Yes, here it comes. If any of Tempestus is going to step over the line, it will be now. They will know my severe displeasure, and that will set them straight.

<What a strange question, Theron. In support of the Mechanicus, of course,> Gearhart canted back.

<Define that support, Lord of Invicta,> demanded Lenix Devo, princeps of *Cullador Braxas*, the senior surviving Tempestus engine now that *Orestes Magnificat* was lost.

<I don't believe I have to define anything, princeps,> canted Gearhart. <You are still, I take it, a Mechanicus engine? You will not question me. You will walk with me.>

<Not against my own forge,> replied Devo. <You trivialise this 'provocative data' but it is central to Orestean orthodoxy. Are the engines of Tempestus to understand that you intend to crush our beliefs under your heel because they defy the *new way*?>

<Watch your words, Princeps Devo,> Gearhart canted back sourly. <We are Mechanicus, one and all. We are bound to a single god. Our faith isn't a binary state. We are one.>

<One divided,> replied Devo. <I admire your might, Lord Gearhart, and I worship the spirits of your engines. But

understand this: if you take Invicta against the forge, Tempestus will stand in your path.>

<Will you? Will you *really*, Devo?> Gearhart canted.

Monitoring the address from his crawler, Crusius moaned softly. 'Oh, be careful, my lord. They're not playing.'

'Is this brinkmanship?' asked Etta.

He glanced at her. 'I fear so. Gearhart is standing his ground, just as I believed he would. But I think he underestimates the depth of Tempestus's resolve.'

'Didn't you warn him?' asked Etta.

'Of course I did, you–' Crusius took a deep breath. 'My most sincere apologies, Mamzel Severin. The moment seems to have robbed me of composure. Yes, I warned him. I advised him to handle the allied engines with the finest of haptic touches. But–'

'But?' sneered Gotch, his scar curling his cheek and lip.

'But Lord Gearhart is his own man. He is forthright and honourable. He is not known as the Red Fury because of any modest temperament. He's–'

'So headstrong he'll drag the Mechanicus into a shooting match, and us along with it?' asked Etta.

Crusius refused to be baited. 'He's his own man,' he repeated. And, I'm most terribly afraid, he's not quite the man he was. Please, my lord, don't do anything precipitous.

<Why aren't you listening to me?> Gearhart canted furiously. <Your beloved forge has been usurped, Devo!>

<Usurped by the truth, Gearhart!> Devo canted back.

<Enhort has acted illegally. He has overstepped the limits of his authority!>

<Adept Seniorus Enhort has all the authority he needs!>

<For cog's sake, Devo!> blurted Krugmal of *Lupus Lux*. <My lord Gearhart just decanted the truth to you via the feed. This Adept Feist saw it all. How much more proof do you want?>

<Adept Seniorus Enhort warned us of this dangerous deceit personally,> canted Ku of the Tempestus engine *Vanquist Solace*. <The so-called *Feist-decant* is a shamefully manufactured lie!>

Gearhart swam back in his casket, exasperated. 'Oh, Deus. Crusius was right. They're wilfully blind to the truth.'

He looked over at his moderati. Bernal and the rest of the bridge crew were watching him intently. Gearhart saw the alarm on their faces.

'Engage the drive train, Bernal,' he ordered.

The bridge crew scrambled into their seats.

'Drive train engaged, aye, my princeps.'

<Stand with us or oppose us.>

Gearhart peered back into the Manifold. <Did you just issue me with an ultimatum, Devo?> he canted.

The code-fuzzed image of Devo's face nodded. <I did, Gearhart.>

<Would you care to repeat it?>

<I said, stand with us or oppose us, Gearhart.>

Gearhart shivered. <Have you any idea what your ultimatum might be about to start, Devo?>

Devo slowly nodded again. His face was drawn with the tension of the moment. There was no doubting his seriousness or, noticed Gearhart sadly, his burning conviction.

Lenix Devo composed himself. <I have, Lord Gearhart of Invicta. It appals me. The idea of standing in contention with you horrifies me. It dismays me that we would not part from this theatre as friends. It terrifies me that the Mechanicus could be so divided in its loyalties.>

<Then why do this, Lenix?>

<Because I love the forge and I would die for the forge. Deus Omnissiah! I cant again, stand with us or oppose us.>

<I see. Tell me this, Tempestus. If I oppose you, exactly what are you prepared to do?>

'We have just been target-selected by three Tempestus engines, my princeps,' Bernal cried. 'Multiple pings. *Braxas*, *Beati* and *Phantoma*!'

'Oh, those brave fools,' Gearhart murmured. 'Moderati? Light the shields.'

'Shields lit, my princeps!'

'My lord!' shouted the sensori. 'All of the other Tempestus engines have locked weapons on Invicta machines. Targeted Invicta machines have responded by locking back!'

'Moderati! Inform all Invicta engines that they may light shields but they must, I emphasise must, cancel any auspex locks!'

'They are so informed, my princeps,' Bernal yelled.

If someone's going to take that first, taboo shot, Gearhart thought, it won't be one of mine. If Tempestus wants this, let them show how much. Let them get their hands dirty. I'd rather die than be the one who triggers schismatic bloodshed.

I'd rather let the blackness consume me.

I'd rather be unplugged.

'Invicta engines report shields lit!' the sensori sang.

'He's called their bluff,' Crusius whispered.

'Yeah, will that work?' asked Major Gotch. 'I've called bluffs in my time. How do you think I got my face so messed up?'

'It might work,' Crusius said, smiling at Gotch's remark

darkly. 'Tempestus has the utmost respect for the Lord Gearhart. You see? Gearhart has even ordered the Invicta engines to cancel any auspex locks.'

He pointed at the holothic display.

'Invicta's engines are just going to stand there and wait to be shot at?' asked Etta.

'They've lit their shields, Etta. They'll take the pain of the first shot without flinching.'

<Executor!> Lysenko blurted, hurrying over from the crawler's main console.

<Not now, man!>

<Magos Navis Kovenicus–>

<I said not now and I meant it!>

Lysenko grabbed Crusius by the sleeve and pulled him aside. Crusius reacted instinctively and almost ripped Lysenko's arm out of its socket. He restrained his rage.

<Not now!>

<You really have to see this. At once!> Lyskenko blurted.

Oblivious to the quiet tussle between executor and crawlermaster taking place behind them, Etta Severin and her bodyman peered at the graphic display.

'Crusius said that all of the Invicta engines had cancelled their auspex locks,' said Gotch.

'Yes. Why?'

Gotch pointed. 'That one hasn't,' he said.

>

<I want that lock sustained right now!> Prinzhorn yelled.

'You won't get it from me,' Tarses replied, undoing his restraints and sliding his chin-seat back.

<Give me an engine lock now, moderati!>

Tarses rose to his feet and turned to face the casket. 'No,' he said. With a wince, he yanked out his hard-plugs.

<Sensori!>

'Kalder's not going to help you, either. An Invicta engine would never fire on another Invicta engine.'

<This Invicta engine will do as it's told,> warned Prinzhorn. <I thought we had an understanding, Tarses. I was beginning to like you as a moderati.>

'And I was beginning to like you as a princeps, my princeps,' Tarses replied. 'But I will not be a part of this.'

<So stand down, moderati. Resign your station. I can replace you.>

Tarses heard the autoloaders click into place. He felt the buzzing song of the auspex as it painted its targets.

'Target lock, *Ajax Excelsus*,' Fairika called out, clambering into Tarses's vacated chin-seat to man the controls.

'Voice command, Tarses, moderati. Disengage lock!' Tarses cried.

The auspex systems faltered and shut down.

<Re-establish lock!> Prinzhorn demanded. The auspex restarted.

'Disengage lock!'

<Re-establish lock!>

Tarses clambered past Kalder and slid over to the auspex bank. He turned it off at the root switch. The sensors went blank.

Fairika got out of the chin-seat and threw herself at him, clawing. Tarses fought her off. Anil and Kalder disengaged their harnesses and struggled to drag her away and restrain her.

'This isn't going to happen, my princeps,' Tarses told the casket, wiping blood from the scratches that Fairika's fingernails had torn across his cheek.

<I am not your princeps,> Prinzhorn canted. <You should have been put down for your murder-crime. Executed! You are no servant of the Mechanicus!>

'I am a true servant of the Mechanicus,' Tarses contradicted. He looked over at Kalder and Anil, fighting to keep the thrashing famulous pinned. Tarses slowly walked up the bridge space, and pressed his hand against the biometric key of *Invicta's* weapon's locker. The small hatch opened. Tarses took out a loaded pump riotgun, and racked it with a snap of his wrist.

He walked towards the casket. Floating, illuminated from above, Prinzhorn glared at him.

'I don't know how many souls I've killed in warfare,' Tarses told him quietly. 'It's a lot, I would imagine. Outside of war, I killed one man, in rage and despair, and I will regret it for the rest of my life. Either way, it's quite clear I'm capable of killing, in war and in peace.'

Tarses pressed the snout of the riotgun against the cold surface of the amniotic casket.

'As far as I'm concerned, this is war, and my conscience is clear. Shut *Victrix* down now, or I'll shoot you where you float.'

<This is mutiny.>

'Oh no, my princeps,' replied Tarses, 'this is duty.'

>

Go on take the first shot, take the first shot, or stand down, Gearhart willed.

<My lord?>

<Go away, Crusius.>

<I'm inloading this to you anyway, broad spectrum.>

The data poured through the Manifold. Every engine saw it. It was vivid, precise, utterly sharp.

<Crusius?> Gearhart stammered. <Where did this come from?>

<The fleet, my lord. Orbital scans. We are now able to determine that the storm patterns battering this region of Orestes were artificially manufactured by a climate tower constructed by the enemy. For reasons unknown, that tower has suddenly ceased operation.>

<Am I reading this right, Crusius? It looks like… sixty at least.>

<Kovenicus has confirmed the data, my lord. It is authentic, if that's not a term too over-used of late. A host of sixty-plus Archenemy engines is bearing south-south-west out of the Western Prospection towards us at full stride.'

<Lenix?>

<Lord Gearhart?>

<Are you seeing this?>

<I am, my lord.>

<Tell me, Princeps Lenix, what happens now? Do we rise, shoulder to shoulder, and confront this shared enemy, or will you start taking principled pot-shots at my engines?>

Lenix Devo did not reply.

<I anticipate your immediate response,> canted Gearhart. <And, Devo, so does Orestes.>

10010

Afterwards, it became known as the Battle of the Prospection.

Bohrman's battle group, already striding into the west on the hunt for fugitive machines, formed up and made a fluid, cohesive turn to confront the second host. They were the first to engage.

Seriously outgunned, Bohrman kept his distance and maintained mobility. He began a harrying action, bombarding the enemy host from distances of up to fifteen kilometres. The enemy seemed determined to keep pushing east, and resisted the temptation to divert some or all of its strength to tackle Bohrman's engines, though blanket fire was returned with increasing ferocity as the skirmishing attacks became more intense.

Lau's skitarii division moved overland at its most aggressive deployment rate. Within three hours, the first cataphractii units were setting up on the north-western border of the Jeromihah Sub, and beginning to shell. The infantry and the weaponised servitor detachments deployed along a six kilometre-wide front ahead of the cataphractii positions. The orbital scans had painted a considerable skitarii ground force moving alongside the engine host.

Bohrman's group kept up its running bombardment for five hours until it was forced to fall back for munitions resupply. The enemy host, like a mobile forest of dirty steel and ceramite, began to broaden its spacing and extended into a wide, line formation. As the host came within five kilometres of the Jeromihah border, accurate scans put its number at sixty-two, despite the multiple kills made during Bohrman's valiant action. The ground shivered continuously as if enduring some low-level, never-ending seismic discomfort. Black hordes of troops ran ahead of the Chaos engines, braying scrapcode. Even to the eyes of seasoned skitarii like Lau and Gunmagos Dorentine, it was a sobering sight.

The cataphractii began saturation shelling. Immense lines of explosive destruction rippled through the Archenemy formations. Wailing shells threw tonnes of soil litter into the air as they struck. The line of contact flickered crazily with pulse and beam emissions.

The enemy host began to fire as it advanced. The horrific power of engine-class weapons mauled Lau's forces, and amid the catastrophic destruction, the first skitarii elements met and clashed with unbridled fury. Lau was right in the thick of it.

Chaos had unleashed chaos.

Gearhart was still twenty kilometres away. Moving at full stride to catch up with his loyal skitarii forces, Gearhart began distance firing at the main mass of the enemy host, and the engines moving in formation with *Invictus Antagonistes* lit off in support of his bombardment.

Everything had come with him. Every last engine of Invicta and Tempestus, their differences erased by the common threat, strode behind the Red Fury into war against an engine force almost twice its size.

<No quarter, my young devils,> Gearhart canted.

Shields rose to full power. Charge reservoirs and accumulators throbbed at capacity. Autoloaders cleared and chambered. Gun-boxes and rocket pods opened their hatch covers.

Legio met host: engine to engine.

None of the unmodified human witnesses to the battle ever forgot the spectacle. Etta Severin observed the engine war from Crusius's crawler. The executor had brought his command vehicle and supporting elements to within three kilometres of the Imperial line, to allow his heaviest ranged weapons to contribute what they could to the bombardment. Etta flinched every time the crawler's gun towers howled or the Hydra and quick-gun platforms slaved to the crawler fired, despite the fact that the external shutters of the observation bridge were sealed and the voids lit.

Crusius had supplied Etta and Gotch with visors so they could access a Manifold view of the battle. The sensory input was completely overwhelming. Despite the comparatively ponderous pace of the engines, the speed of the battle was stunning. Etta couldn't cope with the inhuman rates of fire, the rapidity of blast-patterns and shot exchange, the blink-fast alterations of target beams and auspex tracks, and the constant streams of code chatter. Only modified minds and augmented reflexes could properly process that kind of data inload and still operate with any degree of efficiency. She finally understood how engine crews could lose themselves entirely to their mind impulse units.

Competing with the streaming data was the shock: light shock, noise shock, pressure shock. Every weapon discharge, every shield impact, every solid hit resulted in retina-scorching flashes, jumbled streams of rapid neon flashes, concussive overpressure, and unimaginably loud sonic disruption.

The worst thing of all was the scale. Etta had never really appreciated the sheer size of Titan engines before. As she piggy-backed her visor link to the gunbox feeds of Warlords and Reavers, she felt like an almost ridiculous towering giant, like some ogre out of a fairy-tale book, so top-heavy and lumpen she might, at any moment, trip and fall flat on her face. An engine brought everything up to its own scale: distances became vaster, impacts harder, destruction more grotesquely immense. As she watched the feed inload through dizzy, fast-blinking eyes, she had to remind herself that somewhere far below her point of view, down through the billowing smoke and the shield chop and the slicing beams of razor-sharp light, the skitarii were locked in an equally ferocious combat, a combat that on any other occasion would have been the main spectacle. As it was, the bruising, tearing warrior-clash was an afterthought. The skitarii and their fighting vehicles were mere ants, milling and racing around the massive feet of the contending monsters.

It was too much. She pulled off the visor and set it down on the console.

'Is the device malfunctioning, mam?' Lysenko asked.

Etta shook her head. 'It's just too much. Too much to bear. I don't know how you even begin to…'

'Even for the modified, it is hard, mam,' Lysenko replied. 'Engine wars are usually lost because of human frailty.'

'What do you mean?'

Lysenko shrugged. 'The machine is a near-perfect thing. The

human component is its one true weakness. If a princeps or one of his bridge crew makes an error, or is momentarily confused, or misses a small detail, then the machine suffers. It's a split-second thing. Life or death in an instant. One mis-code, one track-error, and it's over. That's why only the very best make it through selection to active engine work. That's why we value our princeps and senior moderati so highly.'

'Because not everybody can do it?' she asked.

'Because, even with modified enhancement, barely one in ten million possesses enough natural ability to make the grade.'

Etta looked at Gotch. He was still cheerfully watching the battle-feed through his visor. His scarred mouth was hooked in a half-smile, a mixture of grudging respect, professional empathy and quiet awe.

'Impressed, Zamual?' she asked.

Gotch nodded. 'Yes.'

'You ought to be impressed, major,' said Crusius. 'A massed engine engagement like this is a comparatively rare thing.'

'Meh,' said Gotch. 'I'm watching the skitarii. Those buggers can fight.'

Crusius laughed.

'This is a rare thing, you say, executor?' Etta asked, looking over at Crusius.

'Very rare. An entire legio ranged against a rival engine force in open battlefield conditions? Actions on this scale are the stuff of legend. In the last few centuries, Invicta has seldom engaged its full strength at a single location. Most executions call for individual actions across a broad theatre, perhaps half a dozen engines walking in concert at most. Such is the military advantage of engines. A few are usually enough. Whatever happens here today, this clash will be remembered as extraordinary.'

'But it used to be more common?' she asked.

'An engine on engine fight of this magnitude? Yes. In ancient days, when the numbers of active engines were greater.'

'Such as when?' she asked.

Crusius smiled. 'The Heresy.'

'What an unfortunate connection,' Etta said.

'Quite.'

She looked at the tactical display projecting up from the central chart table they were standing around. 'I'm sorry, but I really can't tell any more,' she admitted. 'Are we winning yet?'

Crusius looked at her. 'It's too early to tell,' he replied.

>

They watched the ragged, disjointed feeds bleeding in from the edge of Jeromihah via a strategy table in the Lord Governor's inner office.

'Your assessment?' Senior Commander Frenz asked Sonne.

Sonne frowned. 'I'm not actually tactically modified, sir,' he replied. 'I can make as much sense of the infeed as you.'

'It looks like hell,' said Frenz.

'Oh, it is most certainly that,' said Sonne. 'Adept Feist is Analyticae. He has better modifications for this kind of work.'

Aleuton turned from the strategy table. 'Feist?'

Feist had been left sitting with Kalien in the nest of leather sofas near the Lord Governor's massive gilded desk. He rose to his feet.

Sonne beckoned him over.

'Famulous? My lord?'

'We're enjoying our ring-side seats, adept,' said Aleuton, 'but we were hoping for some more incisive analysis.'

Feist glanced at Sonne nervously. Sonne nodded.

'With your permission, my lord?' said Feist. He extruded a dendrite and plugged himself into the table's systems. Ignoring the table display, Feist looked into the middle distance, scan-reviewing the noospheric version of events.

'Full engagement is underway at the Jeromihah border. Cog, so many engines! There are so many feed tracks! I'm sorry. Give me a moment to sort…'

'Take your time,' said Aleuton.

'Invicta and the Tempestus engines have made full contact with the enemy host,' reported Feist. 'Our skitarii forces have been severely diminished. Lord Gearhart has brought his engines right into the host, close quarter. There– *Ohhh*!'

'What?' asked Aleuton and Frenz together.

'We just lost an engine. *Stratus Conquist,* Defram's princepture. Reactor explosion. I apologise, the code-blast dazzled me.'

'Keep going, Feist,' said Sonne. Kalien had come over to join them, hanging back behind Feist.

'If I'm inloading this correctly,' said Feist, 'we've lost four engines so far, including *Conquist*. The collated feed from *Invictus Antagonistes* tallies fourteen confirmed engine kills, and a total of seven partials. Correction, fifteen. *Lupus Lux* just brought down a Reaver. Correction, seventeen. *Vanquist Solace* just killed an enemy Warlord and the death blast ruptured the shields of the Warlord beside it. *Vanquist Solace* was able to make a second, opportunist engine kill before the Warlord could relight its voids. There… there are reports that Lau has been slain in the ground fighting. Unconfirmed. Too much confusion at ground level. Eighteen kills. *Cullador Braxas* just blew out a Reaver. *Morbius Sire* is confounded by three enemy Warhounds. *Invictus Antagonistes* just made a kill. So did *Tantamount Stridex*. *Stridex* is attempting to cut through the melee to support *Morbius Sire*. Oh, Deus!'

'Tell us, Feist!' Sonne urged.

His modified eyes wide open, Feist scratched at his chest anxiously with clawed fingers. 'The clash is packed so tight, several engines are engaging in close combat fighting. The cockpit mount of *Victrum Splendix* was just torn clean off by a blow from a fusion mace. The crew's gone. *Splendix* is still walking, uncontrolled. *Ferrus Castigatus* has just been brought down by sustained bolter fire. The crew has ejected. They... oh dear cog, the enemy skitarii have got them. They're... they're...'

Feist looked at Aleuton. His face was drawn and pale. 'I'd like to unplug now, my lord,' he said.

'Stay linked, adept,' urged the Lord Governor. 'Just a while longer. I know it's hard. Give me some kind of overall appraisal.'

Feist nodded obediently. 'The enemy line is beginning to swing around. It's retaining cohesion, but it's being driven back in the north-east, and the whole line is being forced to rotate away from the Jeromihah boundary.'

'Is that a tactic,' asked Frenz, 'or just the result of melee pressure?'

'If it's a tactic, then I can't read the purpose,' Feist replied.

'In simple terms, how are we doing?' Aleuton asked.

Feist hesitated.

From behind them, Kalien said, 'It's too early to tell.'

>

The sink streets outside had gone eerily quiet. Stefan really didn't want to go out, but he was aching with hunger. He had a few coins. He wondered if he had enough to score a crust and soup or a bowl of rice from a street vendor.

He scurried down the vacant pedestrian walks of Sink Hollow. There was absolutely no one around. *Why is it so quiet? Where has everybody gone? Is this a war measure?*

Stefan slowed to a halt outside a bakery on the third level. The smell of baking pastry alone, expelled through the shop's vents from the kitchens, had arrested him. Here, at last, were people. Servitors were helping three hauliers to load trays of fresh-baked goods into their transport. Early morning. They were off to supply the sink's dining halls.

Stefan gazed in through the bakery window, his mouth watering and his stomach groaning. He re-counted the coins in his pocket. The bakery window displayed a glorious array of stuffed breads, pasties and pastries ready for work-crew lunch pails. Stef couldn't even begin to afford the cheapest wares.

'Crazy day, huh?' said a voice.

Stefan glanced around. There was somebody beside him.

'I said, crazy day?' said the Magistratum officer, munching on the hot pasty he had clutched in a sheet of unstarched paper. 'Word is, the engines have gone to it outside Argentum. World'll probably end before nightfall. Am I right?'

'Yeah,' said Stefan.

'What comes comes, that's my motto, citizen,' the officer went on, taking another bite. 'Whatever comes comes. Am I right?'

'Yeah,' said Stefan.

A horn blared down the sink row. They both turned. Twenty metres away, another officer was standing in the open side-hatch of a Magistratum carrier. The officer waved impatiently.

'All right, Garling!' the officer standing with Stef shouted. 'I'm coming! Yeah, yeah, I got one for you too!'

He glanced back at Stefan with a grin. There were flecks of pastry and smears of grease on his chin. 'Some people, eh? So eager.'

'Some people,' Stefan agreed.

'You have a good day now, you hear?'

'Thank you, officer.'

The officer wiped his mouth and turned. He took a glance back at Stefan Samstag. 'You sure you're all right, citizen? You look a little frazzled.'

'I'm fine. Really.'

'Hey, don't take off. What's your hurry? You have to be somewhere?'

'No.'

'Take it easy. Come back here a moment. I just want to make sure you're all right. You really don't look all right to me. You scared of something?'

'No. Leave me alone.'

'You scared of me?'

Stefan started to run.

'Hey! Biometric! Show me your biometric! Citizen, that's an order!'

Stefan ignored the command and kept running. He crashed into the hauliers and sent a tray of baked goods flying into the air.

'Settle down!' the officer yelled, coming after him. 'You settle down right now! Halt! Show me your biometric! I won't tell you again!'

Stefan Samstag kept running.

'I won't tell you again!' the officer declared. 'Halt right now! Right now!'

* * *

>

<Engine kill! Engine kill!> Tarses canted. <Retrain targetters!>

<Adjusting track!> Kalder responded. <Reaver bearing 327!>

<Come about two points!> Prinzhorn augmitted, utterly focused. <Missile spread!>

<Missiles locked, my princeps,> Tarses canted. *Dominatus Victrix* shook violently as heavy weapons blasted its shields.

<Void impairment!> announced Kalder. <We're losing cohesion on anterior nine!>

<Boost the rate, moderati!> Prinzhorn blurted. The engine shook again. Warning alarms rang. <Fire those damn missiles!>

<Missiles away! Hit! Hit! Hit! Target is damaged!>

Prinzhorn seized control of the destructor and opened fire. Grimacing, he emitted a strangled growl of code.

<Engine kill!> Tarses canted.

<Warlord, bearing six-seven-seven!> Kalder howled. <Brace for impact!>

Victrix rocked brutally as its shields took a broadside. Tarses felt her stumble.

<Traction failure!> Anil canted, fighting with the controls.

<Stabilisers, steersman! Now!> Tarses demanded.

<It's firing again!> Kalder warned. <Brace! Brace!>

The impact was immense. The cockpit lights went out for a moment. Several panels of secondary systems blew out in a shower of sparks. Smoke boiled up through the floor hatch. Fairika activated the extinguisher systems. Tarses speed-reviewed the damage reports, diverting back-up and auxiliary processors to accommodate. They'd just lost a weapons servitor and taken serious damage to the carapace.

<The reactor is showing signs of mis-fire!> Tarses canted.

<Vent power if you have to! Keep it stable!> Prinzhorn responded. He was firing at the Warlord. Tarses could feel the haptic echo of the main weapons discharging in his forearms.

<Come around three points!> Prinzhorn demanded. <Give me a clean shot!>

<Yes, my princeps!> the steersman canted.

<Tarses?>

<Yes, my princeps?>

<Can you keep that reactor stable?>

Tarses glanced back at the casket. Prinzhorn was almost curled up in a ball. Psychostigmatic wounds covered his face and shoulders.

<Yes, my princeps, I can.>

<Thank you, my moderati. Now let's see if we can kill this scrapshunt son of a bitch.>

>

In the heart of the forge, Enhort sat back from his desk.

<The engines have walked with Gearhart,> he canted quietly.

<So?> canted Tolemy.

<It's a show of loyalty.>

<In extremis,> growled Tolemy. <We retain the upper hand.>

Perched on a stool, Egan shook his head. His hands and dendrites tugged nervously at the folds of his gown.

<You have something to cant, Egan?> blurted Tolemy.

<Nothing you don't already know,> responded Egan. <The engines have sided with Gearhart. We should acquiesce.>

Tolemy turned and glared at him. <We've come this far!>

<Too far, I think,> canted Egan.

<When the engine war is done, we will reassert our authority,> Tolemy augmitted.

<I think you're wrong,> canted Egan, fretfully. <If the engines win the fight, they will be bound by a common purpose. We could not sway them then. If they lose–>

<Everything becomes academic anyway,> Enhort finished. He rose. <I'm going to cancel situation one and signal to the Lord Governor that we are standing down.>

<You're what?> Tolemy canted.

<You heard me, master of the archives,> Enhort replied.

Tolemy's face was fierce. <No!> he canted.

Enhort turned.<'No'?>

Tolemy moved towards him. <Enhort, my dear executor, I haven't worked this hard to throw it all away on a whim.>

<We're not throwing anything away.> Enhort responded. <Gearhart has the backing of the engines. He has popular support. Simple logic demands that we stand down and allow him to assume control of the situation.>

<That would be the sane thing to do,> canted Egan from his stool, <but Tolemy won't let that happen, will you, Tolemy?>

Tolemy and Enhort were face to face.

<I have laboured for years to engineer this moment, executor,> Tolemy hissed. <That effort must not be discarded.>

Enhort shook his head. <It's done. Over. Finished.>

<Years!> Tolemy blurted. <Years of my life, manipulating data, editing this, subwriting that, just to get us to this place in history! I will not allow you to throw this opportunity away!>

Enhort backed away. <You've manipulated data to serve us? How much?>

Tolemy shook his head. <Not so much. Very little.>

<How much, Tolemy? This truth we've been championing? This great revelation of yours? Did you manipulate that?>

<No! It's the truth! It's the pure, given word of the Omnissiah!>

Enhort took a deep breath, looking back down at Tolemy. <You've tainted everything, haven't you, you stupid scrap-shunt. If you've altered so much as one code term in the data that's brought us to this point, then we are undermined. To hell with your truth! Even if it's genuine, we are impeachable! What did you manipulate, you code-wipe? I challenged Solomahn on the basis of your data! The integrity of your data! Are you telling me that you falsified it?>

<The truth is the truth, no matter how it is conditioned,> Tolemy replied.

Enhort turned away. <Servitors!> he commanded. <Open links with Lord Gearhart of Invicta and the Lord Governor!>

<No!> Tolemy uttered a scream of code. He snapped out his mechadendrites and wrapped them around Enhort's throat.

Enhort choked, falling backwards. As he hit the floor, squirming on his back, he managed to tear some of the dendrites away, but the others flexed and tightened.

Tolemy lifted one of his free dendrites up and extended a blade from the manip. He plunged it down towards Enhort's right eye.

There was a spray of blood. It splattered the wall of the chamber.

Tolemy fell. The back of his head was missing. Enhort pulled himself out of Tolemy's twisting, spasming dendrites.

Egan lowered a bolt pistol and sat back down. He rested the pistol on his knees.

'He didn't know I had this,' Egan whispered in his flesh-voice. 'Knowledge is power.'

Unsteady, spattered in blood, Enhort walked over to Egan.

<What have we done?'> Enhort canted.

Egan shrugged. He put the bolt pistol to the side of his head. 'All I know is, I've done too much,' he replied.

He pulled the trigger.

>

Cally shoved open the loose doors of the stow barn. As she entered, Golla and Lars Vulk shrank away in fear. Robor, standing beside the cart, did not look up.

The skitarii shoved Cally and she fell to her knees, rain water dripping out of her hair.

The skitarii plodded over to the cart. It examined the body of the princeps. It uttered something in code.

'What are you saying?' Cally stammered.

'He is still alive,' the skitarii replied. It tilted back its head and augmitted a long, complex code burst.

'Just kill us,' Golla growled.

'Kill you?' the skitarii asked her. 'I have just summoned recovery. Are you Activated Twenty-Six?'

'Y-yes,' replied Lars Vulk.

'We intercepted a code transmission from one of your party. Janny Wirmac. We read that a Tempestus princeps was urgently in need of casualty evacuation. We responded immediately. A princeps is too valuable a thing to lose.'

Cally rose to her feet. 'You're Tempestus?' she asked.

'Of course,' replied the skitarii, looking up from his attentive inspection of the princeps on the cart. 'What? Did you mistake us for the Archenemy?'

'Something like that,' said Golla Uldana. She burst into tears.

'Who's in charge here?' the huge skitarii asked.

Cally wearily made the Icon Mechanicus. 'Samstag, Cally, acting officer, Activated Twenty-Six.' Then she added, 'Sir.'

The skitarii snorted. 'As you were, Samstag. You'll probably get a medal for this.'

>

If he were going to die, this seemed like the perfect place, wrapped up in the consuming wrath of war, engines all around him, firestorms engulfing them as if they were walking across the face of a sun.

But if he were going to die, he wasn't going to let it be an easy death. He would fill himself with the red fury that had become his name, and unleash every last dreg of it at the abominated foe.

His left hand slew a snarling Warlord. His right hand felled a howling Reaver. His feet crushed the tumultuous hordes of enemy ground troops beneath them. He ignored his wounds and the smoke he was trailing, like victory banners, from the punctures and gouges in his pitted metal skin.

Gearhart checked the tactical array. Though they had not broken the enemy line, they had turned it, turned it until it was facing north.

He began to smile.

<As soon as you like, Bohrman,> he exloaded.

The first princeps signalled his acknowledgement. Rearmed and resupplied, Bohrman's battleground was bearing in on the enemy line from the south, from behind.

Gearhart's smile broadened.

Now there would be fury.

10011

The engines limped in a long, majestic procession through the gates of Orestes Principal and ascended through the streets towards the forge and the Field of Mars. Few came out to see them return. The citizens of the hive, at the order of the Lord Governor, had kept to their habs and domiciles. The engines were returning, and a resolution would be made.

The Imperial Guard cordon around the forge parted respectfully as the first engines came through. Their hulls were scarred and battered. The proud martial banners and victory pennants strung from their gunlimbs were scorched and tattered. Formations of gunships, like flocks of birds, flew past the marching giants.

Invictus Antagonistes, blackened and wounded, yet still regal, led the way. It advanced across the empty Field of Mars and came to a halt facing the main gate of the forge. It sounded its warhorns.

The vast main gates of the forge slowly opened. A single

figure, dressed in black robes, walked out into the sunlight, his head held up, without shame. He had no intention of running or hiding.

Enhort walked out into the great open space alone. He kept walking until he was standing directly in front of the massive Warlord. Face to face, two figures, separated by scale.

Enhort looked up at the engine towering over him. He could read its courage and its faith and its deeds in the thousands of dents and holes that covered its armour.

He got down on his knees, and bowed his head.

>

Crusius walked into the office of the Lord Governor. Aleuton made the sign of the cog.

'The execution is complete, my lord,' said the executor. 'Invicta has delivered Orestes from jeopardy.'

'As you promised you would.'

'I see you've been taking good care of my famulous,' Crusius smiled. Sonne came over to the executor and made a quick bow.

'Sonne is a diligent boy,' said Aleuton. 'You should be proud of him.'

'I have always been proud of him,' said Crusius. He looked back at the Lord Governor. 'The forge is stable, my lord. We may consider the crisis averted. There will be elections to select a new Adept Seniorus. My money is on Keito. You should also know that a Mechanicus fleet is en route from Holy Mars. It expects to arrive within three months. The magi will perform a complete purge and data audit of Orestes Forge to ensure that no… no *heresies* remain.'

'Then in the spirit of full disclosure,' Aleuton replied, 'I should tell you that an Imperial Navy flotilla is also en route to Orestes at my invitation to ensure that the situation is contained.'

'I would have expected no less, my lord,' said Aleuton.

'You used the word "heresies", executor. Am I to understand that the data that triggered the crisis has been discredited?'

'It is evident that the master of the archives manipulated a great deal of data to support the claims. We may never be able to tell exactly how much, but it must all be treated as suspect.'

With Sonne at his side, Crusius left the governor's office. There were a great many duties to be performed, not least the preparations for departure. Crusius knew he would have to contact Warmaster Macaroth and make full account of Invicta's endeavours on Orestes. The Warmaster would be, as Sonne might put it, pissed off.

Etta Severin was in the anteroom, awaiting a summons to debrief the Lord Governor.

'We probably won't meet again, executor,' she said.

'Probably not, Etta. It's been a pleasure.'

'It's been an education.'

Crusius turned to leave. 'Executor?'

'Yes, Etta?'

'There was rather more truth to the revelations than anyone wants to admit, wasn't there?'

'I couldn't possibly comment, mamzel.'

She smiled and shook her head. 'Answered like a true executor.'

'Magos Tolemy was conspiring to achieve very personal goals, Etta. His was not a high-minded crusade.'

'Even so, isn't it possible that he was using the truth to get what he wanted?'

'Knowledge is power, mamzel. Tolemy knew that. Sometimes it is too much power. Occasionally, even a great truth must be sacrificed for a greater good.'

'Like now, Crusius?' she asked.

'I couldn't possibly comment, Etta,' he replied.

>

Cally Samstag, her pack slung across her shoulder, walked up to the door of her little hab in Makepole. Nothing felt quite real. The ordinariness of her surroundings seemed extraordinary. She could smell cooking, and the voices of children playing on the landing.

'Stef?'

The little hab was empty. It didn't look as if anyone had been there in days. She put her pack down, and took off her jacket. She touched the little gold medal on the chain around her neck and discovered, to her dismay, that at some point in her adventures, the little wheel of dark gold had broken in half.

She saw the message packet lying beside the door slot. It was an official notice from the Magistratum.

She tore it open.

'With regret, the office of the Magistratum writes to inform you that, during a routine biometric exam in Sink Hollow, Stefan Samstag became agitated, resisted arrest and assaulted a Magistratum officer. The officer was therefore obliged to draw his weapon...'

Cally sat down, the message paper crumpled in her hand, and began to cry.

* * *

>

Two small boys were playing in the Worthies Garden. They had a tinplate Titan, red and gold, that they had bought from some commercia shop, and they were winding it up and letting it walk along the garden paths.

Riik! Riik! Riik!

Zink watched them for a while. He half-remembered what the toy was supposed to resemble. He took up his broom, and began to sweep. Zephyrids were twittering on the lawns.

Horns boomed across the city. Zink looked up. The great ships were moving in over the city again, filling the sky. He had a feeling that something was over, but he wasn't sure what.

Stiff-legged, at low stride, he went on his way down the path.

>

With a hiss, the amniotic casket disengaged from the cockpit socket and lifted clear. The tech-priests murmured their incantations.

It was time to rest again. It was time to make shift to the next walk, time to slumber through the cold hours of the voyage. It was time to heal and repair and rebuild strength.

Gearhart would sleep in his hiberberth. *Invictus Antagonistes* would sleep in its scaffold frame in the carrier hold.

They would share the same dreams.

>

The halt was silent. Thin afternoon sunlight hazed in through the dirty window slits. On the wall, the last, handwritten entry read:

Erik Varco came here, with others. We came here in great need, and we have been obliged to take food, power, the food drums and several other items. Please forgive the fact that we have little to leave in return. The only thing I have that is precious, I have left as an offering.

On the cluttered shelves, in the hazy light, between a rebreather mask with the face of an engine, and a faded sun charm woven from dried desert grass, lay a small medallion of the Omnissiah that had once been fixed to the skirt armour of a tank.

10100

Eyeless and screaming, the regiments of the dead shiver their burned bones together at the sound of your tread. Foul vapour clots the sun. Oh machine! Oh divine engine! Photo-bright the discharge of your weapons, shattering the fragile vault of the sky and smiting the dirt of the ground to dust. The princeps, adrift in liquid data, a beautiful monster, feels the glory of your great walk as surely as if he had been precision-made in the forge as one of your component cogs. Oh metal god! The union is entire, closer than kin or family, closer than brothers, closer than blood. A pact of divine metal, no start of one, no end of another, but both admixed, like an alloy. To be part of a god! To share that majesty and that strength! Oh lucky man!

Do you ever really sleep? In the long between-times, in the silences wasted in oily holds and scaffold frames, do you sleep then? When the enginseers reduce you to dormancy, is that sleep for you? Do you dream then, great engine?

What do you dream about?
What secrets do you keep?

ABOUT THE AUTHOR

Dan Abnett has written over fifty novels, and is well known for the acclaimed Gaunt's Ghosts series including *The Warmaster*, and the Eisenhorn and Ravenor books including *The Magos*. He is the author of the Horus Heresy novels *Horus Rising*, *Legion*, *The Unremembered Empire*, *Know No Fear* and *Prospero Burns*, the last two of which were both *New York Times* bestsellers. He also scripted *Macragge's Honour*, the first Horus Heresy graphic novel, as well as numerous audio dramas and short stories set in the Warhammer 40,000 and Warhammer universes. He lives and works in Maidstone, Kent.

YOUR NEXT REA

WARHAMMER
40,000

KNIGHTSBLADE
ANDY CLARK

KNIGHTSBLADE
by Andy Clark

Now fighting as a Freeblade, Imperial Knight Luk Kar Chimaeros fa
his past and a dreadful decision that will decide his future.

For these stories and more go to **blacklibrary.com, games-workshop.com,** Games Works
Warhammer stores, all good book stores or visit one of the thousands of independent r
worldwide, which can be found at **games-workshop.com/storefinder**

YOUR NEXT READ

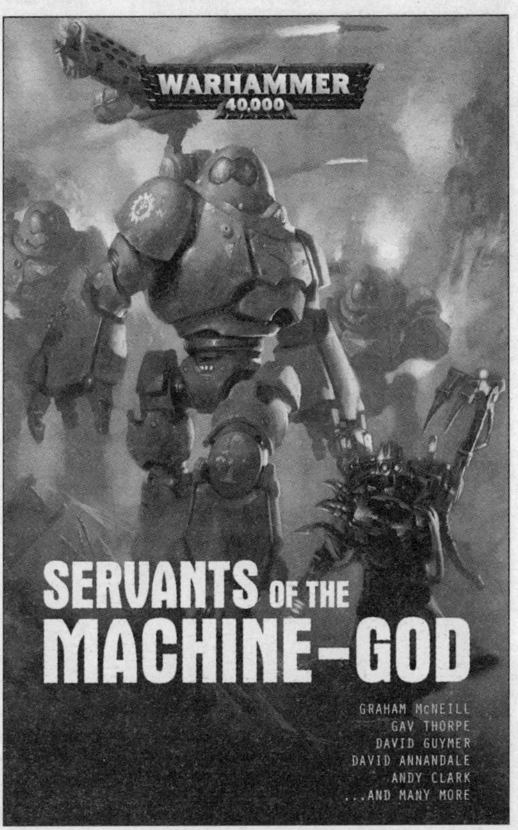

SERVANTS OF THE MACHINE-GOD
by Graham McNeill, Gav Thorpe, David Guymer,
David Annandale, Andy Clark and many more

[T]he forces of the Adeptus Mechanicus – Titans, Imperial Knights, [s]ervitors and skitarii legions – march in a dozen tales showcasing how the servants of the Omnissiah wage war.

stories and more go to **blacklibrary.com**, **games-workshop.com**, Games Workshop and [...]nmer stores, all good book stores or visit one of the thousands of independent retailers worldwide, which can be found at **games-workshop.com/storefinder**